PENGUIN BOOKS

THE SIEGE

'Dunmore slowly and relentlessly guides us deep into the territory of
famine and winter as motherless Anna, her small brother Kolya and her
father, a dissident writer, endure the inexpressible attrition of the Siege
of Leningrad ... In this wise, humane and beautifully written novel she
has written a masterpiece' *Independent*

'A searing historical novel. Dunmore vividly evokes the unbelievable
cold, privations and violence as people struggle to survive ... an extra-
ordinary description of the horrors of the time' *Sunday Express*

'Terrifying and absorbing ... Dunmore skilfully evokes the perilous
fragility of the city as Leningrad is surrounded by German troops and
the supply routes are cut off. An impressive, disturbing novel. Read it,
and give thanks for your warm, well-provisioned home' *Tablet*

'Enthralling ... A woman's-eye view of war, with the daily struggle to
find food and fuel raging through her characters' bodies and minds ...
An important as well as a thrilling work of art' *Independent on Sunday*

'A moving and powerful novel in which Dunmore employs all her
celebrated descriptive and narrative skills ... beautiful' *Daily Mail*

'Tragically haunting and unforgettable' *Big Issue*

'A harrowing, urgent narrative of cold, starvation and the battle to
survive' *Sunday Times*

'Dunmore captures the siege's sense of estrangement and disorientation
in bold, unexpected images' *New Statesman*

'Beautiful writing, brilliant imagery, expert pacing … we are pinned to the page by exquisite descriptions of starvation, cannibalism and frozen corpses … an important novel' *Sunday Tribune*

'Convincingly narrates a horrifying war story from the point of view of the hearth, not the trenches' *Observer*

'Dunmore describes what is happening in language that is elegantly, starkly beautiful … Without a trace of sentimentality, Dunmore manages to sound a fierce note of humanism that relieves the relentless grimness … The Siege is both quieter and more powerful than her earlier work.' *New York Times*

'This is a novel of psychological delicacy and poetic strength as well as a meditation on suffering and endurance' *Washington Post*

ABOUT THE AUTHOR

Helen Dunmore has published seven novels with Penguin: *Zennor in Darkness*, winner of the 1994 McKitterick Prize; *Burning Bright*; *A Spell of Winter*, winner of the 1996 Orange Prize for Fiction; *Talking to the Dead*; *Your Blue-Eyed Boy*; *With Your Crooked Heart*; and *The Siege*, shortlisted for the 2001 Whitbread Novel of the Year Award and the Orange Prize. Helen Dunmore is also a poet, children's novelist and short-story writer. Her two collections of short stories, *Love of Fat Men* and *Ice Cream*, are also published by Penguin. Her poetry collections include *The Sea Skater*, winner of the Poetry Society's Alice Hunt Bartlett Award; *The Raw Garden*, a Poetry Book Society Choice; and *Secrets*, winner of the 1995 Signal Poetry Award.

Helen Dunmore was born in Yorkshire and now lives in Bristol.

HELEN DUNMORE

The Siege

PENGUIN BOOKS

PENGUIN BOOKS

Published by the Penguin Group
Penguin Books Ltd, 80 Strand, London WC2R ORL, England
Penguin Putnam Inc., 375 Hudson Street, New York, New York 10014, USA
Penguin Books Australia Ltd, 250 Camberwell Road, Camberwell, Victoria 3124, Australia
Penguin Books Canada Ltd, 10 Alcorn Avenue, Toronto, Ontario, Canada M4V 3B2
Penguin Books India (P) Ltd, 11 Community Centre, Panchsheel Park,
New Delhi – 110 017, India
Penguin Books (NZ) Ltd, Cnr Rosedale and Airborne Roads,
Albany, Auckland, New Zealand
Penguin Books (South Africa) (Pty) Ltd, 24 Sturdee Avenue,
Rosebank 2196, South Africa

Penguin Books Ltd, Registered Offices: 80 Strand, London WC2R ORL, England

www.penguin.com

First published by Viking 2001
Published in Penguin Books 2002
1

Set in Monotype Garamond
Printed in England by Clays Ltd, St Ives plc

To Ros Cuthbert

Naval Staff   Berlin
Sk1 Ia 1601/41 g.Kdos. Chefs.   29 Sep. 1941

Top Secret

<u>Re</u>: The future of Leningrad

. . . The Fuehrer has decided to have Leningrad wiped from the face of the earth. The further existence of this large town is of no interest once Soviet Russia is overthrown. Finland has also similarly declared no interest in the continued existence of the city directly on her new frontier.

The original demands of the Navy that the shipyard, harbor, and other installations vital to the Navy be preserved are known to the Armed Forces High Command, but in view of the basic principles underlying the operation against Leningrad it is not possible to comply with them.

The intention is to close in on the city and blast it to the ground by bombardments of artillery of all calibres and by continuous air attacks.

Requests that the city may be handed over, arising from the situation within, will be turned down, for the problem of the survival of the population and of supplying it with food is one which cannot and should not be solved by us. In this war for existence, we have no interest in keeping even part of this great city's population . . .

Naval staff

[From the Fuehrer Directives and other top-level directives of the German armed forces, 1939–1941. The original US army translation from the German is held in the Naval War College, Newport, R.I., USA.
With thanks to the Militärgeschichtliches Forschungsamt, Potsdam, Germany.]

I

June, 1941

It's half past ten in the evening, but the light of day still glows through the lime leaves. They are so green that they look like an hallucination of the summer everyone had almost given up expecting. When you touch them, they are fresh and tender. It's like touching a baby's skin.

Such a late spring, murky and doubtful, clinging to winter's skirts. But this is how it happens here in Leningrad. Under the trees around the Admiralty, lakes of spongy ice turned grey. There was slush everywhere, and a raw, dirty wind off the Neva. There was a frost, a thaw, another frost.

Month after month ice-fishermen crouched by the holes they'd drilled in the ice, sitting out the winter, heads hunched into shoulders. And then, just when it seemed as if summer would forget about Leningrad this year, everything changed. Ice broke loose from the compacted mass around the Strelka. Seagulls preened on the floes as the current swept them under bridges, and down the widening Neva to the sea. The river ran full and fast, with a fresh wind tossing up waves so bright they stung your eyes. Everything that was rigid was crumbling, breaking away, floating.

People leaned on the parapets of the Dvortsovy bridge, watching the ice-floes rock as they passed under the arch. Their winter world was being destroyed. They wanted spring, of course they wanted it, more than anything. They longed for sun with every pore of their skin.

But spring hurts. If spring can come, if things can be different, how can you bear what your existence has been?

These are hard times. You can't trust anyone, not even yourself. Frightened men and women scuttling in the dusty wind. Peter's great buildings hang over them, crushingly magnificent. In times like these the roads are too wide. How long it takes to fight your way across Peter's squares, and how visible you become. Yes, you're a target, and you don't know who's watching. So many disappearances, so much fear. Black vans cruise the streets. You listen for the note of their engines, and your heart pumps until it chokes you as the van slows. But it passes this time, and halts at the doorway to another courtyard, where you don't live. You hear the van doors clang and the sweat of relief soaks you, shamefully. Some other poor bastard is in that van this time.

Spring stripped everything bare. It showed the grey and weary skin of everyone over thirty. It lit up lips set in suffering, with wrinkles pulling sharply at the corners of the mouth.

But the lime trees' bare branches were spiked by the glitter of sunlight and birdsong. The birds had no doubts at all. They sang out loudly and certainly into the still-frozen world. They knew that winter was on the move.

Now it's June, and night is brief as the brush of a wing, only an hour of yellow stars in a sky that never darkens beyond deep, tender blue.

No one sleeps. Crowds surge out of cafés and wander the streets, not caring where they go as long as they can lift their faces and drink the light. It's been dark for so many months.

A line of young men, arm in arm, drunk, stern with the effort of keeping on their feet, sways on the corner of Universitetskaya Embankment and Lieutenant Schmidt's bridge. They won't go home. They can't bear to part from one another. They'll walk, that's what they'll do, from one end of the city to another, from island to island, across stone bridges and shining water.

These are the nights that seal each generation of Leningraders to their city. These nights are their baptism. The summer light will flood every grain of Leningrad stone, as it floods every cell of their own bodies. At three o'clock in the morning, in full sun, they'll find themselves in some backstreet of little wooden houses, miles from anywhere. There'll be a cat licking its paws in a doorway, a lime tree with electric-green leaves hanging over a high wooden fence, and an old woman slowly making her way down the street with a little bunch of jasmine pinned to her jacket. Each flower will be as white and distinct as a star against the shabby grey. And she'll smile at the young men as if she's their grandmother. She won't disapprove of their drunkenness, their shouting and singing. She'll understand exactly how they feel.

However old you are, you can't stay indoors on a night like this. It stirs again, the promise and recklessness of white nights. Peter's icy, blood-sodden marshes bear up the city like a swan. The swan's wings are still folded, but they are trembling in the summer light, stirring, and getting ready to fly. Darkness scarcely touches them.

The wind breathes softly. Water laps under the midnight bridges. And suddenly you know that there's no greater possible happiness than to be here, even when you're so old you're beyond walking. You lean out of your apartment window, with stiff joints and fading strength, over the city that will outlive you.

But Anna is not in Leningrad tonight. She's out in the country, at the dacha, alone with her father and Kolya. She doesn't belong in the crowds of students celebrating the end of their examinations. She doesn't share the jokes any more, or know which books everyone's reading. Hers is a daylight city of trams packed with overworked mothers, racing from work to food queue to kitchen and back again.

The white nights rouse up too many longings. Anna has a duty to crush them. She has five-year-old Kolya, her job at the nursery, and her responsibilities. It's no good letting herself dream of student life. She'll never have long days in a studio, mind and body trained on the movement of hand across paper. It's no good remembering what it was like to be seventeen, only six years ago, with graduation from school a year ahead of her, and a crowd of friends round the table at the Europe, packed together, laughing and talking so loudly that you could hardly hear what anyone said. The words didn't matter. The noise of happiness was what mattered, and the warmth of someone else's arm pressed against yours. There was a smell of sunburnt skin, coffee, cigarettes and marigolds.

Don't think about all that. She's at the dacha, leaning out of the window and resting her elbows on warm, silver-grey wood. It's very quiet. Behind her, Kolya sleeps in his cot-bed. They have a bedroom divided in two by a plywood partition. One half for her father, the other for Anna and Kolya. Downstairs, the living-room opens on to the verandah. Every sound echoes in the dacha's wooden shell.

But to have a dacha at all is luxury. There's no chance of her father ever qualifying for a dacha at the writers' colony, but they have held on to this little place, which once belonged to Anna's grandmother. They come here whenever they can in summer, when the city's airless and full of dust. Anna bikes it, on the precious, battered bike that was her mother's, with Kolya tied on to his seat behind her.

Anna does most of the cooking outside on the verandah. She chops onions, kneads pastry for meat pies, peels potatoes, prepares sausage. She even makes jam outside, on the little oil-stove.

All through each summer Anna builds up stores for the winter. She gives grammar and handwriting lessons to the Sokolov children at the farm, in exchange for honey, jars of goose-fat, and goat's cheese. She dries mushrooms, and makes jams and jellies from the fruit she and Kolya pick. Lingonberries, blueberries, raspberries, blackberries, wild strawberries. She buys a drink made from fermented birch sap, which is packed with vitamins and said to be particularly good for asthmatic children like Kolya. Then there are red cabbages to be pickled, onions to be tied into strings, garlic to be plaited, beans to be preserved in brine, potatoes to be brushed free of earth, sorted, then brought back to the apartment sack by sack, strapped to the back of her bike. You have to be careful with potatoes, because they bruise more easily than you think, and then they won't keep.

Anna doesn't know how she'd have got them through the last two winters without produce from the dacha. Not only are there food shortages all the time, but her father can't get his work published. He survives by translating, but even that might dry up. Editors have got their own families to consider. Her father's near-perfect French and German are dangerous assets now. He can't help speaking like someone who has spent time abroad. A year in Heidelberg in 1912, a summer in Lausanne. He could be pulled in for questioning as 'an individual with foreign contacts'.

Her father wanted to take it lightly, the first time one of his stories was rejected. He was asked to appear in front of a magazine committee, where the shortcomings of his story were explained to him. They told him that his tone was pessimistic. He had failed to take on board and reflect in his work the principles drawn from Stalin's speech of the first of December 1935: *'Life has become better, comrades, life has become more cheerful.'*

'And yet in your story, Mikhail Ilyich, there is no sense that any of the characters are making headway! Publication of this work would do nothing to advance your reputation. In fact, it would damage it.'

'Frankly, we were surprised that you submitted it, Mikhail Ilyich,' said the chairman of the committee. 'We try to be understanding, but really in this case it's impossible, as I'm sure you'll agree.' And he chucked the manuscript face-down on the table, lightly, pityingly, humorously, just as he would have done if a schoolboy had submitted his outpourings to a top literary magazine, and expected to get them published. 'No, we can't have this kind of stuff!'

He twinkled at Mikhail, begging him to see the joke. Other members of the committee looked down at their blotters, or played with their pens. Their faces were dark with the resentment we feel towards those we are about to injure.

Mikhail looked at the familiar faces. A flush of hot blood ran under his skin. Was the shame in himself, standing there with his unwanted manuscript, unable to accept the criticism of his contemporaries? The room itself seemed washed with shame. Even his story was stained with it.

'No,' he muttered, 'I should never have brought it here.'

'Ex—actly so,' said the chairman, rising. 'But allow me to say, dear Mikhail Ilyich, that I've always been an admirer of your work. All you need is a little –' his fingers sketched adjustments – 'a little less gloom and doom. That's not what people want these days. That's not what we're here to do.'

He smiled, showing white, strong teeth in healthy gums. The

room prickled with agreement. The room knew what was wanted these days.

Mikhail continued to submit stories, which were always rejected. One evening a colleague from the Writers' Union appeared at the apartment.

'Don't send anything else in just now. It's for your own good, Mikhail Ilyich.'

'I'm writing as I've always written.'

'Yes, that's it, that's exactly it. Do you really not see? We all have to make adjustments.'

'They are good stories.'

'For God's sake, what has that got to do with anything?'

On his way out, he paused. He was waiting for something, but Mikhail couldn't think what. After the man had gone, it dawned. He'd expected to be thanked. He'd taken a risk. He'd tried to help. Not many did that these days, because it was too dangerous. Each person taken in for questioning could drag a hundred more down. *'Who was in the room with you when this occurred? Their names. Write them here.'*

'Better put it in the drawer,' Anna's father would say, as he typed out the final draft of a new story. His fingers pecked at the keys. He had never learned to type properly. When Vera was alive, she typed for him. *'Let the drawer read it. Well, here we are, Anna, I'm back to my youth again, pouring out rubbish that nobody wants to print. People pay thousands for rejuvenation treatments, don't they? I could sell my secret.'*

His attempts at humour make her wince. All this is changing him, month by month. It's scouring him out from the inside. He even walks differently. Anna can't think what it all reminds her of, then one day she's at work and she sees little Seryozha hide behind the bins as a gang of big boys charges round the playground, windmilling their arms, bellowing, knocking into everyone. They're the gang. They're the ones who count. Seryozha shrinks against the wall.

In the nursery, you can sort it out. You can break up the gang. You can put your arm around Seryozha. There, in her little world within a world, things still make sense. But then out comes her boss, Elizaveta Antonovna, with the latest directives in her hand. Her eyes are fixed to the text. She has got to take the correct line. She must not make an error.

Elizaveta Antonovna doesn't even see the children. She's frightened, too. The bosses are all frightened now. How should she interpret the directive? If she gets it wrong, who will inform on her?

Anna's father still goes to the Writers' House on Ulitsa Voinova, but not very often, although as a member of the Union of Soviet Writers he's entitled to eat there every day. 'I don't feel like it today, Anna,' he says. 'And besides, I've got to rewrite these last two pages.'

He had a dream one night. He dreamed he was lying in bed and someone clamped a hand over his mouth and nose. A firm, fleshy, well-fed hand. The fingers were thick and greasy. They squeezed his nostrils until he couldn't breathe.

'What did you do?'

'I twisted my head from side to side to try and shake him off, but he pressed harder. And then I —'

'What?'

'I bit his hand. I could taste his blood.'

'Whose hand was it?'

And then his whisper, in the frightened room that held only the two of them: 'Koba's.'[1]

Anna didn't answer. She knew there was more.

'And then I woke up. I looked in the mirror and there were marks on my face. Dirty fingerprints. I tried to wipe them off but they wouldn't come off. I filled a basin with water and dipped my head into it and when I looked in the mirror my face was streaming with water, but the marks were still there.'

He looks at her. She half-expects to see the fingerprints rise to the surface of his skin and show themselves. But there's nothing. 'It was a dream, that's all.'

'I know that.' He raps it out. There she goes again, stating the obvious, not thinking before she speaks.

'A nightmare,' says Anna.

'Don't shut the door.'

1. A nickname for Stalin.

'No, I'll leave it open.'

Her father has always been afraid of a shut door. He was afraid of getting trapped in a lift, that was why he always took the stairs. When they went to the cinema he had to sit near the exit.

Her father's income is down to a fifth of what it was three years ago. Each summer Anna has increased her vegetable plot at the dacha. She's dug up all the flowerbeds now, except for her mother's three rose-bushes.

Three rose-trees, bearing dark-red, velvety roses which open helplessly wide and spread out their perfume. Before winter her mother packed straw around them, then sacking, and bound it with twine. Anna can see her now: the quick, expert fingers, the way she brushed soil off her knees as she stood up. There, it was done for the winter. Strange, how easy it is to remember her doing that, and yet there are long, blank patches when it seems as if Anna's mother never lived at all.

But she lived. Remember it.

Anna and the sledge. Little Anna on her sledge, long ago. Mammy loved sledging as much as Anna did. They would go out, the two of them, while Anna's father worked. He would have liked to come with them but he had a deadline to meet.

Walking through snow, with the red sledge bumping along behind them, Anna wished that everyone she knew was there to see what a beautiful sledge she had. There were curls of green and gold on the smart, bright red. The rope was new and Anna was allowed to pull the sledge herself. Her mother swooped down to pick up Anna when snow went over the top of her boots. When she set her down again, Anna took up the thick, new rope. A bit farther on, near the park, someone stopped them. She stood so close that Anna smelt her smoky perfume. Her boots had shiny silver buckles on the side, and Anna wanted to touch them.

'Hasn't she grown! How are you all, Vera?'

'We're well,' said Vera. Her hand squeezed Anna's tightly. There was a silence, but Vera didn't put any more words into it.

'I haven't seen Misha for weeks – he's not ill, I hope?'

Her mother's voice was steady. 'He's perfectly well, Marina Petrovna. We are all perfectly well. And now, if you'll excuse me, Anna mustn't stand in the cold . . .'

'Of course –'

When Anna looked back she was still standing there. She didn't move, and no one said goodbye.

When they had turned the corner, her mother stopped and placed Anna carefully on the sledge. She wrapped the shawl around Anna in the usual way, making sure that her chest was covered.

But suddenly she changed and did something new. She dropped on her knees in the snow in front of the sledge. She grasped Anna and pulled her close. She pressed her tight, tight, so that Anna felt the cold of her mother's cheeks burning her.

'Mammy, you're hurting me.'

Her mother moved back. Anna saw her face close-up.

'Mammy, are you all right?'

Her mother stood up, brushing snow off her coat. 'I'm fine. Don't worry, Anna.'

Anna said nothing. Carefully, she tucked in the ends of the shawl which her mother had forgotten. She looked up and she saw that her mother's face was stiff with anger. She was drumming her fingers on the rope, staring up the street as if she'd forgotten about Anna.

'Mammy?'

'What?'

'Can we go?'

'You want to go back home?'

'I'm cold, Mammy.'

'I'm sorry. I was thinking about some things at work. Let's go. Hold on tight now, Anna.'

How old was she then? Five, six? All through that spring and summer there was trouble hanging in the air like thunder. At night Anna woke up and there were voices slashing the dark. When holiday time came her mother took Anna away to the dacha, but her father didn't come with them. He had things to do in Leningrad.

'Too much work to do, Anna. I want to come, but –'

Her mother had two weeks' holiday, and every single minute Anna was with her. Nobody came to visit. Her mother belonged entirely to Anna. In the morning, they ate their breakfast on the verandah, and Anna put a lump of sugar in her mouth and sucked it before she drank tea, exactly as her mother did. Her mother read, while Anna cut out paper dolls and painted their clothes. Sometimes it was hot, high noon before they dressed. Toys and paper scraps lay on the verandah where Anna dropped them, and two days later they were still there. There wasn't a breath of wind.

Her mother sat on the verandah, stretched her bare feet into the sun, and read to Anna. Her mother's feet were tired and lumpy, but she stretched them like a dancer.

'Did you ever dance, Mammy?'

'Oh yes.'

'With Daddy?'

'Your father never liked dancing.'

'Show me how.'

'Not now, Anna, I'm reading to you.'

They slept in the same bed. Anna would roll over and grasp her mother's waist, pretending to be asleep so her mother wouldn't be cross with her. She would say in a sleepy, just-woken voice, 'Mammy?'

'Sh. Go back to sleep now. It's late.'

But her mother didn't push Anna away. In Leningrad, in the apartment, there was no room for Anna in her parents' bed. Here, the old iron bedstead creaked as her mother turned over and settled to sleep, with Anna curled at her back, and Anna's arm around her waist.

'Are you all right, little pigeon? Go to sleep.'

'I love it when you call me little pigeon.'

In the middle of the night, Anna woke. There was her mother's shoulder, warm and broad. She was turned away from Anna. Anna moved her mouth across her mother's back. She licked her mother's skin and smelled it. It smelled quite different where she'd licked it. Her mother tasted good. Anna swam up her mother's body until her mouth was against the soft, creamy pad of flesh behind her shoulder. She opened her mouth and, without knowing what she was going to do, she bit. Her mother startled all over, throwing Anna off. But she still didn't wake. Anna wanted her to wake. Squaring her mouth, she began to make a crying noise, and then to cry. Her mother sat up and lit the bedside candle.

'Anna, what's the matter?' Her mother's plait swung forward and touched Anna's face. 'Are you ill?'

Anna doesn't remember any more. Her mother was herself again, calmly in charge. It was like a change in the weather. Anna settled neatly back to sleep, on her own side of the bed. The next morning, before Anna had even woken, her mother had picked up all the toys, thrown away the dead flowers, and put her research papers into a pile on the table.

'We go back tomorrow,' her mother said.

Back in Leningrad, her parents shared their bedroom again. Every night Anna settled in her cot-bed in her parents' room, and then they moved her into the living-room when they went to bed. But some mornings she woke to find her father huddled in a blanket, asleep on the leather sofa beside her. The thunder growled and rumbled, but far away so she could scarcely hear it any more.

That summer at the dacha grips Anna. It keeps unpacking in her mind. Eighteen years ago. The only time, maybe, when her mother gave way and bound Anna to her, because she needed her. But in all the years afterwards nothing was said. Never again was she as close to her mother as on those summer nights, listening to her mother's breath.

'You won't ever die, will you, Mammy?'

'One day I will,' her mother said, in her usual clear and serious way. 'But not before you are able to live without me.'

'I'll never be able to live without you.'

'Of course you will. You think you won't now, but you will.' Did Vera think of that, when she was really dying?

It was a postpartum haemorrhage. Neither Anna nor her father was there. Vera was unconscious and had already had a heart attack by the time they arrived.

She'd been so practical about her pregnancy, right from the start. Practical, realistic, and humorous with colleagues who teased her about being caught out. Vera, who wrote everything down in her small black memo-book, and never forgot an appointment. She stood there in her cotton maternity smock, and smiled at the teasing. She said, rather oddly, 'Well, none of us is immortal.'

'Immortal?'

'No, I don't mean that, do I? What's the right word?'

'Infallible?'

'Yes, that's it.'

Her colleagues laughed with her. It was nice, the way Vera never tried to know everything. They suspected that maybe she'd wanted this last-chance baby, now that Anna was seventeen. After all, think how good Vera was with the younger members of the team. Always encouraging, taking time, able to teach people without them noticing it. Never losing her temper when they made mistakes.

But Anna knew that it was not her mother who had wanted this baby. She was forty when she became pregnant, almost forty-one. She was an expert in her field, and was beginning to travel, lecturing in Moscow, Odessa, Kiev.

'Are you going away again?' her father asked.

'It's only five days, Misha. You knew about it, it's been planned since last August. It's in the diary.'

'You're never here these days.'

'Anna is old enough now.'

'Is that all you think about?'

Dark stains grew under Vera's eyes. Her ankles swelled so much that the straps of her sandals cut into her pale, puffy flesh. The baby was due in late summer.

'Go and lie down, Mammy. I'll cook.'

'It's all right, Anna, I'm fine. I've just got to finish this.'

Work went on as it had always done. Vera was writing a paper which she would give at a conference in Kiev, three months after the baby was born. Nothing was going to change, she said to her colleagues on the telephone. She would fulfil her responsibilities. When her eyes met Misha's across the room she stared him down.

Kolya's birth was easy, and immediately afterwards everything seemed fine. He was a big baby, a strong, fine child they said to her, slapping the soles of his feet to make him cry. Vera sat up and took the baby. A nurse told Anna about it afterwards.

'I want to know everything that happened,' said Anna. *'Don't leave anything out because you think it will upset me.'*

The nurse looked at her, frightened.

'What is it?'

'It's only – it's just that you sound exactly like your mother.'

Anna brushed that away. Don't think of it now, think of it later.

'Go on, please. Tell me what happened.'

The delivery of the placenta was difficult. Immediately afterwards, before Vera's uterus had contracted fully, there was an emergency in the next ward. A prolapsed cord, it was. They had to leave Vera alone for a few minutes. *'It was only a few minutes, Anna Mikhailovna, no more than seven. I swear it.'*

Vera would not have been frightened when she lifted her sheet and saw blood, even though she'd have known what the bleeding meant. This was her world, the hospital world. She'd have guessed what had happened. Part of the placenta had not been expelled. Now she would continue to haemorrhage until it could be removed. The situation was urgent, but not yet dangerous.

She rang a bell beside the bed. A nurse came. Vera said calmly, 'I think I'm bleeding.'

'Is that exactly what she said?'

'Yes, it was me who came, you see. Those were her words.'

So Vera was frightened. She said 'I think' when she knew. Or perhaps she didn't want to frighten the nurse. The nurse lifted the sheet. She looked and then she said, 'It's all right. You're fine,' and then she ran, her feet striking the hard floor all the way down the ward. Next, there was a metal trolley and porters lifting Vera on to it. The nurse ran alongside the trolley as it clattered down the corridor to the lift. Vera said she felt faint, then closed her eyes.

And then what? Then the clean, shabby hospital wall, and the shut door. Anna can't go any farther with her mother. And then there was her father, kneeling by Vera's bed with his hands over his face. Anna touched her mother's soft, warm cheek, but the gaping face belonged to someone else. All the sense had gone out of it.

Vera was forty-one.

'There's always a greater risk, you understand,' someone said.

But how could it be Vera who had died in this way? It wasn't like her at all. She knew about bodies, and hospitals. She understood the limits of what should happen to people. Health was her job and her life. She knew what Anna should eat, and how many hours she should study. She'd talked to Anna about her periods before they started, telling her just enough and not too much. 'When you have children,' she'd said. Not 'When I have children.' Vera's days of children were over, it went without saying. She had Anna.

But she died at forty-one. She left her child to Anna. In the end, instead of freeing her daughter, she put a child into her arms. That red, squirming thing they were swaddling in the next room. Kolya.

Little Anna stayed at the dacha with her mother, eighteen summers ago, the two of them alone together for the first time. Every night, when she woke, her mother was there, dreaming, her fist up to her face as she slept.

'Mammy?' said Anna.

'It's all right,' said her mother in her sleep-thickened voice. 'I'm here.' She said it every night, until Anna slept without asking.

2

As soon as the ice melted in the late spring of '41, Anna began cycling out to the dacha on her days off. It was a long ride, with Kolya on the back of the bike, but she didn't mind that. She took bread and pickled herrings, and bought milk for Kolya in the village. The cold, fresh air streamed over her face as she pedalled hard. She went faster, faster, her heart pumping, a smile rising from nowhere and breaking on her lips.

'Look, Kolya, look! The Sokolov farm!'

Out at the dacha, the earth was black and sweet, and it crumbled easily after the frosts. Kolya played in the dirt, making fortresses with stick-and-stone cannon while she got the heavy digging done. She let him play, but later on he could help to plant the seeds. She was too much in the habit of doing everything for Kolya, because it was quicker and easier. She'd made him lazy. An image of her father rose in her mind. His long fine fingers turned a page, and he asked, 'What time are we eating, Anna?' without even looking up from his book. He never knew what food there was in the house.

'You must be more independent, Kolya.'

'In-de-pend-ent . . .' he sang to himself, swinging his feet. 'What's that, Anna?'

He would sit there and hold out his feet for her to put his boots on, even though he knew perfectly well how to do it for himself.

Anna stopped digging to watch him. He crouched over his excavations, running his gun forward, banging out fire at an invisible enemy behind the bird-cherries, then digging furiously with his little wooden spade. All the while he kept up a commentary on his own game.

'Attack! Attack! The Reds are attacking – and the Whites are retreating, their commander fat-ally wounded . . .'

Anna sighed. All the little boys at the nursery were the same, locked into old battles. But she kept quiet. Kolya might say something, and Elizaveta Antonovna might overhear it. *Anna says playing Reds and Whites is stupid.* My God, imagine if she heard that. And she might. Elizaveta Antonovna was always appearing just where you didn't expect her.

Anna is a useful worker, but not useful enough for Elizaveta Antonovna to risk failing to denounce her. She wouldn't hesitate for a second.

But Anna knows that for the time being she's as safe as anyone can be. She's strong, that's the main thing. She's never ill, and almost never late. She does half Lyuba's work as well as her own, which keeps Lyuba sweet. And Elizaveta Antonovna knows she'll stick at the job whatever comes, because it means she can have Kolya with her.

She'll have potatoes at this end: five rows. That should be enough. Onions next to them, those purple-skinned ones her father loves so much. He slices them and eats them raw with just a sprinkling of salt. Plenty of beetroot, spinach, and little rough-skinned cucumbers for pickling. No carrots this year, after last summer's root-fly. Cabbages, dill, parsley, garlic, shallots. Anna pictured the seeds beginning to stir. Plump nubs of green feeling their way up through the earth, unfolding, fattening, changing hydrogen and oxygen and all the rest of it into solid, succulent food.

Kolya looked better already, just from spending a few days outdoors after that long winter in the apartment. He was losing the waxen look of children who've been living inside sealed double windows.

But that moment when the ice-sheath finally loosens, and the brown earth shows, long after you've given up hope that it ever will! At first there's the stink of sour earth, which has been covered all winter with layers of ice. Before the ice melts, it grows grey and rotten. Maybe it's worth having winter, when it leads to such a spring.

'Kolya! Don't roll in the mud like that!.'

He stopped in his play, on all fours on the wet earth, and stared at her.

'Don't talk in your nursery voice –'

'What?'

'Talk to me in your home voice.'

She laughed, squatted down by him, seized his round little body in its padded jacket, and snuffed the scent of his skin. He laughed back at her, his eyes squeezed into slits.

'I'll show you a nursery voice. *Children, what is the meaning of this disturbance?*' She grates out the words, and sees him flinch.

'You sound like Elizaveta Antonovna.'

'Let's not talk about her. Listen, do you know what radish seed looks like? Because I'm going to need you to plant some. Radishes, spring onions and lettuce. And then, before you know where you are, we'll be eating our first salads.'

'Can I pick them?'

'First you have to plant them. We'll start in this bit over here, where I've dug. You remember, you have to rake it over carefully, then make the lines with a stick to show where the seeds have to go . . . they're called drills.'

'I know.'

'And then you can put in the seeds. But not all at once, mind – just a little pinch of seed in your fingers, like this.'

Kolya peered into the brown-paper bags which held the seed, some of it saved from last year, some bought at the market. He poked a finger into the radish seed.

'It's all dry and dead.'

'No, it's not dead. Don't you remember last year? Inside the seed there's a tiny germ of life, waiting until we put it in the soil. Once the sun warms it up, and the rain softens it, it'll start to grow –'

Kolya yawned, showing the rosy inside of his mouth, and his milk teeth.

'Never mind, Kolya. Just put the seeds in and see what happens. Maybe you'll find radishes growing by magic.'

'By magic,' he repeated. 'Is this drill deep enough, Anna?'

'It's perfect. When the radishes are big enough, you can pull them up. You know how Dad likes them on a saucer, with the leaves arranged round them. You could do that.'

17

'He'll be surprised that I grew them all by myself, won't he?'

'If you're going to say you grew them yourself, then you have to take care of them. Weed them, and water them if they need it. I'll show you what to do.'

But Kolya was losing interest. He dumped the last of the seed into his drill.

'Can I go and play?'

Anna went back to the potato patch. She wasn't going to make any mistakes this year. She would plant as much as possible. As long as you've got potatoes, and onions, and a bit of sausage, you'll always come through.

Kolya's commentary had started up again. 'Attack! Attack! Attack! The tanks are on their way –' After a while she stopped hearing it. Spade into the earth, lean forward, press your weight down, lift. A spadeful of earth thrust up into the light, fresh and glistening, to be turned again and broken. Worms twisted, spiders scurried, little beetles ran off the spade and plopped back on to the earth. She was getting hot. She'd take off her jacket, but Kolya would want to take his off too. A blackbird sang in the lilac bushes, then another, staking out territory with all the fierceness of spring. Farther off, behind the screen of budding leaves, Anna heard someone sweeping a verandah with a broom of birch twigs, brushing with long, steady strokes into every corner so that all the muck left by the melting snow would be gone. Sweeping away the winter.

And now it's the twenty-first of June, and Anna has four days' holiday ahead of her. The whole garden is dug, planted, and fuzzy with green. The early crops of lettuce, radish and spring onion are coming on beautifully. She counts over her crops in her mind like a miser counting money. She thinks of how they will be eaten during the dark months.

The white lilac below Anna's window is flowering late, after the cold start to the year. In the last few days its tight cones of white bud have begun to loosen and release their perfume. A chaffinch has built its nest there, so close that if she leaned out a little farther, she could touch it. But she must hurry. It's more than twenty kilometres to Marina Petrovna's dacha, and on the forest roads that'll take at least three hours' cycling. Marina Petrovna wants her to come at nine o'clock.

'And for God's sake, don't be late,' her father said last night. 'She's quite capable of refusing to see you, if you are.'

Marina Petrovna sees no one. This has been an article of faith for years. Sometimes her father receives a letter.

'Who's that from?'

Her father pauses before answering. 'Marina Petrovna.'

'Don't keep it in the house, Dad, will you?' She wants to say, *burn it*, but doesn't quite dare. At least these letters don't come through the post, so it's less of a risk. Has her father been to see Marina Petrovna? Better not ask. She is invisible, for the same reasons as Anna's father is unpublishable. She had years of fame, and then fame vanished between one day and the next. Her name was wiped from posters, programmes and reviews. But how lucky she was, considering that she'd been associated with Meyerhold as well as Tairov. She was formally criticized by the Committee for Artistic Affairs 'for her inability to adequately incorporate the fundamental method into her technique', and for 'lack of discretion over her choice of artistic associates'. She was called in for questioning, and actually released. Even a year later, she couldn't have got away with it. She'd have disappeared, along with her name.

But an actress can't burrow down and work alone, hidden. She's got to have stage, cast, director, lighting, and above all an audience. She grows older. Her best years pass, and the list of roles she's never played grows longer. She is silenced.

Marina Petrovna stays in her dacha, not far from the village where she spent every summer as a child, where her old nurse still lives. Her nurse doesn't even try to understand how people who thought they were actors and poets can suddenly find they have turned into appeasers and left-right mongrels. She wipes her hands with an invisible cloth, and mutters that things have always been like this. High-up people get ideas into their heads, but it's us who have to bear the brunt. *So just you stay here with Nanny. Keep your head down and lie low until it's all over and done with.*

The dacha is only thirty kilometres from the centre of Leningrad, but it might as well be three thousand. No one is invited there, and no one goes. Marina Petrovna doesn't push her luck. She went to ground, and they seem to have forgotten about her. But they could remember her at any time.

You have to look straight ahead. Don't look round at the black vans, or the men who climb out of them, mount the stairs with heavy boots, and stand in silence for thirty seconds before the chosen door. Then they raise their fists, and knock.

People tell themselves that the worst is over. And it's true that it's better now than in the worst of the Yezhov terror. You have to believe in something. Even in the Yezhov years, people still trusted in an unbroken record of Party membership, or hoped that influence and contacts would protect them. Or pretended to themselves that they still hoped and trusted.

Sometimes they were released while further evidence was gathered. Fish with hooks in their mouths, waiting to be jerked out of the water, like Olya. She'd been one of Vera's colleagues. One day in the bread queue, someone tapped Anna on the back. Anna turned, stared, but did not recognize the woman.

'It's me. Olya. Don't you remember me? I used to work with your mother.'

'Oh yes, yes, of course –'

'Don't pretend. You didn't recognize me, did you?'

'I'm sorry.'

'Don't be sorry. Would your mother recognize me, do you think? Sometimes I think Vera had all the luck. She got away in time. No one betrayed her, and she didn't betray anybody.'

Of course. Olya. One of her mother's protégées. She was twenty-two when she joined the radiology department, but she'd looked eighteen, even sixteen. She had very short, wildly curly brown hair that everyone made excuses to touch. She was brilliantly intelligent, and had been the best student of her year.

'We won't keep our Olya for long,' Vera had predicted. 'She'll go on to great things.'

'I lost my job,' whispered Olya in the bread queue.

'What are you doing?'

'Nothing. Just waiting. They've chucked me out of the Party as well. You know, Anna, work was everything to me. My colleagues were my family.' She glanced behind her, scanning the street. 'I shouldn't talk to you. It might be dangerous for you.'

'Olya –'

'No. I've got to go.'

All over Leningrad they lie frozen in the hours before dawn, listening for the knock that comes to other doors, but never, surely never, to your own. Not to you, with your next promotion on its way, and the holiday in the Crimea planned, and little Mitya's fourth birthday next week.

Even Anna's boss, that perfect supplier of statistics and ever-ready follower of Party directives, even Elizaveta Antonovna was grey with terror that February four years ago, after Stalin's speech to the Central Committee. Wreckers, traitors, enemies and saboteurs were not only to be found in the opposition. They had infiltrated the Party itself, and were among its élite, masking themselves as irreproachable Party activists and committee members. But how could you ever prove it wasn't a mask, Anna wonders. Only by ripping off your own flesh . . .

Behind Anna, Kolya stirs. He sits up, instantly wide-awake.

'I want to come with you!'

'You know you can't. We talked about it yesterday.'

'I'll be so quiet she won't even know I'm there.'

'No, Kolya. Marina Petrovna hasn't asked you. And anyway, you're going fishing with Dad, aren't you?'

He'd forgotten that. She watches the two pleasures fight in his face.

'And when I come back you can show me what you've caught.'

'You're better at catching fish than Dad.'

'You'll be fine. Just don't let the fish see your shadow.'

'Why not?'

'Because if he sees your shadow he knows you're waiting to catch him.'

'Anna.'

'What?'

'I won't move. I'll be so still the fish will think I'm a tree. Like this.'

He lies perfectly still, with his hands crossed over his chest. Anna is about to tiptoe out of the room, but somehow she can't leave him like this, lying on his back, with his hands folded, so still. It looks wrong – unnatural –

'Kolya?'

He springs up, glaring at her. 'I shut my eyes so you could go! You keep saying goodbye and you never go. I hate it when you do that.'

3

The track narrows to a path. She's going to have to get off her bike. Birch, bird-cherry and larch have given way to the deep green gloom of fir, and the trees meet overhead. Anna dismounts, and takes out the sheet of directions her father has written down for her. 'Turn left at the Tutaev farm (watch out for the dogs), then carry on for about six kilometres until you come to the crossroads . . .'

He was right about the dogs. Two Alsatians ran out after her, snarling and snapping round her wheels. But they were half-starved, and couldn't run fast enough to catch her as she raced downhill away from the farm. What if she'd had Kolya on the back, with his plump legs hanging down and his weight slowing them just enough for the dogs to outrun them? She must remember to go back another way.

There should be a wooden gate in the wall which runs along the track here. The wall is crumbling, held together by moss, ivy and creeping tendrils of bramble. She could climb it, but that would mean leaving her bike. She'd better keep going.

Anna half-lifts, half-pushes her bike. The sun is hot now, and under the canopy of firs the air is warm, resinous and sleepy. You could lie down here, with your head on a cushion of pine-needles, where the trees' roots arch above the forest floor like arthritic fingers playing the piano. You could shut your eyes.

Anna never gets enough sleep. There's Kolya to rouse and wash and dress. He ought to do it himself, but there isn't enough time. She makes his porridge, tidies round and does some washing if there's time. Her father never wakes. He sleeps like a stone in the mornings, in a thick, dead sleep that doesn't refresh him. It's not surprising, since he's up most of the night. She hears him moving about. A shuffle from room to room, very quiet, so as not to wake anyone. The clink of a glass. A cough, a sigh. Sometimes she could swear she hears the pages of his book turning as she listens, frozen and on edge, unable to go back to sleep herself because it feels as if she's abandoning him. And then for a long time, as much as an hour sometimes, he doesn't move at all. She pictures him sitting there, head bowed towards his chest, book slipping to the floor, worn out and sleepless, with a glass of tea cooling by his side. But she must get some sleep – she's got work in the morning.

She has to be at the nursery by seven. She sets the tables, scrubs the little toilets that Lyuba never cleans properly, checks menus and food deliveries and does as many of the dozen jobs on the list inside her head as she can, before the children start to arrive at seven-thirty. And here they come, six of them, seven, a dozen, fifteen, a flood of little bodies packed into padded trousers, jackets, caps and boots, swaying sleepily on their feet and quite unable to take off their own boots, or put their jackets on the correct pegs.

Their mothers have been up since five and even so they'll be late if they don't rush off now, this minute, unpeeling the hands of little Vasya or Maya who clings on tight to mammy's legs and won't let go without a screaming session. Above the din, Anna says over and over again: 'Don't worry, he'll be fine as soon as you've gone. I promise you, he'll be smiling again in five minutes.' *If only I keep my job here. If only I can keep Kolya with me.*

All day Anna deals with runny noses, tired tears, biting and hair-pulling, lessons in hygienic hand-washing, and socialization at playtime. Demarcation lines are strict. Anna is an unqualified nursery assistant, not a teacher. Elizaveta Antonovna Zamirovskaya, with her pedagogical qualifications and anxious, pedantic sticking to theory, never forgets for one instant that she is the expert and she is in charge. 'I have to deliver the type of education which will develop the children's concept of Soviet citizenship to its full extent. I don't expect you to understand the nature of that responsibility, Anna Mikhailovna, but I do expect you to cooperate with it to the best of your ability.'

'Allow me to assure you of my fullest cooperation, Elizaveta Antonovna!' Anna shouts back eagerly whenever this speech comes round, as it does two or three times a month. She has realized some time ago that Elizaveta Antonovna lacks confidence, for all her degrees. She needs bolstering, and the best way for Anna to do this is to assume the manner of a zealous factory forewoman receiving her morning orders. 'And may I report that the children's toilets are still overflowing. I don't think that plumber we had last week was much good.'

But after all, poor Elizaveta Antonovna, it's a struggle for her. She doesn't like the children much, and they don't like her at all.

Anna is becoming anxious. Still the same crumbling wall. Still no gate. Maybe Marina Petrovna never meant her to find the place. It isn't going to happen. No need to have selected and sharpened her drawing pencils so carefully, and spent so much more of her wages than they could afford on a new block of drawing-paper. And all this, because her father had written about Anna's work in one of his letters to Marina Petrovna. He was too conscious that she'd had to leave school to take care of Kolya, and he tried to make up for it with praise and encouragement that sounded false in her ears. He thought she was turning into a worker bee. But wasn't that what he wanted and needed? Anna to queue for him, and mend Kolya's clothes, and run from shop to shop until she got hold of fresh milk.

'You've got real talent, Anna. You must develop it.'

'Yes, for getting hold of an extra hundred grammes of sausage . . .' But she didn't say it aloud.

What was the use of talent, without training? She was making no progress at all. Her technique was poor. What she needed to learn could never be learned in spare moments in between her job and the house and Kolya. She needed teachers. She needed contemporaries, who would drive her on. But then, did she need to learn to be 'national in form, socialist in content'?

Without telling her, Mikhail packed up Anna's pen-and-ink portrait of Kolya, and her pencil sketches of Lyuba working in the nursery kitchen, and sent them to Marina Petrovna.

'What did you do that for!' Anna shouted at him when she found out. 'You should have asked me first. I'm not a child.' The flare of humiliation surprised her. Suddenly she hated that portrait of Kolya, which was the best thing she'd done. She wanted to disown it, and the sketches too. But then Marina Petrovna sent the work back, padded and packed with extreme care, as if Anna's drawings were rubies. With it there came a letter. She'd liked Anna's work. Would Anna accept a commission? Because if so, Marina Petrovna would very much like Anna to come and draw her.

'Draw Marina Petrovna! My technique's not good enough. I'm an amateur, can't she tell that? I can't even afford materials.' Again her father's hurt, conscious look. He thinks she's blaming him, because he contributes so little to the household now.

'No,' she says. 'All I meant was –' And breaks off. What's the point? One circle of her father's pain only leads down to another, until it reaches the freezing floor of his lost sense of self. He has wanted this for her so much. He has written a long letter to Marina Petrovna, 'explaining everything', no doubt. Anna's talent, the impossibility of her studying as she should be studying, his own guilt. Does he really know her well enough to spill all this out to her? Yes, he knows her well enough.

'What did you write?' she asks more gently.

'Nothing,' he says. 'It was just a note. I thought Marina Petrovna would like to know how you're getting on. She would remember you. And she was very close to your mother.'

'Was she?'

'Of course. I thought you knew that.'

But was she really close to my mother? I don't think so. She wrote letters to my parents with both their names on. My father always passed the letter to Vera, so that she could read it first. And she would tap the envelope on the table, and raise her eyebrows, and then hand it back to him, unopened.

It's you she writes to, isn't it?

Anna stops. She's almost pushed her bike straight past the gate. Perhaps she didn't really want to find it. Marina Petrovna Berezovskaya is one of those legends everyone knows and no one talks about. But she's also her father's friend Marina, who wrote letters her mother didn't want to read.

'Isn't she your friend as well, Mammy?'

'Not really. She's your father's friend. He's known her for a long time.'

'But she wants to be your friend, or she wouldn't write to you.'

'I daresay. But friendship doesn't work like that.'

4

The creak of the gate flushes out a pair of woodpigeons from the birch-scrub. The birds go up, clattering their wings, and then settle again on a branch way up above Anna's head. Prr-*coo*, they say, prr-*coo*, as they smooth away the noise she's made. The path is so narrow that she'd be better off leaving her bike here, just inside the wall where it can't be seen.

Anna is prickling with excitement now. In a few minutes she'll be at the dacha. Marina Petrovna will be in front of her.

Anna has studied a dozen photographs, trying to become objective, trying to separate the woman she is going to draw from the woman who was her parents' friend. Her father's friend. There she stands, in a pale dress, beside a chair where her father sits. Here, she is in trousers, crouched over a pail of berries, looking up. The sun must be bright, because she's shielding her eyes. Anna's father is slightly out of focus, behind her. He looks young. Another photograph shows Vera and Marina Petrovna together, side by side. But Vera seems to be pulling away, as if she'll be gone as soon as the shutter clicks. These photographs, with many others, are pasted into her father's scrapbooks. He ought to get rid of them.

A bramble snags on Anna's arm. The path is overgrown, and the trees are loaded with ivy and wild clematis. Anna treads softly, as if someone is listening. In the green rankness of the trees she catches shadows making faces. The path turns, and turns again. She might go on like this for ever, making her way soundlessly towards the house on this perfect summer morning. She might never reach it at all.

After weeks or months, someone might find her bike with its tyres sagging into the dust. But not a trace of Anna anywhere. Not a note, not a bone, not a scrap of her clothing. Like all those others.

Anna glances down at the crumpled sheet of instructions. *Follow the path to a second gate . . .*

The second gate. Even more ramshackle than the first, this one is hanging off its hinges. Briars have closed around it. She steps over the gap.

There is more light coming through the trees. Fir gives way to birch. There is rowan, and cherry. Sun streams between the tree-trunks, on to last year's fallen, skeletal leaves. There is an acrid smell of fox.

Anna stops. So far she's been heading uphill, but from here tracks spill in all directions. Some of them are animal tracks.

Surely there must be an easier way to the dacha. Perhaps she's testing you. Marina Petrovna's face rises in Anna's mind. The sweep of her eyelids, the lift of her cheekbones, the downward glance. Her beauty is cool, not warm. Black hair, dark eyes, pale skin. She is said to have had a Tartar grandfather.

They could slam that head against a cell wall. They might still. Think of what happened to Professor Kozlovsky. They let him out but he'd gone crazy. He couldn't give lectures any more.

Now the trees are thinning. The path must be coming out on top of the hill. Yes. Yes. A clearing, a thicket of lilacs, and through them the grey, quiet bulk of Berezovskaya's dacha.

Anna slips through the lilacs. A verandah runs the length of the house. There's a door, and it's half-open. She's expected.

Marina Petrovna is dressed in a cream-coloured wrapper, as if she's just finished taking off her stage make-up at the end of a play. She is smoking nervously.

'Anna,' she says, taking Anna's hands, searching her face as if for something she recognizes. She's too close, and the smell of her perfume makes Anna uneasy. 'I've been waiting for you.'

'I'm not late, am I?'

'No, you're not late. But I don't see many people. It's always a shock, so I prepare myself.'

The hand which holds the cigarette is trembling slightly. Her skin has a parchment look, and her curly black hair is greying.

'I know, I'm looking older. Country air is supposed to be good for you, but I'm not so sure.' She smiles, and takes another drag at her cigarette, half-closing her eyes. 'And you've grown up, Anna. I can still call you Anna, can't I?'

'Of course you can.'

'You must have been fifteen or sixteen when I last saw you.'

'Sixteen. I'm twenty-three now.'

'And your father tells me you work as a nursery teacher.'

'I'm not qualified to teach. I'm an assistant, that's all.'

'But you draw. I've seen your work. It's good.'

'I'm an amateur. I've no training.'

'You've come, that's what matters.' Her voice is exactly as Anna remembers it. 'Come and see the house, and then you can decide where you want to draw me.'

They walk together from room to room. Upstairs there are two bedrooms, and Marina Petrovna opens the shutters wide in each, so that they spring from gloom into light. The wooden floors are polished, but the rooms have a dry, unopened smell.

'It's bright in here at this time of day, isn't it? I'd forgotten . . .'

The light flows over the face, neither cruel nor kind, but accurate. The skin that looked so velvety in the photographs is drier now, stretched over bones. She lights another cigarette, draws the smoke deep, lets it trickle out.

'The light's good in here,' says Anna. Marina Petrovna pauses, and looks around the room with her eyes narrowed to see what Anna sees. There's very little furniture: a faded blue sofa, a rug, a stove, a window-seat. The walls are cream, the wood dark. Now that the shutters are open, Anna can see how high the dacha stands. From here you look out over forest to a line of shallow blue hills. Marina Petrovna goes to the window and stares out. Her hand slides up and down the satiny wood of the window-frame.

Anna knows that this is the room. This is where she comes, to sit on that sofa or in the window-seat, to look out at the distance. This is her place.

Anna's gaze flickers round the room, fast, excited, scenting possibilities. That big mirror above the fireplace, which is on the wall opposite the window – if you pulled the sofa forward and she sat just here, with her back to the mirror –

'I want to try something, Marina Petrovna. Is it all right to move the sofa?'

She nods. Anna drags it forward, pulls it to the angle she wants. 'Could you sit on here for a moment?'

She sits with a stiffness which shows how little she likes being told what to do. She's on the edge of the sofa, knees together, dissociating herself from her own body as if to say, *This is your idea, not mine.*

Anna's taken things too quickly. But here is the composition, exactly as she'd known it would be: the reflection, the back of her head, her arm lying across the back of the sofa, and beyond it the line of forest, bluer and more enigmatic in the mirror than face to face. And yet clearer, too.

'I don't want to be drawn sitting down,' she says.

Anna looks again at the curve of Marina Petrovna's arm against the sofa's rough blue cloth. It is perfect. Marina Petrovna stands.

'It feels wrong.'

She isn't going to be shifted on this one. These early moments are dangerous, when a sitter recognizes that you haven't just come to mirror her. You've come to penetrate. You're a threat to her private world. And with Marina Petrovna it will be more difficult than usual. She's used to controlling the way she's seen.

'A standing pose is tiring,' says Anna.

'I don't mind that. We can have breaks, I suppose.'

'Of course.'

Anna shoves the sofa back against the wall. Marina Petrovna remains standing, in a pose that isn't a pose at all. Arms loose at her sides, head plumb straight to the line of neck and spine.

She's right. This is how she should stand. She came into the world with so much that everyone wanted. All she ever had to do was enter a room and offer herself. It doesn't matter that years have passed, or that her skin is fading and her hair going grey. The curve of her lips suggests that happiness will begin any moment.

'I'll do some preliminary sketches,' says Anna. 'Just to get the pose and the room, the basic composition. Can you stay like that for twenty minutes?'

'Of course.'

Anna draws quickly, making thumbnail composition sketches as Marina Petrovna relaxes into the pose. She'll be disappointed when she sees these sketches. Sitters always are. They want the likeness, and they won't get it yet. They hate being a shape among other shapes.

It needs something more, but Anna don't know what yet. She draws on.

Lilac. A bowl of lilac. On that table, where the mirror will double it. 'There,' says Anna. 'That's it for the moment. Rest.'

Marina Petrovna looks closely at the sketches where her face is a blank disc. Then she says, 'It's going to be good.'

'Yes,' says Anna, but at this moment she doesn't care. She's swamped by the tiredness she always feels on starting a new piece of work. The thrust of beginning will land her somewhere she doesn't want to be. She can get free only by drawing her way out of it.

'After all, you're the one who has to live with it,' Anna says at last. Marina Petrovna looks startled. 'The drawing, I mean.'

'Yes. Yes, of course.'

She walks to the window. Anna watches her outlined against the light. She knows Anna's watching, but it doesn't make her self-conscious. She's grown up with being watched.

Everyone Anna has ever drawn has been nervous at first. Perhaps they are afraid that she'll prise out hidden things, and put them down on paper for everyone to see. But Anna would say that the best portraits don't work like that. They're not about exposure, they're about recognition. Anna wouldn't voice her theories aloud, because she's an amateur, and untrained, and hasn't the right to speak. She is trying to work her way towards what she thinks. But it's hard work, and drawing itself is hard enough. The line cuts its way down the paper like the arm of a swimmer doing butterfly stroke. It looks easy, but how the arm aches afterwards.

There's something each sitter doesn't like about herself, or himself. Lyuba screeched when she saw the sketches Anna had done. 'My God, Anna Mikhailovna, is my bum really that big?'

'You were bending over to mop the floor,' Anna pointed out. She had loved the line of Lyuba's spread, straining haunches. She would have liked to draw her naked. But Lyuba continued to gape at the paper, offended and fascinated.

Her father said, his voice light but pained, 'Are my lips really as thin as that, Anna?'

'I never knew I did that with my hands.'

'Are my eyes as glassy as you've drawn them?'

'I thought I was smiling.'

But what is a portrait but the scrutiny of light on form? When Anna first read this, she didn't understand it at all, but now she likes to repeat it to herself. *Light – on form. Light . . . on . . . form.* Elizaveta Antonovna filling in her reports: light on form. The children racing in the playground, their screams rising into the air like winter smoke: light on form. Her father's hand hanging at his side while he reads: light on form.

'We'll have tea,' says Marina Petrovna. 'I've got some cherry jam my Nana made last season. You must be hungry.'

She doesn't grow any food, realizes Anna, leaning out of the window and scanning the overgrown garden. Not so much as a bunch of herbs. How can she manage?

'And then I'll sit for you.'

'You mean stand, Marina Petrovna?'

'Yes, I mean stand. But now I want you to tell me all about your father. What does he think of the situation?'

'The situation?'

Marina Petrovna draws herself up. She counts on her fingers, snapping out the names. 'Poland. France. The Scandinavian countries. Greece, Austria, Belgium – need I go on?'

'Oh, I see.'

Yes, I see, thinks Anna. But I've got Kolya to think of, and the nursery children, and I've got to find a way of keeping rabbits out of the lettuces, and pickling enough cabbage for the winter, and keeping Dad from getting too depressed, and Kolya's grown out of his shoes again, and he needs vitamins, and the girls in white dresses have graduated while I –

I can't, I simply can't think about everything else on top of that. 'We're at peace,' she says. 'We have a pact with them.'

5

The green and gold evening passes like a hundred others. It seems nothing special at the time. Anna's tired after the bike ride back, with a long detour to avoid the dogs at the Tutaev farm. She's washed away dust and sweat, put on her favourite green cotton dress, and made a casserole of potatoes and anchovies. Kolya and her father are late back from fishing, but it doesn't matter. The casserole will be a little crisper on top, that's all.

'Anna!' she hears Kolya shouting through the garden. 'Anna, we got two! Two real beauties.'

The fish are brown trout. She could wrap them in wet muslin and they'd last until tomorrow, but she decides that for once they're going to have a real feast. Casserole first, then the trout fried in butter. Her father has already cleaned the fish and they lie on the kitchen table with the patient, helpful look a trout takes on after its death.

If only she'd known at the time how important every detail of that evening was going to become. Kolya boasting that the trout he'd caught had been this one, the fatter of the two. Her father, sunburnt and relaxed after his day at the lake. The taste of the trout.

Anna peels back the salty, delicate crust of scales. Each of them dips forkfuls of trout flesh into the foaming butter Anna has swirled around the pan. And her father says as he does every summer: 'There's nothing like fresh-caught fish. By the time it gets to market half the flavour's gone.' Sharp, smoky taste of anchovies, potatoes rich and savoury with anchovy oil. A handful of early lettuce. Kolya's red lips greasy with butter as he reaches for another chunk of bread to wipe round his plate.

No, she doesn't really notice any of it. After Kolya's gone to bed, she and her father drink tea on the verandah. He smokes while they talk, and a warm breeze shivers the birch leaves. Plumes of flower toss on the lilac, and now its scent is strong. They sit up until long after midnight, because neither of them wants to break the spell of the summer night. The only unusual thing is that when at last her father rises to go to bed, he doesn't shuffle off with a mumbled goodnight, his shoulders bowed by the thought of the night to come. He stands beside his daughter for a moment, with his hand on her hair.

'What a night, eh?' he says.

'Yes.'

'Your mother's roses will be flowering soon.'

'Kolya helped me to weed them.'

'That's right. That's how it should be.'

He strokes her hair again. 'That's how it should be,' he repeats.

'Well . . . Goodnight, Anna.'

'Goodnight.'

Anna sleeps. In her dream, her father is reading her a bedtime story. He has the book open on his knee but he isn't really reading, because he knows the story by heart. It's a very frightening story but Anna doesn't want him to stop. Her father says that it is about a war that happened a long time ago, when the French invaded Russia.

'*How long ago?*'

'*Oh, more than a hundred years, Anna. You'll learn about it in history one day.*'

Once, long ago, General Hunger met General Winter. General Winter, as you would expect, was sheathed in snow. His fingers were daggers of ice, and where his boots struck the earth they left blackened footprints in the grass. When he bent to smell a rose, his breath scorched it. But he loved roses, and rippling fields of wheat, and naked, suntanned children. He loved them all, because he had power over them all.

General Winter stood in his greatcoat of snow, and greeted General Hunger, as all great generals greet one another, once enough of their people have died and they can open their talks.

General Hunger, on the other hand, was not what you would

expect. His cheeks were rosy, his hair sprang from his head, and his eyes were moist and bright. He was in his element. The two generals sat down on their chairs, planted their tall polished boots in front of them and leaned towards one another. They began to boast of what they could do to their enemies.

'This is what I can do,' said General Hunger. 'I make their skin flake and crack at the corners of their mouths. I make sores break out on their lips. They screw up their eyes and try to focus, but they never see me. They don't realize that it's I who have changed their eyesight.

'I whittle most of them down to skeletons, but with some I play a trick and fill their bodies with liquid that keeps them pinned to their beds. What I like best is a big, strong, well-muscled lad of eighteen, who burns up food like a stove. You should come back and see him after I've been keeping him company for a few weeks. He melts faster than a candle, in my hands. His muscles waste away. All those big strong bones stand out. I can turn him into an old man, I can make his eyes weak and watering, I can loosen his teeth in his gums until a crust of bread will pull them out. No one eats himself up quicker than a fit young man.

'I turn old men into children whimpering for food, and I turn five-year-olds into old men. It's all the same to me if they're young or old, ugly or beautiful, and I make them all the same. I've seen a lovely young woman of twenty-five shrink back from the sight of herself in a mirror after she's been living with me for a month or two.

'If I can't finish them off on my own, I groom them for my friends. A little cold that wouldn't keep them in bed for half a day soon proves fatal when it visits them after I've been staying.

'I strip them of their thoughts. I take away their feelings. I get into their blood. I am closer to them than they are to themselves. They can think of no one else.

'My dear cousin, you have got to admit defeat.'

'Very good,' said General Winter, scratching his ear with a nail of ice. 'But now hear what I can do. I hide the earth so they cannot see a single shoot of green. I drive the sap down into the trees' roots. I search out everyone who has no shelter. I fill roads with snow, I cut off retreats, I block all movement. I ensure that nothing can grow and nothing can thrive.

'If they leave a hand or a foot uncovered, I seize it. I scorch their skin to red and purple, and then I blacken it. I make their flesh rot like the flesh of turnips when frost gets into a clamp. I harry them with wind and I blind them with blizzards. I freeze the seas so they cannot travel, I blow through the holes in their windows. I make them slow, and miserable, and afraid. I cut off their water supplies, and take away their light. I make them wade waist-deep in snow to find a handful of fuel. When they are ill and off-guard, I creep into their beds and rock them to everlasting sleep. I send gales and ice-storms. I drown them in mud. My greatest power lies in the fact that each year they forget how strong I am. In summer, when they lie under trees bathed in sunlight, they cannot believe in me. They make their plans, and they leave me out. But I have already made mine, and mine are always the same.

'So, Cousin, what is hunger without winter? Without me, they would be able to eat the green shoots, and catch fish from the streams. Without me, the sun would keep them warm.'

General Hunger frowned, and folded his arms. His face was dark with thought.

'There is something neither of us have mentioned,' he said. He glanced around, but no one was listening. The two generals drew closer, so that their heads were almost touching.

'Without the help they give us, we could do nothing,' whispered one general to another.

'Yes, it's true, without them . . .'

The two generals thought of the armies gathered to do their work for them. General Hunger broke into a smile, and slapped his thighs with meaty palms.

'Let's join forces!' he said. 'What one of us misses, the other can take care of. Together, we will be invincible.'

And the two generals stopped arguing. The talks were over. From that time on, they have always worked together.

'*Who wrote that story, Daddy?*'

'*I wrote it down, Anna. But I didn't make it up. It's a true story.*'

Inside Anna's dreaming flesh the child stares at her father. Anna twitches as if a mosquito has bitten her, and turns over in her sleep.

The next morning, Sunday morning, the weather stays fine. Little Mitya Sokolov comes over to play with Kolya, while Anna finishes her mending. Two shirts of her father's, her red blouse, and that pair of last year's shorts which will do Kolya for another summer if she patches the seat. She can hear the children's voices from among the trees, where they're building a camp. Her needle flashes in and out with quick, impatient stitches. Her father's poking about with a bit of guttering which has come loose. She'll go and give him a hand in a minute, because she's pretty sure he hasn't got a clue what he's doing. But it's good to hear him whistling like that. She'll just finish Kolya's shorts, and then she'll have a hunt for the twine. That'll fix the guttering for the time being, at least, and stop it clattering at night when the wind blows. But where did she put the twine after she'd finished using it in the garden?

This is when she hears Mitya's mother yelling. 'Mitya! Mitya! Mitya! Where are you? Come here this minute!'

Stupid woman. What's she bawling like that for? She knows perfectly well Mitya's up here, playing with Kolya.

'Mii-tya!' The voice rises to a panicky shriek. Anna bundles up her sewing and runs to the verandah steps. Something's wrong. An accident –

'Darya Alexandrovna?'

But the woman is so out of breath she can't speak. She must have run all the way from the farm. She's fat, like all the Sokolovs, and she smells powerfully of sweat. There are beads of it on her broad forehead. Her breasts heave under her overall.

'Mitya's fine, Darya Alexandrovna. He's only playing with Kolya – look, they're just over there. I thought you knew he was up here with us –'

'Haven't you heard? Haven't you heard the radio?'

'No –'

'It's war. They've attacked, the devils, just when we weren't expecting them.'

Looking terrified, Darya Alexandrovna wipes her hand across her mouth, as if to spirit away the words that have just left her lips.

'War, don't you understand?'

'The Germans?'

'Of course it's the Germans! You don't think we'd be attacking ourselves, do you? They're dropping bombs on us already, the bastards.'

Anna stares up at the clear blue sky.

'They've bombed Kiev,' gasps Darya Alexandrovna, words tumbling out of her mouth like betrayed secrets. 'Holy Kiev, would you believe it? And other cities, they say. It was Molotov himself who told us.'

'Molotov? Are you sure?'

'Of course I'm sure. Wasn't it I who heard it? Bombs and shells, dropping on everywhere.'

But the perfect sky is empty. War doesn't belong here, in the country. War. Everything will change.

'The children –'

The children's voices are piercing. 'No, Mitya! That's *my* piece of wood. You've had your turn.'

A tussle, a wail of rage. 'It's not fair . . .'

'I'd better sort them out.'

But Darya Alexandrovna detains her, pressing a hand on her arm.

'At least they're the age they are, my Mitya and your Kolya. They're too young to get dragged into it. But my nephew – you know, our Vasya – he's your age, twenty-three. God alone knows where they'll be sending him off to.'

The image of Vasya rises in Anna's mind. Plump buttocks straining the cloth of his too-tight trousers, stiff bristles of blond hair and little, cunning grey eyes. A Sokolov all right. He'll look after himself.

'I'm sure Vasya will be fine, Darya Alexandrovna.'

'It's always the same,' mutters Darya. 'The high-up ones start things, but it's us who have to finish them off.' And she glares at Anna as if suspecting her, too, of being a 'high-up one' who will expect Darya, Vasya and the whole tribe of the Sokolovs to put right her mistakes. Then she goes pale, obviously realizing that a different construction could be put on her words. She's dropped her guard in the panic of the moment.

'No offence, mind – when I say "high-up ones" I don't mean anything by it. You know that, Anna Mikhailovna.'

'I know. It's the shock. You don't know what to think.'

'They'll be swallowed up, those Fascists, that's what they'll be. They won't get away with it. Our lads'll soon beat them off, under Comrade Stalin's leadership.'

'Of course,' says Anna mechanically. She knows this is not the way Darya Alexandrovna really thinks, or talks. It's just the usual stuff everyone has to spout the whole time. Like the way old people in the village thank God every second sentence, if they haven't been taught how backward it is. Luckily, the words form themselves into clichés so naturally that you don't even have to think about it. Out here in the country, those words sound even more grotesque than they do in the city.

Darya Alexandrovna's right when she says we weren't expecting the Germans. But why weren't we? Why didn't those 'high-up ones' know anything? They know whose stories should be published and whose not. They even know people's thoughts. They know that Olya's got to lose her job, and hang around the bread queues like a ghost. But they don't know that the German army's about to drop bombs on us.

And here comes her father, hesitating when he sees Darya Alexandrovna. He doesn't like her, and she doesn't like him. Writers are useless articles, in her opinion. Her father holds a broken bit of guttering in his hand.

'Anna Mikhailovna,' says Darya is a hurried undertone, 'I don't reckon I'm going to be able to oblige you with that honey after all.'

'But –'

'It's the bees. I ought to of told you before, our bees've not been doing as well as they should. It's those late frosts. We had to light fires in the plum orchard to drive the frost away. I thought we'd have honey to sell this year as usual, but the way things are, we're going to need it all for the family.'

I bet you are, thinks Anna. Dark, rich honey, full of calories and vitamins. Honey that will last all winter. You'll keep it for yourselves. You're not stupid. But I am. What a fool I am, wasting time, standing here talking to you. We ought to be back in Leningrad, looking out for ourselves, the way you are. They'll all be in the streets by now, stripping the shops bare. There'll be nothing left. If Dad takes Kolya, and I get back as fast as I can on the bike –

'Father!' she says. 'We must leave straight away. We've got to get back to Leningrad as soon as we can.'

6

30TH JUNE

It never ceases to amaze me that people can hold two completely opposed beliefs at the same time, without feeling the slightest sense of contradiction. We are told that there is no real threat to the city. The bulletins may not be good, but that's only temporary. Our forces will turn back the German aggressors, and run them all the way to Berlin. And we both believe this, and don't believe it. The locusts have already settled on the shops, stripping the shelves clean of oil, buckwheat, sugar, dried peas, tinned goods: anything that will keep. Prices in the market are doubling and trebling.

My poor Anna was beside herself when we got back from the country to find the local shops already empty. However, she's made up for it since, pedalling from one side of the city to the other, bargaining in the market, chasing each fresh rumour of a sausage delivery. Usually these turn out to be only rumours. If the goods actually exist, they are much too expensive for us to buy them.

The banks closed down as well, because people were taking all their money out in order to stuff it under their mattresses for the duration. Although they've re-opened now, you can't withdraw more than a certain amount. But for a while nobody could get at their savings at all, not a single rouble of it. We've got no savings left anyway, but it was depressing to see such crowds, their faces animal and desperate, waving their pass-books, fighting past each

43

other to get to the bank doors. For once our lack of money was a blessing. Imagine if I'd felt it was my duty to Anna and Kolya to shove everyone else out of the way and yell and bang on the bank doors along with the rest of them until I was chased off by the police.

You have a certain idea of yourself: what you'll do, and what you won't do. It's hard enough to hold on to it.

Anna doesn't know whether they'll keep the nursery open or not. People have been sending their children out of the city since the first Sunday, and now organized evacuation is starting. No one seems sure where the children are going. South of the city, somewhere, out in the country where they'll be safe from the bombing. But Kolya is staying here. I haven't got the slightest faith in our 'organization'. There'll be some sort of muddle, that's for sure, and I don't want Kolya caught up in it. We're waiting, all of us, to see what happens.

(Why do I keep writing 'we'? I don't know. These past years, I'd come to believe that 'we' had finally disintegrated. Fear does that. And by the time we got to the Yezhov years we hardly dared be human in public. Old friends made excuses when they met you on the street, or they scuttled past you, heads down. You'd ask for news of a former colleague. There'd be a quick glance round, perhaps a whispered, 'Haven't you heard?' You'd know that your colleague had evaporated.)

But here we are, looking into the face of something even more terrifying than the misery we've been able to pile up for ourselves. We scurry about like ants with a stick poked into their ant-heap. Why the stick's been poked, we don't know, but our lives and houses are upside-down just the same. That's what war means: blunders and muddle, and doing things without understanding why you're doing them. A long time later, if you're lucky, someone comes along and writes things down so that they make sense, and calls his story history.

This I should not be writing down. How can a man with children be so criminally irresponsible? But there's something deep within me that says: Write, whatever happens.

So I keep on writing. I have a little place under the floorboards, big enough to hold a couple of these notebooks. There's a rug over the floorboards, and a table covered with work planted on top of it. Anna would never dream of disturbing my work.

We've had a few siren alerts, but no bombing so far. Everyone's talking about London, and the aerial bombardment there. Are we going to get the same? The barrage balloons are up, there are fire-fighting units being trained everywhere, and every apartment block has a kid perched on the roof with a bucket of sand to throw on to incendiary devices. Anna is on the fire-watch rota for our building. Nothing stops her. When she gets back from scouring the city for food, she starts pasting paper strips crisscross over all the windows, according to instructions. The rooms aren't exactly gloomy, but it's nothing like the light of a June day.

Anna and Kolya sleep in their clothes, in case of a raid, but I still get undressed. I sleep badly anyway – why make things worse? If there's an air-raid, who's going to care about Mikhail Ilyich's patched vest? We'll be too busy 'making our way to shelter in an orderly fashion'. There aren't enough places in the air-raid shelters, though, so I doubt if I'll bother to go.

And yet nothing happens. We're all waiting. Was it like this in London? Leningrad still floats in its usual sea of summer calm. Any minute now the bands will strike up in the parks, the ice-cream girls will come out, and everyone will start talking about swimming and rowing and berry-picking in the forest. That still seems like reality. War is the dream from which we could wake, if we made enough effort.

This morning I went out at five o'clock and walked along the embankment, then down the Nevsky. I walked for hours, it seemed, but I wasn't hungry, and I didn't grow tired. I couldn't have swallowed anything, not even a sip of tea. I must write this down, although it's almost impossible to put into words. These heightened states all sound banal once you write them down. For instance, there's nothing more tedious than lovers writing about being in love. You need to be outside the experience, not caught inside it. And for once it seems I'm caught inside.

But this is what happened as I walked. The last years fell away. I saw only our city, as it always was and always will be. It was as beautiful as before, but it wasn't fierce any longer, or proud. Rather than crushing us down, it seemed to be asking for our protection. Everything looked newborn, as if the city had dipped itself into the waters of the Neva overnight and then risen again, naked and vulnerable, with water streaming from it. As if to say, *You know that all my masterpieces are built on bones, but I am human, too.* Even the columns of the Kazan cathedral no longer looked like elephants' feet ready to crush the human ants that run this way and that way, trying to escape.

I stood there for a long time, looking at Kutuzov's statue. There he was, with his sword still pointing at Napoleon's army, ready to drive it back. And he drove it back. He played his part. He saved Russia, there's no arguing with that. Kutuzov, along with General Hunger and General Winter.

There were just the two of us, me and Kutuzov. It's all very well for you, I thought. I may even have said something aloud. You are stone. You are safe inside history. But we are still flesh, trapped in a present we don't understand, and being shoved towards a future we can't predict. The times are scared, and so are we. If only I could forget what human blood smells like. Hot, and rank. And then after a while, as it sinks into the ground, it changes and begins to smell of iron. You knew all about that, didn't you, Kutuzov? All those men you ploughed into the earth, like a farmer.

We have to face the Germans this time, instead of Napoleon's army. More blunder and muddle, and who can tell how it's all going to turn out? Maybe you know, Kutuzov. Maybe that's why you are still holding out your sword.

I'd have liked to shout up to him: 'What's going to happen, Comrade Field Marshal? Do you know, up there? You're still with us, aren't you? With us all the way!'

And perhaps those stone lips would have moved.

But you don't do such things, unless you want to get carted away. The 'black crows' are still out on the streets, never mind about the German advances. Police business goes on as usual, and once they get you into one of those vans, you don't come out again.

All the same, I found myself smiling as I walked on. Me and Kutuzov, eh? Each step I took seemed to give me the strength for a hundred more.

Well. All very high-flown, isn't it? The upshot was that I came home and told Anna I'd decided to report for duty on the Luga line, with the People's Volunteers. Even an old man whose stories are unpublishable can dig a tank-trap. The Luga line's where we'll hold them, if we hold them anywhere. Strange how the name of a river can suddenly turn into a defence system. The Luga line, we say to one another, nodding, as if we've known it all along. That's where we'll stop them.

But the stupid thing is that I'm still elated. I still feel as if I'm walking through my city in the dawn, and it's lying there, beautiful and naked, asking for my protection. Mine! – as if I mean anything.

As I said, it never ceases to amaze me that people can hold two completely opposed beliefs at the same time, without feeling the slightest sense of contradiction. Whatever happens now, those frozen years are over.

Anna has got hold of a kilo of salt cod, and some smoked lard.

7

The statues are disappearing. They are covered in sandbags, or wooden planking. They've been carried down to cellars, or camouflaged. Peter's bronze horse no longer rears above the city, smashing the air. His hooves beat against the sand which packs against him and the planks that mask him.

The whole city is going into disguise, and its people are going into disguise with it, carrying pickaxes, spades and entrenching tools over their shoulders, smearing their faces with sweat and dirt, clodding their boots with mud. They've taken trams and trains out of the city, to work on its defences. They sleep in hay, boil water for tea over twig fires, and bandage their blistered city hands with rags. Students, schoolchildren, women, old men: they're all here, digging for their lives.

This is the Luga line. No one can imagine beyond it. River, forest, villages, shallow hills. Woods smell richly of pine resin, just as they have always smelled when Leningraders go out to the country on their summer excursions. There are the little huts, empty now. There should be peasant children clinging to their mothers' legs, peering at the summer people. Look, here's that fantastic place for bilberries! And didn't Sasha get a whole pail of horse-mushrooms behind that grove of birches last year? Little Sasha, staggering out with the pail so full the mushrooms bulged over the top and he kept dropping them.

If they can't hold the German army here, it will drive straight on to the outskirts of Leningrad. There's nothing to stop it. Only flat, forested land, little hills, villages.

Anna digs. She remembers a dam she built across the stream that runs by the Sokolov place, years ago, when her grandmother was still alive. And her mother, too. Someone was helping her – who? Vasya, of course. Vasya Sokolov, long before he had

49

whiskers like pig's bristles. That was when he was her friend, and they banded together to outwit his family, who wanted him to work on the farm every hour that they weren't forced to put him into school.

Vasya used to come up and knock on the door for her to come out and play. The stream was running fast, with a winter's weight of water behind it, and the water was icy to their bare feet. It must have been early in the year. They built their dam of earth and sticks and stones, plastering more and more earth on to the structure while freezing water gushed between their legs. Her hair flopped forward over her face. Her hair-grip fell out, and flicked into the water. She peered between the stones, trying to find it. Hair-grips were hard to get hold of, she knew that.

'My hair-grip, Vasya! Can you see it?' But he didn't hear her. He was watching the dam.

'It's holding,' Vasya yelled, as a pool began to swell behind the dam. 'We've done it!' And he screamed and hopped up and down on the bank, jeering at the stream that couldn't flow any more. But Anna was watching more closely. Prickles of water were coming through the dam. As she watched, their plastered mud began to crumble.

'It's coming through! It's coming through, Vasya!'

And the water was spurting now. It swirled through a crumbling gap. Mud eddied, thinned, and disappeared. Anna slapped on handfuls of earth, but they flowed away between her fingers.

'Quick, Vasya, help me.'

The sticks began to move. Even the stones were going now, as the water elbowed away the dam. The water ran thick, muddy, fast. Their dam was gone.

Anna is digging again. She's digging for her life, but the sounds and smells of summer keep confusing her. If there are woodpigeons turning over their sleepy song, surely someone will come soon, and say it's all over, you can go home now. Spread out, have a picnic if you like, enjoy yourselves. But there's the crumple of artillery, far off, then suddenly not so far off. There are aeroplanes like black crows, searching the fields for grain. By now she can spot a Junkers when it's still a pinhead in the sky.

Anna thrusts her spade deep, turns up a spadeful of stony earth, throws it behind her, digs in again. There is burning pain between her shoulder-blades. Suddenly a roar rises from a group of workers hauling timber. 'Get out of the way, can't you?' But it's not her they're shouting at. She digs on. Spade in, bear down, turn. They're butchering those trees.

Her shirt's soaked with sweat. She's worried about one of the blisters on her hands, which looks as if it might turn septic. She soaked her hand in salted water this morning, and bound the blisters with rag. But everyone's hands are raw with blisters. If you smear honey on they heal quicker. Honey's an antiseptic. Position the spade, bear down with full weight, turn, lift. Over and over, a hundred times and then a hundred more, all through the long summer day, as long as the light lasts. They were on anti-tank ditches yesterday, today they're back on trenches.

'All right, girls, you've reached your target here. We're moving on. You're being assigned to fortifications at the railway station. Get going!'

Little Katya, on Anna's right, scrabbles out of the trench like a kid who's afraid she's taken more than her turn in the sandpit. She's terrified of getting things wrong and drawing attention to herself. She doesn't realize that it's precisely her nervous quickness to obey orders which makes her stand out. But then she's only fifteen, so what can you expect?

'It's all right, Katinka, there's no big rush. Here, have a swig of my tea.'

'Are you sure? Don't you want it yourself?'

'I'm offering it to you.'

Katya's brought nothing with her. Only herself, and her small, rather delicate hands which have certainly never held a spade before these past weeks. She was crimson with shame when her period started and she hadn't 'got anything'. Anna had to sort her out with some borrowed rags, and show her how to wash them in the stream. Katya's blood unrolled and ran away with the clear water. Luckily, in this weather everything dries quickly. Anna rinses out her own sweat-sodden shirt and underwear every night, and sleeps in her jacket.

Katya takes a small, polite sip of the cold tea.

'Go on, have some more. The sugar will give you energy.'

But by now Arkady Konstantinovich is looking for blood.

'Do you ladies think this is a tea party?' he scorches them. 'Get your backsides over here now! Get in line.'

They stumble over the rough ground. It's a couple of kilometres to the station, but at least they're not digging. A change of position is as good as a rest. With your spade slung over your shoulder, a different set of muscles takes its turn to ache.

Not a tea party . . . Anna glances at Katya, at Evgenia beyond her, at the whole line of them tramping forward, boots caked with earth, hands wrapped in rag bandages, sunburnt faces streaked with mud and sweat. Hair is tucked into scarves, or plaited and pinned out of the way. As their line advances under the trees, shadow dapples them. Evgenia's red hair sparks, then dims as she goes on into the shade of a fir tree. What a lot of different colours there are in red hair, when you look at it. Rust, copper, black. Evgenia's sleeves are rolled up, showing strong, creamy arms which the sun has splashed with freckles. As she works, her strength and bulk become grace. No one can dig out a section of trench faster than Evgenia. She doesn't hurry, she doesn't grunt with effort. She makes her way look like the only possible way of digging a trench. Why is it that some people make you want to watch them, while others – like Katya – have the effect of chalk squeaking up a board?

Katya is pretty, unlike Evgenia. Her fair hair can't help escaping from its plait and curling around her small face. It's one of those rosebud faces which don't stand up well to dirt and exhaustion. Her eyes are frightened. She stiffens when she hears shell-fire, and she's terrified of enemy planes. No wonder, when the first thing she saw on her way here was a girl about her age, stitched to the ground by bullets. She hadn't made it into the ditch with the others. *'They just left her there,'* Katya told Anna. *'They didn't even put anything over her. We all had to file past her.'*

'It's all right, Katinka,' Anna soothes her now. 'They're miles away. You can tell from the sound of the engines.'

Katya gives her a pitiful, grateful smile. At least it's as easy to cheer her up as it is to frighten her. She ought to be at school, frowning over her geometry like a good girl. Instead she's here, along with every Leningrader who's capable of holding a spade, and plenty who aren't. God knows how many thousands there are altogether. You only see your own bit, but no doubt there are thousands of Annas and Katyas and Evgenias, stretching the length of the Luga line.

Everything becomes normal so quickly. It's normal to get up at dawn, and queue for the hastily dug latrines, and not mind if someone else is peeing alongside you. It's normal to sluice your face in a stream, bundle your hair into a headscarf, gobble down a couple of slices of bread and stumble to work. Your eyes are bleary, your back aches, your arms ache, the muscles in your neck burn. But just get going, and you'll soon warm up. That's the way to deal with stiffness, Evgenia says. Work your way through it. Just keep on digging and don't give yourself time to think about it.

It's normal to run for cover at the sound of aircraft. It's normal to see someone who didn't move fast enough, sprawled in a ditch. Sprawled there, they look as if they're still running for shelter, deep into the earth. But when you pick them up they have a strange, warm floppiness and their heads fall back.

There are two realities now. There are summer trees, flights of startled birds, the smell of honeysuckle in the depths of the night. This is the old reality, as smooth as the handle of a favourite cup in your hand. And then there's the new reality which consists of hour after hour of digging, and seconds of terror as sharp as the zig-zag of lightning. Lightning that's looking for you, seeking out warm flesh on the bare summer fields.

'We could die out here!' Katya cried the first time the planes came over. She stared in horror, as if it had never occurred to her. Someone is trying to kill me, me, Katinka, with my top grades in physics and chemistry, me, with my ambition to become a doctor, me, with my new summer-dance dress waiting at Gostiny Dvor.

'Yeah,' replied Evgenia sarcastically. 'Ain't that a shame?' And she went on shovelling earth.

When they reach the railway station they fall out immediately and begin work. Anna is assigned to a work-group which is to dig a tank-trap on the station approach. There's rubble to be cleared first, and a stretch of wall to be knocked down. An older woman with glasses and grey hair begins to recite as she swings her pickaxe into the side of the wall:

> 'And so he brooded:
> From here, we shall menace the Swede,
> Here shall we raise a city that will taunt
> Our haughty neighbour . . .'

'Pity it isn't the Swede this time,' someone else interrupts. 'They were nothing compared to these Fascist bastards.'
'Don't spoil it! Let her go on,' other voices shout.

> 'Nature has fated us to cut here
> Our window on to Europe, gain our foothold
> To stand firm by the sea . . .'

'Only the window's got broken, and now the rain's pissing in,' mutters Evgenia in Anna's ear. But as the recitation continues, surely Evgenia is working even more powerfully than before, her redhead's sweat staining her shirt. Working alongside her, Anna smells Evgenia's sharp, foxy scent, which seems to belong to the forest and be part of it.

Trains are still leaving from here, taking evacuees to the north-east, out of the danger zone. A crowd of kids is being bundled on to one. Kids are packed into every corner of the carriages, kids are jammed against the windows. They're being taken back to Leningrad again, having been evacuated out here for safety, at the end of June. Evacuated straight into the path of the Germans, as it turns out. The children are dressed in layers of clothes which are much too thick for the weather. This is how their mothers must have dressed them for the first evacuation, so that they'd have their winter clothes with them. Very few are crying. They look dazed, and the little ones press up against the bigger ones as they wait passively to be boarded. Anna searches along their faces. Maybe she'll spot one of the nursery children. But it's probably better if they don't see her, even if by some tiny chance she sees one of them. It's terrible to see someone familiar, and then lose her again. They are already doubly lost, and there's nothing Anna can do.

'Poor little sods,' says Evgenia.

'Have you got children?'

'Me? No. I had a kid, but my mum looked after him, and now he thinks my mum's his mum, if you see what I mean. So I don't interfere. It would only upset him. What about you?'

'I've got my little brother, Kolya.'

'Your mum's dead then?'

'That's right. She died when he was born.'

'So you've brought him up. I bet he thinks you're his mum, really. It's the one who sticks around that counts, with kids.'

'We do talk about her. Our mother.'

'Yeah, but talk doesn't add up to much, does it? Where's he now?'

'Back in Peter. A friend's looking after him.'

'He'll be all right, then. You a student?'

'No, I'm a nursery assistant.'

'I'd have had you down for a student. You've got that educated look about you. Watch out, those bricks are coming down.'

The brick wall bulges and bursts outwards. They jump back, all of them except Katya, who is in a dream as usual.

'Katya! Get out of the way!'

But Katya still doesn't see. She blinks and smiles, looking uncertain, as the wall sways behind her. And although it's only a bit of a wall, it's still big and heavy enough as it comes down around her, one wave of bricks knocking her to the ground, the second raining on the back of her neck, her head, her fallen body.

'Oh my God.'

'Get her out quick.'

They pick the bricks off her, their hands fast and frantic. They drag her clear, as gently as they can with the smeared thing covered in blood and brick dust. But their thoughts can't catch up with what they see. Katya's been and gone and done it again – why doesn't she ever listen?

She isn't listening now. A thread of blood seeps out of her right ear. Her face is bluish-grey. Evgenia bends over her.

'She's gone.'

'Gone?'

'Dead.'

They carry Katya's body into the shade by the station waiting-room.

'Somewhere the kids can't see it,' Evgenia urges, and someone goes inside, finds a curtain, and wraps it over Katya. The curtain smells of stuffy rooms, and dust.

'Someone'd better tell Arkady Konstantinovich.'

'We ought to pull the rest of that wall down first. The tank-traps've got to be finished by tonight.'

It's not that we don't care –

It's not that we don't feel for you, Katinka, under that heavy curtain when you ought to be in Gostiny Dvor, trying on your new dress and frowning and saying it doesn't quite fit on the shoulders –

It's not that we wouldn't have done anything for you, anything, if you'd still been alive and we could have helped you –

Sun moves around the corner of the waiting-room. It touches the bundle in its thick curtain. It plays on the exposed tips of rather white, rather delicate fingers. We didn't wrap the curtain round her tightly enough. From close by there comes the shrieking whistle of a train, panicky now, as if there's not much time left. And then the children on the train begin to cry at last, as the carriages judder and the wheels slowly turn. The small familiarity of the station pulls away from them, gathering speed.

But you understand, don't you, Katya, that we had to go on digging the tank-trap?

8

It's dark. The packed barn smells of women. Flesh, sweat, blood, dirty clothes, swollen feet. The heavy smell of work sweat, and the sharper, acrid stink of fear.

The light of a hurricane lamp sends shadows stretching and sprawling. They'll have a couple of hours sleep, maybe three, just enough to stop them falling over as they dig.

Everyone's hungry. A pail of cabbage soup with dried mushrooms is hot and tasty when it's fresh in your belly, but the fullness doesn't last long. And too much cabbage soup makes you shit. Shadow after shadow dodges out of the barn to crouch among trees, guts twisting. *Only hope nothing splashes on these trousers, there's no chance of washing them tonight.*

The bread supply didn't arrive this evening. Four trucks shelled yesterday, someone said. The green and golden land of summer is changing. It smells of raw earth from hastily dug fortifications. It smells of sap where the pale-yellow inner flesh of birches quivers as the tree is chopped down. Trucks and tanks have gouged their way up to the Luga line, leaving the fields churned up behind them. They are ploughing next year's food back into the earth before it has grown ripe. The German front line is close, but no one knows how close. There are rumours that the Luga line won't hold. It's bulging, like a dyke before it gives. Those motorized Panzer divisions can smash through anything.

Not the whole length of the Luga line, for God's sake: surely that can't be. After all, we've got tanks and artillery too, and all these fortifications. There are tens of thousands of us, digging until we can't stand up. And then there's the Red Army, and the People's Volunteers besides. What do you mean, the People's Volunteers have only got one rifle between six of them? What kind of talk is that? My Piotr's out there with his mates from the Sanitary Department. Don't tell me they'd take all those men if they hadn't got enough rifles for them.

'Some people will believe anything,' Evgenia hisses in Anna's ear.

Nothing seems to stop those Fascists. They're not human, if you ask me. No matter how many get shot, there are always more of them, great grey waves of them racing inland, swallowing up our fortifications as if they were kids' sandcastles. One minute they're standing, the next they've crumbled away and then they disappear. You can't even see where they were standing.

They are shelling close tonight.

'How close was that?'

'If you count after the flash, like thunder, you can work it out.'

'Don't be so stupid, of course it doesn't work like thunder.'

'Oh my God, that was close.'

'Come on, girls,' says Evgenia. 'I want my sleep if you don't. Here, this is what you do. Wrap your blanket round your head, tight, that's the way. Fold it over your ears, just like your mother used to do – then you'll soon drop off.'

'Until they drop something on the barn.'

Evgenia draws herself up. 'What sort of talk is that?'

Instinctively they are silent, glancing at one another. Who said it? Who's the *defeatist*? Even here, thinks Anna, we're still at it just the same.

'If they drop a shell on the barn you'll be fine,' goes on Evgenia, 'as long as you've got your blanket round your head. It's just a question of having the correct attitude.'

A tiny gasp. Can she really have meant to mock Party talk like that? Jokes are the worst thing, everyone knows. Nothing gets you disappeared faster than a joke overheard by the wrong person. Or even the right person, someone you trusted but who can't stop herself weaselling off to the authorities like a kid in the playground trying to get in with the teachers. *'Mi-iss, do you know what Evgenia said?'*

'All I do is put my blanket round my head, think about the high-up ones who are looking after us the way they always do, and I drop off right away,' announces Evgenia. 'Just like a baby. Nothing to worry about.' A look of calm, virtuous stupidity spreads over the broad planes of Evgenia's face. She thumps her fist into the pillow she's constructed from straw and a liberated waiting-room curtain. Not the same one, of course, as Katya's – but better not to think of that now.

'Here, Anna, there's room for two on this pillow. Bring your blanket over here. This is proper luxury, this is.'

Luxury. The smell of Evgenia's thick red hair, the tickle of her plait as she switches it over her shoulder. Evgenia's big, solid body hunches in purposeful sleep. Evgenia won't lie awake counting shell flashes. That's not going to stop a German tank, is it? The thing is to get what rest you can, and then be ready to crack on again in the morning.

Yes, she really is asleep. A tiny snore, a snuffle, and then Evgenia flings out her arm across Anna. It lies there, heavy and warm. Why does it feel so good, like the answer to a question? Night and terror dissolve. Anna relaxes, lapped against Evgenia's soft, warm flesh. The white, freckled arm that drives the spade into the ground faster than anyone.

Evgenia has that effect on everyone. Somehow, with Evgenia in your work-team, things don't seem quite so bad. You believe that the Germans will be stopped, as long as everyone does her bit, gets as much sleep as she can and doesn't swill down the cabbage soup so fast that she ends up with bellyache. You have to chew that little bit of bread which you've kept over from yesterday's ration, then have a swallow of your soup, then another bit of bread. Nice and easy, that's the way, no gobbling. Give your digestion a chance. And as for the Germans, there's no sense wasting time making them bigger in your mind than they really are. They're only human, in the end, Panzer divisions or whatever. They've got to eat and sleep and shit and keep themselves warm, and once all that starts getting tough it won't matter how many tanks they've got.

Anna lies still, thinking in Evgenia's voice. She smiles in the darkness. It'll be light in less than an hour, and they'll start work again, and she won't have had any sleep. Normally she'd worry about that, but not now. She can sleep walking along, if it comes to it. You don't walk straight, but there's usually someone there to shove you into line. She hasn't yet worked out a way of sleeping and digging at the same time, but perhaps that'll come, if she gets into the rhythm.

If only Kolya's getting on all right with Marina Petrovna. How strangely things turn out. Who would have thought, a month ago, that Marina Petrovna would be the one to send Anna off to the war? There she stood in the door of their apartment, perfectly at home, hoisting up Kolya on to her hip so that he could wave goodbye to Anna as she disappeared down the stairwell.

The knock came late at night, just when the blue gloom of a Petersburg summer midnight gives way to morning. Anna stumbled to the door, face sticky with sleep, afraid.

'Who's there?'

'It's me. Marina Petrovna.'

Even in the middle of her fear, Anna had to smile. Did everyone in the whole world say 'It's me' before they said their name? She slid back the bolt, and grated the key round once, twice. Marina stood there, a bundle in her arms.

'Can I come in?'

'Quick.'

If only no one's seen her. What if they recognize her. Oh God, what's she come here for? What's she after now?

'Your father . . .' said Marina.

'No, he's not here. He's gone off with the People's Volunteers.'

They stared at each other. This wasn't the woman Anna had gone to draw, safely out of the way in her dacha. Here she was, wanting something from Anna.

'I'm sorry,' said Marina. 'I'll go.'

'You can't go now, in the middle of the night. You'll get picked up. Or they'll trace you back to us and we'll all get picked up.' Anna knew how hard her voice was, but she didn't care. How could she cope with yet another person who wouldn't be practical, who refused to come to terms with the way things were? She'd got enough of that with her father. Why couldn't they have a bit of sense? Why did they think she could have sense for all of them? 'Come on in here,' she said. 'Let me take that.'

The bundle was terribly heavy.

'Be careful, there are glass jars in there. But I shouldn't have come. I wouldn't have come if I'd known. I thought your father would be here.'

In the electric light, Marina's face was drained. The grey in her hair showed thickly.

'He's gone. Everyone's gone to fight. I think he's somewhere near Kingisepp, but I'm not sure. You know they called for volunteer reinforcements?'

'Yes, of course.'

'And so he went. He's in the People's Volunteers.' Anna kept her voice flat, hiding the fear she felt. Her father was the last man who should have gone.

'Of course, he would go . . .' said Marina, as if to herself, as if drawing on layers of knowledge Anna hadn't known she had. 'That's just like him. Have you heard anything from him?'

'No. But I didn't expect to, with things the way they are.'

Marina Petrovna looked like a ghost. She stared around the apartment, as if challenging its reality.

'So here I am,' she breathed, 'after all this time . . .' And she picked up a photograph.

'It's very like her.'

'I know.'

Anna wanted to pick up the photograph and hold it to her, the glass against her body so that Marina Petrovna couldn't see her mother's image. What did this woman want? Memory curled inside Anna like smoke, making shapes she didn't want to recognize. Her mother had not wanted to be this woman's friend. And why was that, when Vera believed so passionately in everything women could do for one another? All the women who worked with her loved her. She understood that they had to spend their lunchtimes in queues, because that was what she had to do herself. She knew that after work they would have to take a tram and then a bus to the nursery, then another bus home, and then immediately start to prepare the supper out of the heavy bag they'd been lugging around half the day. But had Marina Petrovna ever lugged a lunchtime shopping-bag, or peeled potatoes with her coat still on so as to save time, because the children were whining with hunger?

In the photograph, Anna's mother glanced up and smiled, unaware of them both. She was still picnicking in the forest near Tolmachevo, still sitting on a rug spread out in a birch grove where shade dappled her face. Under her summer dress Anna saw the swelling roundness that would become Kolya. It was hot that day. Vera's ankles were swollen, and her face puffy. In her hand she held a hard-boiled egg which she had just finished peeling. In a minute she would stretch out her arm and offer it to someone who was just outside the frame of the picture. *There's a screw of salt in the basket . . .*

But Marina Petrovna doesn't know anything about all that. She can pick up the photograph and stare at it as much as she likes, but she'll never know my mother. And I shan't tell her anything. *What is she here for? What does she want from us?*

'Thank God,' said Marina Petrovna, 'that Vera knows nothing of all this.'

'No.' Anna stared at her smiling mother, lost in summer peace. *You died, and you left me to deal with it all. When I show Kolya your picture and say, 'That's Mama,' he doesn't even want to look at it. He just says 'I know,' in a bored voice, and rushes off to play. But I know that you didn't mean to die. You had no patience with the idea.*

'Anna, I've got something to ask you,' says Marina Petrovna. 'A great favour. But you must say no, if it's impossible. I shan't be offended.'

Marina's eyes shone as if she had just blinked away tears. She was still much too beautiful, even now with the lines driving deep into her skin as she smiled, and her hair showing coarse and grey under the electric light. She was an actress, wasn't she? That's why she could throw out so much emotion that she took up the entire room. Imagine living with that force. You'd feel crowded. It would crowd you out. Everything you felt would be less important than anything she felt. Perhaps that was why she went on battering Vera with offers of friendship, when the friendship was gone.

'You want to stay here,' said Anna.

'Yes. Only for a day or two. I've had to leave the dacha. A friend has offered me a room, but I'll have to wait until her children are evacuated. It should be on Wednesday. And with the Germans breaking through, I wanted to be sure to get into the city as soon as possible, before I was cut off.'

The matter-of-fact way she said it unnerved Anna.

'They'll never get as far as your dacha. They can't get that close to Leningrad.'

Marina smiled in much the way Anna smiled when Kolya made one of his wild, childishly confident assertions. *Fine, if you don't want to join the grown-ups, I shan't spoil things for you.*

'My old nurse has gone up to Mga. She's got family there. But this is where I belong. This is where I should be, here in Leningrad. So if you could let me stay, just for a couple of nights – I can sleep anywhere. And I shan't go out, so there won't be any risk to you. And look –' she dived into her bundle. 'Food. I brought everything I could. Here, have these jars of honey.'

Two jars of dark honey. Two sealed jars of lard. A greasy packet of smoked trout. Dried mushrooms, dried cherries –

'This is pork fat. And the bilberry jam is last year's. It's full of vitamins.'

Marina Petrovna laid the jars and packets out on Anna's table. Her face sparkled with triumph.

'I brought as much as I could carry.'

Anna's mouth prickled. Here it was, everything she'd searched for in the empty shops. She could smell the musk of the cherries. Already, in her mind, she was storing the food and portioning it out. But she said what she had to say.

'Marina Petrovna, we can't take this –'

'Don't you know that food is the only thing that matters in a war? The only thing. You must put all this away, Anna. You're going to need it. You're too young to remember what it was like last time. Such terrible sufferings . . . but you were only a baby then.'

'I can't let you give us so much,' said Anna, but she knew she would, and she thought that Marina Petrovna knew it too. And perhaps Marina Petrovna wasn't going to be so bad after all. At least she wasn't so completely lost in how things used to be that she never bothered to find out how they were now.

'Don't worry,' said Marina Petrovna. 'There's still some food left in the bundle. I shan't go to my friend's house empty-handed. But I'm not making any conditions, Anna. Whether I stay here or not, this food is for you and Kolya, for your mother's sake.'

If only she hadn't tacked on that last bit, about my mother. But then she is an actress. That's why her sentences always end properly. It's important not to forget that. And then Marina Petrovna smiled, a sudden, naked, timid smile, unlike any expression Anna had seen on her face before.

'Of course you can stay here,' Anna said, before she knew that she was going to say it.

They made up a bed on the slippery leather sofa, and then sat at the table by the window and drank tea as dawn washed between the crisscross strips of sticky paper.

'Thank God you don't live in a communal apartment any more,' remarked Marina Petrovna. 'Do you remember it, Anna? All those little Slatkin children crawling around under the table, pinching people's ankles while your mother and Lydia Maximovna talked about childcare theory. And there was that poet – what was his name, the one who was no good and kept plonking himself down at the end of the table to copy out his poems, just when the supper was ready. He had a perfect instinct for it. And then someone would have to go and unblock the lavatory on the landing for the hundredth time, because the little Slatkins kept throwing things down it. What an impossible life, for a woman like your mother.'

She keeps coming back to my mother, like someone feeling a hole in a tooth with her tongue.

'We liked it,' said Anna. 'At least, I think we did.' She remembered the packed, moist warmth in the kitchen, the taste of sugar lumps which had been dipped into the grown-ups' tea, the unexpected people huddling there for hours over their tea-glasses. There'd been a constant, noisy flow of talk that washed back and forth above the children's heads. Beneath it, under the table, Anna and the Slatkin children had done exactly as they liked. Anna remembered the forest of adult legs, the different shoes, the way a woman's foot would suddenly slide out of its sheath of leather and her toes would wriggle.

And then everything had changed. People had stopped being idealistic about communal living. It became something you only did if you couldn't climb any higher. If you had influence, or money, you measured it in square metres of privacy. The Slatkins had separated, and the children were sent off to their granny's in the country. Otherwise, Lydia would never have been able to finish her novel.

'I haven't thought about them for years,' said Anna. 'The Slatkins, I mean. I wonder if they're still in Leningrad.'

'Lydia Maximovna's doing very nicely, writing screenplays for Lenfilm. She'll have been evacuated, with the rest of the company. But of course she hasn't come near your father for years. She's much too canny for that.'

'What about the children?'

'You wouldn't guess that she'd ever had any children. She's remade herself, Anna – she's an object lesson to us. What a pity that we can't all do the same.'

Anna looked sharply at Marina Petrovna, then allowed her a small smile of recognition.

Anna packed all the food carefully away at the back of her store-cupboard. They would touch none of it yet, not even the dried cherries that Kolya loved. Something came to her, a fleeting thought as stray as a fragment of a dream, but alive with terror. She saw Kolya's mouth wide open, his pink mouth with the milk teeth that Anna brushed so carefully. Suddenly Kolya's white teeth were brown, and rotting. Kolya opened his mouth for food, but there was no food. Without allowing herself to think about what she was doing, Anna fetched the empty glass jars she collected throughout the winter for next year's preserving. She built a parapet of empty jars in front of the food Marina Petrovna had given her. A fortification.

Marina Petrovna did not leave. When Wednesday came, her friend's children weren't evacuated. They would have to wait for the next convoy, and until they left there would be no space for Marina in her friend's apartment. Anna accepted it, not letting herself know how she felt about Marina's continuing presence. She was determined to see it as something impersonal, one more consequence of the war. They did not quarrel. Marina Petrovna seemed to want to be friends, but that wasn't possible yet. Kolya liked her. That was important. It freed Anna for fire-watching and queuing.

And then the call came for more volunteers, not to fight this time, but to go and dig defences. It didn't matter if you were fourteen or sixty, as long as you could hold a spade. A hundred thousand Leningraders were needed. No, two hundred thousand, three hundred thousand. Posters bloomed everywhere. *To the trenches! To the fortifications! Defend the Motherland!* Long lines of schoolchildren waited to register, chattering about tank-traps and fortifications instead of maths homework. New words flew about, words these kids had never even heard before, let alone used. *Strategic defences. Signing up. Immediate danger of invasion. Crisis.*

Now they were off to learn what these words meant, with their bare hands and maybe a knapsack with a bit of food and a change of underwear in it, if they were lucky.

And there was Anna, an outsider again. Neither a student, nor really a worker any more. The nursery had closed, then re-opened, then closed again after the latest evacuations. She'd scrubbed the toilets for the last time, and straightened the rows of tables. The silence was like a holiday. Elizaveta Antonovna had been drafted into a 'vital position in the evacuation service', where her solid Party skills would outweigh her ignorance of the needs of children. Lyuba had vanished. Anna wandered through the empty, sun-filled rooms, and then out to the children's garden, where their sunflowers grew as they grew every year, vigorously and unequally. How disappointed little Vaska Piskov would be to see that his sunflower was completely dwarfed by the thrusting sunflower of Pavlik Orlovsky, who hadn't bothered to water his plot at all, even after a stern lecture from Elizaveta Antonovna.

Anna locked up, delivered the keys, then went off wandering again with Kolya. They took a tram down to the Baltic station, where crowds of students surged and jostled, waiting for trains that would take them where the action was.

'Are we going on a train?' asked Kolya, tugging at her hand. She held on tight to him, afraid of losing him in the rush of people.

'No, we're not going anywhere. Not yet, anyway.'

'I bet I could be a good fighter.'

'They aren't going to fight. They're going to build defences.'

'I *would* fight, if I was grown up. Why don't you fight, Anna?'

'Because I've got you. I can't leave you on your own, can I?'

'No, you can't leave children on their own, because they might get lost and not be able to find theirselves.'

But he said it glibly, by rote, as if it was something that could never possibly happen to him.

And then suddenly it became possible. She could go. Marina Petrovna simply said, 'It's ridiculous, the two of us stuck here looking after one child. I can't dig, with my back – I've never even been able to dig my own garden. But if you go, I'll look after Kolya. He'll be fine with me. We'll get on with building our fort, won't we, Kolya?'

'Will we get it finished by the time she comes back?'

'I expect so.'

How heartless children could be, Anna thought. He was perfectly happy to let her go, now that Marina Petrovna was there to make papier-mâché from wallpaper paste and newspaper, and draw plans for the fort which was going to be built to exactly the right scale for Kolya's toy soldiers. They were going to paint it in camouflage colours.

'But how will you manage? What about the shopping?'

Because you're not a person yet. You haven't got the right papers. You don't really live here. If you can't get your own rations, you'll be eating up ours.

'I'm going to get all that sorted out,' said Marina Petrovna briskly. 'I'm here in Leningrad to release a worker for volunteer duty. I'll get my papers. These aren't normal times. And meanwhile I can do the shopping down at the Sennaya Market. I've got money.'

Yes, it's all worked out right for you, thought Anna. She could not separate out her feelings for Marina Petrovna, or decide which to trust. Was Marina generous, or self-interested? Was she manipulating Anna, or trying to help her? But you couldn't listen to her voice and disbelieve her. That came from her training, perhaps. She was an actress. Doubts came later, worming into Anna's imagination. This was the woman her mother hadn't trusted. Vera had tapped Marina Petrovna's letters on the table, and handed them back, unread, to Anna's father.

So there was Kolya waving goodbye, in the arms of a woman he had never seen a week before, entrusted to a woman whom Anna had wanted to draw, not to live with. Marina Petrovna had won. She'd made her place in their lives. She was there, opening and closing the doors of their apartment, saying to Kolya when they'd finished shopping, 'Come on, it's time to go home.'

Evgenia's arm weighs heavy. But if I move, I'll wake her, and she needs her sleep. I'll just curl sideways, like this, and wait until they come to get us up. It can't be long now.

Suddenly Evgenia heaves herself around. Her breath, sour but not unpleasant, blows softly into Anna's face. Her warm, acrid, redhead's scent enfolds them both. Her arm isn't just lying there now, it's encircling, gripping, remembering some lost lover or child who appears as a phantom in Evgenia's dreams. But there is nothing ghost-like about the warmth of Evgenia. Their bodies lie close, and alive. Katinka should be here too. She ought to be lying on the other side of Anna, moaning on about how she's got straw stuck down her neck and she's never gong to be able to sleep in this place, it's even worse than going on a Pioneers' camp.

Katinka should be examining her white legs for scratches, and saying in a high, aggrieved voice, 'It's all right for you, Anna!' because she knows that Anna is only a nursery assistant, not a student on her way to better things. And therefore Anna was naturally better able to cope with straw and scratches. Katinka's parents were not Party members in good standing for nothing. They'd taught her well.

Katinka, dimpling a smile at her reflection in the morning bucket of water, and then brushing out her fair hair, fifty strokes on one side, fifty on the other, like the well-brought-up girl she was. That hairbrush was about the only thing she'd thought of bringing with her.

'My mother would kill me if I didn't look after my hair. She acts as if it's hers, she's been taking care of it so long.'

All that muddle of a person gone. And they're moving us on today. What if they don't even bury her? No, they won't bury her. There isn't time.

The ground shakes. Women start up, clutching blankets.

'Oh my God, what was that?'

'Just the shelling, same as always,' says Evgenia, sitting up calmly, shaking back her red hair. 'Getting a bit close, though, isn't it, girls? What about you, Anna? Did you have a nice sleep, duckie?'

'Duckie!' says Raisa Fyodorovna. 'Why d'you have to talk like a village girl, when you're a Leningrader like us?'

''Cos I *am* a village girl really, only I came to the city when I was eight, to make something of myself. What's wrong with us village girls, anyway? At least we know how to dig, which is more than I can say for some.' And she mimics Raisa's ineffectual pawing at the earth.

'Can't you think of anything better than making fun of people who are doing their best?' spits Raisa. 'Listen to that shelling. They're right on top of us.'

'That's our artillery, can't you tell the difference? We're answering back. Those bastards aren't going to have everything their way.'

Evgenia stands up, and twists her hair into a knot. 'Come on then, my darlings, that's enough tarting yourselves up – time to get on with the digging. The Germans aren't going to wait while our Raisa cleans her fingernails.'

9

Triumphant return bearing two eggs. Got them from the farm we can see through the trees: just one old woman left, sitting by the unlit stove. She wouldn't take my money, called me *Sir*, and talked about the war as if it was the weather.

'I don't know what'll happen to the hens and pigs with all those armies running around, and no man in the house, but what can't be cured must be endured.'

Two sons in the army, husband dead, daughter-in-law gone three days ago with the grandchildren to walk to the railway station at S—.

'If the trains are still running, they'll go on to Peter,' she said. 'But I couldn't walk so far, not with my legs. So they left me to mind the shop.'

She thrust her legs out to show me. They needed dressing, but there was no one left to do it, she said. Knots of blue vein wriggled down the inside of her calves. The skin was too white, dead white, with raw purple and red sores in it which were eating away at the healthy flesh. One of the sores was suppurating. Andrei would have known what to do.

'I sit out in the yard like this, Sir, so I can get the sunlight. Sunlight's better than liniment.' She pointed to the wooden stool by the doorway. 'I carry that outside, and I sit there, and the hours fly by.'

She hobbled out to get the eggs for me. Very slowly she creaked down on to her knees, opened the hen-house door, and fumbled around inside. At last she brought out

71

two small eggs covered with shit and straw and she came hobbling back, cradling them in the palms of her hands. She blew on the eggs, then rubbed off the bits of straw.

'These are today's eggs, these are, nice and warm. Put them in water, and they'll sink like stones. You try it, Sir. That'll show you how fresh they are.'

She took me round to the pigsty and showed me the sow and four piglets. A solid, bristly sow with wicked eyes slanting up at us to see if we'd brought any swill, or if we were going to be daft enough to get within biting range.

'She's one you want to watch. She's had my son pinned on his back before now, in that corner. If I hadn't of held her off with the pitchfork she'd have had him. But there isn't a sow like her for breeding. Twelve fine piglets she bore in her last litter. We gave four of them to the chairman of our kolkhoz at six weeks, then my daughter-in-law's family had three. We ate one ourselves, and we're rearing these four. The way the wind is blowing, the high-up ones are turning a blind eye to pigs these days, thank God for it. Well, you understand it all, Sir, because you're an educated man.

'We used to have a cow, but she died. My daughter-in-law reckons that if we rear these four pigs, we can trade them for a cow in the kolkhoz market. But now they've put a tax on our orchard, so I don't know how we're to pay that except out of the pig money.'

She knew how it all works. You have to have so much for the kolkhoz chairman, to make sure everything goes smoothly and you don't get into trouble. So much for the tax on orchards. And give thanks to God that they've decided to turn a blind eye to pigs, since the 'model charter' of 1935. She rattled the whole lot off as if these were the laws of nature. And I felt ashamed, even though none of it was my doing. Words like these don't belong in the mouths of old women who can't help crossing themselves when they say the words 'thank God', even though it's been drummed into them that God has no place in our great struggle against backwardness.

Model charters, edicts, labour-days, allotted tasks, 'liquidate the kulaks as a class'. I didn't make up those words. So why did I feel guilty? Perhaps because I'm an educated man. One of those who ought to have given her bread, but instead all she's had is words, dropping on her like millstones. We were going to make everything different, and better. To hear Vera talking about healthcare in the community was like watching the sun come up.

Well, we certainly made things different.

The old woman bent over the pen and scratched the sow's back.

'She's as good as gold with me. It's the men she doesn't like. You can't blame her. She's sharp enough to know that she had twelve and now there's only four left. She remembers that it was my son took her piglets away.'

I could have stayed there for hours. I didn't want to leave the old woman. Not because there was anything I could do for her, but because inside that little yard you couldn't believe in anything but the cluck of hens, the midday heat, and the wicked grin of that sow as she bided her time. There were bluebottles all over the midden, and horseflies. Everything was rotting down nicely, the way it should. She was so sure it would all go on, just as it had always done, season after season. Even if the high-up ones went completely crazy, they couldn't stop apples growing on apple trees. The pigs would grow, the hens would lay, and once the midden was ripe her son would appear to spread the muck on the potatoes.

'This is our "private plot", you see, Sir. They let us grow our vegetables here, and keep our hens. There you are, Sir, that's the way. Wrap the eggs round in your kerchief and you'll get them home safe.'

I fetched the stool for her and she sat down in the yard, and hitched up her skirts to the knee so that the sun could warm her raw, swollen legs. Vera would have known what to put on those sores.

'I must be on my way,' I said. I pressed money for the eggs into her hand, and she got out a ragged handkerchief, tied the coins into a knot in the corner, and stuffed them deep into her pocket.

'Will you be walking this way again?' she asked me, as if I were a gentleman on a rambling holiday.

'Maybe,' I said.

'Well, you'll always find eggs here. I can't eat them myself, never have been able to. I'd give them to you for nothing if it wasn't for my daughter-in-law. They're her hens, you see, and she'll know at once if I don't get the right price for them. The way she can add the figures together, you wouldn't believe it. She keeps herself sharpened up like a knife.'

Her face creased, chewing over the thought of her daughter-in-law. I left her sitting in the yard. By the time I'd got to the gate I'm sure she'd already forgotten about me.

Andrei and I have just eaten our eggs. Little fires are burning, everything's calm and settled and almost like home. That's the main thing I remember from the last war. You had to make a home out of wherever you were, no matter what the place was like.

We lit cigarettes, and Andrei started telling me about camping out in the taiga in summer. He won't hear a word said against Siberia. We're all ignorant and prejudiced, he says. It's the most beautiful place in the world. The air is free and bright, not like our muddy Leningrad air. The water is the purest on earth. When you drink it, out in the taiga, ice-cold, you feel it flowing through your body like new life. And the people there are quite different from city people.

'No wonder, since they're all ex-cons and politicos,' Ilya commented. 'Siberia's not exactly somewhere you'd go to by choice.'

'So you're criticizing the wives of the Decembrists now, are you?' Andrei said. 'Why d'you think they chose to follow their husbands? Typical Leningrad narrow-mindedness. There is life beyond the Neva, you know.'

'So why're you here then, if it's so great in Irkutsk? And let's leave the wives of the Decembrists out of it. They didn't have such a bad time, if you ask me.'

'Are you saying they weren't martyrs?' broke in a Komsomol boy called Petya.

So here we are in the middle of nowhere, in the path of the German advance, equipped with entrenching tools instead of the machine-guns and rifles we need, but still arguing about the martyr status of the Decembrists' wives. Nothing, to me, more effectively sums up both our strength and our weakness.

'I'm saying nothing,' said Ilya, leaning forward so his face was a couple of inches from Petya's. 'Nothing, right? You got that?'

And suddenly there was something so impressive about him that Petya simply said, 'I know. Don't get me wrong.'

Petya's a nice boy. Idealistic, but not the informer type. Meanwhile, Andrei had pulled out the textbook on thoracic surgery he carries everywhere, and started on Chapter Three for the dozenth time. But every time Andrei begins to study, something happens and we have to –

Diary ends. Written in pencil on blank side of folded diary sheets:

Diary sheets found by medical student Andrei A— in the breast-pocket of Mikhail L—, a member of the People's Volunteers wounded in the German offensive of 7–8th August, and taken by the said Andrei A— for safe-keeping and return to his family.

This was the way Andrei wrote: he couldn't help it. All his funniness and liveliness disappeared as soon as he had a pen in his hand – or even a pencil. His grey eyes would cloud with thought. His pen would hover over the paper, then suddenly, rapidly, decisively, he would begin to set down a stream of clichés. He wrote these words, and folded the papers back into his own breast-pocket. Mikhail had a daughter, he knew. A daughter and a son, in an apartment not far from the Moyka. If he concentrated, he would be able to remember the address.

Concentrate. Think of that, not of where you've been.

He's been in an open truck full of wounded men, moaning at each rut in the road, sometimes crying out. Andrei does what he can, without medical supplies, water or room to move. A man bleeds to death who would have been saved by immediate surgery and a transfusion. There's a volunteer who doesn't look more than sixteen, who has received shrapnel wounds to his face. His lower right jaw is shattered, and blood mixed with bone splinters keeps bubbling out of his mouth. Andrei has turned him on his side, to lessen the risk of choking. The boy makes no sound at all; simply breathes in and out, and with each breath the blood swells thickly out of his wound. He is conscious, but so shocked he doesn't seem to feel his own pain. Andrei has torn his own shirt into bandages, and commandeered the shirts of two reasonably clean-looking men with leg wounds. The man with the torn femoral artery dies, and his head falls back on to the shoulder of the man next to him, the man with the crushed foot.

'Is he – you know?' asks the crushed foot quietly. Andrei doesn't pause to answer. Next minute, out of the corner of his eye, he sees the crushed foot pressing down the eyelids of the dead man with his thumb. Catching Andrei's glance, he says defensively, 'Well, you've got to show respect, haven't you?'

Stink of burning everywhere, thick, acrid, tallowy smoke rolling low on the ground, swallowing the line of people. Huts are on fire, either as a result of bombardment, or because their owners have torched them as they fled. Somehow they remember, deep down, that it's the thing to do. Retreat if you have to, but leave nothing for the enemy but ashes. Leave no food for them, and no shelter.

They crowd the road, men, women, terrified children clutching their mothers' skirts, goats, stampeding pigs, flocks of hens that have been let loose. The truck bumps past a man crouched at the side of the road, wringing a chicken's neck. Andrei will always remember his big, meaty, red hands as they wrung the life out of the flailing bundle of feathers. *That's one at least those bastards won't eat.*

A round, doll-like couple wrestles a mattress along. They can't bring themselves to leave it behind, it's a real feather mattress after all, though they're choking with the effort and everyone's shoving into them and cursing them. Finally they stumble to the edge of the road and sit down on the mattress, legs stuck out, gazing vacantly in front of them.

The road leads to the station, six kilometres away. They say there are still trains running. They say if you've got something to barter, you stand a better chance of being squeezed on board.

Among the peasants there are soldiers, grey-faced, mongrel-looking in exhaustion and defeat. They're walking, walking, walking into nowhere, like patients coming out of anaesthesia who scramble off their mattresses, remembering tasks they've left far behind, on the other side of health. You have to press them down between the sheets. *Sleep now, you'll be all right.*

The soldiers walk on and on. Each group is alongside the truck for a while, and then it falls behind. The truck may not feel as if it's moving at all, but it's still going faster than the column of refugees and fleeing soldiers. Somewhere there's a place where there's no bombardment, no tanks rearing over the crest of ploughed fields and making straight for you with the wicked little snouts of their guns swivelling to get you in their sights. No Junkers shitting flame, no parachutes coming down like thistle-heads with a beautiful, rocking, side-to-side motion. Then they spit out men with machine-guns. No din of bombardment that crowds the inside of your head and can never be shaken out.

What did Mikhail say? 'For Christ's sake, I'm one of the few men round here who know how to use a rifle, and they won't even give me one.'

There weren't enough rifles. One between six, to start with. Mikhail got one in the end. Someone died, and his rifle was handed over, still hot.

If only the children wouldn't cry like that, on the same thin, high note of misery as they run along beside the truck, begging for a place. Some of these kids are on their own. The bigger ones heave up the little ones and try to hoist them on to the truck.

'I can't, don't you see? There are wounded men on here.'

A man appears, thrusting a baby at him. 'My wife can't walk any farther. He's only two weeks old, he won't take up any space.'

'I've got to tend these men. Your baby's safer with you.'

The truck driver puts his hand on the horn and accelerates, scattering people out of his way on the road ahead. Andrei looks back and there's the man with the baby, dwindling, his arms still held out in front of him, offering the baby. Its rhythmic shrieks stick in Andrei's ears.

Mikhail's still unconscious, over there in the corner of the truck where he won't get jostled. He's concussed: possible skull fracture, but at least there's no bleeding from mouth or ears. The wound to his shoulder and upper arm looks bad, and it's certainly bled a lot, but it's not dangerous. A piece of shrapnel has ploughed through the flesh, and there are bone splinters. That wound needs to be probed under anaesthetic. Scorch marks and soot and blood everywhere make things look worse than they are.

Andrei feels a sudden, overwhelming longing, as powerful as sexual desire, for the carbolic smell of the Erisman Hospital. There, everyone knows what to do. You work as a team, moving like a corps de ballet. The more urgent things are, the more quietly people speak, throwing out a few words as they fight cardiac arrest or haemorrhage.

'Soon, we'll be there,' he promises a man who 'got a real kick in the guts when I wasn't expecting it'. His skin is grey, with a sheen of sweat on it, and he is strangely garrulous. 'The thing is, Doctor, I can't feel a thing. Only I'm so effing cold. If this is summer I want my money back.'

The cart bumps on. The man's pulse changes. He is blue around the mouth now. He says in a changed voice, 'Hold me, I can't seem to feel myself.'

Mustn't let anyone else get hold of Mikhail's diary, thinks Andrei with a small, cool part of his mind as he works on. Could be dangerous. They'll find the papers when they undress him in hospital, if I leave them in his pocket. Better give them to the daughter – what's her name, Anna. She'll know what to do.

The diary sheets don't crackle in Andrei's breast-pocket. They are soaked with sweat. Later on, he will take them out to write his pencilled note, and see that they are also stippled with blood. Maybe Mikhail's, maybe another man's. Andrei will be unable to remember whose blood it was that suddenly jetted into his face, making him flinch with instinctive revulsion. It was the memory of his own revulsion which would return night after night to haunt him, not the blood.

In his second year at medical school, Andrei wrote down these precepts in his private notebook:

A good doctor always works with method.
   A good diagnostician does not speak of theories. He begins with what he sees, feels, touches, tastes and hears. A doctor who neglects to smell a wound in order to judge if it is infected will never be a good doctor.

Andrei refuses, and will always refuse, to speak from anything but his own experience. What he has touched and talked to: that he believes. He believes in one truckload of wounded men, one road blocked with retreating soldiers and desperate refugees, one baby whom he was unable to rescue. He believes in what he can see and touch and smell, what he has held in his own hands.

Andrei will never regard himself as a witness to the collapse of the Luga line. He did not see 'desperate counter-attacks' or 'valiant resistance', or understand that 'the Luga line was collapsing into a shambles'. What he saw was men without weapons, fighting with their bare hands, snatching up spades, pitchforks and the rifles of the dead. He saw fourteen-year-old boys crouching in dugouts, pretending they knew what came next. What he felt was the give of cheap cotton as he ripped it into bandages, and what he tasted was the golden-yellow yolk of an egg so fresh that if it had been put in water, it would have sunk like a stone.

10

Andrei stands in the empty, sunlit street. No one about. Of course, it's still very early. Not even six yet. He keeps forgetting. The days have been pulled out of shape and they won't go back.

This is the right street. That building over there, fourth from the end, with its entrance door open. Behind the façade, there'll be the courtyard and staircases with the apartment doorways leading off it. Third floor, then the door on the right. It's exactly like a thousand other Petersburg apartment houses. Dark staircases give way to cramped, subdivided rooms, where parents sleep behind a curtain and grown-up children can't leave home because there is nowhere for them to go.

Andrei's lucky. He shares a fifteen-square-metre room in a communal apartment, and gets on well not only with his room-mate but with most of the other people in the apartment. Even Frol the drunkard, who lives in the stair-cupboard, has taken a fancy to him for some reason. When Andrei's trying to study, Frol bawls at anyone who's making too much noise: 'Shut your faces, can't you? How's the boy going to learn anything? Where do you think you're going to get a doctor from, when you're dying?'

It's all very different from Irkutsk.

'How I envy you,' his father said the day before he left. 'There's nowhere in the world like Petersburg.'

His father had been a Petersburger, an idealistic young engineer who took up a post in Irkutsk soon after the revolution. Andrei grew up on the legend of his father's brilliance and youth.

'Your father could have done anything.' The little boy was quite happy with that. His father could have done anything, but he'd come here, where the only family he could ever have had awaited him. He'd married Andrei's mother, and it can't have taken him long to realize there would never be any question of separating her from Siberia. It was her blood and her life. When Andrei was four years old, she would take him camping in the taiga with her. They would hike for hours, then pitch their tent. His mother knew every inch of the ground. What he loved most was the sound of the wind, moving softly over the face of the earth, stirring the grasses and delicate fronds of summer moss. When he lay on his back, he could feel the earth moving under him as the wind blew faint clouds over the clean blue face of the sky. He used to believe that the rushing sound he could hear was the turning of the earth.

There's nothing like that in Leningrad. Here, the wind is funnelled down avenues of stone. It blows dust into your eyes, and the air tastes as if it's been breathed before, hundreds of times, by hundreds of people. Leningrad air isn't a living thing, caressing you through your clothes, moulding you to the earth.

But people here in Leningrad have strange ideas about Siberia. They talk about cold, but what they don't understand is that it's an entirely different kind of cold. Mist gathers on the Neva, and thickens into dank, bone-piercing fog. But in Siberia, at twenty degrees below, the cold sings. Siberia's more than a place, it's a spirit which can't be translated anywhere else. People talk more openly there. They're not so scared.

In Siberia, there is too much of everything. Too much space, too much sky, too many thousands upon thousands of trees marching away towards a horizon that never grows closer, too great a crowd of stars on winter nights. But when you know it, it's not frightening at all. Siberia becomes the only place where you can really breathe.

But he's here, in Leningrad. Andrei's head is light with sleeplessness. The silence makes his ears ring. On his way, the morning calm was so uncanny that he wanted to shatter it. He wanted to yell until they opened all the shutters and hung out of their windows to listen.

'Don't you know what's happening?'

But he walked on through quiet streets that smelled of bakeries. An old woman, who was sweeping her steps with a worn-out knuckle of a broom, stopped and stared at him. Did he look strange? No, old people stare at everything.

This is where she lives, the daughter. Anna. He takes off his cap. They're a trusting lot here. Not only is the outer entrance door to the courtyard open, but the inner staircase door as well. No one's about. He climbs the staircase that smells of onions and cabbage, with its feeble electric lightbulb cased in a mesh of wire. Quite a nice place, though. Stairs clean and well-swept, no rubbish in the courtyard. The handrail is old, smooth wood that's been polished not long ago. This must be the door. Yes, it is. He hesitates. It's very early, but after all he's bringing good news.

Andrei raps firmly on the door, and stands back two paces, as his mother taught him to do when he was a child.

'Don't crowd up at the door so you fall into the house when they open it. It's not a cultured way to behave.'

A light goes on, but no footsteps come to the door. Don't they know that he can see the thread of light under the door? He can hear somebody moving about inside the apartment, with light, quick footsteps. What are they doing?

He knocks again, and this time feels a draught at his back. The door opposite has opened. He turns, and there is a man, watching him. A big, pale-haired guy in his vest, with bulging muscles. He says nothing, just stares at Andrei, and then slowly closes his door. Andrei's skin prickles. This is Leningrad for you. Everyone watching and listening, but saying nothing. Boldly, he steps right up to the door, and lances his voice through the wood: 'I'm a friend of your father's.'

The door opens so suddenly that he tumbles in. She must have been listening just behind it. He falls against her, apologizes, clutching at the door-handle, trying to right himself. He fell against her breasts. He felt them against him, soft and full and warm. She is naked under that cotton dressing-gown. And then he pulls back from the sensation, for she's the daughter of his friend.

'Who are you? What are you doing here?'

'It's all right – I'm a friend of your father. Andrei Mikhailovich Alekseyev.'

She shrinks back from him, her eyes narrowing as if he is her enemy. 'Oh my God, you've come, you've come –'

'No, it's not that. He isn't dead, I promise you. He's alive. He's in the Erisman Hospital, with a shoulder wound. He came back with me in a hospital truck.'

'Is it bad?'

'It's not good, but it isn't dangerous. He had concussion, which can be more of a problem, but there doesn't seem to be a skull fracture.'

'You're a doctor?'

'Not yet. Fourth-year medic.'

'He got himself shot!' she bursts out. 'I should have known it, I should have stopped him going.'

'You couldn't have stopped him going.'

'What's that supposed to mean? He's got a son who's only five years old, did he tell you that? Or did he just forget about Kolya, the way he always does when it's not convenient? And now on top of everything else, he's got hurt. People are getting hurt all over the place who shouldn't even be there; they're not doing any good, they're just getting killed and then someone rolls them up in an old curtain if they're lucky and they're left for the Germans, like logs of wood. Well, thank God, you brought him back. And now he's wounded and – I'm sorry. I should be being grateful to you.'

Though she's retreated from him as far as she can, the entrance to the apartment is so tiny that he can still feel the sleep-warmth coming off her body. He smells the warm, strong scent of her skin and hair.

'Should we . . . Can we go inside? I've got to get back to the hospital in a minute, but I'd like to talk to you.'

'Don't go in there. Marina Petrovna's asleep. Come in the kitchen. Hush, we mustn't wake Kolya – he's been having bad dreams.'

They actually have their own apartment. He stares round. Yes, they have their own kitchen. It's tiny, but imagine not having to label all your food and put it on the right shelf in case someone else swipes it.

'It's a nice apartment,' he says.

'We have two rooms. Seventy-five square metres. We're very lucky, although I don't know how long we'll be able to hold on to it.'

She flushes, as if she's said more than she intended.

'A man like your father needs his space.'

'What?'

'A writer, I mean.' He pronounces the word 'writer' with a mixture of respect and doubt which makes it clear that there are no writers in his family. 'Even in the dugout, he wrote pages and pages, just as if he was sitting at his desk.'

'What happened to it?' she asks sharply.

'It's all right, I've got it here. That's why I've come – well, part of the reason. I didn't want to leave it lying about in the hospital.'

'No.'

He reaches into his breast-pocket and brings out the sheets of closely written paper, folded, limp and warm with the warmth of his own body.

'Thank you. But why don't you sit down?'

She sits him at the little folding table, and automatically begins to prepare tea.

'And I don't suppose they gave you anything to eat,' she mutters, taking out half a loaf of black bread which has been carefully wrapped in muslin overnight. 'Well, you'd better have something here.'

'Watch that knife.'

'What?'

'You'll chop your finger off if you're not careful.'

She looks down at the loaf she's cutting, then up at him with a small, reluctant smile.

'He's really going to be all right? You're sure about that?'

'Sure.'

'I'll go back with you. There are all sorts of things he'll need –'

'Leave it for a few hours. He's asleep. He's had his wound probed, and they removed the shrapnel. He'll be knocked out at least until this afternoon. Anyway, it's chaos down there. Stretchers all over the corridors, calls going out for blood, temporary theatres being set up all over the place. This is the first time I've been able to get off duty.'

She's rummaging in the store-cupboard, reaching up with her back to him. The sash of her blue dressing-gown is pulled tight around her waist. She's not slim, she's rounded and strong. He takes in the curves of waist, hips, calves. He remembers the feel of her breasts. He's sitting forward, and there's so little space that her dressing-gown tickles his knees as she turns. He looks down quickly, so that she won't see his thoughts in his face. He hears the chink of glass jars, then she brings out a jar of honey, opens it, and spreads honey on the bread for him. 'Here, eat this.'

Bread and honey. It tastes like heather honey, dark and sweet and smoky. And the bread all the better for being a day old, with that chewy texture black bread gets on the second day. She's put butter on it, as well as honey. He can taste the salt in the butter. Delicious. He hadn't know he was so hungry until he swallowed the first mouthful. And the tea, just as he likes it, strong and with three lumps of sugar in the bottom of the glass. How did she know that was what he liked? She must have asked him, though he doesn't remember it. He's so tired. Tiredness is racing through him in waves. The truck, then the train. Hours of waiting on the platform beside the men. There was a crowd of peasants who'd flocked to the station with their bundles, and he made them break off bits of fencing to serve as makeshift stretchers. They didn't want to do it at first.

'We'll get into trouble. They call this sabotage, don't you know that? It's more than my life's worth to touch a railway fence. That's State property, that is.'

'That's right, Sir, State property.'

They nodded self-righteously at one another, as if Andrei were a pitiful fool who didn't know the way things worked.

'I'll give you State property,' said Andrei. 'I know your type. Break up those fences or I'll order you to be shot.'

They believed him, maybe. Anyway, they did it, and so the worst cases got stretchers. And the strange thing was that the man who'd

86

been the most difficult about the fencing fetched a bucket of water and a dipper, and went down the line of wounded, helping the men to drink. One of them was too far gone to drink from the dipper. The man with the bucket knelt down beside him. For five minutes he knelt there, dipping his fingers in the water and letting the wounded man suck them like a baby. And when he caught Andrei looking at him, a helpless, childish smile spread over his face, and he said, 'This is what we do for the calves when they're being weaned, Sir. Always works a treat with the calves.'

The sweetness of the tea spreads through Andrei. If he were alone he'd dip the last crust of the bread in it. Nothing nicer than black bread dipped in sweet tea . . .

'Go ahead if you like. I don't mind.'

'What?'

'Dip your bread. We all do here – me and Kolya, even Marina Petrovna.'

'I shouldn't be eating your ration.'

'I gave it to you. Eat it.'

'When I was in a dugout with your father, I used to dream about sitting in a kitchen, drinking tea.' He doesn't add that in the dream there was always a woman, warm, blurred, moving around the kitchen, brushing against him.

'I know.'

'You know?' He doesn't intend it, but all his meaning comes out in his voice. *How can you know, when only we who were out there can ever possibly know.*

'I was there until two days ago. Farther back from the line than you, but not very far. We were digging an anti-tank-trap when the shells finally came too close even for us. Six women were killed, and then they ordered us out of the sector. We got a train back to Leningrad, just as if we'd been on a camping holiday. Except that the train was so full we weren't sitting on seats, we were packed in so tight that even if we fell asleep we didn't move an inch, we stayed upright. And the guard kept yelling, "Get those heads inside the window or they'll be knocked off!"'

Packed in next to Evgenia. Their faces only centimetres apart.

Sometimes sleeping, sometimes talking about things which were over for ever, as if they were still going on.

'I reckon pickaxe blisters are worse than spade blisters, don't you?'

'No, a shovel's worst of all, until you get used to it.'

'That Lena still stuffing sausage into her face when we were running for cover. She wasn't going to miss a mouthful, was she?'

'Yeah, and shouting, "I'm not wasting bloody sausage!" when you told her to get a move on.'

'Just about sums it all up, doesn't it? "I'm not wasting bloody sausage."'

And Evgenia laughed, showing her white teeth.

But who could explain Evgenia to this young man who has never met her? Evgenia at the Baltic station, when their train had clanked into the platform at last, after spending hours in a siding just outside the city. The crowd of women clung together, even after they'd all got off the train. It was a warm morning, but they were shivering. In the everydayness of the station their filthy clothes and mud-caked boots looked terrible, though they'd seemed perfectly normal before. They were so tired that the station appeared like an hallucination of itself. But they were still in it together, a team, until a woman close to Anna said quietly, 'Well, no use me hanging about here,' picked up her pack, and trudged off alone, towards one of the exits.

They didn't belong to one another any more. There were no orders to follow, no more digging and shovelling and entrenching to be done.

'Not for now, anyway,' said Evgenia, 'though I reckon they'll be needing us again, before long.'

Her red plait was coming undone, and her freckled skin was grimy.

'So you go back to your place, and I'll go back to mine,' said Evgenia, 'and maybe we'll meet again.'

'Wait, I'll give you my address.'

But Evgenia shrugged. 'No need for that. If we're meant to come together, we'll come together. I don't believe in all that giving addresses and keeping in touch.'

'Don't waste bloody sausage, that's what I say,' said Anna.

Evgenia laughed. Still laughing, she turned and plunged into the crowd, her red plait slapping between her shoulder blades as it unravelled. Suddenly she turned and bawled back:

'And don't let those hands get soft! Piss on your blisters!'

'They pulled us back all along the line,' says Anna to Andrei. 'They couldn't use us there any more, so we came home. I don't know what's going to happen next.'

'We'll consolidate –'

'Yes.'

'Did you know them? Those six who were killed, I mean. Were they friends of yours?'

'Not really. Only one, who was killed earlier on. She was like a child, even though she was fifteen. She should never have been out there. She used to get me to brush her hair for her.'

'You must have been close,' says Andrei, trying to imagine the degree of intimacy which would be required before he brushed someone else's hair. But of course, with women, it's different.

'No, I didn't like her much. She was pretty, but she was spoiled. You know the type. Father in the Comintern, food parcels delivered to the apartment, summer camp at government resorts. I don't suppose she'd ever stood in a queue in her life. But it wasn't her fault.

'I keep on thinking about her. You know the way you are at fifteen. Too much of some things, and not enough of others. Nothing had begun to add up for her, she wasn't even really a person yet, and then she was dead. And we wrapped her up in a waiting-room curtain, with roses all over it. The worst thing is that the roses looked so terrible. As big as cabbages, and the colour of mud.'

'Don't think about it.'

'Why not?'

'It'll stick. You can't go on remembering the curtains.'

'Maybe it should stick.'

'But not in you.'

He looks up at her, straight at her, intimate. No one looks at her like that. Even the nursery children, who long for her attention and are always trying to get as close to her as they can. When she tells them stories they creep forward, snuggling against her legs, patting her skirt. They notice everything about her. If she cuts her hair, or wears a new colour, or has had a bad night, they'll pick it up at once.

'*Anna Mikhailovna, why are you looking in that face? Are you sad?*'

She is their support system during the long days. They must check all the changes in her, in order to reassure themselves that she is still the same. And perhaps her father's expression, when he looks at her, is not so very different. She is used to that kind of attention, and she can deal with it. But Andrei's look makes her uncertain. He's curious. He wants to know more. His gaze probes and grows close. Anna feels the warmth of her own skin, and the soft touch of her cotton wrapper on her thighs.

'Have some more tea,' she says, to restore her balance. She always feels safer when she is doing things for people. But he doesn't seem to hear.

'You have to protect yourself,' he goes on. 'Not become heartless, I don't mean that. But when I first went on the wards, there were things that I couldn't get out of my head for weeks. After a while I realized it wasn't possible to be a doctor that way. You have to keep something inside yourself, that can't be used up and taken away from you.'

'And you've got that?'

'I'm trying to. I suppose it's the same for you, working in a nursery, with all those children. Your father told me about it. You must have had to work out a way of responding to them without being eaten alive.'

'You're right. But how strange that you knew it. Most people – my father, for instance – can't see that my work involves anything of the kind. They see the routine and all the physical stuff you have to do – *all that drudgery*, he calls it – but they don't imagine there can be any challenges. We go on and on about the workers, but because we're all supposed to be improving ourselves all the time, and getting qualifications and making progress, we still can't really value work unless it has status. So although my boss doesn't understand anything about the children at all – in fact she doesn't even like them – she's the one who fills in the reports and makes decisions. And everyone accepts that this is the way it should be.'

'Or maybe just that this is the way it is.'

'It's worse than that. We bow down to diplomas as if they were icons.'

'Perhaps you're right . . .'

'No. I'm just prejudiced because I haven't got any. Diplomas, I mean. And I'm sure I'll be as bad as everyone else when it comes to Kolya. I'll be shoving him on to get as many qualifications as he can. It won't be hard for him. He can read already. He's a real Levin.'

'And you're not?'

'No, I'm not like them. All the Levins do brilliantly at school, and they love writing. Nothing is quite real to my father until he's written it down. But I was nothing special at school.'

'Like me.'

'You're a medical student.'

'Yes, but I have to work at it. You wouldn't believe how I have to work. But once we're applying the theory, I'm fine. It's a great feeling when patients come in and you notice a tiny thing about them – the colour of their eyeballs, or the way they stoop to one side. Even before they've started telling you what's wrong, you've got an idea. That's what I like.'

'Yes.'

Without smiling, they exchange a glow of recognition. She watches his hands as he drinks the last of the tea. They are strong and broad, with long fingers. His hands look as if they know things. In the heat of the kitchen he's unbuttoned his collar. There is a triangle of deep sunburn, and then a line of paler skin, fine and close-grained.

He puts down the glass, takes a small piece of folded paper from his breast-pocket and hands it to her.

'This is the ward, and this is the name of the surgeon in charge. I've written it all down. You can come later. He'll be awake then. But don't be alarmed if he's running a fever. It's very common, at this stage, and it doesn't mean there's an infection.'

'Of course, I understand,' she says, even nodding her head as if to show her readiness and understanding. What is the matter with her? Why can't she behave naturally? And why is she wearing this ugly old cotton wrapper of her mother's? And above all why is she so conscious of the fabric against her nipples, rubbing them a little every time she changes position, making them harden until she's afraid he'll see their outline?

'Goodbye.'

'Goodbye.'

'Perhaps, when you come to visit your father –'

'I should have thanked you. It was such a shock when you came, and I thought you might have been –'

'It was stupid to come so early. I ought to have thought. It was just that I wanted to tell you straight away that he was all right.'

He is holding her hand. Her nails are broken, and there are raised welts of callous across her palm. He doesn't look, but he can feel them. He thinks of her digging with those hands. Without meaning to, he folds her fingers gently into a fist.

'Well, goodbye.'

'Yes.'

But they don't separate. They stand close, her hand in Andrei's. He takes her other hand. They stand like dancers: she sways a little, to music he almost believes she can hear. She is warm, fluid, soft.

'Do you like dancing?'

'Yes.'

'Me too.'

'We'll go one night, shall we? If the bands are still playing.'

'They're still playing at the Astoria. We could go there. You have to queue, but it's worth it.'

'All right.'

They smile, too close, blindly. They want oblivion. They want night, and dancing.

'Well, goodbye.'

'Goodbye.'

Dancing in the dark. That's what they call it. Both of us together. I've never done it. Once I nearly did but I thought of Kolya. I thought, what if I get pregnant, and die?

I want to shut my eyes with him. Andrei Mikhailovich Alekseyev. Imagine, both our fathers are called Mikhail.

I want to shut my eyes with him. I want to see black velvet in front of us, and prickly stars. I don't want to make tea for him, or take care of him. I want to dance in the dark with him. Can he tell that I want that?

1 1

'Elizaveta Antonovna, two more unaccompanied children –'

'Can't you see I'm in the middle of important calculations?' snaps Elizaveta Antonovna. The tip of her nose twitches. 'Now I'll have to add up these columns again. Take them into Hall Two with the other processed children, but for pity's sake don't go and mix them up with the unprocessed groups. And if you could *kindly* stop those boys running in and out of the end room. I can't concentrate with all this noise.'

Elizaveta Antonovna ought to be in her element. She hasn't had her clothes off for two days, as she's already told Anna several times this morning. She just grabs a few hours' sleep, then carries on. And where's Anna been? Oh yes, of course, working on defences. But Elizaveta Antonovna doesn't want to hear about that. What matters is what's happening here, where she is.

'So you're back, are you? About time.' Building defences has got nothing to do with the all-important crisis that circles around the vital figure of Elizaveta Antonovna. Lists, figures, snatching up of telephones, respectful listening to superiors and barking of orders at inferiors, that's Elizaveta Antonovna.

The telephone cord has got twisted around the stand of her in-tray. Let her snatch it up one more time, prays Anna. Let the cord pull tight and the tray slide off the edge of her desk. Let it fall on the floor and scatter all her important papers so that she's got to spend an hour putting them in order and she won't be able to stop us getting on with the work. But Elizaveta Antonovna notices the cord, frowns, untwists it.

Elizaveta Antonovna has been seconded to the District Evacuation Centre, and now she's battling against all odds to fulfil her quota of processed children. Hundreds, thousands, hundreds of thousands of children, who are now to be evacuated from Leningrad

94

as soon as possible, into the deep rear. The Germans are going to attack from the air, everyone says. It could be worse than the blitz on London. Suddenly there is a cityful of children to be herded into buses and trams for the railway station.

Never has there been such an opportunity for lists, forms, quotas, processing and delegation. Rarely has a knowledge of the needs of children been of so little use. It's a handicap, in fact.

Anna takes the two children by the hands. Girls aged three and five, they were pushed into her arms by their mother.

'I can't go with them, I'm an essential worker. Here, take them. Remember, Nyusha, keep a hold of her hand, don't let her run around or gobble up all her sandwiches before you even get on the train. Do what the lady tells you and you'll soon be back home again. Quick now.'

You would have thought she felt nothing, but for the staring pallor of her face. The children, too, seemed numb. They were stuffed into their winter coats, as round as little cabbages. The little one held a bit of grey cloth, and stroked its silky edge against her face.

'Put that back in your pocket. *Only when you're in bed*, remember, or they'll take it off you.'

The little girl whipped the cloth into her pocket, and huddled against Nyusha.

'What's this lady going to think of you, carrying round a bit of dirty old rag?'

The mother spat on her handkerchief, bent down, and briskly polished her daughters' faces. 'There. There's good girls. Now then –'

But as she straightened up, Anna saw her face, tight with anguish.

She whispered, 'Is it true what they say, that they're bombing the railways the kids are going on?'

'I don't know. We haven't heard anything.'

'But our kids'll get out safe, won't they? I mean, you won't be sending them anywhere there's bombs?'

'They'll be safer out of the city, away from air-raids.'

The mother nodded convulsively, putting her hand up to her throat.

'Please, don't worry. We'll look after them.'

The mother seemed about to speak again, but instead she made a gesture with her hand, as if pushing something away, grabbed both children in a clumsy hug that knocked their heads together, then turned and rushed out of the room.

The little one began to wail. Her sister scrabbled in the child's pocket, and fetched out the rag. Flushing, she explained to Anna, 'Mum lets her have it when she cries.'

'It's the best thing, Nyusha. Your mother wouldn't want her to be crying all the time. Give her the rag whenever she wants it.'

The little girl had stopped crying. She was rubbing the silky edge rhythmically over her lips, slipping away into safety, her eyes wide, dark and unfocused.

'Now, let's get you two sorted out. You'll be going into that room first, with all the others, so you can be divided into groups for the journey. We'll make sure you stay together. You'll be going on a train, you know that, and we're sending plenty of food with you, so you don't need to worry.'

'Mum's made our sandwiches.'

'I know. But maybe there are children who haven't brought anything. We have to look after everyone. What's your little sister's name?'

'Olenka. She doesn't talk.'

'But you can tell when she's hungry and when she wants to go to the toilet?'

Nyusha nods importantly. 'Yeah, I can tell. She sort of pulls me when she wants things.'

'That's good. Now, in here, just wait on these benches and we'll be as quick as we can. Move up a bit, the rest of you, there are two more here who want to sit down.'

The unaccompanied children sit in rows, packed together. Only their eyes move. They watch the accompanied children enjoy the luxury of naughtiness. Those children who still possess their mothers wriggle out of their grip, jump up and down, and invent a game called Dead Man, which involves standing in a row and leaning sideways hard but without falling over, until the child at the end topples on to the floor. Other children play the usual games of tanks, Red Army, and being evacuated.

'This is your number. Don't take it off or you'll have to be processed all over again.'

'Wait a minute. I've got to put my doll back in my knapsack. She's being really stupid, because she doesn't understand about bombs.'

Many of these kids are experienced evacuees, having been withdrawn from the Luga area already. Frazzled, frantic mothers shout at them, but don't dare leave the queue for the tables where they will receive billeting details. Queues snake everywhere. There's a queue for processing, which ought to be confined to the end hall, but has got too long and now winds in and out of the queue for mothers of accompanied, processed children to receive their billeting details.

Suddenly a big woman dressed in trousers and a Party blouse comes in and claps her hands.

'Transport is leaving for Sortirovochnaya station NOW, with a capacity of fifty accompanying adults and one hundred and fifty children. Form queues in the courtyard immediately, processed adults and children only.'

'Quick,' says Anna, 'all of you get off that bench. Follow me.' A sense of panic has seized the halls. There's transport, but who's going to get on it? The queue for billeting details quivers, as mothers hesitate, step out of it, then back. Then they surge. Children, bags and mothers jam the door to the courtyard. Just get on the train, that's the main thing, and then worry about where you're going afterwards. As long as you've been processed, you'll be all right.

Mothers shove past Anna, dragging children. There's a smell of sausage, wool and armpits. They can't possibly all cram through that doorway at once, but people are still elbowing forward. Bodies struggle in the bottleneck towards the bright doorway that leads to the courtyard. And the children –

'Mind the children! They're getting crushed.'

The unaccompanied children have no mothers to lift them above the crush and force a way through for them.

'Get in tight behind me,' shouts Anna to the children. 'Hold on to each other. Citizens, please, for heaven's sake – these children can't get through. They're going to get hurt.' No one takes any notice. Behind her a child begins to wail in terror.

She will not let this happen. Above the crowd, beyond her, she sees the woman in the Party blouse. Fixing the woman with her eyes, she yells above the noise: 'Comrade! These are the children of essential workers!'

The words reach the ears of the woman in the Party blouse. Her arm sweeps up. Her voice booms above the children's crying. 'This is no way to behave! All of you, stand to one side and let these children through at once.'

And they do. Not grudgingly, but willingly, as if they have been recalled to themselves. Everyone stands still, and suddenly there is room enough for everyone to get through. It's as if fear had swollen them. *Shoving kids out of the way like that – that can't have been us, can it? It was just that we didn't realize –*

The smallest children are lifted carefully above the crowd, and passed from hand to hand until they reach the courtyard.

The courtyard is cool. Already, in the third week of August, there is a tang of autumn in the air that has collected here, along with the rasping smell of diesel fumes. Most of the evacuees will go to the station in trams and buses, but there are three lorries here as well, tailgates down, engines running, belching out exhaust. Elizaveta Antonovna immediately goes to the cab of the first lorry and begins to argue with its driver.

'Comrade! Not only are you choking us, but you're wasting precious fuel.'

The driver doesn't take offence. He leans down and says tolerantly, 'No, the way it is with these engines, it's more *efficient* to keep them running.'

His words silence Elizaveta Antonovna. 'Oh, of course, if it's a question of *efficiency* . . .' And she frowns at the milling, inefficient mass of children and mothers. Mothers are scrambling into the lorries, balancing babies and toddlers on their hips, pulling older children after them. A stream of instructions flows as they settle the children down.

'And don't start messing about with those buttons. Next thing someone'll pull your coat off and you'll lose it.'

The children sit in rows again, solemn, bundled. They don't cry, or cling to their mothers. They give each other little sideways looks, expressionless, as the grown-ups step off the lorry backs. So many children packed into the lorries, and so few adults to look after them. But it's all properly organized. *They* know what they're doing, *they* will make sure everything's all right.

A boy calls down, 'Have I got to keep my coat on all the way, Mum? I'm too hot.'

'Yes, but where you're going, the weather might be different. And besides –'

She doesn't finish the sentence. Besides, winter's on its way. It comes so quickly, once it starts. Yes, I know we said you were only going away for a week or two, until things settled down. But all the same, when I got you ready, I put on everything. Those lined boots I queued for most of a day last January. Don't be stupid, they're not too tight, they still fit you perfectly. They'll do for the whole winter, and don't scuff them like that – Mitya's got to have them when you're finished with them. A pair of mittens on strings round your neck – no, all right then, you don't need to wear those yet. Tie the strings of your hat round your neck. Once that's gone, it's gone. Vests, jumpers, woollen trousers. Yes, *I know* you're too hot. But better too hot than too cold, as you'd soon find out if I didn't look after you properly.

These children should be bare-legged and rosy, wearing shorts or a cotton dress. They should be running in the park, tasting the last of summer.

The lorry engines roar. A man jumps out of the passenger seat of the front lorry and goes round to the tailgate. He lifts it, holds it in position, fastens one set of bolts, then the other. As he works he leans over the back and jokes with the children. *'No undoing this, mind, or we'll have you lot bouncing all over the road.'* Then he goes to the next lorry and does the same, and to the next, shooting the bolts home with a clang that echoes above the noise of the engines.

As he jumps back into the cab, the driver puts the lorry into gear, and it rolls slowly towards the archway that leads out of the courtyard. They're going. They're really going now. Most of the children are hidden by the lorry's sides, but one or two older ones climb up until they can just see over the side. Four or five faces show, pale, staring, and terribly young. As the lorry swings into the dark under the courtyard gate, these children search the crowd for their mothers. All the mothers wave back, whether or not they can see their own children. They wave and smile, and call out goodbye as if the children are leaving for a summer picnic. On the faces of the children who have climbed up there is a blaze of delighted recognition, as if they are not leaving at all, but coming home.

'Don't just stand there!' snaps Elizaveta Antonovna. 'We've got another hallful to deal with.'

Thousands and thousands and thousands of children. Leningrad children, children who've already been evacuated once, as the Germans advanced, children who've slogged their way to Leningrad past bodies in ditches, and burning huts. Some of them play ferociously in the halls of the evacuation centre, and band together to make trouble for the adults. Some are passive, and will not look directly at anyone. They'll piss where they sit rather than ask to go to the toilet. These children know that lorries are the easy way. They know about walking for miles, until the soles of their shoes flapped and their blisters burst, and the grown-ups screamed at them: *'Keep up, can't you? Do you want us all to get shot?'*

So many children, and so little time. The railways are being bombed. Packed trains full of children wait in sidings, creep forward, wait again, then slowly glide back to the station they passed through ten hours before. By that time all the sandwiches have gone, and no one knows if they should touch the food stores that are packed and labelled to go with the children to their destinations. Food is pouring out of Leningrad, as well as children.

'It's chaos!' snaps Elizaveta Antonovna at last. Her pale hair is stuck to her forehead with sweat, her eyes are red-rimmed, and none of her columns of figures will add up. Whining, mithering children clutter every step she takes. 'It's complete chaos! If only people would follow instructions.'

Parents besiege Anna, wanting to know if it's true that a train full of children was bombed somewhere near Mga two days ago.

'We haven't had any information. I swear I'm not keeping anything from you. I'll tell you everything as soon as we know it.'

'Think they'll tell you anything? They'll tell *her*, but she's the sort that's so uptight she won't even let her own shit go down the pan.'

And sure enough, there's Elizaveta Antonovna, face to face with a sweating, half-demented mother who has run all the way from the Lepny machine-tool factory at the end of a twelve-hour shift, on hearing the latest bombing rumours. Elizaveta Antonovna is wagging her lists at the mother. 'You're simply making things more difficult for everybody. I shall have to put in a report –'

'Elizaveta Antonovna, allow me to inform you that you are urgently required by a Party official in Hall Three,' breaks in Anna, shoving between them. Thank God, Elizaveta Antonovna spins round, a tiny spot of crimson on each cheek, and marches from the room.

'Please, come and sit down; forgive us, she doesn't know what she's saying. In this little room here.'

'I suppose you're another of them who doesn't know anything about anything,' shouts the woman, but she allows Anna to lead her into the cleaner's cupboard. In the stuffy darkness, her shoulders bow. She breaks into heavy sobs.

'I only sent her away for the best, I didn't want her to go.'

Anna does not attempt to comfort her. If only Elizaveta Antonovna keeps out of the way. If only they can have a few minutes' peace in this cupboard that smells of damp mops.

'I didn't even say goodbye properly, in case it started her off crying.'

'Listen, you stay here as long as you like. I've got to go and sort out the children. But I promise you, as soon as we hear anything –'

'You won't hear anything. The ones like you never do. It's the ones like *her* that they tell everything to.'

Parents bring their children to the evacuation centre, change their minds, take them home again. And the system is completely overloaded now. There aren't enough trains, and no matter how many children are processed, most never leave. Suddenly six busloads of children reappear, whom Anna had thought must be well on their way to the Urals by now. An exhausted mother explains, 'The line was torn up by a bomb five kilometres ahead. They kept waiting and waiting to see if they could get us through, but then we ran out of food so they had to send us back.'

News comes of the bombed train. Not the train near Mga: that was just a rumour, although it's true that the Germans are still trying to cut the railway line there. But a train *was* bombed, with nearly two hundred children on it, and forty adults. There are thirty-two survivors. Perhaps the children on that train were among those whom Anna squeezed on to the benches, and told to line up for transport. Children who were too hot in their winter hats with flaps that tied over their ears, and who started eating the sausage and apples in their knapsacks as soon as they were out of their mothers' sight.

That night Anna lies awake, listening to Kolya's breathing. Leningrad still bulges with children. For every evacuee sent away to the east, it seems that another arrives from the south and west, fleeing the German advance. And Kolya remains here. The room smells of his sleep. Has she made the right decision? If Marina Petrovna wasn't here, she would have had to send him. Anna's working sixteen hours a day, and with her father coming out of hospital as well, in a couple of days, it would have been impossible to keep Kolya. How strange to think that it was only by chance that Marina had come here at all. Yes, she's beginning to think of her like that, dropping the patronymic even from her mind: Marina.

She would never have thought she could be grateful to Marina. But day by day, steadily, Marina has earned her right to a place in their lives. She queues, she makes meals, and she even manages to keep Kolya happy too, with stories, pretend games, and drawing, while the queues slowly move forward.

Marina is obsessed with food, even more so than Anna herself.

She will walk halfway across the city on the chance of a bag of sugar for their store-cupboard. The sun is still shining, there is still food in the shops, and the rations aren't too bad. Prices have shot sky-high, though, and if it weren't for Marina, Anna would no longer be able to buy sugar or fats off the ration. Eighteen roubles for a bag of sugar, can you imagine? But Marina pays it. She has money.

'You mustn't spend so much, Marina. I'll never be able to pay you back.'

'We are not going to be able to eat money,' is all Marina will reply.

She gets Kolya walking too. They set off, the pair of them, Kolya bouncing along, his black eyes glistening with excitement as Marina breaks off her story just at its most exciting point.

'I'll tell you the rest when we've walked as far as that building down there – look, the one with the brown doors.' She points away into the distance and Kolya, instead of grizzling and dragging at her hand, as he might do with Anna, bounds forward with a squeak of pleasure.

Anna crushes the stir of jealousy she feels. But how quickly Kolya has transferred his attention. Not his love, no, she doesn't believe that. But every morning he rushes to Marina as soon as Anna has finished helping him to dress. Their laughter spills out as he helps Marina to fold her blankets, push back the sofa and make the room ready for the day. There's something magnetic about Marina. Anna has to remind herself that her mother didn't feel it. Vera wasn't attracted, she was repelled. And she must have had her reasons. What were they?

Marina bends over her shopping-bag, and pulls out a jar.

'Two hundred grammes of lumpfish roe!'

'Marina! What did it cost?'

'I keep telling you, money's not going to mean anything soon.'

Kolya and Marina crouch over their pot of wallpaper paste, dipping in strips of newspapers and layering them on to the wire bones of Kolya's fort.

'Am I doing it really well, Marina?'

'Really well. Look how smooth you've made that wall.'

'The walls have to be high, don't they, so the enemies can't climb over them.'

'That's right. One more layer should do it, Kolya, then we'll leave it to dry. We can start the painting tomorrow.'

Marina sits back on her heels, and wipes paste and newsprint off her hands. What if I drew her like this? Anna thinks. In her mind the old pose Marina took at the dacha still hangs. That's the portrait she'll finish one day, when all this is over.

But perhaps it isn't. Everything's changed, so why shouldn't her work change too? Perhaps it's better to find a different way of working. Break up the portrait. Turn it into dozens of sketches, quick and fluid, charcoal on sugar paper. Instead of one definition, go for her now, frowning over the wads of dirt packed under her nails. Or now, twisting to warn Kolya not to try and lift the fort yet, let the papier-mâché harden. Or now, noticing Anna's stare and offering back the candour of a face which knows how to change itself into anything it wants.

Anna lies awake. The night is taut, tensed, watchful. All over Leningrad people are awake, as she is. She thinks herself through the walls, into apartment after apartment after apartment. All of them waiting, counting the hours. Up on the roofs, fire-watchers keep themselves awake, too, gripping the metal rims of their sand-buckets, waiting for the noise of aeroplane engines. No one knows what's going to happen next. Even the Germans may not know. We think they know everything, but maybe they're waiting, just like us, for orders that haven't been written yet, and thoughts that haven't even come into anyone's head.

They're waiting out in our woods, smelling the mushrooms that are ready for picking. But they won't know where to find the best ones. They'll trample them underfoot, and the bruised chanterelles will give off their scent of apricots.

And then there's Andrei. He never came back, and she'd been so sure that he would that she hadn't even warned herself not to trust him.

How horrible it is that you can be completely wrong about things like that. You can trust yourself, believe in your own instincts, and then they turn out to be wrong. The other person wasn't even thinking about you. As soon as he got outside the apartment, he had forgotten her. He'd taken his message to her, and he hadn't thought of her again. Finish. But how humiliating it is, to reach out towards someone who hasn't reached out to you. Like running towards a face in the distance, your arms held out, calling, 'How wonderful to see you! I didn't know you were back!' and then getting close and seeing that the face was a stranger's, stiff with embarrassment.

But Andrei doesn't know. He doesn't know that she closed her eyes and danced with him in the dark. He doesn't know that she asked him: *Do you want it, too?*

She twists on her bed. Should Kolya be here at all? If the bombs come – if the bombers come over in wave after wave, as they did over London, and set the city blazing – if the German army advances – if they get here –

German aeroplanes are dropping leaflets, not bombs. Anna does not dare to pick them up. You don't know who might be watching you. But she has listened to the whispers in the evacuation queues, and she knows what those leaflets say.

Leningrad is already defeated. Our victory is
inevitable, and resistance will only make things
worse for you. Your armies are withdrawing to
Moscow, abandoning you. The defeat of Leningrad
is inevitable . . .

She turns over again, and buries her face in her pillow. The nights are growing cool, but each time she thinks of Andrei a wave of heat washes over her skin. She forces her mind back to Kolya. And the other children, those children in the lorries. Nyusha, Olenka and all the others. She can't shake off the feeling of guilt, the uneasy, ominous sense that every action now has a consequence out of all proportion to the action itself. She read a child's name off a list. The child went, or stayed in Leningrad. The train was bombed, or the bomb missed it. Leningrad will be bombed, or not bombed. But whether she feels guilt over the children who were sent away, or over those who stay, she can't decide.

The nights are still warm. These are the last nights of summer, being wasted and thrown away. Anna twists in her bed. She will not think of him.

12

The city has not yet been bombed. It floats under the late summer sky, borne up by the light that seems as much to rise from the Baltic as to shine from above. Floating, lyrical, miraculous Petersburg, made out of nothing by a Tsar who wanted everything and didn't care what it cost. Peter's window on Europe, through which light shines. Here's beauty built on bones, classical façades that cradled revolution, summers that lie in the cup of winter.

As August wears on towards September, its goldenness fools nobody. How many more days like this can there be, before the end of the northern summer that 'mimics the southern winter'? Night steps out, lengthening its stride. The rim of cold slowly rises, and each morning the sun takes a little longer to warm the air. All day the heat of the sun feels shallower. Petals grow crisp, as sap runs back into the stems of trees and flowers. There's a winy taste in the morning air, and in the parks, under the trees, there's the first tang of decay. Rowing boats still knock against their moorings, but this is the Baltic, where in winter you will walk on water. Time to lift the boats, and store them for winter.

No bombs yet, though the city is braced for them. 'BRACED TO RESIST THE ONSLAUGHT OF GERMAN AGGRESSION WITH HEROIC FORTITUDE,' announces *Leningradskaya Pravda*. But sky and earth remain in the same relations as ever, braced or naked.

The city is still undamaged by enemy action, but not untouched. Every park and open space is gashed with trenches for air defence. Train-loads of treasures from the Hermitage have been shipped out, and what can't be moved has been packed into cellars. Statues which cannot be safely moved are wadded with sandbags. Barrage balloons hang in the air, fins all pointing in the same direction, like airships which are going nowhere. The swaddled statue of Peter the Great looks like a hand-grenade you might pick up and hurl towards the enemy. Everything makes you blink, and look twice.

That old woman, sitting on a bundle of bedding in a doorway, is not moving from one apartment to another. She's on her way to the railway station to be evacuated, but she's had to rest. Even though she's left almost everything behind, she has to keep stopping if she's going to manage to drag the essentials along with her. Food for the journey, blankets, her goosedown pillow without which she can't sleep. If she leaves that behind, only God knows when she'll get another, and she can't bear to lose the comfort of it, or the way you can keep your whole body warm as long as you don't get a draught between head and neck.

By the time she reaches the station, the train will be full. Patiently, she will drag her bundle home again, and wait, and set out for a second time the next morning. There she is, resting in exactly the same place, on her second journey. Is she real, or not real? She doesn't move, just sits there on her bundle with her head bowed. Her face is sunk into its lines. She has retreated deep inside herself, trying to gather strength for the next move she must make.

Everywhere there are armed men, moving steadily through the city. They are being deployed from one section of the front to another, as it strains under the German advance. They are the raw guts of the army, exposed, pulled back, exposed again. These are men who have clawed their way back from Kingisepp or Novgorod, who've felt what the Leningraders have yet to feel. The old woman watches them as they pass her, but she doesn't speak to them, and they are mostly too exhausted to notice her. Everything is organized confusion, a city torn out of one rhythm and struggling to find another.

Three men in sweat-stained, filthy uniforms sway with exhaustion on the kerb. They've stuck together all the way.

'Listen, babushka, can you get us some water?'

The old woman raises her head and stares with milky eyes. 'Water?'

'Yes, water. You know, wet stuff, comes out of taps?'

'I don't know. I don't live here.'

The man standing over her is enormous. She cringes as if he's the enemy, not one of our boys at all.

'Leave it, Pavlik. Let's try down here.'

Day by day, news mixes with rumours. The Finns are coming east, taking advantage of the German advance to grab back the territory they lost during the Winter War. They've been waiting for this, those bastards. It's a pincer movement, Finns from the north, Germans from the south and west. Just what they've always wanted.

No, the Germans are planning to sweep round from the south, going east then coming back on us. They're going to encircle us.

That's impossible. That simply can't happen. Look at a map. They would have to take: look – Mga, Volkhov. Those towns are actually on the Vologda railway. Do you think we're going to lose the Vologda line, for God's sake?

It can't happen. Because if it did we'd be –

Not even a city any more. An island. An island of Russia in a sea of Germans. Not to mention those bastard Finns.

Put that map away, can't you?

Late August. The moon swells like a barrage balloon, with the yellowness of harvest. This is the weather to be out in the fields and the little dacha gardens, bringing in next winter's food. That's what this moon is for. Harvest moon.

> The fields were white with harvest
> and the moon was full
> I cut the field by morning
> then I f— with you.

Who'd have thought people would ever be afraid of the moon? They're calling it a bomber's moon now, as if that's what it's for. But it's always been a harvest moon. On a night like this you can work in the fields as if it's daylight, without stopping, a whole row of you getting on as fast as if you had a tractor. Black shadows should be stooping in a silver sheet of barley, or among sharp-cut potato leaves, not running for their lives. You can learn to pick fruit by touch. When you touch fruit at night, it holds the day's heat.

Leaves are cold, but apples are warm. Whoever heard of not bringing home the harvest?

All those rows of vegetables Anna's planted at the dacha. Out there, without her, they're getting fat. She can't bear the thought of them any longer.

'Listen, Marina, I'm going to try it.'

'It can't be worth the risk.'

'It would be. Think of everything I could bring back. I'll take the panniers, and my basket, and I can balance a couple of sacks over the handlebars.'

'But, Anna, the militia are stopping everyone as they come into the city now. What if they think you're a spy?'

'As long as I've got my papers with me, I'll be all right. They'll let me back in.'

'If they don't shoot you first.'

'I'm going to go tomorrow. It'll be fine.'

'What about work?'

'If I volunteer for tonight, I could come off shift at noon. I'll come back here, get the bike, allow three hours to get there, then three hours to come back at the other end. I'll be home before dark.'

'Listen. If you're really going to go –'

Marina kneels down and feels under the leather couch where she sleeps. 'There. You'd better take that. I had it sharpened.'

It's a Finnish hunting knife, a *puukkuu*.

'Where did you get it?'

'Take it, you don't know who might be around.'

'There won't be anyone, they've all left. It's a dead zone now.'

All the same, Anna takes the knife. It is heavy and well-balanced in her hand. She imagines it slicing a ripe onion, spitting out juice as it slides through layers of lilac and white onion-flesh.

'Who did it belong to?'

'No one. I bought it.'

'Don't tell my father that I've gone.'

'Of course not.'

'We can tell him afterwards, when we've got something to show for it. I'll get him some radishes, if there are any left.'

'What are you going to tell me afterwards?' asks Kolya, looking up from the flag he is painting for the fort.

'No, not you, Anna was talking about someone at work.'

Kolya went into his father's room the day he came back from hospital. What Kolya saw on the bed was an upthrust jaw with grey bristle pushing through it. A thread of spit ran from the corner of an open mouth.

'Hush, he's asleep.'

Asleep. Is that what asleep looks like? A snorting breath rattled out of the mouth. Kolya backed towards the door.

'He'll wake up soon.'

Two feet pointed upwards under the sheet. His father never sleeps like that. The thing in the bed didn't look like his father at all. If they hadn't told him it was his father, he would never have guessed.

And in fact he doesn't really believe them. He says 'Daddy' because that is what they want him to say. His own father is away, fighting in the war. In Kolya's mind, his father has changed into a Red Guard, storming a fort.

'He's very tired,' they say. 'He has to rest. Don't stamp round like that, Kolya, it hurts your father's head.'

They go in and out, tending to the silent grey thing on the bed.

Anna tiptoes into her father's room. She takes away the glass of water beside his bed, empties it, and runs fresh water. He's sleeping so much. Marina has got hold of a bedpan and a bed-bottle, because he can't get out of bed. But he's supposed to get out of bed, and walk around to keep his blood circulating. They hoisted him into a sitting position this morning, one at each side, then Anna pushed and they swivelled him sideways. Marina eased his legs off the edge of the bed. He seemed dazed, not really aware of what they were doing. His long, pale feet hung down to the floor.

'Can you stand up?'

'No, I – I'm sorry. I can't stand up.'

'Just sit for a minute. It'll do you good.'

He was wearing his vest and long underpants. The vest wouldn't fit over his bandaged shoulder, so Anna had cut out the sleeve. Tomorrow, they'd have to dress the wound. Take off the dressings, clean the wound with boiled water – and make sure you've boiled the swabs beforehand, so as not to introduce infection – then dry carefully, leave to air, sprinkle with boracic powder, replace with fresh dressings. But it had been impossible to buy fresh dressings. Every inch of bandage in the city was gone. Marina had managed to buy a packet of lint, then they'd cut up a sheet for bandages.

'As long as it's clean,' they told each other.

He must drink. Water flushes out a wound. He must be roused to drink, even if he's asleep. If he doesn't pass urine, that's a sign of dehydration. Water, not tea: tea is too stimulating.

Anna replaces the glass. He's sunk in sleep. It's so tempting to leave him where he is, out of pain, and beyond causing pain. But she gently taps his cheek.

'Father. Wake up. You have to drink.'

It takes so long. His mouth works, as if he is chewing. Under his eyelids, his eyes move, but the lids stay sealed shut.

'Wake up.'

Suddenly his eyelids spring open. To her amazement, he smiles and says in a voice that is so near to normal that it sounds like a shout in the still room, 'Anna. What are you doing?'

'Trying to wake you up. Here, have some water. Your lips are cracked.'

'Anna, make me some tea.'

'You're not really supposed to have tea. It's too stimulating.'

He turns his head wearily from side to side. 'What's that you say?'

To her horror, she realizes that he hasn't understood the word 'stimulating'. Her father, who collects words as other people collect rare coins.

'Don't worry, I'll get you some. A little glass of tea can't do any harm.'

When she returns with the tea, he seems to be dozing, but as soon as she clinks the spoon against the glass, he opens his eyes again.

'Did you put in two lumps of sugar?' But he makes no move to raise himself or take the glass, even though his right arm is perfectly good.

'I'm going to put another pillow behind you, then you'll be able to drink it.'

He struggles into a sitting position.

'Here you are.'

Tremblingly, he takes the handle of the glass, purses his lips, sips the tea.

'Good tea.'

'Try a little more.'

Sip after sip, the tea goes down. His hand shakes with exhaustion, and she takes away the empty glass. He lies back on the pillows, smiling with his eyes closed.

'That was good.'

'We'll try lime-flower tea next time. You know how much you like it.'

'Yes, I do like it.'

'I'll just take this out, then I've got some porridge for you.'

'I'm not really hungry, Anna, *moya dusha*. Just tired.'

Did he really say it? Never in his life has he called her that before. *My soul.* He smiles.

'Onegin's uncle.'

'What?'

'Me. I'm like him. Are you wondering when the devil will come for me?'

In a flash, like a miracle, the passage comes to her, and she knows what he means. She's able to answer just as he's always longed for her to be able to answer, finishing off his quotation.

'No. I'll just carry on gloomily spooning out the medicine.'

His smile broadens. 'At least you haven't forgotten your Pushkin.'

'No, at least I haven't forgotten that,' she answers. He reaches for her hand and grasps it, but the grasp is weak. His mind has wandered off already. How can she be angry with him?

She thinks of it out at the dacha, as she digs up potatoes. Leaves rustle at her back. She turns, scans the crowding trees, puts her hand on the knife which lies on the earth beside her. No one there. But there could be. No one knows how close they are. Her bike is propped against one of her mother's rose-bushes, at hand. A few late roses struggle through a mat of bindweed. The forest is closing in, swamping the garden she's made.

Empty woods, empty dachas, empty gardens which are already overwhelmed by weeds. This is the empty zone now, the dead zone from which everyone has fled. Here are the potatoes. She sets in her fork, presses down, lifts black earth and a nest of potatoes, as white as eggs. They are small this year, because they've had to fight the weeds for nourishment. Each potato clings to the mother plant by a fibrous tendril. She shakes the soil away, puts the potatoes into a hessian sack, and digs again. A tine spears a potato and splits it. As she pulls it off, she hears another shiver of leaves behind her. She plants her fork again and digs, forcing herself not to look round this time. One more row, then those onions, then she'll go. The radishes have run to seed. She'll dig up the parsley and put it in a pot. It's worth having.

Leaves rub together with the hissing sound of late, dry summer. There's no one. Even if she were to scream her breath away, there'd be no one. No smoke rising from the Sokolov farmhouse, no porky, bristling Vasya, no little Mitya. All the Sokolovs have gone. Wonder where Vasya is now. He'll be all right, those Sokolovs always look after themselves. Remember Vasya bringing the nest up to the dacha, carrying it so carefully inside his cap, his head bent. Three baby thrushes inside. Vasya knew they were thrushes, he always knew everything like that.

'Here, look what I brought you, Anna.'

You looked. They were bald and reddish-purple, squirming together.

'I found it down by the stream.'

You peered into the nest, which smelled of mice. Vasya knew more about birds than anyone. He was always watching them. Once you saw him stamp on a frog, but that was only because he was with the other boys.

'We'll take them back now,' said Vasya, 'before she finds they're gone.'

Everyone's gone. She should never have come. Quickly, Anna sweeps together the last pile of potatoes and crams them into her bag, still covered in soil. No time for the parsley, and anyway she can't carry any more. Both panniers are full, and her sacks, and the basket. She'd planned to fetch a few things from the dacha, but she doesn't want to go inside. It's locked up, and shuttered, as if it's winter already. The house stares at her, surprised that she's here, its windows blank. No, this is no longer the place she loves.

Anna fastens the buckles of her panniers slowly and carefully so that no one will see how her fingers want to fumble. Her skin crawls with animal terror. Imagine thinking earlier on that she might even go down and see if there are any radishes in the Sokolovs' abandoned garden. She didn't know what it would be like out here in the dead zone, where everything's waiting, waiting.

A thread of sweat trickles down her back. She breathes out, long and slow, as Marina has shown her. That's what you do for stage-fright, but it works for everything. She must not run.

She's got to get back to Leningrad as fast as she can. Dear Leningrad, a hundred times dearer at this moment than it's ever been, like the mother hive to a bee that's out too late in the year. She's seen those bees fly low, struggling, limping home through thick, cold air.

The leaves shake, as if they know something she doesn't know. What will they see, before this is all over? Who will these trees bend their empty branches over next? The Germans are coming closer, closer. Soon they'll be walking in our gardens. Wasps and birds have had the plums she might have picked for Kolya. There are dry white stones hanging by threads from the cherry tree, like tiny skulls.

But even now that she's packed all her panniers and bags, there are still three rows of potatoes left. And those onions, and the little turnips too. Suddenly Anna's terror hardens. Grimly, she sets her fork in the earth and begins to dig again. This time she doesn't lift the potatoes carefully, cradling them between the tines in case they bruise. She throws each forkful aside, and attacks the next plant. It goes quickly like this. One row, another, then the third. Uprooted potato plants sprawl underfoot. And now the onions. She drags them from where they're sitting plumply, half in and half out of the earth. She twists them to loosen the roots, and throws them on to the path. Good onions, packed with vitamins. Turnips next. They haven't come to much, but they might provide a bit of nourishment. Get them out of the earth. All of it, all that food, out of the churned earth. No matter who invades, they'll find nothing. The land won't feed them.

Anna raises her boots high. She smashes them down on the white potatoes, the onions, and the turnips. Some of them try to hide by burying themselves back in the soft earth, but she's on to them. Her heels grind and crush dirt into white flesh. Juices ooze, smearing the path. They are gone. They will feed nobody. She kicks soil over the food she has destroyed.

13

'Your papers.'

Anna proffers them. She doesn't speak, or smile. The militia know that smiles mean weakness. The militia-man plants his forefinger on her signature, and frowns.

'Your papers appear to be in order,' he says at last, as if this is only the beginning of her need to prove herself. He's about her age, twenty-three or twenty-four. A real Leningrad boy, with his muddy blond skin, grey eyes and sharp cheekbones. But jumpy. They're not just stopping people for the sake of it. The whole city's gun-ready.

'What have you got in all these bags?'

'Produce.'

'Open up the bags.'

She unties the sacks, and opens the panniers. He lifts up potatoes and onions, searching. But not roughly. Like her, he knows that you mustn't bruise potatoes.

'Stuff you've grown yourself?'

'Yes.'

'Off to market with it, are you?'

'No. It's all for personal use.'

'Per-son-al use,' he drawls, looking over the sacks, the panniers, the carrier-basket.

'Yes.' She cracks, and offers him a complicit smile. 'But you wouldn't believe the weight of all these potatoes. I'll never get this lot home. I could do with lightening the load a bit.'

He just keeps on staring at her. Maybe she needs to make it clearer.

'They're too heavy. I've got too much in the sacks.'

'Potatoes, is it?'

They are talking in low voices now, scarcely moving their lips.

'And onions. Onions keep well.'

It is dusk. Thick, grainy dusk settles around them, concealing them. Anna unhooks a pannier from her bike, and passes it to the young militia-man.

'Perhaps you need to examine this.'

He looks at her, a long look, then moves off sharply with the pannier. She waits. Only peasants are permitted to sell their produce at the kolkhoz market. She's carrying too much. If he charged her with bringing in stuff to pass it on at a profit, the charge would stick. Plenty of people do it. They go out to the villages to buy 'private plot' produce, and then add on a hundred per cent and sell it in city markets. Maybe there are people out there now, scouring empty plots from which everyone's fled, making a profit before the Germans take the last villages around Leningrad. There are lots of dead zones, in a war. If you're quick, you can make money out of them.

She could be here for hours. It's dusk, and she said she'd be home by dark. She waits by the side of her bike, her face smooth. You mustn't look anxious. But you mustn't look too sure of yourself, either, or as if you're taking anything for granted. The thing to aim for is a submissive, citizenly look. Meek, but not so meek that anyone will be tempted to stamp on you. These checkpoints at the city limits are to stop spies and saboteurs getting in. People say there are dozens of German agents in Leningrad, who have slipped through the suburbs into the heart of the city. They're Russian-speakers. They spread propaganda and report back on the Leningrad defences and the state of morale. They help the German gunners to correct their sights on to key targets.

The sentry comes out, swinging Anna's bag.

'Everything's in order,' he grunts. She takes it. He's on her side, he's going to let her through. The bag is as empty as air. She fastens it back on to the bike frame.

'But don't try it on again.'

Anna still says nothing. She nods at the militia-man, avoiding his eyes.

'Not bad, your onions,' he says suddenly. 'My gran used to grow onions like that.'

'So did mine. That's how I learned.'

'Yeah, beautiful onions, she was famous for them. All right then, on your way.'

She swings herself on to the bike and pedals slowly down the street.

It is nearly dark by the time Anna gets close to home. So dark that she almost passes Andrei, only a hundred metres from her home. She sees a young man on the opposite side of the road, head down, striding away. She sees him as a stranger, then as himself.

'Andrei Mikhailovich! Is that you?' she calls out, braking the bike.

He looks up at her call. 'Anna.'

He says it as if her name is the end of a journey. His face opens in a smile. 'I thought I'd missed you. I've just been to your apartment, but Marina Petrovna told me you were out.'

'Yes.' She is smiling, too.

'I've got a few hours off. Listen, shall we go and have a drink somewhere? Maybe a dance, like we said?'

'I'll have to take the potatoes home first.' She must, but she wants to stall him, too. After all that getting used to disappointment, it's too easy that he's suddenly here.

'What?'

'All this stuff.' She points to the panniers. 'I've been to the dacha.'

'You've been out of Leningrad?'

'Yes, I told you, to the dacha.'

'Don't you know how close they are? There's going to be another major advance any day. What if you'd got caught up in it?'

'I didn't see anything.'

'And you could have got stopped on the way back in.'

'I knew what I was doing.'

They stare through the gloom into each other's faces.

'Sorry,' says Andrei.

'No one tells me what to do.'

'I can see that.'

'You think I didn't work out the risk? Who is going to look after Kolya, if I don't? Look how much food I got.'

But her skin crawls with goose-flesh, remembering the silence of the dacha, and the rustling leaves.

'Are you all right?'

'I'm fine.'

'You don't look all right.' He falls into step beside her as she wheels her bike to the courtyard entrance. It would be now that he comes, when she's tired and sweaty, dressed in a cut-down pair of her father's old trousers, and the boots which are two sizes too big, even though she's lined them with felt so they are quite comfortable. He must think that her entire wardrobe consists of cast-offs.

'My feet aren't really this big,' she finds herself saying. 'You know how it is, I couldn't get the right-sized boots last winter.'

'You should see mine. But luckily, as it's dark, neither of us need worry.'

At the bottom of the staircase she turns to him. 'If you wouldn't mind waiting here with the bags, while I take the bike up. It's not safe to leave them here.'

'I'll carry your bike up for you.'

He shoulders the bike. She slings a pannier on each arm, and holds the basket.

'I'll have to come back downstairs again for the sacks.'

'You wait here while I take the bike up. I'll come back down and help you with the rest of the stuff.'

Then he does a strange thing. He puts the bike down again, and takes a handkerchief out of his pocket.

'If you'll allow me, there's something on your cheek. Mud, I think.'

He rubs at the mark with his handkerchief, but it won't come off.

'If you spit on the handkerchief –'

'You don't mind?'

'No.'

'There.' He wipes firmly. 'It's all gone.'

There they are. His spit on her cheek, like a seal.

'I wanted to come before,' he says.

'I know.'

'I couldn't. It's been crazy –'

'I know.'

*

Thank God, there is no one in the communal bathroom. Anna strips to the waist and finds the cloth that's kept in the bend of the waste-pipe. She wipes clean the greyish basin with its clot of hair in the plug-hole, and then fills it with cold water. She's forgotten the soap. Never mind, there isn't time. Water will have to do. Anna sluices her face, her arms, her neck. There's a knock at the door.

'Anna, it's me. I've brought you some soap.' In her hand, Marina holds a bar of fine-grained, expensive toilet soap. The soap Anna's seen and coveted, but never touched. 'It's jasmine.'

'Where did you get that from?' blurts Anna, then too late hears that it sounds like an accusation. She sees what she imagines Marina sees: herself, naked, dripping and graceless. 'Thank you. Is Andrei all right?' Is he bored, wanting to leave, being pestered by Kolya – or is he looking at you, Marina, not caring how old you are, caught by your beauty all the same. By your slender arms and legs, your clear, level, grey-eyed gaze. It won't matter that you're old, when you turn your eyes on him.

'He's fine. He's talking to your father. But I don't know where to put the potatoes. If they go down in the cellar, they'll be stolen, but it's too warm for them in the apartment. They'll sprout.'

'I'll think of something.' Anna is conscious of her breasts, wet and slippery, tight from cold water. She is not fine-bodied like Marina. There is too much of her. Her breasts swing heavily, their dark-brown nipples stiffening. She turns back to the basin and lathers up the jasmine soap, but Marina still won't go.

'Let me help you. I'll do your hair.'

'Thank you,' Anna repeats, staring into the mirror to avoid Marina's gaze. She doesn't want her hair done, she wants to be left alone to put on the lace bra that's shabby, though a perfect fit, the matching knickers, the satin petticoat that belonged to her mother, and her own favourite green dress.

'I like your dress.'

'I made it. I'm good with my hands,' says Anna, brushing her hair savagely.

'Here, let me help you. We all do our own hairstyles and make-up in the theatre, you know.'

'I thought someone else did it.' Surely Marina would have had a dresser? She's always imagined Marina in her dressing-room, surrounded by flowers and sallow women in black who shake out costumes over their arms and dip their elbows into Marina's bath to test its temperature. And, of course, those mirrors with a frame of bulbs. Only people who can afford to look at themselves in the strongest possible light would dare to sit in front of those mirrors.

'You need to know how to do everything yourself. There are all those years before you qualify for a dresser – and all the years afterwards, too. There aren't any guarantees in the theatre. A few good years might be all you get. Look, this colour will suit you. Do you like it?'

'I don't wear lipstick.'

'I know. But with your skin, you can take quite a dark red. As long as it's a red which hasn't got any blue in it.'

'I don't like the feel of it on my lips.'

'Try it. You'll be surprised at the difference.'

Marina paints Anna's mouth, blots it, paints again. But the lipstick is shaped to Marina's mouth, not Anna's.

'I'd like to try taking your hair right off your face, and putting it up.'

Marina brushes Anna's hair upward. 'Like this. It needs more lift. I haven't got any setting lotion, but you should be all right without it. Your hair's nice and thick and it's got plenty of body.'

It is strange to have another woman's fingers in her hair. Anna wants to twist and shake them off. It is like being owned. Men don't make her feel like this.

'Did I pull your hair?'

'No, it's fine.'

'There, have a look in the mirror.'

Anna looks without looking. Sometimes she can't bear her own reflection, and this is one of those times.

'Thank you, Marina, I couldn't have done it like that.'

And now go, go. Leave me alone so I can gather myself together.

'Tell him I shan't be a moment.'

Marina understands. Is she disappointed, or not? What does she want from this sudden intimacy she's created: two women in a bathroom, hairstyles, make-up, fingers in each other's hair? What does she think the next scene is going to be? No, thinks Anna, don't come any closer. I am not a girl who's looking for a mother. If you sent me a letter, I would send it back unopened.

I have Kolya. I've become what I wanted.

She shuts the door firmly behind Marina, and returns to the mirror. There's her face, rather pale, her red lips, her pulled-back hair. It occurs to her that by washing, she has washed away Andrei's spit. When he rubbed her cheek, he cupped her jaw in his hand to steady it. His touch was warm. She reaches into her hair, finds Marina's hairpins, and pulls them out. Then she takes a piece of newspaper from the spike by the toilet, and wipes the colour from her lips. She leans closer to the mirror, and smiles.

'It fell down,' she mouths to Marina as she goes back into the apartment, shrugging her shoulders. But Andrei isn't looking at Marina, or anyone else. He's asleep.

'He went to sleep just when I was showing him my fort,' says Kolya. 'Can you wake him up again, Anna?'

She looks down at Andrei. His head has slipped to one side. She must put a cushion there, or he'll have a stiff neck when he wakes. How pale he is.

'It's the heat in the apartment,' says Marina.

'Yes.'

'They've only been sleeping three hours a night.'

'Did he tell you that?'

'Yes. He was explaining why he couldn't come before.'

'He didn't need to explain. I knew there'd be a good reason why he didn't come.'

Kolya fits his toy soldiers carefully into the entrance of the fort.

'There, they're on guard now. Aren't you going to wake him up?'

'Not just yet. But if you're a good boy and play quietly, you can stay up a bit longer.'

Go away, Marina. Go to my father, as you always do when I come home. Andrei will sleep better, if you aren't watching him.

*

123

Later, Andrei and Anna walk together in the blackout.

'We're talking as if they're bound to attack.'

'What else can happen now? It's inevitable.'

'How many more nights like this will there be?' says Anna, almost to herself. 'Don't you feel it? It's like a weight pressing down on us.'

'It's the blackout.'

'I was never afraid of the dark when I was little.'

'I can't stand it. It's like living inside a box.'

'That's because you're Siberian.'

'Of course. Everything's because I'm Siberian.'

'Do you wish you were there?'

'No.'

He turns, clasps her. He rubs his face into her hair, scrubbing away the images that pack around his mind like shadows, leaving only a small lit-up core that belongs to him. The shadows stretch and sway. He makes himself look at them, because if he looks they don't grow larger. They are the wounded, brought back to Leningrad in trucks and carts.

All those bodies he's seen opened. The smell of gangrene in stomach wounds. The glistening, blue-purple slide of intestines. He has seen a man try to pack his own intestines back into his body. He's seen a frill of bubbles around the eyes of a man with facial burns, who had also had a leg amputated above the knee.

'Remember that patients always pick up your reaction,' said the surgeon in charge, before they went into the ward. Andrei watched him take the wrist of the burned man, and talk to him about his amputation. He looked directly into the frilled, sightless eyes. When he released the hand of his patient, he patted it gently, turned to Andrei and remarked, 'Very good progress in this case.'

She smells of soap and of her own hair. Her body presses against his, whole and unpenetrated. Now there's nothing but their two quick, hot bodies, pumping with life. He wants to dive deep into her, part her flesh, put his face between her breasts, open her buttocks. He wants to penetrate her, sinking deep into flesh that is made to be opened.

She makes a noise in her throat. They're alive, hungry, tasting the salt and spit of each other's mouths. Suddenly Anna twists in his arms, pulls back, puts her hands on his shoulders and pushes him sharply away. 'Not like that. Not yet.'

'I'll be careful.'

'You won't. I've already got Kolya, I don't want to get caught for another baby.' She says it crudely, as Lyuba would say it.

'But I'm –'

A burst of sound cuts across them.

'What was that?'

'Only a whistle.'

'There's something going on.'

They freeze, listening. He hears the pant of her breath. The whistle blasts again.

'It's the militia.'

Far off, to the south-west of the city, there's the drone of a plane.

'Is it theirs? Can you tell?'

'They'll only be dropping leaflets.'

The blackout stands thick around them, blotting out what they strain to see. She's still in his arms, warm and damp, but she's already gone away.

'You must get back.'

'And you.'

'There's a doorway here.'

They back into the doorway. Several streets away, there's a burst of anti-aircraft fire, then silence. They wait, but nothing else happens, and the engine noise dies into the distance.

'It's coming soon.'

'Yes.'

'They'll need you at the hospital.'

'Yes, I must go.'

'Tell me why you didn't come before.'

'I couldn't come,' he says, stroking her face then holding it between his hands and kissing her on the mouth, with slow, deep kisses, between the words. 'I couldn't leave the hospital.'

'How bad is it?'

'I can't tell any more. It all seems normal to me now.'

'Yes, that's it, isn't it? Everything becomes normal so quickly, until you look back and see how far you've come away from how things used to be.'

'Maybe not so far at all yet, compared to how far we've got to go.'

'Don't say that.'

They stand close for a while, not touching, but breathing each other's breath. The city is silent now, as if at peace. She combs Andrei's hair back with her fingers.

'You know I wanted to?' he says.

'To come? Yes.'

'And then I saw you today, on your bike, with all those sacks.'

'I didn't think you'd seen me, that's why I called to you.'

'But I had.'

'You're just saying that.'

'I swear I had. I knew you were there. Didn't you see me smiling?'

'It was dark.'

'Not quite dark.'

'We must go.'

'Yes.'

They step out of the doorway, and turn right.

'You know, in the blackout, the pavement feels so uneven. And yet it looks smooth by daylight.'

'There's going to be a curfew any day. This might be the last time we can walk round like this.'

'Tell me about Irkutsk.'

'You're not interested in Irkutsk. You're a Leningrader.'

'You're a Leningrader now. You live here.'

'Yes, but I can go away. Real Leningraders can't. Wherever they are, no matter how beautiful it is, no matter how happy they are, they're always pining to be back. They can't live without a cold in their head, and someone's boot on their neck.'

'You're telling me there's no boot on your neck in Irkutsk?'

'It's a question of degree. God and the Tsar are farther off, as they say.'

'But here in Leningrad, they're our next-door neighbours. You're right. We're all packed in together, and we don't trust one another. We have to suspect everyone. If you've got a bigger room than someone else in a communal apartment, you've got to watch your back in case he denounces you to get hold of it himself. I keep thinking, how did we get to where we are? Nobody wants it, so how did it ever happen? I look back, and I just can't see how we got here.'

'It's not so bad. The people in my apartment aren't like that.'

'Only because you don't notice it. It's that pure Siberian air you carry around with you. Don't be fooled. There'll be someone in your apartment who's watching you. There always is.'

'With the Germans so close, all those other things will stop.'

'Let's not talk any more.'

They hurry on, through the blacked-out city that crouches beneath a blacked-out, starless sky. At the entrance to Anna's apartment building, they stop. There's a smell of rubbish and drains. A drop of water tocks off the roof, and then another.

'Here we are,' says Andrei.

'I know. Not the Astoria, is it?'

'We'll get there one day, I promise.'

'We always seem to be standing in doorways.'

He pulls her up, close to him. They shut their eyes, drifting. One drop of water falls, then another.

'It's raining.'

'Yes.'

A sharp wind teases Anna's bare legs. The end of summer. It's come suddenly, just like this, as it always does. He pulls up her dress, sliding the ruck of fabric over her thighs.

A big, pale-haired guy in a vest, with muscled shoulders, leans out of an upper window. He thought he heard something. He thought he caught movement. The Germans are sending agents into Leningrad, infiltrating. He peers out, snuffing the air which smells of autumn. Nothing. Nobody there.

A rat darts across the courtyard entrance, but Anna neither sees it nor feels it.

'You know I wanted to come.'

'Yes. Yes.'

*

In the apartment, Marina sits by Kolya's bed until he's asleep, and then goes into the other room, the dark room where Mikhail lies. She switches on the shaded, low-watt lamp beside his bed, and examines his face. Although he's breathing steadily, she doesn't believe he's asleep.

'It's me,' she says. 'Do you want to talk?'

'What about?'

No, he doesn't want to talk, or eat, or move. The process that began in him years ago, when Vera died and they stopped publishing his books, is now completing itself. He opens his eyes, and looks at her sternly and critically.

'What are you doing?'

'Nothing. Kolya's asleep. Anna's gone out.'

He blinks impatiently at these names which force him to come back into the present.

'She's gone out with your friend Andrei.'

'Yes.' He moistens his lips. He'd like to tell Marina to go out too, and leave him alone. Why is she always hovering over him like this, expecting things of him? Doesn't she know that all he wants is to sleep? No, not to sleep exactly. But to drift, to let go, to cease to feel.

'Is your shoulder hurting?'

'No.'

Marina considers him. Then she says clearly and deliberately: 'You know that the Germans have broken through.'

He moves again, more restlessly. 'They took Kingisepp. We couldn't stop them.'

'They are almost at Pushkin.'

'That's impossible,' he whispers.

'You would think so. But they are there. They have encircled us.'

'Why are you telling me this?'

'Why not? Why should you be the only man in Leningrad to have the luxury of not knowing it? You have a son who is five years old.'

A flicker of amusement lights his face. 'You're a hard woman, Marina.'

'It's about time someone was hard on you. I'm not going to let you lie here and give up. You aren't dead yet. You haven't lost your children. You haven't been arrested. You've got your papers and your ration card, and God knows there are enough families jammed into one room who would kill for this apartment. You've got Anna out slaving morning to night, and on top of that carting back potatoes and onions so you won't starve to death – at least, as long as you deign to open your mouth and swallow the food she puts in it – and all you can think of is what a pity it is that she's not an intellectual. Well, thank God for that, when you look at the way most of the Writers' Union have behaved over the past few years.

'You could get up. You could be better. You just don't want to. You *refuse* to heal yourself.'

'My God, Marina, this is like having Jesus in the bedroom. You'll be telling me to take up my bed and walk next.'

'You may laugh. All right, look at me. My career is finished. I'm turning into an old woman. I've lost years when I should have been playing roles I'll never play now. There may be Germans in my dacha by now, smashing up my furniture for firewood. Here I am back in Leningrad, worse off than when I was eighteen. But Misha, for God's sake, let's stop making such a tragedy out of it. We've done far too much of that. Other people have lives, but we just keep on having emotions. We think things have been so terrible for us, but we're alive. We're not even in prison. With any luck our former colleagues will be too busy filling their store-cupboards to spare any time for denouncing us.

'I've got a ration card on the black market, and I've got somewhere to live, because your daughter's had the generosity to take me in. I'm in good health. I know how to keep Kolya happy. And I want to be here, with you. But you –'

She stops, breathing hard. What began as an attempt to stir him from his lethargy now shocks her. It is much too close to what she really feels.

'You are not trying,' she finishes, keeping her voice even.

'I'm dying, Marina.'

'By choice.'

129

'You can't say that.'

'I can say anything I want to you. You are letting it happen. *I know*, you loved Vera. *I know*, they stopped publishing you. *I know*, they wounded you.'

'Marina –'

'You don't even notice the people who love you. To you, they are nothing. You don't value yourself, and that belittles everyone who loves you.'

His eyes are open now, round with surprise and fixed on her. The childishness of his expression makes her want to relent, but she won't. How dare he lie there like a stone, cold and withdrawn?

'But you know, Marina, it does hurt.'

'I do know. It hurts because you're not dead yet. You've got to promise that you'll let us help you. No more letting soup dribble away down your chin into that scrub of a beard you won't let us shave.'

'Dribble?'

'Yes, dribble. And very unattractive it looked, I have to tell you. People of our age, Misha, can't permit ourselves to behave like useless old fools. It was one thing wiping your backside when you first came back from hospital, but I'm sure Anna doesn't want to make it a permanent arrangement.'

'Marina, I – I really don't know what to say –'

It is hard work to fight down her pity. 'You must get up,' she says. 'Every day you spend in bed is weakening you. Your muscles are wasting. Even if it hurts you must get up and walk around the room.'

'Did Andrei tell you all this?'

She pauses, stroking his hand. 'In a way. He said there's a point in every illness, no matter how serious, where the patient has to cooperate. And you've reached that point.'

It's enough. His face is the colour of tallow.

'Go to sleep now.'

He nods. She continues to stroke his hand as his eyelids seal down over the prominent eyeballs. The beard sprouts, dirty grey from greyish-yellow skin. He is old and sour and battered. She would defend him with her last breath, and he is the only man for whom she has ever bothered to become angry.

'We'll be fine,' she says. 'You'll see, Misha, it'll all be all right, as long as you don't ever believe that you're going to be beaten.'

14

Sugar burns. It sends up columns of black and acrid smoke into the night air. It hisses, crackles, runs like a river of flame. A volcano of sugar spews smoke and sparks into the night sky until its white-hot molten core drives back the fire-fighters. This is the devil's kitchen. The flaming wooden carcasses of the Badayev warehouses are ovens which devour the food they were built to protect. Smoke seethes from the city's stores of cooking-oil, lard, butter, meat and flour. Leningrad's food reserves are burning, sending up gouts of flame, sweeping thick, greasy smoke low over the rooftops.

Thousands of tons of sugar, flour, fats and meat vanish overnight. A coating of soot and food-grease lies on window-ledges all over Leningrad. If you lift a hank of your own hair you can smell the stink of burnt fat.

It's the night between the eighth and ninth of September. Mga has fallen, and now there are no more road or railway links to the rest of Russia. The only way out is over the still, grey water of Lake Ladoga. Leningrad is surrounded. Built on many islands, it has become an island, packed with people who need their two thousand calories a day, but haven't got so much as a window-box to grow a handful of parsley, or a pet rabbit to skin for Sunday dinner. These are urbanites who forage in queues, not in the earth. They're used to food shortages, unofficial rationing and making do, used to insufficient vitamins, poor-quality meat and erratic supplies of fresh fruits and vegetables. They're used to coping.

But in a strange way a state of perpetual shortages can make you feel secure. You believe that because things are bad enough, they won't get any worse. After all, *they* can surely manage to keep this up, as a bare minimum. It's not much to ask. Food will keep on coming in from elsewhere (although never enough of it); it will keep getting distributed (although inefficiently); it will be obtainable in the end (although at high prices, and after long and laborious queuing).

For years, working the food system has taken up so much energy that you rarely have any spare to question the system itself. You grumble, automatically on good days, bitterly on bad ones. If a queue forms, you join it instantly. Never mind what it's for, as long as you're in it, clutching your just-in-case shopping-bag that you carry everywhere, always. Since the beginning of the thirties, the food situation has grown steadily worse, like a winter that keeps looking as if it's over, before darkening into another grey, obliterating snowfall.

Your boots wear out, but you mend them somehow, and even if you never get used to the cold, you put up with it. So here you are in one of the richest, most fruitful countries on earth, and grateful if you can get a couple of onions to go with that precious half-kilo of fatty sausage. Georgia may be overflowing with lemons and apricots, roast lamb shanks and sweet wine, but you certainly don't see any of that up here. Cabbage, a bagful of wizened apples, soup. *Kasha and cabbage soup, that's our grub.* The kolkhoz market has better stuff, but it costs a fortune.

Of course it's different for the high-up ones. They have special shops with white bread, fresh meat, caviar and everything you could imagine, spread out like on a magic tablecloth. You can tell who shops there just by looking at them. How do you think they get those plump, rosy skins, without a spot or wrinkle on them? And their children have smooth, glossy hair that bounces around as if it's got a life of its own. You only get hair like that by eating butter and oranges.

But this time everyone's been caught out, even the high-up ones. They didn't see it coming. The Badayev warehouses: they're Leningrad's big store-cupboard. You've often joked, just like everyone else: *I don't think I'll bother with the queue. I'll just pop down to the Badayev warehouses. They'll have everything I want.* It's always been nice to think of those vast wooden shells, packed to the gills with food. Comforting. Like thinking of money in the bank, even if it's not yours.

It seems like the Germans knew about our big store-cupboards, too. They had a special kind of bomb for them, one that doesn't just explode, but sets fire to everything. It's a new type of bomb you can't put out with water, because it just starts burning again as soon as the water runs off it. And that's the way they cooked the biggest cake you've ever seen, out of the flour and sugar and fat that was in store to last us all winter.

They say there's a way of getting back the sugar that's melted down through the warehouses and sunk into the soil. *Reclamation*, it's called. There are some of our scientists down there working on it already.

But a shock like that kicks you in the stomach. The Badayev warehouses. You didn't believe it when you first saw the flames go up. Fountains of greasy, black and orange fire. You feel empty. You went to have a look in the morning, but there was nothing left except bits of building jagging up out of black ash. The ash was still smouldering, and every now and then little spurts of flame ran across it. The space where those warehouses were is as big as a park.

You ought to be thinking of all the poor souls who lost their lives in the raids, but you can't help thinking about all that butter and flour and God knows what else they kept down there. How many bags of flour would there have been, for example? 'A ton of flour' doesn't mean a lot, but if you can work out how many bags there might have been, then that really means something. Same with butter and sausage.

It'd take whole shopfuls of bags of flour and sugar and fat to fill a park. In fact it's not just a question of space, because you could never put all that food in the shops at once. So you have to think about the time it would take to use it all up. The number of days those shops would have been filled. Or even weeks.

But now it's just – not there. All burnt up. Weeks and weeks of food. Months of it, maybe, for all Leningrad's millions of mouths. Those Germans knew what they were doing. All gone, apart from the sugar in the soil, which our scientists are going to get out by a special process.

Aeroplanes coming in from Moscow now approach Leningrad from the north-west, to minimize the chance of German attack. They fly in low over swamp and forest. They skim Lake Ladoga. It's come to this, that Russian planes fly like thieves in the night over their own land.

The plane tilts and banks. Layers of green and grey appear in the windows, then disappear. But Pavlov doesn't look out of the window. He has briefly considered the possibilities of German attack or pilot error on this dangerous, unfamiliar route, and then dismissed them. He thinks about nothing except what needs to be thought about now, at this moment. His job is to take over the administration of all food supplies and distribution in Leningrad, in the present crisis. He is jotting down columns of figures, making lists. Reserves, military rations, civilian rations, rates of consumption. He has nearly three and a half million mouths to feed. The plane lurches. Tree-tops, much too close, punch into view. Pavlov straightens his paper, which has slipped sideways, and rapidly adds up another column.

'We'll be landing in five minutes.'

'Excellent.'

The plane lands heavily, throwing its passengers back against their seats. They are here, in Leningrad. Whatever happens, they are part of it now.

15

Two sharp knocks on the door. It's his signal.

'Anna.'

The apartment smells of onions and his mouth floods with saliva. But she doesn't ask him in. They stand in the tiny, stuffy hallway, just as they stood the first time he came here. Suddenly he is afraid that she is no closer to him than she was then. The breasts he has touched are hidden by her ugly jacket. Her face is pale, her lips dry.

'I was just on my way out.'

He touches her cheek.

'I've got to go straight away, Andrei. I'm late.'

She's always late. Always on her way somewhere, rushed and frowning. The evacuation centre has closed, since there's no question of evacuating anyone for the foreseeable future, now that all the railway lines that connect Leningrad to the rest of the country have been cut. She's working in a labour battalion, building fortifications again, but this time they're inside the city. Sector by sector, building by building, barricades are going up. Pillboxes, bunkers and machine-gun nests are being set up, trenches are being dug, and key defensive positions identified. A new map of the city is emerging, which has nothing to do with homes, shops, schools, parks or restaurants. It is to do with patrols at every crossroads, with mined bridges, with sight-lines, steel tank barriers, pillboxes, and the artillery positions which everyone calls Voroshilov hotels. Trams filled with sandbags are positioned to block junctions. Street names and house numbers have vanished from this map.

Even the trees in the parks have become something else. Now they are defensive positions, behind which a man can crouch, watching, alert, his cheek pressed against bark which is carved with lovers' initials. Each prospect of stone and water yields a second meaning which seems to have been waiting, hidden, since the city was first conceived. Was it this that Peter had in mind when he built?

'Let me see your hands,' says Andrei. He turns them over. 'You must cover those blisters, and put some iodine on them. They'll become infected if you get soil into them.'

'They'll soon harden.'

'I'm trying to help you.'

'I'm fine. Come in and see Kolya for a minute. He was asking when you were coming.'

'But you haven't got time.'

'No.' Suddenly she grabs him, pulls his head to her, and kisses his lips, running her tongue into his mouth. After a second she withdraws and nips the cushiony softness of his lip between her teeth. They rock together, their eyes shut. Anna draws away first, and rubs her cheek against his.

'You never shave. Isn't that always the story with us, no time to do anything or go anywhere? As soon as I wake up, I already feel as if I've been running all night. I never do anything properly. Last night I dreamed I was booked on to the Moscow train, but even though I knew it was leaving in less than an hour I had so many things to do that I couldn't stop myself doing them. I was cutting up a blanket to make a lining for Kolya's jacket, and my mother was standing in the doorway with her arms folded, watching me. And then she said, "Don't you know what time it is, Anna?" just as she used to do when I was running round the apartment trying to find my homework on a school morning.'

'Imagine if you could really be booked on to the Moscow train.'

There are no trains to Moscow any more. There are no trains to anywhere. They are both silent, thinking of ripped-up track, bombed trains, and sleepy stations full of yellow, gluey sunlight, where you used to step down into nowhere, and go walking. All those stations are occupied.

'They brought in two little boys last night,' says Andrei. 'Brothers. They'd been sleeping in the same bed when their apartment was shelled. One of them had his legs crushed, the other had a ruptured spleen.' He stops, and strokes her cheek. 'I don't think they'd have had much chance anyway, but all the theatres were full when they were brought in, so that was that.'

The children actually did not look like children. They were black with smoke, and their hair stuck out, crisp with heat from the fire which had torn through their apartment building.

'Did you get the morphine delivery?'

'It's supposed to be coming in on a military flight tomorrow. Anna, please, don't go for a minute. Let me hold you.'

He grasps her through the wadded cloth of her jacket. Her neck smells of flowers. Which flowers? He's sure that he knows. He breathes in again, closing his eyes.

'Anna, what perfume is that?'

'It's Marina's soap. There's only a sliver of it left.'

'I'll get you some more.'

She puts her hands on his wrists. 'Andrei, please.'

'You love me. Say you love me.' He shivers at the softness of her hair, tickling his face.

'It's not the right time.'

He pulls back. Her face is sullen.

'You think I can do everything,' she says. 'Well, I can't. I have Kolya in there, and my father. They've got to be fed, and kept clean, and their clothes have to be washed, and Kolya's boots have holes in them. They're too small anyway, but I can't get another pair. I've got to find felt boots for him for the winter, or he'll get frostbite, but God knows where I'll get those. And now the bread ration's going down again. I hear things –'

'What things?'

She leans closer. Her frightened breath stirs in his ear.

'It's not just the bridges that are being mined. It's everything. So – if the Germans do break through – they won't find anything left. It'll all be blown up. The whole city. Rather than let them have it –'

'That's just a rumour,' he says, so quickly that she knows he's heard it, too. 'How could we destroy Leningrad?'

'The person who told me is a Party member. He was at school with me. He says they're mining everything there in the northern sector. If they're doing that there, then it must be the same across the whole city. There are detonators ready, just waiting . . .'

'The whole city . . .'

'Yes.'

They stare at each other.

'But how can there not be Leningrad any longer? It's impossible.'

'Yes, it's impossible,' says Anna. 'But I believe him. He knew what he was saying. We'll blow it up rather than let them have it.'

'You can't think about all that, Anna. You've just got to think about now.'

'That's what I'm trying to do. But then you come – and you wake everything up – and you make me feel things again, and I want to talk to you about them –'

'That's good, isn't it? What's the point of being alive if you don't feel it? You might as well be under an anaesthetic.'

'Andryusha, it's different for you. I've got my father, and Kolya. I've always had a child holding my hand, and I'm not even a mother. Sometimes I think I never will be. This'll be my life, this'll be what I have if we don't all die. Don't you understand? I'm not complaining, I'm just telling you how it is. They are my responsibilities. Look at my father. Do you think he'll ever be –'

He sees her feel for the difficult word. *Normal*, perhaps. *Himself. All right*. All those shorthands women use to him when they come into the ward with their baskets of bread and soup clutched in rough, red-knuckled hands.

'He won't be able to work again,' she says at last. 'And he'll need someone at home to look after him when I'm at work. I won't be able to leave him alone. How can we afford that, on what I earn? Or is Marina going to stay? That's good in a way, but on the other hand I'm never alone, I've never got time when someone isn't wanting something, expecting something –'

'You don't need to think about it all now.'

'Why are you saying that? Are you saying that because he's going to die? Is that what you're trying to tell me?'

'No, Anna, of course not.'

'Well . . . I'm sorry, Andrei. I get angry. I'm not angry with you, but you see why I can't let myself think about other things now. I can't think about how I feel.'

'You want to. I know you want to.'

'Yes, but that's not the point. Anybody can give way sometimes.'

'For God's sake, Anna, what's that supposed to mean?'

'I don't know how to say it. It's this. You make me weak. I'm afraid of it. I'm afraid you'll weaken me.'

'I would never let you get pregnant. You know how careful I am.'

'That's wonderful. That solves all my problems. Doesn't it occur to you that not being pregnant really isn't all that much to hope for out of life?'

'Anna,' he says, in the tone she loves. Two drawn-out syllables, as if he doesn't want to let go of her name: An—na. 'Anna. Let's not quarrel.'

'I know. But you should be with your patients, and I should be digging ditches.'

'In a minute.'

'You know I want you to stay. You know that.'

'Yes.'

'But we have to make sacrifices.'

'Mm.'

He is unbuttoning her jacket. Her breasts are squashed by the tight, ugly blouse she's wearing to match the ugly jacket. He undoes the buttons of the blouse, and there is the warm, deep crack between her breasts. He touches the line where her tan ends, then slides his hand down and finds her nipple. She kisses him, arching her back so that her breast fills his hand. Then she says, 'Marina, Kolya and my father are all within three metres of us. They can even hear us breathing.'

'You don't want to make any more sacrifices.'

'You know I do. But I can't. I must go.'

He watches her as she buttons up her blouse. She glances up and smiles a sudden, naked smile.

'It's so stupid, isn't it? All the things we want, and all the things we could have – and we might never be able to have any of them.

You remember Katinka, the girl who died – the one I told you about? She was *outraged* by the idea that she might be going to die. Because that wasn't what she'd been promised. After all, she was only fifteen, and all her life everything had gone so well. Death was something that happened to other people, like failing an exam.

'Sometimes I think we should do everything, now, all at once, without stopping to think, because this might be the only time we've got. And I don't know if I hold back because I'm sensible, or because I'm scared.'

'I would never hurt you.'

'You might. And I might hurt you. I don't want any of that to happen.'

'It won't happen.'

'But sometimes I think I'm better on my own, Andryusha. Safer. I know this will sound stupid, because as you see I'm surrounded by people all the time. But I've always felt as if I were alone – no, that's not right, I mean *on my own* – ever since my mother died.'

He folds his arms around her. He wants to make them so close that there is no room for words to come between them. In the little hallway, silent, they're safe.

In the next room Marina Petrovna is making onion soup and listening to Radio Leningrad, while Kolya sprawls on the floor drawing pictures of tanks. His tanks are tiny, like insects crawling across white paper. There are houses and streets in his picture, but no people.

There is a smell of onions and sickness in the room. Kolya's father lies on the sofa, exhausted by the effort of getting out of bed. From time to time he sips from the glass of tea beside him. There is the tea-glass. There, his hand. Slowly, by an immense effort of will, he joins one to the other. The glass shakes as he lifts it to his lips. The tea slops, but doesn't spill. He sucks in a little. Sweet, sweet. Suddenly the effort of holding the glass outweighs the bliss of sugar. He puts it down, and lets himself sink on to the pillows Marina has packed around him. He feels himself falling, but with another effort he steadies himself. He is on the sofa. There are his legs, under the

141

blanket. Everything is just as it should be. He patrols his thoughts until it is safe to relax and watch his son.

He's going to be good at drawing, like Anna. But he's coming to the stage when they aren't satisfied with those sweeping, intuitive early drawings which we adults think are so wonderful. He wants to learn. How do you draw eyelashes? How do you draw a man so he looks as if he's really running? For a while his drawings won't be as good as they are now. He'll be struggling, and he'll get cross with himself, and hurl his paper into the bin. I remember that stage so well, with Anna. 'That's beautiful,' we'd say, but she'd screw up her face and say, 'No, it's not. It's all wrong. It's rubbish. I'm going to tear it up.'

Vera thought it might help if she had drawing lessons, even though she was only seven. And it turned out to be just the right thing. She stopped getting into a rage with herself, and all her enthusiasm came back. I would never have thought of the drawing lessons, but Vera had a feeling for things like that.

When the sun gets as far as that cushion there, I can go back to bed. But not before.

But the terrible thing about coming back to life is that you can't be at peace any more. There are a thousand things to torment you. Before, I didn't mind what happened. I could let it all slip away. I didn't listen to the radio, even though Marina has it on all the time. But now I'm afraid, just like everyone else. When Marina takes the boy down to the air-raid shelter, I'm afraid that I'll never see them again. I lie here: that's all I can do. I listen to the anti-aircraft guns and sometimes I can hear planes. They aren't our fighters. They drum above the roof and I find myself praying, even though I never pray. Always the same words: if it falls, let it be a bomb, not an incendiary. The sheets stick to me with sweat.

I am not afraid of bombs. But if an incendiary took hold here, I wouldn't be able to get away. I'm afraid of that.

Last night I dreamed of Marina and the child. They were trying to wade towards me through a river which was full of fire instead of water. But he slipped and went down and then he floated away, slowly at first then faster and faster, with the fire lapping around his head. Marina kept on looking at me. I knew she wanted to tell me why she hadn't rescued him. It was because it was too late for him. He would suffer too much if he was brought up into the air again.

When I woke up I was wet with sweat and the guns were still crackling. They drop phosphorus bombs. Water can't put out phosphorus: it burns and burns.

Last night there was a terrible screaming that went on and on, and I think it was that which made me dream about Kolya, and the fire. Marina says they weren't human screams. A bomb hit the zoo and the animals were wounded. Some of the cages were blown open and the animals were running up and down the streets. I suppose they had to be shot in the end.

Marina says they're not selling any food off the rations now. The restaurants are closed. She sits on my bed and tells me how many potatoes we've got left, how many onions, how many grammes of lard. She counts them over aloud, then counts them again. We both enjoy it. If she stops, I ask her more questions. 'How many potatoes did you say exactly, Marina?'

Kolya loves peeping into the store-cupboard and seeing how many jars there are. He doesn't try to touch anything. He stares solemnly for a while, and then he says, 'We've got lots of food, haven't we, Marina?' She answers, 'Yes, we're very fortunate,' and he nods, satisfied, and goes back to his game.

There's been further bombing of food stocks, but no one knows exactly where. Now we know that they don't just want to defeat us. They want to destroy us. Nothing in Leningrad matters to them at all. Not a stone, or a child. Carthage must be destroyed.

But there's freedom in knowing it. We can't make deals with them any more. So much for our pact. We have no choice left. We have to resist.

So I get out of bed and lie on the sofa for two hours. Doesn't sound much like resistance, does it? Wouldn't it terrify the Germans to know that Mikhail Ilyich Levin is staying alive, and repeating poetry to himself.

> Onegin, do you remember that hour
> Picked by fate for our meeting
> In the alley, in the garden . . . ?

I can recite page after page. I close my eyes, and it's as if I had the book in front of me. I go through the section where Tatyana is lost in her dream. The plains, the fir trees, the ghostly light and the creak of her footsteps through the snow: all these come to me so powerfully that it's as if I'd never really read about them or thought about them before. I almost say aloud that I'm sorry I didn't understand until now. My eyes fill with tears, and I don't know why. But I know that it's by these things, and nothing else, that we survive. Poetry doesn't exist to make life beautiful. Poetry is life itself.

Tatyana will go on walking, the snow will fall, and Onegin will go on failing to love her until it is much too late. Suddenly he'll recognize her for what she really is, and she'll explain to him why nothing more can happen between them. Everything that seems arbitrary has been laid down since time began. Soon the brown, earth-coloured landscape will be covered by snow.

Always, every winter, there's a certain moment when you think that this time it will go on for ever. The spring has forgotten us. Frost sinks deeper and deeper into the soil, driving out every sign of life. The sap will never rise again. And in a way you don't even want it to rise. Spring is painful, and messy, and the earth smells foul when the crust of ice finally melts and breaks.

'Onegin, do you remember . . .'

And the ice starts breaking.

'That's very good, Kolya. Just look at the way you've drawn that tank turret.'

'But I can't do the guns properly, Dad. Do you know how to draw guns?'

'Give me your paper. Gently now. I'll have a try.'

16

Impossible arithmetic. No matter how often you do the sums, they can't work out. Evacuation started much too late, and too many people were evacuated into the path of the German advance. They poured back into the city, just ahead of the Germans. For every evacuee who left Leningrad for the Urals, three or four came in from the south and west, driven by the German advance. The city is packed. There are close to three million civilians, and then there's the military, nearly half a million of them. Divide Leningrad's food by all those mouths, and see how quickly it vanishes, once the supply-lines are cut.

Here's a market stall, loaded with cabbages, buckwheat, lard, rye flour, wheat flour, sugar, honey, potatoes. The potatoes are solid, with firm, yellow flesh. The lard is of the finest quality, and the honey is on the comb, with its wax intact. Those fat, sweet cabbages with their crisp hearts are heaped up like chrysanthemums, green and bluish-purple, with first touch of frost prickling on their outer leaves. It's a dream-stall, which could never really exist in a world of queues and shortages. But even if it did, how many could it feed? Imagine that a hundred people crowd around it, grabbing the food and stuffing it into their bags. Suddenly there are a thousand, and now the crowd swells out of the square to pack the surrounding streets. There are ten thousand, fifty, a hundred thousand. The imagination halts. It cannot grasp a million flailing hands. Besides, the dream-stall has long since been stripped and overturned. There's nothing left.

But the hands are still there. They're held out, and they've got to be filled. For city people, it's hard to grasp that the supply chain has broken. It's kept them going all their lives, even though the system sometimes dissolves into chaos, and prices go up and down like an undertaker's hat. Leningraders don't talk about shopping, they talk about 'getting hold of things'. It's an art-form you learn at your mother's side, queueing. But there's never just *not been anything*. We're not peasants in the Ukraine.

Suddenly and sharply, it's obvious that cities only exist because everyone agrees to let them exist. It's crazy, when you think of it, for millions of mouths to pack themselves into a couple of hundred square kilometres, without a pig or a potato patch between them. It only works in the way that fiction works, by making people collaborate. All its life, the city has had the power to demand. It asks for milk, and before dawn milk arrives. Field after field furs over with rye and barley, pigs die choking on their own blood, apples swell and fishermen drown. In the black-deep reaches of Lake Baikal the sturgeon turn their snouts and swim into nets. The city doesn't ask for details, as long as the food keeps coming in.

Leningrad mobilizes countryside, villages and towns for hundreds of kilometres around. Thousands of peasants who will never see the city spend their whole lives working to provide its food. Its web of trade relationships curls into millions of lives.

Within the city, the process of transformation never stops. Raw wood-pulp is transformed into books, raw small-town boys are transformed into doctors and engineers. Would-be actors and filmmakers and dancers, bursting with chaotic talent, are shaped into finished artists. Leningrad can take anything, swallow it, and make it new.

In packed trams and buses, members of the Writers' Union are jammed up next to steel-workers from the Kirov works, who transform rivers of molten metal into KV tanks as the writers struggle to strike out words at white-heat and pour them into new stories and poems. Leningraders deal in finished products. They are high up in the chain that leads from raw earth to luxury goods. Most of them will never eat caviar, but they know that caviar grows in jars in GORT stores, not within a fish. They understand that milk doesn't come from cows, but from shops.

Years of food shortages, rations and queuing have had the odd, contrary effect of making them less likely to panic when times get tough. They're so used to bread queues and scoured, empty shelves in shops. They believe in their bones that if you walk far enough, have the right contacts, join every queue and wait for as many hours as it takes, in the end you'll go home with something in your shopping-bag. It could be a few frostbitten turnips, a precious, fragrant hundred grammes of coffee, a few gnarled apples from a kolkhoz stall, or a piece of sausage. Sometimes it won't be much more than a couple of onions and fifty grammes of lard to make onion soup. But tonight, at least, you'll eat.

And tomorrow is another day. The wheels will turn, the web will stretch, there'll be an unexpected delivery of pickled cucumbers, or cranberries from the Ladoga marshes, all drawn to the magnet of the Leningrad markets. With any luck you'll be there, bag at the ready, first in the queue. This is how it has always worked. Like a body that cannot stop believing in an amputated, ghostly limb, so the city continues to believe in its supply chains long after they have been severed.

All those millions of mouths. Lips open, teeth bite and grind, salivary glands flood mouths with rich saliva to moisten the food and begin its digestion. Rhythmic waves of peristalsis send the food into the centre of the body. Energy begins to flow. Starches convert to sugar, and the body floods with warmth, energy and hope. Lips shine with grease, the skin temperature rises slightly, and a faint pearling of sweat appears on the forehead. Life is good.

The mouths of Leningrad continue to open and swallow. The gummy, toothless mouths of babies fasten on to their mothers' nipples. Old, toothless mouths mamble black bread dipped in tea. Ravenous seventeen-year-old boys, still growing, cram their mouths with anything they can find.

The question which arithmetic can't answer has got to be addressed by someone. There is this much food, and it is not being replaced. If no further supplies come into the city, how long will it last? How many times can these three and a half million mouths open, and still be filled?

Dimitri Pavlov, newly arrived from Moscow, is the man who must attack the question, even if he cannot answer it. The brutal truth of the situation belongs to him, and he knows it to the core.

Before long, the rest of Leningrad will know it too, not with their brains but in their bellies. The entire city is a stone island now, and has got to depend upon its own resources. But you can't eat stone, or the magical prospect of the Neva at dawn. Nor can you derive calories from apartment buildings, armaments factories, icons or munition works. The history of Leningrad, Petrograd, St Petersburg may stretch back to the moment Peter put his iron mark on the marshes of the Neva, but you can't eat history.

Pavlov has the power to do anything, though nobody, as he observes, can fold a piece of paper more than seven times. 'Really? Can't you? But of course you can, if it's a big enough sheet.'

Silently, Pavlov hands over a large sheet of high-quality, thin paper, and watches his colleague fold it. Once, twice, three times. This is easy. But at the eighth fold the man looks up, pained, although still smiling.

'Do you know, you're quite right. I would never have believed it.'

'Even if that paper were as big as Lake Ladoga, it still wouldn't fold. We cannot change the laws of nature.'

Pavlov writes more lists, calculates figures, and works out his plans. There is silence, except for the scratching of his pen, the crackle of papers as he checks statistics, and the sound of typing from the next room. In the outer office the phone rings constantly, but Pavlov pays it no attention. The calls will be from managers of local food-storage units, slaughterhouses and depots, ringing in with the latest statistics which he has requested. He wants to know exactly what Leningrad holds. No rough calculations. He doesn't want any fantasies about how many cabbages may still lie unharvested in suburban gardens. Above all, he doesn't want optimism. He wants the detail. No rounding up of figures. No hoping against hope that somehow supplies may 'get through' when it is impossible for them to get through. For that is what the besieging army intends. Pavlov has grasped that from the beginning. They have dug in, and they'll hold on, relying on hunger and winter to open the gates of Leningrad to them. The Panzer divisions may have been transferred away from the Leningrad front, but a ring of steel holds Leningrad tight.

Every so often a young woman comes in from the outer office

with a long, flimsy strip of paper covered in typewritten columns, and lays it down at his side. Pavlov drinks in these statistics at a glance, and adds them to his calculations.

'It's the same with our reserves,' he announces suddenly, to the colleague who keeps glancing at the folded sheet of paper as if perhaps he might have done it another way, and succeeded with the eighth fold.

'I'm sorry?'

'Our reserves. Here. According to these figures, at present we have twenty-five thousand pigs in the Leningrad area. Some on the hoof, some already slaughtered. Sounds a lot, doesn't it?'

'I should say so.'

'But we are consuming meat at the rate of two hundred and fifty tons a day. Tell me, how long will we be able to continue to fold that particular piece of paper?'

'Forgive me, I don't know exactly how much a pig actually weighs –'

'Then find out. These are the things we must all know. Facts. We have got to know the facts, not what we think will happen or hope will happen. For a start, we must put out of our minds any expectation of further supplies reaching us in the foreseeable future.'

'But, excuse me, surely it's still possible to bring in supplies by water, over Lake Ladoga.'

'Not enough. The supply chain is too weak, and we haven't got the infrastructure. There are not enough landing-stages or barges, and the railway line is hopelessly inadequate. We'll exploit that route as far as we can, but our boats are sitting ducks for German bombers. For the time being, I have decided to discount from my calculations any supplies which may reach us via the Ladoga route. We must be realistic. Facts are our business, not pious hopes. We have three and a half million people to feed for an indefinite period, and at the present rates of consumption we won't do it. The ration must be cut again.'

Both men would say, if you asked them, that they are working in concentrated silence. They have long since ceased to hear the sirens, the screech of fighter planes struggling to defend the city, and the explosions which are so loud that they seem not to be heard but to thud deep into the stomach, like blows. They do not try to put what is happening into words. If they did, they would probably reach for clichés. 'Leningrad is fighting for its life.' 'The people of Leningrad will defend their city to the last drop of blood.' 'The Fascist invaders will be repulsed by the determination of the Soviet people.' Pavlov would reach for the clichés, simply because to do so saves time.

Pavlov is a man in his prime. He reaches out for a paper without looking at the woman who brings it, and she plants it eagerly in his hand. From time to time he blinks, and runs his fingers through thick, vigorous hair which is gritty with dust. Hair, skin and mouths are full of dust these days, from the bombardment. When these old buildings are shelled, they send clouds of blackened, ancient dust into the air, which drift and settle everywhere. Pavlov's skin has a faintly kippered smell, from the smoke which hangs low over Leningrad. He coughs, and seizes another strip of figures.

'Excuse me,' ventures the colleague at last, 'how long do you calculate that the blockade will continue?'

'How should I know?' snaps Pavlov. 'The duration of the blockade is not within my area of competence. Not only do I not know the answer, but the answer doesn't even interest me. I have not been sent here to speculate. Facts are what I need.'

He sits back, and knuckles his eyes with his fists. His eyes are raw with sleeplessness, and they itch all the time. It's the dust. Sometimes lines of figures dance as he studies them. Already he is afraid that mistakes have been made. If the decision to implement tougher cuts in the rations had been taken two weeks ago, thousands of tons of supplies would still be held in reserve. It's no good making cuts on an ad-hoc basis, in response to each new crisis. There must be a properly thought-through and managed policy to deal with improper, unmanageable realities.

'We must continue to fold our piece of paper,' he says, without opening his eyes. 'Even when it becomes impossible.'

He begins another list, heading it with the words 'Other resources':

Warehouses, depots, freight trucks, etc. to be swept and sweepings sifted for grain
Soil at Badayev warehouses to be processed for reclamation of sugars
Edible cellulose content in bread to be increased

FOR URGENT ACTION:
Slaughterhouse by-products
Edible barks, fungi, berries, peat
Harvesting of vegetable plots from dead zone
Brewers' malt
Domestic pets
Laboratory and zoo animals – guinea pigs, rabbits, etc.
Edible wild plants, especially anti-scorbutics, e.g. nettles, pine needles
Wallpaper paste
Leather articles . . .

Pavlov hands this new list to his colleague. 'Please add your thoughts.'

'Leather articles?'

'Some nourishment can be obtained from leather. Of course we have to set against that nourishment the energy which is required to boil the leather until a stock can be extracted. Apparently a type of beef jelly can be made from top-quality leather. This is the type of information which people will require, as time goes on. So please add your thoughts. It's possible that I have missed something.'

17

Anna has always loved the first snowfall of winter. She knows as soon as dawn comes that it'll be today. The sky remains dark, with a yellow tinge to the clouds. The light has a sharp, raw edge. Everything is waiting, silent and expectant.

Snow will come. The shrivelled leaves of autumn, the dying grasses, the chilly, dun-coloured earth, will all be covered. The snow will wipe away all mistakes. Light will stream upwards from the immaculate white of the ground.

When the first snow falls, Anna always goes to the Summer Garden. There, the noise of the city is muffled, and the park is eerily luminous. Small, naked-looking sparrows hop from twig to twig, dislodging a powder of snow. The trees are lit up like candelabra by the whiteness they hold in their arms. Underfoot, she hears for the first time the squeak of snow packing into the treads of her boots. She bends down, scoops up a handful of the new snow, throws it up into the air and watches it scatter into powdery fragments as it falls for the second time. And although she's cold and she ought to get home, she always stays much longer than she means to, because she knows that this feeling won't come again for another year. The snow will continue to fall, thaw, freeze, turn grey with use, be covered again and again by fresh blizzards. But nothing again will have the freshness, exhilaration and loneliness of the first snowfall. She's the one thing still warm and alive in a world which is going to sleep.

She looks up, into the snow which spirals down the steep funnels of the sky, whirls into her face, lands on her eyelashes and melts into tears. And then she goes back to the apartment, along streets where trams are already thrashing the new, soft snow into slush. Children skid around street-corners, yelling, their faces blazing crimson. Soon it'll be time for skis and sledges. And tomorrow, when she wakes, the snow will be thick and crusted with ice. The sun will be out, and all the shadows will be blue. This is how she has welcomed the snow every year of her life.

But not this year. The first snow falls on the fourteenth of October, drifting down through the sky and settling on the ruins of shelled houses, on to tank-traps, machine-gun nests and heaps of rubble. The snow is silent, but ominous. No one knows, this year, whether it will be an enemy or a friend. The Russian winter defeated Napoleon, people say to one another. Perhaps it will defeat Hitler, too.

A ring of siege grips the city. Nothing comes in, nothing goes out. And in the suburbs, within sight, the Germans have dug themselves in. There they stay, hunkered down for winter in deep trenches, behind defended firing-positions. The Germans have always been good at digging trenches, say older Leningraders who fought in the last war. Luxury trenches, they have, with carpets and chairs and pictures hanging on the walls. There they squat in the outskirts of Leningrad, like wolves at the mouth of a cave. They pour shells on to the city, but they do not advance any farther. This is blockade.

The Germans eat. Of course they eat. Through binoculars our boys can see that they are well-muscled and healthy. They move briskly through the chilling air, swinging their arms. They write letters to their families, saying that they'll be home soon, when they have won the war. Behind them, unbroken supply lines stretch all the way back to Berlin. The Germans are altering their rolling-stock to fit Russian railway lines. They have got the harvests of Estonia, Latvia and Lithuania on hand, and they can wait as long as they have to. An iron ring squeezes around the besieged city, slowly throttling it.

'It's snowing!'

Kolya runs to the window, but the exertion makes him cough and he grabs the back of Anna's chair. She pulls him on to her lap. His face is dusky, and his eyes stream with tears.

'How many times have I told you not to rush about like that! Now, breathe out slo-o-wly. That's good, you're doing fine. Another big breath.'

He lies back against her shoulder, eyes shut, exhausted. She chafes his hands.

'You should keep your gloves on, Kolya. Yes, I know you don't usually wear your gloves indoors, but see how cold it is.'

There is no fuel. The electricity is off. The apartment is cold with the kind of cold you usually encounter on coming home after a long absence in winter. It's a cold that penetrates clothes and upholstery, and makes furniture icy to the touch. The beds will not warm. You clamber into them, shivering, and in the morning you ache from trying to keep yourself warm. Your sleep is shallow. It is packed with dreams, and refuses to deepen into the bliss of oblivion.

Anna puffs out her breath and a white cloud forms, then disappears.

'Marina –'

'Yes?'

'What do you think about the *burzhuika*?'

Marina sighs, knitting up her face into lines. She's been trying to read, but her eyesight hasn't been so good these past few weeks. She ought to have reading-glasses, if they could be obtained. Her eyes tire quickly, and the lines of print fizz and dazzle. I am turning into an old woman, she thinks. The thought of not being able to read frightens her so much that she pushes it straight out of her mind. 'I don't know. How much are they asking for it now?'

'Three days' bread ration, or a kilo bag of sugar and two hundred grammes of lard. Plus five hundred roubles.'

'The money's no problem. I've got that.'

'You can't have much left.'

'No, not a lot, but I've certainly got five hundred.'

'But a kilo of sugar! A whole kilo.'

Anna cuts Kolya's bread ration into three small chunks. Three times a day she smears a chunk with sunflower oil, then scatters a thick icing of sugar on it. Kolya loves sugar. They have only two kilo bags left.

'But without the *burzhuika*, and with winter coming . . .' Anna continues. This is how she and Marina solve the hundred daily problems of shortages. They think aloud, until the words make some kind of pattern in their tired and hungry minds, and then they find that they have made a decision. They've got to make their minds up, because now the snow's come the price of these little stoves is shooting up every day.

'Is it extra for the stove-pipe?' asks Marina.

'Yes. Another two days' ration, or you can make it up in sugar or coffee.'

'But on the other hand, if we wait until it gets colder, the price will go up. And maybe they'll run out of *burzhuiki* and we won't be able to get one at all.'

Kolya begins to cough again. Marina rises, fetches a blanket from the sofa, and wraps it around him, tucking in the edges carefully. 'He should be wearing his fur cap,' she observes. 'A high percentage of heat is lost through the head.'

'I know. But he keeps pulling it off, don't you, Kolya?'

'It's stupid, wearing a cap in the house. Everyone will laugh at me.'

'I bet they're all wearing their caps now,' says Anna. 'Alyosha, and Shura, and all your friends. They'll all be wrapped up, just like you.'

She strokes his hair. 'Listen, I'll pull up a corner of this blanket and that'll keep your head warm. Like a soldier's helmet. No, don't wriggle. You'll feel much better.'

'Tell me what Alyosha's doing now. Will he be at nursery?'

'Nobody's at nursery now. It's closed.'

'I thought I was at home because I was ill.'

'No, you've been at home since long before you were ill, don't you remember? Because of the Germans. It would be too dangerous to go to nursery, with all the shelling, even if it was still open.'

'I wish you *would* buy us a *burzhuika*, Anna. I'm so cold.'

'I know.'

'When's it time for dinner?'

'Not yet. But Marina's going to make you some of her special drink.'

Marina rises. She looks into the other room, where Mikhail lies on his back, very still, apparently sleeping. He hasn't managed to get up today. It isn't that he's given up again, it's just that he's so weak. She goes into the kitchen. Although there's no electricity today, they've still got a little oil left. It will last another day, perhaps, not more. They desperately need to get a *burzhuika*, which can burn anything. Chopped-up furniture, books, banisters. They can go scavenging in the parks. They'll be able to keep one room reasonably warm, and heat water for tea as well as cereal.

By the time Marina brings back Kolya's drink of hot water with a spoonful of honey and a grating of nutmeg, both women have come to the same decision.

'I'll go now,' says Anna. 'You're right, all the stoves might be gone in the next few days, with this snow falling.'

'We'll have to move your father in here. We can't possibly keep more than one room warm, and it's much too cold for him in there.'

'Where are you going, Anna?' asks Kolya anxiously as she settles him on the sofa, still wrapped in the blanket.

'I'm going to get something wonderful for us. A little stove with a long pipe that goes out of the ventilation window. We'll be able to burn wood in it, and keep warm even when there's no electricity.'

'Can I light it?'

'Of course you can. But you have to be very careful, because we can't waste matches.'

'Anna, will you bring me something to eat?'

'I don't think I can. I don't think I'll be able to carry anything on the sledge except the stove. It's very heavy.'

'But I'm so hungry. Please, Anna, can't you just get me a few sweets? You can put them in your pocket and they won't weigh anything.'

She sits down on the sofa beside him, and puts her arms around him under the blanket. He is still cold, in spite of the layers of clothes and blankets around him. And he's getting thin. Those fine hairs on his legs and arms seem thicker. Isn't that a sign of malnutrition?

It didn't help, his having that cold. At least he didn't develop a chest infection. As long as she can keep his chest clear, his asthma won't get too bad. She needs goose-fat to rub on his chest at night. It's an old wives' remedy, but it really works. And some eucalyptus oil. But it was wonderful that Andrei managed to get hold of the vitamin C powder.

She hugs Kolya more tightly. The shape of his ribs is clear under her hands. When she last undressed him to wash, she saw that the fat had slipped off his buttocks to reveal the distinct outline of his pelvic bone. The bread ration for a child of five is only two hundred grammes a day now. The temptation is to use up their reserves too quickly. There is a sack of potatoes left, fifteen onions, two jars of honey, the sugar, a jar of lard and a half-bottle of sunflower oil. Before the weather turned cold Anna searched everywhere for nettles, but she's not sure how much nourishment will remain in the few semi-dried leaves which she has hung between the inner and outer windows for the cold to preserve them. There's been no difficulty in storing the potatoes after all, now that the apartment is virtually unheated. But if it freezes too hard, they'll blacken, and rot.

They are well-off, compared to many. Anna plans to allow one of the onions to sprout, because Kolya needs the vitamin content of the green shoots. This is the kind of thing she talks to Marina about now. There's no more fake intimacy, no pretending. They are a unit, in spite of everything. If they're going to survive, they'll only survive together. Marina looks after Kolya and her father, while Anna rakes Leningrad for fuel and food.

Thank God, her father eats very little. For a while she kept on trying to persuade him to eat, preparing cereal with a little honey for him, and moistening his bread with sweet tea. But now she senses a change. He wants life more than he's ever done, but it's not his own life he craves any more. It's hers, and Kolya's. He takes less than his share of the rations, and she no longer tries to persuade him.

'Don't tire yourself, my little one. Conserve your energy,' he says to her, following her with his eyes as she moves through the cold, dark apartment like someone wading in deep water. Words which she has never heard before flow from his lips. It's as if a spring has been released within him, which was tamped for years so that the water ran deep underground and never surfaced. *My soul,* he calls Anna, and *my bird.* His eyes follow her, and they glow with a life she's never seen in them before. His shoulder wound, which was beginning to heal well, has opened again, but Andrei says there's no infection. It's only that the healing process will be very slow.

'Thank you, my darling,' he says when she washes the wound with boiled water, and dresses it. The words creak hoarsely in his throat, because he doesn't seem able to draw deep enough breaths any more. But Anna doesn't hear the failing of her father's voice. To her, everything he says now is bathed in meaning, even if she can't understand it, any more than she understands the last bubbling of a blackbird's song on a spring night. After she finishes the dressing, she sits and holds his hand.

Even when her mother was alive, she never heard these words. Her parents didn't use sweet words. Her father is going back a long way now, to his own grandmother who took care of him when he was a child, who stroked his cheek, rubbed his chest with goose-fat in winter, told him stories by the stove, and lavished words on him like caresses as he drifted between sleep and waking. *My little pigeon, my blossom, my treasure trove.*

For Anna's father, the spirits of the past have come alive. They cluster thickly in the icy spaces of the apartment. Sometimes he can see them, sometimes not. They are not impatient. Sometimes they shift position, and when this happens he always discovers that they have come closer to his bed. He believes he can hear their thoughts. While he watches frost gather on the inside of the windows, their faces appear out of the patterns. They watch him eagerly, waiting for him to notice them and speak to them. His grandmother's face is there, and the stern, intelligent, bony face of his mother. Only Vera does not come, not yet. He lies and waits for her. He is sure that she will come, because her children are here. Why has it taken him so long to see that Anna moves just like her mother? Look at the way she bends over Kolya to massage his chest.

When he was still well enough to get out of bed he would lie on the sofa and watch Kolya swallowing his *kasha.* His eyes followed every movement of Kolya's lips, and his lips moved in unconscious mimicry, chewing on nothing. As the child swallowed his food, so the father swallowed on air.

'Good boy, keep eating. You'll grow strong.'

He's living on tea with sugar. 'It doesn't take much energy to lie around,' he said, and smiled at Anna, a curiously sweet smile which showed how far his gums had drawn back from his teeth. His skin was yellowish, tight over prominent bones of his forehead and nose. But Kolya wasn't frightened of him any more. He knew who he was. Sometimes he was allowed to carry his father's tea. 'As long as you do it very carefully, Kolya, and don't spill a single drop.'

'Dad's getting better!' he announced cheerfully, each time he brought back the empty tea-glass with a few grains of sugar left in the bottom. Kolya always swept his finger round the glass to gather the last drops of sweetness, and sucked blissfully. Only once did he spill the tea. He had his eyes on his father's face as he carried the glass towards the bed, but he tripped on a ruck in the rug, and hot tea spilled on to his father's chest. Anna heard Kolya cry out, but her father made no sound. When Anna pulled up his woollen undershirt, she saw his waxy skin stained red with the scald.

'Don't worry, Kolya,' her father said slowly, wheezing from the shock. 'You didn't mean to do it. You'll bring me another glass, eh?'

'I'm off, then,' says Anna. The roubles, sugar, lard and bread are in a cotton bag tied around her waist. Anna made the bag a few days earlier, out of a sheet which was too worn out to be turned sides to middle. She's sewn a flap which buttons down to secure the bag. A bag which you can wear under an overcoat is safer these days than a shopping-bag. She'll take Kolya's little sledge to carry the stove, the rest of the sheet to cover it, and some torn strips of hem to tie the sheet down. It's best if people don't see what you've got.

'Be careful,' says Marina. 'You know how rough it's getting down there.'

'I'm taking my father's silver cigarette box, in case there's any more vitamin powder.'

'Does he know?'

'No.'

She has known the wording of the inscription on the silver cigarette box since she was four years old. Before she could read the words, she used to trace them with her fingers.

'To my beloved Misha, on the occasion of our marriage . . .'

Inside, it smells of real tobacco, not *makhorka*. A spicy, luxurious scent has lingered there for years.

'He would want us to sell it. But I don't think he needs to know.'

Marina sucks in her lower lip as she examines the cigarette box. 'I wish you weren't going alone. Listen. Take this.' She pulls off the ring Anna has admired so often, a rich, glowing ruby, set in dark gold. Because the ring has become loose, Marina has wedged a little piece of silk under the gold band to keep it on her finger. Marina twists the ring, and the wad of silk falls to the floor.

'But Marina, this ring must be worth thousands of roubles. You can't just give it away – '

'It's worth a stove-pipe, anyway. Put it in your pocket, not in the bag, so they don't see it. Then you can bring it out if the bargaining gets tough. But take care who sees it.'

Anna turns the ring over. Inside the band, there is an inscription in minute lettering: *For My Cordelia.*

'Did you play Cordelia?'

'Obviously.'

'You should keep this.'

'Oh Anna, I played so many roles. I kept it for the stone, not for the inscription. Besides, I never identified with the character. I am much too aggressive. I would have taken Lear by the shoulders and shaken some sense into him. That kind of vanity amounts to madness, don't you think? All of us are to grovel on the floor declaring our love for our great leader. But of course, you have to find a way into every part.'

How thin her fingers are, Anna realizes. The bones are skeletally clear on the back of her hands. If it weren't for the silk, the ring would simply have dropped off.

Yes, she's thin, and she looks old. I would draw her differently now. It would be a better drawing. Marina, my father, Andrei, Kolya, me. We can't separate now, even if we wanted to.

'I'll be back as soon as I can.'
'Be careful. Take care of yourself.'
'Don't forget Kolya's massage.'
'No, I won't forget.'

18

The wind has dropped. Snow falls straight down, in large, soft flakes that blur footprints as soon as they are made. All sounds are muffled, except for the whump of German artillery. The shell-bursts are just irregular enough to tear nerves which are already raw with cold and hunger. They are shelling the south side of the city today, at close range.

The streets are quiet. A few figures struggle along, muffled into shapelessness, keeping to the safer side of the street. Because the Germans have dug in to the south of the city, the northern sides of the streets are said to be the most dangerous. On the 'safe' side, there is some protection from overhanging buildings, as long as there isn't a direct hit close by. This is the theory. The facts of life have been torn up and scattered, so you might as well believe in theory and rumour as anything else. Very probably injuries from blast would be equally bad on both sides of the street. Everyone has stories of people a few metres from the site of an explosion who were miraculously thrown clear, unharmed. And there are stories of others, stripped naked by blast, who died at what should have been a safe distance. If you started trying to find logic in any of it, you'd go crazy.

It is hard work walking through the snow. Already, after a few hundred metres, Anna's heart is thudding painfully. She stops to cough. She's out of breath, and a sweat of weakness starts out over her body, trickling between her shoulder-blades. She ought to have tried harder to get hold of some horehound pastilles for this cough, which has been dragging on for two weeks now. But when they get a stove, everything will be better.

Because she can't walk fast, she isn't keeping warm. Usually her blood seems to flow more brightly in winter. She's buoyant, glowing, always the one who stays in the park long after dusk, hauling children up slopes on their sledge. Winter suits her. Her eyes are bright, her skin clear, her lips red. More than anything she loves winter nights, with their scent of tangerines and frost, and the staring brilliance of stars. But today the snow is oppressive. Anna's not even sure that she's moving forward. Perhaps only the veil of falling snow is moving and she herself is treading in the same footprints, over and over again.

She forces herself on. She's so hungry. Somehow the hunger feels sharper out here. Indoors, you become torpid. You're weak, but you don't understand quite how weak until you try to do something which demands energy. You move slowly, and rest a lot, like an invalid. You take time to build up to making tea, and lean against the table while the water boils. Hours drift past, glazed.

But out here it's frightening. She mustn't rest, not even for a minute, or the cold will get her. Even though there's no wind, the snow seems to be pushing her backwards.

Across the street she sees Klavdia from the nursery laundry, dragging a heavy canvas sack. But Klavdia's eyes stare blankly, or even with hostility, and Anna's greeting dies in her mouth. Was it really Klavdia, or just someone who looked like her? Or perhaps there was no one there at all. You can easily imagine things. Sometimes grains of blackness thicken in front of her eyes. A cluster of falling flakes takes on the shape of a face. At the corner, snow devils are dancing, in spite of the lack of wind.

Heads down, scattered on the white streets like flakes of soot, a few figures fight their way onward. If she collapsed, no one would be able to help her. No one has the strength. It's hard enough to survive, to get the bread ration, to fetch water if you're in an apartment where the pipes have already frozen, to toil from empty shop to empty shop in search of milk for a sick child.

'But I'm fine,' Anna says aloud, and tastes a flake of snow on her lips. It's only being alone in the snow that makes her nervous. Her heart's beating so hard. If only she had some valerian drops, to calm herself. Even though the snow is moving, and she is moving, it's all like an icy dream from which life has fled. She could look down on herself and watch herself struggling on, an insect which doesn't know that it's winter and it shouldn't be out. It's quite funny, when you look down on yourself like that.

There's life in the Sennaya market. It has become the crossroads where those who have meet those who want. Those who want bring their jewels, rolls of paper roubles, icons, silver knives and forks, velvet dresses, rolled-up canvases cut from paintings, Venetian glass wrapped in layers of woollen cloth, war medals and porcelain plates. Journey by journey, they bring the accumulated wealth of several lifetimes. On each journey, they get less back for it.

The prices are never fixed. Here, the laws of supply and demand apply in their purest form. A woman who possesses lard, bread, oil or a scrap of bacon can set them against whatever her heart desires. If she has a jar of sugar, she can cover herself with rubies. The market operates with ruthless force, inflating its prices day by day and sometimes hour by hour. As Anna moves close to the stalls, she sees a stallholder flip an offered gold locket with his finger. He has bread to sell.

'I'll give you a hundred grammes for it, that's all. Take it or leave it.'

'But it's worth –'

'Take it home and eat it, then.' And he turns huge, bored shoulders on the trembling woman whose locket has slipped through her fingers into the snow.

No one says, 'I'll sell you this bread.' They say, 'I'll give you this bread.' The brutal truth is that before the Tsar of bread everything else must sink to its knees. Everyone knows it. Your jewels? Your father's life-savings? Can you eat them? No. What use are all your possessions, if you haven't got the means to keep life in your body? Hand over everything, and I might give you life for another half a day.

Everyone now knows what it takes to keep life in a body. You can be separated from your life so easily. It might happen in the street, or in the bread queue, while you're typing or while you're sleeping. You can die from a cold, an ear infection, or a miscarriage. If you have a stomach ulcer, it will open and bleed. You can die so casually these days.

The stallholder attends to another customer, while the woman with the locket grovels at his feet, scrabbling for gold in the snow. When she holds it out to him again, submissively this time, he simply nods, pockets it and hands her a little chunk of bread. She stares round, unfastens coat and jacket, and thrusts the bread into her blouse. Then she stands still for a moment as if she has forgotten where she is and what she is doing. Her blue-tinged face is vacant. She's a goner, Anna thinks, making the rapid, automatic assessment she's learned in the past few weeks.

Anna skirts the stalls, making eye-contact with no one. Her cotton bag of bread, lard and sugar bumps against her waist. She is sure that others can see the bulge it makes in her coat, and so she hunches forward, walking more slowly than ever, hiding herself in the shroud of falling snow. She hasn't yet seen any *burzhuiki* for sale. Three men stand guard over a stall where a few small pots of meat pâté are on display. She walks on, lowering her eyes, dragging the empty sledge which hurts her arms as much as if Kolya and two of his friends were packed on to it and she were pulling them uphill. For a moment she almost believes they are there behind her: Kolya, Alyosha and Shura, squeaking and giggling, their cheeks burning crimson with frost and health, their plump little legs encased in winter trousers and felt boots.

'Please, Anna, please, just give us one more turn!'

But her empty sledge sticks in a snowdrift, shudders, and then comes free.

'Anna!'

'Oh my God, Evgenia, you frightened me.'

'I saw you by Lavra's stall. Don't go near there again. He's dangerous.'

'Who's Lavra?'

'Don't look. The one with the meat. What're you doing down here, anyway?'

'I'm looking for a *burzhuika*.'

Evgenia glances at the empty sledge, then at Anna's empty arms.

'Got the price? They won't take money, you know.'

'I've got it.'

'Come with me. I know the woman who trades them. She had two, last time I went by. Her name's Galya, not that she'll want you to know her name. But she knows me. She doesn't want to get in wrong with me, in case things turn out different from expectations.'

'What d'you mean?'

'Galya's canny enough to realize that we might not all die. She's done all right out of the war so far, but the customers she's screwed into the ground won't forget her, if any of them are still alive, that is. The only thing people like her are afraid of is life returning to normal. She knows I'll be back to see her, unless she treats me right. I'm not going to die.'

They are standing very close, but even so, flakes of snow are falling between them. Evgenia's red hair is wound up in a thick shawl. The planes of her face are flattened by hunger, and her freckles stand out yellowly. In normal times you'd say that she looked terrible. You'd ask her what was the matter, and what she was doing out of bed. But Anna believes her. Evgenia will live, and not die.

'Is your kid all right?'

'He's at home.'

'You keep him there, Anna. Don't let him out. The streets round here aren't safe for kids. Let's go and get that stove.'

The woman with the *burzhuiki* is tucked away, standing in the shadow of a wall. As Evgenia and Anna approach she glances round, darting her head this way and that with a strange, inhuman movement.

'Looking for her bloke. Her minder. She got set on the other day when she wouldn't sell for a kilo of bread.'

'Do you come here a lot?'

'I'm here most days,' says Evgenia. 'Here, Galya, this is a friend of mine. She wants a stove, and a stove-pipe. She doesn't want any of your rubbish either.'

'Stoves and stove-pipes are sold separately,' chants the woman, staring at Anna with flat, expressionless eyes. Then she retracts her head into the folds of her scarf. She's a lizard, that's what she is, Anna realizes. Lizards are cold-blooded.

'Not to me and my friends they aren't,' says Evgenia.

'What's she got?'

'I've got a kilo bag of sugar,' begins Anna, when a shove from Evgenia silences her.

'My friend'll give you the sugar for the stove and the stove-pipe.'

The stove-seller just shrugs. 'Don't make me laugh. I could get twice that. These *burzhuiki* are like gold-dust these days.'

'You could, but it wouldn't do you any good,' says Evgenia quietly.

'What are you saying? Are you threatening me? Piotr, come over here!'

'I'm not threatening anyone. We're neighbours, aren't we? Good neighbours. And we want to go on being neighbours. Neighbours've got to sort things out themselves, haven't they? We can't always be running off to the authorities, or our lives won't be worth living. Did you know, Anna, they aren't bothering with arrests or trials or any of that stuff now? Anyone who looks like a speculator, they just get shot. Stopped on the street, open your bag, and if you've got stuff in there you shouldn't have, that's it, you're a speculator. No more questions: bang. Galya knows that, don't you, Galya? Neighbours need to stick together in times like this. We've all got to help each other, that's the way it goes.'

Evgenia speaks so quietly that Piotr, hulking outside the little cluster of women, can't hear a word.

'A kilo of sugar and three days' bread ration,' says Galya rapidly. Her tongue flicks over her lips. 'I'm giving it to you.'

Anna half-turns, so the stove-seller won't see the contents of her bag when she opens it. She extracts the sugar and bread, and pushes the rest of the stuff to the bottom of the bag.

'Give us the stove first,' says Evgenia. The woman reaches down, and pulls out a stove from under the stall.

'Where's the stove-pipe?'

'Here.'

'That section's cracked. Do you want to poison her?'

'Most of those I sell to don't even buy a pipe.'

'My friend's buying a pipe, one with four sections. The other one, the one you've got tucked away behind the stall. The one that's not cracked. That's the one she's paying you for.'

Grumbling, Galya crouches down and ferrets out a second stove-pipe.

'Get it on to the sledge, Anna.'

'I want my payment first.'

'You'll get your payment when my friend's got her stove fixed on her sledge.'

Evgenia stands over Anna, arms folded over the sugar and bread, while Anna packs sections of stove-pipe beside the squat body of the stove. She wraps her torn sheet over stove and stove-pipe, and ties it down with her strips of hem.

'You ready now, Anna?'

'Yes.'

'All right then, Galya, there's your sugar and there's your bread. Mind out for those patrols on your way home. They don't think any more of shooting a speculator than shooting a pigeon. There aren't any pigeons around any more, 'cos they've all been eaten, and there's plenty of speculators. Not many as nice and plump as you, though, are there, Galya? Maybe we can eat speculators for a change? We could have a little chat with Lavra about it.'

Galya's head darts out of its collar. She looks as if she's going to hiss like a lizard.

'Watch what you're saying,' she mutters, almost inaudibly.

'I know what I'm saying,' says Evgenia, 'and so do you. You mind what I say, Galya. Bang!'

Side by side, Evgenia and Anna walk across the market. The stove feels heavy, but already snow is falling on to the sheets that cover it, disguising it.

'You'd better get off home quick,' says Evgenia.

'Evgenia, here.' Anna fumbles with the flap of her bag, and gets out the lard and the five hundred roubles. 'You have this. I'd never have got the stove without you.'

Evgenia takes the lard and tucks it into her coat pocket. 'I don't need the money,' she says.

'Evgenia, how's your mother, and your little boy?'

'He's had this same cough everyone's had. Mum bought some cod-liver oil for him, but it's all gone. There's nothing else wrong with him, once he gets rid of his cough. Only hunger.'

'If that woman had been on her own, I'd have taken the stove, knocked her into the snow, and run.'

'Yeah, I reckon she knows that. That's why she keeps Piotr close at hand. She has to give him a cut, of course, but I should say he's worth it. If even a nice girl like you is thinking of bashing Galya over the head and running off with her stoves, there'll be plenty who'd do much more than think about it. Me, for a kick-off.'

'Have you got a *burzhuika*?'

'I got one off Galya two weeks ago, when it turned cold.'

'So you're doing all right? I mean, you've got money? You're still working?'

'I've got my job, though the power's been off so much we're only on about twenty per cent production. I'm still on a worker's ration, which is the main thing. But I'm working with my left hand as well.'

'Where?'

'You know. Down the market.'

'Oh. I see.'

'Quick, aren't you? Mind you, they say hunger slows down the brain. Two hundred grammes is the going rate at the moment. You can guess what type of man has two hundred grammes to spare these days. They're a real portrait gallery. But I'm not much of a one for men anyway, as you know, so it doesn't make a lot of difference to me. Whereas bread does. And I don't really –' Just for a moment, Evgenia's tone falters. 'I don't really notice it at all. D'you ever get that feeling, Anna, as if things won't still be there when you reach out to touch them?'

'Yes.'

'It's lack of vitamins, that's what it is. We're suffering from what polar explorers get. Only we're not going to discover anything except that if you don't eat, you end up dead. When I was short for the stove, Galya found me a bloke with a thing about red hair. So she's not all bad, is she? Even though I agree that she'd be a lot better-looking arse-over-tip in a snowdrift.'

'We'll fix that up for her one day, shall we?'

'Just wait till all this is over. The German bastards'll be running in one direction, and those Sennaya bastards in the other. There'll be some arses kicked then, I can tell you. But listen, Anna. Don't you even think about going in for what I'm doing. Shits like Piotr will mince you up in a week, if you don't know how to deal with them. And you don't, anyone can see that. You get home with that stove. I'll see you again. On the Patriotic Day of Workers' Arse-Kicking, if not before.'

Evgenia's strong teeth gleam in her pallid face, then she turns and is swallowed up in the falling snow.

It takes a long time to walk home. Already the temperature is dropping again. Tomorrow there'll be a glossy crust of ice on blue mounds of fresh snow. No one is clearing the streets. There's no sign of the old women with their brooms who should be out by now, sweeping the doorsteps and the strip of pavement in front of their apartment houses. They haven't got the strength to come out. They're huddled in their apartments, which have turned into cells of ice. They sit in hats and boots, gloves, shawls and coats, with their blankets piled over them, and they are cold.

Anna trudges past a building where an old woman has lain with flu for a week. She lies alone, although at her side there is a half-drunk glass of tea made for her by a neighbour the day before. But now the neighbour is ill herself, and cannot come. There's ice on the tea. As Anna passes, and as day wheels round into night, the old woman's lungs cease to resist the secondary infection which she has been holding off for the past twenty-four hours. Pneumonia takes hold, although the old woman feels nothing much, except that she is very weak. In the centre of each grey, seamed cheek there is a small purplish-red spot. It hurts to breathe deeply, so she breathes in shallow pants, sipping the icy air into her body.

'Mama, please light the stove,' she begs. Pain comes alive in her body, penetrating every grain of her flesh. Slowly and painfully she begins to rock herself from side to side, side to side, in the rhythm of her mother's heartbeat. It consoled her seventy years ago, when she was in the womb. It consoles her now. She rocks and rocks, sipping in breath. Soon it will be better. The aching will go away, and she won't shiver any more once her temperature rises. She will burn for a while, and then she'll die down. There are no sounds in the cold little room but the sounds she makes. Once, very faintly, she hears the flop of new, unstable snow falling from the roof into the courtyard, but she thinks it is something else. The ice on her half-drunk glass of tea grows thicker.

By the time she gets to the Moyka, Anna is seeing people who aren't there again. A group of students, arm in arm, the girls in short-sleeved summer dresses, crosses the bridge. They laugh, they look down at the sparkling water. Anna hears their voices ring over the canal, bright with summer happiness. Where are they going, and why so happy? She drops the rope of the sledge and strains to see where they've gone, but they have disappeared.

It's not snowing so heavily now. Immediately below her on the ice there's an old woman crouching, drilling a hole with the kind of hand-drill ice-fishermen use. Perhaps she's going to fish. No, there's a bucket beside her on the ice. She's come for water. She ought to go down to the Neva, the water will be purer there. But perhaps it's too far. Anna listens to the squeak of drill on ice. As if the woman senses her presence, she glances up, and sees Anna leaning on the canal wall. Recognition passes between them.

Anna knows the old woman, because she was at school with her.

'Tanya!' she calls. 'Is that you?'

'Yes, it's me. How are you all?'

'All well. What about you?'

Your brother, Seryozha, the handsome one. Your little sister, Masha, with her pulled-back hair and startlingly deep blue eyes, who played the piano so well.

'Masha was evacuated. Seryozha's in the army. It's just me at home, with my mother.'

'The water's gone in your apartment, then?'

'Yes, all the pipes are frozen, even the courtyard pipe now. There was a man who came round with a cart, and you could buy water, but he doesn't come any more. You've still got water?'

'Yes.'

'Well, I'd better get on.'

But Tanya doesn't start drilling again. She stares at Anna, her dark eyes hungry in her drawn, sexless face. Starvation has catapulted her into old age. She used to complain that it was so unfair, the way Masha had those beautiful eyes while her own were a sort of grey, nothing special. But Tanya's eyes seem to have grown larger, carving out pools of darkness in her face. Suddenly she looks a long way down, like someone at the bottom of a cliff. Will she ever be able to climb back up those steps from the canal ice?

Anna picks up the sledge rope. 'See you again.'

'Yes. Good luck.'

'Good luck.'

The sky flares briefly into sunset as Anna trudges on. The snow burns blue and crimson, then the light dies. There are only a few wild-looking streaks of red left in the sky. And over there, that red that burns more fiercely, it must be a fire started by German shells. They are using phosphorus incendiaries. Because there is no water to put the fires out, they burn until they die of their own accord. The wind is rising, though it's not fierce yet. It burns Anna's face as she makes her way onward, back bent, dragging the heavy sledge. Only a few hundred metres now. Soon she'll be home. They'll have to help her carry the stove upstairs, piece by piece. She can't do it on her own, she just can't do all those journeys up and down the stairs on top of this. Maybe Marina will be able to manage the sections of stove-pipe, one at a time, if Anna carries the stove itself. But Marina's so weak.

Anna stops. She looks up at the sky, and fine, icy snow patters into her face. Her legs shake. Is it just the snow falling, or is she losing her balance? She clenches the rope. She's still standing. She won't fall. She'll make it to the corner, then to the first lamp-post, then the next.

An explosion tears through her. She doubles up, dropping the rope. She's down in the snow, on all fours, like an animal. Slowly, realizing herself, she clambers up. It wasn't close. It's all right. Blood beats hard in her head as the shock spreads through her flesh. She bends down slowly and picks up the loop of rope. It's all right, it wasn't close. Just the usual shelling, pounding from the south-west.

'Bastards,' says Anna. 'Bastards, bastards, bastards.'

Last month they shelled the department where her mother worked. But all the equipment Vera had fought for was saved, because it had already been moved into the cellars. Komarovsky told Anna about it when she met him one day, crossing the Anichkov bridge. He said things were difficult, but they were still able to carry on.

'How's everyone?'

'We're managing. We have to improvise. There's no chance of getting spare parts, and of course there's a shortage of trained personnel. So many away sick. But we keep going. I often think of your mother.'

She will get this sledge home. She will get the stove upstairs, and light it. She will make sure that Kolya does his breathing exercises. She will put food in his mouth, whatever it takes. Nothing is going to stop her.

'Bastards!' she shouts at the grey sky. 'I don't care what you do! You can all go and fuck yourselves, you fucking bastards. See if I care!'

19

Kolya kneels by the stove. Yellow light flickers on his face as he touches his lighted taper to a curl of newsprint. His breathing is heavy with responsibility.

'Hold it there. Wait till it catches.'

Kolya holds the taper still. A blue skim of flame races over the paper, and deepens to yellow.

'It's lit! It's lit! It's on fire!' He turns round to Anna, his face triumphant. 'I lit it properly, didn't I, Anna?'

Flame burrows deep into the coils of *Leningradskaya Pravda* with which Anna has packed the stove. Among these coils is the front page from one of the worst days of the September bombardment. *Leningrad: To Be, Or Not To Be?* it asks. Her father had stared at that headline for a long time when the paper came out. On that day he didn't have the energy to read the article, but he folded the newspaper and kept it by his bed. From time to time he reached out and touched the headline.

'Leningrad,' he muttered. 'And we're asking if it will be, or not be.'

After a few days she had taken away the newspaper, and he hadn't seemed to notice. She thought she would keep it, and she folded it inside her father's copy of *Oblomov*. One day, when all this was over, she would show it to Kolya.

But now everything that can burn must be burned. Flame crackles at the handful of splintery wood from a chopped-up packing-case. Kolya kneels there, swallowing the warmth of the fire like food. He's taken off his gloves, and spread his hands to the heat. How thin they are now, not like Kolya's hands at all. They look older and more knowing than they should, now that the rosy flesh has disappeared. So does his face, with its sharp little nose and big eyes. Now he knows what grown-ups can't do. You can ask for food, but they won't give you any.

'I'm hungry, Anna. My stomach hurts.'

'Let me rub it for you.'

'I don't want you to rub me. I want some sausage.'

'There isn't any sausage, Kolya.'

'Why?'

Her face is tight when she looks at him. Is she angry? Is she cross with him? He grizzles, to wear her down.

'I'm hungry, Anna. I'm so hungry. My stomach hurts.'

She pulls him on to her knee. She rocks him, too tight and too hard. She doesn't go into the kitchen and open the cupboard and get food for him.

He doesn't ask any more. His hair is dry and dull under the fur cap which she keeps pulling forward to make sure his ears are covered. His hair needs cutting. Wisps of it stick out from under his cap. He crouches there like a cave-boy, worshipping flame.

'We've got loads of stuff we can burn, haven't we, Anna?'

'Yes, loads of stuff.'

The crackle and hiss of flame is life in the cold room. You will live, it says. You will live, and not die. Once the *burzhuika* gets going, its fuel will be their mother's oak dressing-table. It's a solid, well-made piece which will give hours of heat.

Anna swallows the sudden memory of Vera at her dressing-table, twisting up her heavy dark-brown hair and pinning it at the nape of her neck. The hair was newly washed and slippery. Her mother made an impatient sound, dipped her fingers in a jug of water, then damped her hair. Anna leaned forward, and smelled her mother. She smelled her mother's warm skin, and the rosemary rinse she used on her hair to make it shine. Vera's face stared at itself in the mirror, but Anna knew she was thinking about something quite different.

'Mama, you look prettier when you don't bunch up your hair like that.'

'It wouldn't be practical, Anna.'

Vera was already thinking of her work. There, she glowed with life. There she had her team, her responsibilities, her patients. There was always some problem to be solved, or new technique to be explored. At work, Anna saw, her mother laughed. There were jokes which flickered over Anna's head, and she basked in them without understanding them. Vera's colleagues knew everything about Anna, and they had brought in cakes because she was coming. Vera explained the work of the radiology department to Anna, drawing diagrams and showing Anna the machines.

'This is why you have to work hard at your maths, so that when you're grown up you can get a job you love.'

Love was a rare word in her mother's mouth. She praised Anna for what she did, rather than for what she was. Suddenly she placed her hand on Anna's hair.

'I want you to have this. I want you to have work that makes you happy. It's especially important for you, because you're going to be a woman. You'll need something that is your own. I want you to keep studying hard, until you fulfil your potential.'

And here I am, thinks Anna, contemplating the well-made joints of the dressing-table. And your dressing-table's about to fulfil its potential by keeping us warm for a couple of days. She feels a perverse, angry desire for her mother to see this. Maybe I haven't fulfilled my potential, Mammy, but watch how I'll keep us alive.

She wanted me to have something that was mine and didn't depend on anyone else. She turned round on her stool, away from her mirrored image. She put her hands on either side of my face, and pushed my hair back, and looked into my eyes. She was half-smiling.

'Work is what keeps you going, Anna.'

If only Anna had thought to bring the axe from the dacha. They have a tiny chopper in the apartment, but it won't cut anything much thicker than the packing-case. They are borrowing a saw from the Sergeyevs across the landing, but this means that Anna has had to offer them a share in the wood. Zina didn't want to take it at first. 'No, go on, we're not using the saw today anyway.' The Sergeyevs have no *burzhuika*, but they have rigged up a lethal little brick fireplace close to their ventilation window.

'There's no fire risk,' Zina assured Anna. 'You see, there's a layer of stones under the brick, and my Fedya's put a sheet of steel underneath that.'

But Fedya's hardly ever at home now. He works, sleeps and eats at the Kirov works.

'My Fedya's a wonderful worker. Practically a Stakhanovite,' Zina said to Anna once, not long after her marriage.

Fedya won't speak to Anna if he meets her on the stairway, or in the queue for the bathroom. He's a big, solid, handsome man, fair-haired and strongly muscled. A real Leningrad boy, who grew up in the courtyard with his mates. His mother hung out of the window to yell him in for supper, like all the other mothers. Echoes, screams, whistles, shouts, smells of cabbage and soup.

Anna sees him in singlet and trousers on the bathroom landing, with his towel slung over his shoulder. He pushes his way into the bathroom first, because he's got to get going, down to the Kirov works. He's got a real man's job. But he's decent too, the kind who would do anything for you if he was on your side.

Fedya's a Party member, the real thing. When he sees any member of the Levin family, his face closes over. He doesn't trust them, doesn't like them being in the building, and certainly doesn't want them on his landing. The Levins are trouble.

'We were living here when you were just a kid!' she wants to tell him. But he swings his way down the stairs, whistling, proprietorial, and she says nothing. There's nothing to be said to this young man in his prime, a respected worker with a wife and child, who has done everything right and has very little sense of humour. What can you say to him that will change his mind, when he believes so absolutely in what he is and what he does? By definition, his thoughts become truths. He knows that if there are enemies of the people still waiting to be unmasked, then they will behave exactly like Anna's family, coming in and out at odd times, reading books in the bathroom, smiling when there is no reason to smile, and possessing two whole rooms and a kitchen.

Fedya certainly believes that enemies of the people exist. He reads his paper thoroughly, and scans the staring little photographs of engineers and university lecturers who have been unmasked as spies, Trotskyites and saboteurs. They thought they'd fooled him, did they? Well, look at them now, and a good thing too! Yes, when she passes Fedya on the stairs, Anna can see in his face the thought of their two-room apartment, and her own unworthiness to live in it when a whole raft of decent workers could be put in there. And how he'd love that, she thinks.

But there's a shamefully weak part of her that still wants Fedya to like her, even though she knows that he never will. What a fool she is. She remembers the time when she was standing aside in the hallway, waiting while he helped old Masha downstairs with her kerosene. When he saw Anna, he shot her an unfriendly look, as if to say: What are *you* hanging about for? Why did that look burn her? She'd wanted to spread out her arms, barring the stairs, and not let him go by until she'd told him: 'I work too, you know! I'm a nursery assistant and I've got more bums and noses to wipe than you've seen in your entire life. And I'm bringing up a child as well . . .'

But it wouldn't make the slightest difference. He knows her origins. She's the daughter of a member of the intelligentsia, and a dodgy one at that. No amount of toilet-scrubbing will get rid of that stain.

In spite of Fedya's fireplace, the Sergeyevs' room is as cold as a tomb. Theirs is a single room, but the biggest on the landing, and it faces north.

'Why don't you come in to us, you and the baby?' Anna suggests. 'Once we've got the *burzhuika* going, it'll be a lot warmer than in here.'

But Zina shrinks back. 'Oh no, thank you, we're fine as we are. With our little fire, it gets quite warm.'

She wouldn't dare come into their apartment. What would her Fedya say? He's always telling her that she's politically naïve. She can't help it, he knows, because of her lack of education, so he's undertaken to keep her on the right tracks. The trouble is that the tracks seem to keep swerving all over the place, and then doubling back on themselves. Zina's given up trying to work out where these tracks are going. Although she looks and listens and nods in all the right places, really she has switched off.

But Fedya has dinned into her that the Levins are not safe neighbours. It's one thing to meet on the stairway, but she mustn't take it any further.

'You see, Zina, with people like that, you get drawn in. They seem friendly enough, but that shows how artful they are. And of course you're judged by who you associate with, that's only natural.'

She knows that Fedya would go mad if he knew she'd been into the Levins' apartment. Quite apart from questions of right or wrong or political education, you can't be sure who might be watching you. Even now, when you'd think people would have enough to do with trying to find the next meal, there might be someone with enough energy to denounce you. There's one in every apartment building.

The baby writhes in her arms. Its head wobbles on scrawny folds of neck as it lets out a mew and butts feebly against Zina's clothes.

'He's hungry . . .' she says to Anna.

'Are you still feeding him yourself?'

'Yes, but I don't know if he's getting enough. Can you remember what your Kolya weighed at three months?'

'About eight kilos, I think.'

'He only weighs four and a half. And he was such a big baby when he was born, do you remember?'

'Yes, he was. Let me have a look.'

Gently, Anna draws back the shawl. The baby's hands are crossed on his chest. They are purplish and spider-thin, like the hands of a newborn. She touches the baby's cheek. He's suffering from dehydration, as well as malnutrition.

'Is he drinking water?'

'No.'

'You could boil a little on your fire, and let it cool. Have you got any sugar?'

'No.'

Anna touches the baby's cheek again.

'Or honey? Anything sweet?'

'We haven't got anything.'

But to put sugar into this baby's mouth is to take it out of Kolya's. The baby mews again, its old, small face screwing up. Its mouth works against the palm of Anna's hand, rooting for food. She'll give Kolya an extra share of her own bread ration to make up.

'Zina, I can let you have a hundred grammes of sugar. Have you got a baby's bottle?'

Zina nods. 'I got one when he was born, but I've never used it.'

Zina doesn't seem surprised or grateful at Anna's offer of the sugar. She doesn't in fact seem to understand what it means.

'Boil up the water, and quarter-fill the bottle. While the water's still hot, add a teaspoon of the sugar so it dissolves. Then give him that every hour, even if you have to rouse him. If he doesn't suck at first, put the water on your finger until he gets the taste of it, and then he'll suck.'

'But he's sleeping so well. He's sleeping right through the night now.'

'That's because he's so weak. He shouldn't be sleeping like that. You have to rouse him. Flick the soles of his feet with your fingers if he won't wake: like this. Once he's got a bit of energy he'll start to suck more strongly. The stronger he sucks, the more milk you'll make. And you must rest all you can. Wrap yourself up in everything you've got, and drink plenty of water. You'll make more milk if you conserve your energy.'

Zina is only nineteen. Four years younger than Anna, and not even a Leningrader. She's got no family here, and now she's landed up in the middle of all this, and with the baby too. Zina's a Kiev girl, and she hasn't seen her mother since the baby was born. Her dark eyes fix intently on Anna's face.

'Anna Mikhailovna, tell me,' she whispers, 'when are they going to lift the blockade?'

'I don't know.'

But Zina's eyes continue to search her face.

'Doesn't your father know anything? He's a writer, isn't he?'

'We don't know anything. How could we?'

Zina asks no more, though Anna can tell she wants to. Maybe she really believes that there is a layer of people left in Leningrad which is in control of what is happening, and knows what's coming. Maybe it's less frightening, if you believe that. Whether her father comes into that category because he's a writer, or because Fedya's told her he might be a German sympathizer, Anna can't guess. But she's still angry, even though there is no point in being angry with Zina.

'My father was wounded defending the Motherland. He can't even get out of bed,' she says. 'How do you think he can possibly know anything?'

How strange to hear herself talking of the Motherland, using words that belong on posters, not in real life. And yet she means it. Words are regaining their meanings, after years of masquerade. Hunger means hunger, terror means terror, enemy means enemy. It's not like trying to read mirror-writing any more. Everything gets clearer day by day, as siege and winter eat into their lives. The coils of Soviet life are losing their strength. There's only the present left, and it has burned away both past and future. There's only the dark, besieged, freezing city, and the Germans outside, dug into their winter positions, waiting, stamping their feet.

But they will never come in. Her friend in the Party was right. We will destroy everything, we will blow up our own city and let it burn as we let Moscow burn before Napoleon. We've mined bridges, steelworks, palaces and power stations. If we have to, we'll press the buttons that detonate those fuses. Once Anna saw an apartment building dynamited, because it was in the way of a new road. In the second of detonation it hung in the air, silent, holding shape like a mirage of itself. Then the noise of the blast rolled over it and flattened it.

We will do that. We will eat horses and pigeons and dogs, we will burn our books and our furniture, we will consume ourselves rather than be consumed.

'I'm sorry, Anna Mikhailovna, I didn't mean anything –'

She's terrified I won't give her the sugar now. No, it's more than that. She really is sorry. I have got to stop being so suspicious of everyone.

'I'll go and get that sugar. And thanks again for letting us use your axe. I'll bring you your share of the wood once we've finished chopping up the dressing-table.'

'A dressing-table – how nice! I've always wanted one of those.'

'It was my mother's.'

At the thought of the dressing-table, Zina's eyes fill for the first time with tears of weakness.

'It doesn't seem right, does it, all this?'

'You go and lie down. When I come back with the sugar I'll knock on the door twice so you know it's me. Tuck him in beside you, and open the shawl so he gets the warmth of your body. They can't maintain their body temperature as we can.'

She sounds like Fedya, thinks Zina. So sure of herself, and knowing things, and having the right words. But it's different with Anna, because I can understand what she says. I don't keep drifting off.

In the apartment the *burzhuika* is burning strongly, eating up Anna's schoolbooks.

'It's getting hot!' shouts Kolya as she comes into the room. Her father is on the sofa, swaddled in blankets. On the floor Marina has pushed together the big mattress and Kolya's little mattress. She is busy heaping them with blankets, pillows and shawls. In the light of the candle-stub, huge shadows of Marina leap from wall to wall. It is five o'clock.

Anna goes to the kitchen with a spill of paper lit from the candle, lights another stub, and opens the store-cupboard. There's the last bag of sugar. Without allowing herself to think about what she's doing, she opens it carefully, and measures a hundred grammes into a cup.

'What are you doing?'

'Oh! – Marina. You nearly made me spill it. I'm just measuring some sugar.'

'For whom?' Marina raps out.

'For the baby next door. Zina's baby. He's starving.'

Marina is silent while Anna refolds the top of the sugar bag. Then she says, with cold certainty, 'You can't do that.'

'I've got to. He's malnourished, and he's dehydrated. In this cold he could easily die.'

Marina draws herself up. 'So what are you going to do about it, Anna? What about all those other babies? Are you going to trawl up and down the street knocking on doors until you've given away all our food to people who are going to die? And then you can come home and watch Kolya die.'

'It's only a hundred grammes.'

'A hundred grammes is a hundred grammes. It's not "only" anything.'

'But Zina's our neighbour. We can hear the baby crying. She's only across the landing, and she hasn't got a clue what to do. He's going to go to sleep and not wake up at all if he doesn't get some calories into his body soon.'

Marina lays her hand on Anna's arm. Her voice changes, taking on a seductive, vibrant, 'cello-note that Anna has not heard before.

'Anna,' she says, 'you are the ones who matter. You and Kolya. Don't you understand that?'

'Only us?'

'You still don't see, do you, what it's going to be like? You still don't understand. It's going to go on like this, getting colder and colder, and with less and less food. No one's going to come and help us. And I don't intend to watch you all die.'

'You might die first.' A grin stretches her face. She can't really be standing here with Marina, talking about their own deaths. She can't really want to burst out laughing.

'People don't die just when they want to. I'm the type who'll go on to the end. It's pure selfishness, you're quite right. I can't face seeing you die one by one before me. So put the sugar back in the bag.'

Marina's eyes glow in the light of the candle-stub. Anna can't read them, but they draw her in. She wants, suddenly, more than anything, to yield and become what Marina wants. She wants to be carried on the warm wave of Marina's voice. To let Marina decide. They are almost touching, in the tiny space of the kitchen. She wants to give in, and Marina knows it. It's like sex. The other person always knows.

But the baby cries. In spite of his weakness, the cry is piercing. It is like Kolya's cry. She would get up in the night to him, sick with tiredness, those first days after Vera died. She didn't know the first thing about babies then.

'No,' says Anna, with stiff, clumsy lips. 'I can't do that. I've told Zina she can have a hundred grammes. But that'll be the end of it. She'll have to manage on her own after this. Everything else is for Kolya.'

Marina has drawn back. It's over. 'Even if she comes knocking on the door with that baby?'

'Even if she does.'

'Good. Because you have a responsibility, you know.'

'To what?'

Anna is sure she knows the answer. Marina will say that her responsibility is to Kolya, and to her father. But she doesn't. Instead she looks closely at Anna and says, 'To stay alive, of course.'

To what? thinks Anna later, when the sugar is gone, and the candle is burning down. But the *burzhuika* really does give out some heat, now that she's been able to feed it with wood. Kolya's looking better already. And tomorrow she'll attack the other half of the dressing-table. She couldn't do it all at once. The effort of chopping the wood made her heart beat so fast that she thought she would vomit. Marina made her sit down and take valerian drops.

She is drawing. Kolya is asleep, curled on his mattress close to the stove. Anna has a stick of willow charcoal, and she is drawing Marina as she sits by the sofa, reading to Anna's father. *A responsibility – but to what?* thinks Anna again. What did Marina really mean? To stay alive is not enough, if everything else has gone. She's right about that. I should have waited, and helped Tanya to climb the canal steps, but I couldn't do it. I had to get home, and carry the stove upstairs.

Her father lies still, with his eyes closed, but Anna knows he is awake. Marina is reading a Shakespeare play, in English, which she speaks better than any of them. It is *A Winter's Tale*. Anna can understand some of it, but she's not really listening. She has cut out the too-seductive sound of Marina's voice, so that she can draw. Her fingers are clumsy with cold, even though she's wearing a pair of old woollen gloves. Their tips are cut off, because she can't draw with gloved fingers. She draws with long, firm strokes. Tonight, the charcoal seems not just to sweep the paper, but to understand every grain of it.

How strange it is that she should be drawing Marina's portrait now. Marina's face is so much changed, or maybe it's Anna's perception which has changed. Marina does not look beautiful. Her glasses perch on her nose, and she wrinkles up her eyes to focus on the text in the poor light of the candle. Her eyes are watering. Anna knows she's worried about her eyesight. From time to time she stops reading, and fixes Anna's father with a long look, as ruthlessly protective as the stare of a hawk circling its nest, scouring the sky for danger to its young.

She loves him. Of course she does. It's as simple as that. She has loved him in this way, and he has loved her in another. She is his dear and brilliant friend, of whom he has always been very slightly afraid. But she loves him. It's been going on for years, nearly twenty years, way back before Kolya's birth, back to when Marina tried to make herself into a dear friend of their mother's, too. But Vera wouldn't let her. Vera refused to be party to any of it. She would never collude. How strange it all is, how painful and lopsided.

But when you look at Marina, you can't help believing that this is the only way she could ever have loved. There would always have to be something impossible at the core of it.

And I would never have known about it, if it hadn't been for all this. She would have remained my father's old friend, wonderful actress, beautiful too, you know, in her time. You should have seen her, but of course these days . . .

I would never have folded blankets with her, hand to hand. I would have drawn her portrait at her dacha, and never known her at all.

It has got to be a double portrait. Her father, and Marina. Rapidly, Anna sketches the sofa, the outline of her father's body blurred by its pile of covers, the sharp edges of nose and jaw, the sunken hollows of his eyes. She draws his protruding eyeballs, with the veined skin of his eyelids sealed down over them. She draws the angle of Marina's neck as she fixes her gaze on him again. The poise of that head closes a circle which contains only Marina, and the man lying on the sofa. One hand holds the pages of her Shakespeare, the other rests on the pillow, close to his shrunken cheek.

Anna draws on. She shapes the pointed shadows that spring out on the wall behind Marina. She draws the patchwork blanket which is drawn up under her father's chin. She knitted that blanket herself, coloured square by coloured square, before Kolya was born. It wrapped him on his first outing. Her fingers remember the warmth and scratchiness of the wools. It was spring, and cold. She held Kolya awkwardly, not yet used to him, as she walked in the park. The black buds were swollen, bursting with leaf. The baby screwed up his eyes against the strong spring light.

She draws on. The stove sighs as a lump of wood collapses into ash. Soon its warmth will be gone. Quickly, quickly, before her fingers stiffen, she draws her father's jawbone.

Only Anna hears two taps at the outer door. She gets up, putting her drawing aside. It can't be Andrei, because he's already said he won't be able to come tonight. Perhaps it's Zina. Something wrong with the baby again.

But it's Andrei, pale, with soot marks on his face.

'What's happened?'

'That crazy idiot Borya made a fire in our apartment, and then he fell asleep and it went through to the floorboards. They managed to put it out, but the smoke's wrecked everything. Both mattresses caught fire.'

'Oh my God. Is Borya all right?'

'He's inhaled smoke, so he's not feeling too good. But he'll survive. The Antonovs will take him in.'

'He didn't lose his ration card?'

'No.'

Without a ration card, you die for certain. It's as simple as that. With one, you may die too, but the land of not-dying remains open to you. Andrei stares down at her with his Siberian eyes. Even when he's as kicked-in as he is now, he still seems to bring with him the taste of a different, more open-handed air. She rests her mouth on his cold cheek, which smells of smoke. Her lips open. She tastes him.

'You can stay here. Of course you can. But it's too far for you to walk all the way to the hospital from here. Surely they'd give you a bed there?'

He seizes her and holds her. He is trembling all over. He's stalled with exhaustion, and then the shock of the fire and finding everything gone.

'All the way I was thinking what I would do if you weren't here.'

'Where else should I be?'

'I know. But anything can happen these days. I suppose I could find a cot somewhere at the hospital, but it's so full. We've got patients on the floor, in the corridors, jammed up next to dead bodies.'

'You can stay here. We'll work everything else out later. Come on in. My father and Kolya are sleeping, but Marina's awake. You wouldn't believe how warm it is now we've got the *burzhuika*.'

She takes him in, and moves her drawing off the arm of her chair. Andrei sits down, closing his eyes.

'He's staying here,' says Anna to Marina. 'He hasn't anywhere else. His room's been burnt out.'

Marina nods silently. Then, in the voice that still comes clear from her shrunken mouth, she continues to read from the play:

'Tis time; descend; be stone no more; approach;
Strike all that look upon with marvel. Come:
I'll fill your grave up: stir; nay, come away;
Bequeath to death your numbness . . .'

'Feel in my pocket,' says Andrei.

'Your coat pocket?'

'Yes.'

His coat is cold. She reaches into the pocket, and brings out a jar.

'What is it?'

'It's for you. It's honeycomb. A patient's mother gave it to me.'

Anna takes the jar over to the candle. Sure enough, there it is, a dark comb of patterned cells that drip with honey. There's quite a lot there. The small jar is at least half-full. She turns it round, so that the light catches it.

'I wonder where she got it from.'

'I didn't ask.'

'You have some of it, to keep your energy up.'

'I get my meals at the hospital. I'm fine. Anna, I can't believe you've got the *burzhuika*. It's like heaven here. Is it all right if I sleep in this chair?'

'Of course.'

She steps over the mattress, sits down at his feet, and rests her head against his knees. She feels his hand begin to stroke her hair. His hand is still trembling. After a few minutes it slackens, and weighs heavy. Marina and her father are within touch, but she feels as distant from them as if she were on another star. Those stars that hang over Leningrad, bitingly sharp, when the dust and smoke from the shelling clear. They look down and they see everything. A smell of antiseptic clings to Andrei. She knows how carefully he scrubs his hands and arms before he comes to see her, so he won't smell of blood.

'I'll make you tea in a minute,' she says.

'Just let's sit.' His voice is blurring. The stove-warmed, people-

188

warmed air is working on him like a drug. His hand on her skin is growing warmer.

'So nice,' he says, as he falls into sleep.

Slowly, a fug thickens in the little room. The temperature must be at least eight degrees. Maybe even ten. She can't put any more wood in the stove, or there'll be none for tomorrow, but it'll be a while before it cools. They'll have warmth to get them through part of the night. Marina's head has drooped, though she is still sitting upright. Perhaps she's fallen asleep, too. How good it is to fall asleep, and not to feel hunger any more. You should never wake anyone once they've got away, deep into their dreams, where there's food.

But Anna can't sleep. Her stomach hurts, and the candle's nearly burned down. She can think about her drawing. The figures are sharp on the surface of her mind. She can shut her eyes and see them. Who will ever finish drawing all this? The gaping mouths, the heavy coats hung on racks of bones, the shell-shattered streets, the purple faces of old women, the white snow falling, the uncleared snow in the streets, the children scrabbling in piles of rubbish while tongues of ice poke out of the gutters. A whole city is going to sleep. A forest of ice is growing around us.

No one can see us any more. Do they even know what's happening here? Are they being allowed to know? Radio Leningrad tells the truth, or part of it, but that's because it's local. The people who speak on the radio are hungry too, you can tell. It shouldn't make any difference whether they know in Moscow what we're going through in Leningrad, but it does. They may not be able to do anything for us, but to be lost from people's thoughts is like a second death.

When this drawing is finished, she'll do another. She'll draw until her paper gives out. It doesn't matter if her hands are clumsy. She'll draw Evgenia's face with the freckles standing out on it, and her big wide mouth smiling. Zina holding out the baby as if she wanted to give it away. The baby's shrivelled face. Andrei leaning against the inside of the door. The wound in her father's shoulder that won't heal. She shuts her eyes and tests herself. Yes, they are all there. She can see them in every detail.

Anna wraps a blanket around Andrei, on top of his coat, and tucks it in. He doesn't stir. Those soot marks are still on his face, so she spits on her handkerchief and gently wipes them off. Then she blows out the guttering end of the candle.

20

What are days? You wake hours before it's light, from hunger. Hunger has burrowed deep into your stomach and is eating away at you. You turn, moaning, trying to dislodge it. You taste the foulness of your breath.

The day begins like a day of fever. Strange dreams and voices march over your mind as you slip in and out of sleep. Someone laughs close to your ear. Suddenly, you catch the scent of coffee. Blue smoke drifts from a ventilation shaft. Inside, they are roasting coffee beans, then grinding them and packing the grains into stiff brown-paper bags which are sealed with white labels. They stack the bags plumply on shelves. It is morning, and it isn't winter any more, but summer, with light streaming through the shop window. The fragrance of coffee wreathes around your head like smoke.

You wake yourself, snuffling around in the bedclothes. A load of blankets and coats weighs you down, but you're still cold. Your feet are numb and your breath comes short. The cold settles in your back and makes your spine hurt. You must breathe gently. You must not be restless. Every movement destroys energy which you no longer possess.

In the next apartment a baby cries steadily from hunger. The crying goes on and on, threading its way into the innermost coils of your brain. If only he'd stop. Whatever it takes, make him stop.

There is no electricity. There is no running water. It is the twelfth of December. Leningrad is garlanded with ice, pinned down by heavy blankets of snow. Later, the low, slanting light of winter will glide along the blue banks of the Neva. There will be streaks of rose on the snow.

The bread ration is now 250 grammes per day for workers, and 125 grammes for everyone else. How much is that? A couple of slices of bread. One, if you cut thickly.

But you don't cut thickly. You cut the bread into tiny cubes. You moisten each one with saliva. As long as it lasts, you have food in your mouth. But your stomach tears at you. It's not fooled.

In bread queues people talk about the ice road over Lake Ladoga. A road made of ice, tracking over miles of unstable ice, the one route that now connects Leningrad to 'the mainland'. Lake Ladoga, north-east of Leningrad, is the only way out. The young ice has already swallowed up dozens of trucks and men, but it's freezing hard, and the ice is getting thicker. Soon they'll be able to bring in supplies. Food will come. It's early days yet, and of course they're losing trucks and men. Ladoga's ice is still treacherous, freezing solid enough to take a tank in one place, and then opening into a crevasse a couple of hundred metres farther on. The Germans know that it's the only supply route left, and they started shelling it almost as soon as the first trucks rolled out on to the ice.

But whatever's sacrificed has got to be sacrificed. The ice road is all we've got. It must be believed in. They are already calling it 'The Road of Life'. The bread queue mutters its creed, and blue lips pray for the temperature to drop, the ice to thicken further, the route to become faster, safer.

'Now we've recaptured Tikhvin, the crossing won't take so long. They won't have to go all that way round.'

'They're working day and night to get the stuff to us. I heard there are thousands of tons of flour backed up at Novaya Ladoga.'

'They're opening up new tracks over the ice all the time. They've got fuel stations and first-aid posts all the way, every kilometre. That'll speed things up.'

But what they believe in remains invisible: there's no food here. They have been queuing for two and half hours, and there's still no sign of bread. There were problems with the ovens this morning, someone says. Anna huddles deeper into her coat, stamps her feet, and listens to the distant noise of shelling. She thinks of Lake Ladoga, beautiful in summer with its glistening iron-and-silver water, its cranberry marshes, birches, wild duck and reeds. The lake is deep, packed with fish and legends. But Andrei says that Ladoga is nothing to Lake Baikal. It's no more than a puddle. He'll take her to Baikal one day, when they go to Siberia together.

'We have fish as big as whales,' he says. 'And the water of Lake Baikal is the purest in the world.'

He explains why this is so, but she doesn't bother to take it in. She imagines them both, in summer, on a wooden jetty which thrusts out far into the waters of Lake Baikal. They are not fishing or swimming. They are just sitting there, doing nothing, close together. Her head is on his shoulder, and his hand cups her cheek. The sun is on their backs and their breathing rises and falls in time to the distant cluck of water on the far-off grey stones of the shore. Andrei tells her that stones from the Baikal shores bring good luck, so she's put a handful in her pocket. She reaches in and touches their round, smooth surfaces. The air smells of spice and pine, and the water breathes out its own virgin sweetness.

'You see, I told you you'd love it here,' says Andrei. Without looking at him she knows that his Siberian eyes have squeezed up into slits as he smiles at her.

'Yes,' she says. 'You're right. I love it here.' Across kilometres of water there are mountains, marching away into wilderness. No one goes there, says Andrei, apart from hunters.

'I'll take you up to the snow-line tomorrow.'

But the sun on her back is warm.

'No,' she says. 'Let's not go anywhere. Let's just stay here.'

The woman ahead of Anna in the queue is wearing a heavy fox-fur coat, and a fox-fur hat. But in spite of her clothes she is trembling so much that the little fur tail on her hat bobs up and down and bounces on her shoulders as if it's alive. Suddenly the woman turns and grasps Anna's arm. Her face is the colour of old candle-grease, and her hands grip hard, digging into Anna.

'Help me, I don't feel well –'

Anna staggers. Her body will not take the weight of this woman. 'Sit down,' she says. 'Rest for a minute. The queue's not moving.'

But suspicion lights in the woman's blurred, starved eyes. It could be a trick, to steal her place in the queue. One hand lets go of Anna, to scrabble inside her coat and check if the ration card is still there. Maybe Anna has used this moment of weakness to slide a hand in and take it. Without a ration card, you die. There's no getting another, not now Pavlov's tightened everything up. The woman gives a sob of relief as she finds the edge of her card and rubs her finger against it as if she's touching a holy medal. But she still glares suspiciously at Anna.

'Rest for a minute. I'll keep your place,' says Anna.

The woman's gloves, too, are made of fox-fur. The fur is reddish, soft, glistening. It looks so much more alive than the woman who's wearing it. You can't buy a fur coat of that quality in any shop Anna's ever been into. The woman's colourless lips open. 'I want to live,' she whispers, as if it's the biggest secret of all. She leans all her weight on to Anna.

'Quick, the queue's moving,' says Anna. The woman lets go and lunges forward. The queue stirs, shifts, but does not move, while Anna steps back out of the reach of the woman's preying hands, and folds her own arms across her chest. Her head hurts. She tries to recapture the jetty with its warm, sunlit wood, the feel of Andrei's shoulder, and the muscled leap of a fish far out on the water. But they will not come.

Someone behind her is whispering about the ice road now. 'The rate we're losing trucks, there won't be any left soon.'

'But some of them they're getting through, all the same,' replies another woman. 'They know how bad things are here. They're doing the best they can. Working night and day . . .'

As long as people know about us, we are not alone. Not left in the dark like abandoned children, to freeze and starve.

'They're getting through,' Anna repeats under her breath. They will come. We will live, and not die. She sees the ghostly whiteness of the frozen lake, swept by mist and snowstorms, and the wavering track the supply trucks have to follow. Perhaps there are flags stuck in the ice, to guide the trucks from station to station. The Finns believe an ice-woman lives there, far out on the ice, where the water is deepest. She calls through the storms to draw to herself a human lover. Male or female, she doesn't care. What she wants is what she hasn't got: warm flesh and a beating heart. Each lover can only warm her for a moment, before she freezes him.

The trucks churn on over the ice. There are weak patches, and crevasses. There is wind that stings with driving snow. It hisses, carrying sound. *Doroga zhizni . . . doroga zhi-ii-izniii . . .* This is the Road of Life, the only chance you've got. Broken-down trucks litter the sides of the track. But although the blizzard is dangerous, it's less dangerous than the German planes which it keeps on the ground.

Sacks of flour, meat essence, butter, tinned fish, cereals, ammunition, baby-milk. Anna wills the trucks forward. They must come whatever happens, over hundreds of kilometres of emergency track built across the Ladoga marshlands, and over the ice on to the railway that will bring them to Leningrad. The Germans pincers can't quite close on this last supply-route. They bomb it whenever the sky clears, but winter is on our side. The ice grows thicker. Engines groan as the trucks labour on. It is twenty degrees below zero out on the ice, and the wind blows hard, stripping heat from men and machines. The sacks of flour are tightly packed, but even so they judder as the trucks judder.

These are not sacks of flour, but days of life. If a truck rolls into a crevasse, this number of people will die. If a truck gets through, this number will live. Kolya will grab his bread. Anna will give it to him bit by bit, to make sure that he chews it properly instead of swallowing it like a dog. He must chew, in order to extract every morsel of goodness from the bread. She will smear it with a few drops of the sunflower oil she bartered for her mother's sheepskin coat. Kolya's whole life is in his mouth.

The bread queue surges. It's arrived, the bread which is still called bread even when it's mostly cellulose and warehouse sweepings. The smell of it drifts out as if from the lips of heaven. In front of Anna the woman in the fox-furs begins to cry and laugh, crossing herself over and over. She had believed there would be no bread today. That today the ration would simply cease to be. It would disappear, like the last little circle of water that a wild duck struggles to keep open in winter, by constantly swimming round and round in the same spot.

Anna shuffles forward, feeling for the ration cards where they lie in the secret pocket she has sewn into the lining of her coat. She won't take the cards out until the moment when she's at the head of the queue. Ration cards are not like gold: they are so far above gold that you can't even make the comparison. Before she even picks up her bread, she'll hide the cards again. If there are thieves about, better lose one day's ration than the cards. You can survive a day without bread, just about, but you can't survive without ration cards until the end of the month. She and Marina have discussed over and over again the risks of Anna collecting the rations for the whole family. What if she fainted, and was robbed of the cards? It would be safer if she and Marina went together. But someone must stay with her father, and Kolya. And although Anna doesn't say it, she knows she is now the only one with the strength for the daily walk to the bakery, and for hours of queuing. Marina's cough is bad.

Anna prepares for her daily walk to the bakery as carefully as a marathon runner. She eats the quarter-slice of bread she has saved from her ration, and tucks another quarter-slice into her pocket to eat if she begins to feel dizzy. She drinks a glass of hot water with a pinch of salt. She warms her jacket, coat, gloves and scarf at the *burzhuika* before putting them on. She heats foot-cloths, wraps them around her feet, and then puts on her father's felt boots. She does everything slowly, according to a set pattern. Whenever her heart beats too fast, she stops, and rests.

She always takes her father's cherry-wood walking-stick to the bread queue. If she slipped on the uncleared ice and snow, she might never be able to get up again. And besides, the solidity of the stick in her hand is good. If someone tried to rob her, she would hit them with it. She's seen people grappling in the snow, fighting in slow-motion over a crust of bread.

She swathes her face with her shawl until only her eyes show. Each time, before Anna leaves, Marina makes the sign of the cross over her. The gesture means nothing to Anna, and a few weeks earlier it would have irritated her, but now she lets Marina do it. It's another part of the ritual of setting out.

'Be careful!' they all say.

'Be careful, Anna!' pipes Kolya, staring at her from the mattress where Marina has laid out the fort and the toy soldiers. Sometimes he strokes his toys, but he hasn't the energy to play with them any more.

The bread is in her hands. A second later she has stuffed it into the cloth bag around her waist. Both bread and ration cards are invisible as she makes her way back through the frozen streets. The light is already fading. The grip of frost hardens, and the tip of her walking-stick skids on ice. Anna rights herself, breathing hard. Sweat springs out all over her body as the bread ration knocks against her, under her coat. She must not allow herself to fall. They're waiting for her, counting the minutes until she comes back. The *burzhuika* will be cold by now, but they'll be huddling together under the blankets to share their warmth. Marina might be singing to Kolya. She knows a lot of songs, and although her singing is more like a sort of rhythmic talking, it always calms him down. Funny that Marina can't sing. But she can soothe Kolya when he has one of those fits of hopeless, hungry crying that make Anna feel like jumping out of the window.

Or maybe Kolya's doing his breathing exercises. When they get *Leningradskaya Pravda* they read every word, stripping it for meaning. Sometimes there are four sheets, sometimes only two. When everyone has read it, they spread the newspaper on the mattress and Kolya does the breathing exercises that are supposed to help his asthma.

'Swim with your arms, Kolya. Make the paper crackle.'

Kolya's arms move stiffly. Anna turns him over, and lays her hand on his diaphragm.

'Breathe in, Kolya. That's right, slowly. And now out, all the way. Watch my hand go up and down.'

Kolya peers down his chest to watch her hand. When it moves, a fleeting smile crosses his old man's face.

'I'm good at breathing, aren't I, Anna?'

After that, they put away the newspaper, to light next day's fire.

Kolya will be looking out for her.

'Where's Anna?' he'll ask, and Marina will say, 'Don't worry, she'll be back soon. It's a long way to the bakery.'

'But I'm so hungry.'

She fights her way onward. A man passes her, pulling a sledge on which the starved contours of a human body poke through the sheet that covers it. One of the runners catches on a lump of ice, and the sledge sticks. The man jerks it free. She sees what lies there with terrible clarity, as if the man has stripped away the sheet. Forehead, nose, jaw, shallow breast, jutting ribs and pelvis. It's a child's body. The sledge runs lightly over the snow, bouncing a little.

Anna feels in her pocket, and touches the emergency quarter-slice of bread that rests there. She hasn't felt dizzy today. Once again, she hasn't had to eat the last quarter-slice of bread. Once again, she'll be able to add it to Kolya's ration.

21

It was too late for the little girl. Her veins collapsed, and before they could get a line in, she died. A camphor injection hadn't done anything. As far as cause of death, you could take your pick. Dysentery, dehydration, shock . . . But she'd died of hunger. There are only two causes of death left: shelling and starvation.

The mother is still crouching by the iron cot, holding her daughter's hand. She is silent. Andrei straightens himself slowly, easing his back, and puts a hand on the woman's shoulder. But he doesn't say anything either. What is there to say? What words of comfort for the loss of a child who need never have died at all? The little girl's name was Nadia. Ten minutes ago he spoke her name into the bluish, shrunken face, although he already knew there was no calling her back.

'Talk to her. She can still hear you,' he said to the mother. For a while she sat there, bundled up, impassive. She looked sixty, but was probably thirty-five. Suddenly she seemed to realize what was happening. Her face quivered. She threw herself forward so that her mouth was almost touching the child's, and words began to pour out of her. 'Stay with me, don't leave me, my treasure, my little soul. Look, I've brought you your little woolly cat, the one you love . . .'

But the child's face remained rigid.

It's over. Andrei sways with tiredness. Nine o'clock, and there'll be a cup of barley soup for him in the canteen. Never mind that it'll be water haunted by barley rather than the rich, hot, savoury soup his body craves. He has a half-slice of bread in his pocket, for Kolya. Anna's face will unclench when she sees it. She'll prod the bread with her quick fingers, as if it might not be real. And then she'll frown and interrogate him about what he had to eat at the hospital. 'Because you've got to have your ration, Andrei, when you're on your feet all day long and then you've got to get home afterwards.'

Home. That's what they both call it now. Home isn't the apartment, or even the room warmed by the *burzhuika.* It's the mattress where they curl together at night, with Kolya breathing beside them. They don't kiss. She doesn't sigh, and press her body against his. They don't ache for each other any more. They rest, wadded in their winter coats, like climbers bivouacked on an icy mountain. They lie cupped against each other, and still. His training tells him that this is because their starving bodies have shut down in order to survive. Their bodies know more than they do. If she weren't there, would he ever be able to sleep?

When he lies like this, close to Anna, breathing her sour breath, he feels as if they are no longer separate at all. They are the same. When she sighs or moves, it's as if this is happening inside his own flesh. When she swallows a crust of bread dipped in tea, he feels the warmth of it flushing his own skin.

They are high on the mountain, and ice tears at their flesh. He doesn't know if they will live. Her face is sallow, her lips cracked at the corners. In the mornings her eyelids are stuck together with yellow crusts. He is the same. Slowly, slowly, they creak into life. They mustn't keep on lying there. He's heard too many stories of whole families sinking together into the stupor of death. She lights the *burzhuika,* and warms a pot of water which has frozen overnight. She dips a cotton rag in the water, and wipes his eyes until the crust is gone. He blinks. There she is. They look at one another without speaking. The day is in front of them, stretching out, a wasteland of hunger that they must shape. She nods at him. They are together. She is with him.

'I'll go and change your father's dressings.'

'Good. I'll make tea.'

They can make tea out of anything. Often they make it out of plain water, with a touch of sugar or salt.

'Kolya,' she says then, 'Ko-olya. Time to wake up.'

She won't let Kolya sleep on too late into the morning. She insists that the days keep their shape. There's not enough warm water to wash properly, but they can at least wipe themselves clean. She combs Kolya's hair, massages his hands and feet to get his circulation going, and brushes his teeth very gently because Kolya's gums bleed and his teeth are loose. By then the water is hot, and he can have his tea.

'The bakeries will be open already,' she tells him. 'They opened at six o'clock. They'll be baking your bread now, Kolya.' Then, because they've got a stub of candle, she does a little reading with him. He's so quick, a real little Levin. A few months ago he'd have zipped through the pages. But now he doesn't remember the words. She points to them. 'What does that say, Kolya? Can you remember? And that one?'

That is *home*, where Anna is. 'Yes,' Andrei promises himself, 'I'll finish all this, and then I'll go home.'

Andrei is swallowing the last of his soup when the surgeon he worked under last spring stops by his table.

'I've been looking for you.' Pavel Nikolayevich is a chunky man with spatulate fingers. He looks more like a tram-driver than anyone's idea of a surgeon. But Andrei's seen those fingers at work, and knows the skills built into each of them. Pavel Nikolayevich takes a small packet out of his coat. 'Here. Something for you.'

'Thank you.' Andrei reaches out and takes the packet, which is squashy and heavy for its size. He doesn't ask what it is. These days, you say your thanks and don't ask questions.

The professor leans close. 'Guinea-pig,' he whispers. 'Incredibly enough, Tamara was still keeping a few of the lab animals alive. Giving them hay and so on. So there you are. The South Americans regard guinea-pig as a great delicacy, I believe.'

'I can't thank you enough . . .'

'Rubbish. If we don't keep you young doctors going, who'll look after us when we're old men? Besides, you know, I have no dependants. These days that's a blessing. Now, put that away before anyone sees it. They'll all be wanting some.'

He pats Andrei's shoulder and walks on.

'What's that, Andryusha?'
'Meat.'

'Meat! What meat? Where did you get it?'

'Someone gave it to me.'

'But what is it? Dog? Cat?'

'No, better than that, wait a minute –'

He's already unwrapped the packet once, in the hospital, and seen the little stiff, furred corpse.

'Let me see it! Andrei!'

'No, not yet – why don't I cook it first?'

Her face blanches. She steps back from him. 'What kind of meat is it?' she whispers hoarsely. Her face is stiff with horror. At once he knows what she suspects.

'No, Anna, no, I swear, it's not that. It's nothing bad. It's a guinea-pig.'

'A guinea-pig!' She puts her hand over her mouth. 'You're sure, Andrei? Who gave it to you? You hear such things.'

He has heard them too. In the market, and in the bread queue. Even among the doctors. Andrei believes in what he's seen, not in rumours. People whisper of corpses with missing limbs, and of children who disappear. They say there are cannibals trading in the Sennaya market now, hawking unidentifiable meat pâté. Quickly, he turns his mind away.

'Of course it's a guinea-pig. Look at it. Fur and all.'

'Oh yes –'

'But we'll have to skin it.'

'You can do that. You're used to dissecting things. I'll work out how to cook it. We haven't lit the *burzhuika* yet, because there's only one bookshelf left.'

The room is icy. Kolya, swathed in blankets, is perched on Marina's knee. She must have been reading him a story, but she has fallen into the sudden sleep that keeps overtaking all of them. Anna's father, under his mound of blankets, is also sleeping.

Kolya's sharp little face turns to Anna. 'Marina's been asleep for a long time, but I didn't wake her up.'

'Good boy. Guess what, Kolya, we're going to have meat! Andrei's brought it. You can help me get the stove ready.'

'Meat,' says the child, as if he doesn't quite remember what it is.

'Yes, and then I'm going to make soup from the bones, like we do. When Daddy and Marina smell soup, they'll soon wake up.'

But Marina is already struggling out of sleep. 'Soup? Let me make it. You and Andrei must rest. You both look exhausted.'

As she crosses to the kitchen she checks Mikhail, as she always does, and pulls the blankets closer around him. Anna won't believe it, she says, but her father was awake for a quite a long time, earlier. While you were in the bread queue, Anna. He even talked, didn't he, Kolya? Your father was talking to us, wasn't he?'

'Yes,' says Kolya, but uncertainly.

Anna massages Andrei's legs while the meat cooks. They've decided to make a stew, so as not to lose any of the meat's goodness. They can eat strips of meat today, then the soup tomorrow. The rare, savoury smell of cooking meat fills the apartment. The next moment, there's a knock on the door.

'Someone smells meat,' says Marina.

'I'll go.' And whoever it is, I'll stop them at the door. They mustn't come in. If word gets out that we've got meat . . . What if it's Zina? I can't give her any more – I promised Marina –

It is Zina, with the baby in her arms. She stands in the doorway and holds him out to Anna, as she did before.

'I think he's ill. Do you think it's a cold, or maybe an ear infection?'

The baby has been dead for at least three days, Anna judges, as she takes him into her own arms. The icy cold of Zina's room has preserved him, but he is dry and blue and his half-open eyes show slits of white.

'Zina . . .'

'He's cold. I wondered if we could come in. You said it was warm by your stove.'

'Zina, where's your Fedya? Has he seen the baby?'

'He hasn't been home since last week. You know he's on the Defence Committee at work. My Fedya never stops – he's practically a Stakhanovite.'

'Zina, you know, don't you, that the baby –'

Zina reaches up, and puts her hand over Anna's mouth. 'Don't say anything, Anna. It brings bad luck.' She takes back her baby and rocks him gently. 'He's so beautiful, isn't he? And we haven't even got a photograph of him. My mother's never seen him, you know. So I came to ask you, Anna Mikhailovna. You know that drawing you did, the one you showed me, of your little Kolya when he was a baby? I wondered if you would draw my baby, so I can send the picture to my mother.'

The smell of meat floats into the tiny hallway.

'Wait here a moment, Zina.' Anna goes back into the apartment, snatches up paper and pencil, whispers in Marina's ear, and returns to Zina, who still stands in exactly the same position, her face peacefully bent over the baby.

'We'll do the drawing in your apartment. It's quieter there.'

In their coats, boots and hats, the two women sit opposite one another. Zina cradles her baby. From time to time she bends and whispers to him.

For the first time in her life, Anna doesn't attempt to draw what she sees. She draws the baby as she remembers him in his early weeks, before the siege began. A breast-fed baby, already rounding out nicely, with a few feathers of damp, dark hair. One plump hand clutches the edge of his shawl. His eyes are open, and they find his mother's gaze. She draws quickly, because Zina is beginning to tremble.

'There you are. I can do a copy later on, if you like, so you've got one to keep and one to send to your mother.'

Zina stares at the drawing.

'It's just like him. That's exactly the way he looks at me. And his hands, look. That's just the way they hold the shawl.'

Anna does not look at the baby's purple claw, curled over the edge of the blanket in which Zina has wrapped him.

'My mum's going to be so thrilled when she sees this.'

Zina shifts the baby into her right arm, takes the drawing and puts it carefully away under the bed.

'My Fedya'll frame it. He can do anything like that.' Then she returns and faces Anna.

'I know he isn't –' she swallows, 'looking his best just now.'

'No, because he's –'

'I know. Don't think I don't know. It's just I don't want to talk about it. And when my Fedya comes home he'll do everything that should be done.'

'Of course he will.'

Anna, Andrei and Kolya eat the tender, savoury meat, while Marina spoons broth into Mikhail's mouth.

'This is funny meat,' says Kolya. 'I've never tasted it before.'

'It's a special kind of meat they've brought in over the ice road.'

'Can we have it again?'

'Tomorrow, you'll have meat soup with your bread. I don't want my last bit, Kolya. You have it.'

Later, after the others have gone to sleep, there are just the two of them again. They lie face to face, whispering, feeling each other's dry lips move. His breath smells of meat, and she knows her own must, too.

'We stink,' she says. Now the pipes are frozen there's no running water in the apartment. For some reason a tap in the courtyard is still working, although water is so heavy that they carry only the bare minimum upstairs. But they're lucky, not like Tanya. Every day she sees more people on their way down to the Neva, stumbling with their buckets, clambering down to the ice. God knows what's in that water now.

Anna dreams of a steam-bath, her naked flesh red with heat, her sweat trickling down breasts and thighs and prickling at the roots of her hair. Women wade through clouds of steam, their heads small above mountains of breast, belly, buttock and thigh. They sit on wooden benches and snort with content. Every particle of dirt is steamed out of their pores.

Anna's skin itches. It's days now since she has taken off her clothes. She disgusts herself.

'I'm so dirty,' she says.

'I love you more and more.'

'Don't go to sleep yet. I'm afraid.'

'What are you afraid of?'

'My father's going to die soon. Marina says he wakes up, but I don't think he does. Only in her mind. I feel as if we're somewhere else, not here on earth at all.'

Andrei shifts his swollen legs. 'That's because it's night. But tomorrow I'll see if I can get a spoonful of cod-liver oil for Kolya. Masha at the dispensary said they might have some. A few drops a day will make all the difference. And you'll go for the bread ration, and we'll come home and eat. We'll get through another day. We'll still be on earth. As long as you're alive, I'll stay alive.'

'You promise?'

'Yes, I promise.'

'But my father will die.'

'Yes. Yes, I think he will.'

Frost and snow gather, thickening centimetre by centimetre on windows, roofs, parks, railways, and the bodies of the dead. Slowly, the city sinks down, like a great ship sinking in an ice-field. Its lights have gone out. Its water no longer flows. Production in factories has all but stopped. The ship is poised, ready to dive into the blackness of death. Only its people keep on stubbornly living, as if they don't know that it's all over for them.

The next morning, Anna finds a small onion which must have rolled off the store-cupboard shelf and hidden itself among the bristles of her broom. She grabs Andrei's arm with a cry of joy. Sobbing, she says to him, 'You were right, you knew all the time. We're going to be all right, I know it. This is a sign, that's what it is. A sign.'

He looks at her dry, swollen lips, her sharp cheekbones and sunken eyes. He looks at the little onion which she is holding out in triumph.

'Yes,' he agrees. 'It's a sign.'

She slices the onion finely, and adds it to the meat broth which she has saved for Kolya, with a pinch of salt and a cup of water.

'The vitamins will do him so much good.'

She lights the stove with kindling from the last bookshelf. Soon the soup is simmering. Marina, Andrei and Anna gather round to watch Kolya swallow his meat soup with onion. Anna spoons it into his mouth. 'There you are. It's good, isn't it? Now you'll grow up to be a big boy.'

After eating, the child goes back into a fuddled drowse. Sometimes he whimpers. Anna notes that Marina has not even suggested keeping back any of the broth for her father.

'I was listening to the radio,' says Marina. 'There was a nutritional expert on last night. She said there's nourishment in wallpaper paste.'

'But we haven't got any.'

'We have. Kolya's fort. We used wallpaper paste to make the papier-maché. If I strip off the painted layer, we could cook the rest of it. There's bound to be some calories in it.'

'But what will Kolya say? He got so upset when I said we might have to use it for fuel for the *burzhuika*.'

'Yes, but if it's for food, that's different.'

While Kolya sleeps, Marina works for hours, peeling off the thinnest possible layer of painted papier-maché from the fort, and putting the rest to soak in water.

'The paper will float to the top, and the goodness of the paste will remain in the water. We can make it into a kind of soup for him.'

'Don't tell him.'

'No. We'll say we've put the fort away for safety, until the blockade is lifted.'

'Yes, let's say that.'

22

Again, it's the dead of night, but this time she's alone. The others are in the room, of course. Kolya, on the mattress next to her, pressed against her. Marina, on the other side of Kolya, sleeping. They lie like this, the adults sandwiching the child, so that their body-heat will keep him warm. But Andrei's not here, and without Andrei she feels cold and fearful. She's restless, thinking of him at work. He's sleeping at the hospital tonight. She made him promise. Outside it's minus twenty, and she's afraid that on a night like this he could collapse on the way home and freeze to death.

There is typhus in one of the nearby children's homes, he says, where orphans are crammed together. What if Andrei gets typhus? In his starved state, he'd have no resistance. What if he simply didn't come home from the hospital one night? Would anyone there think to inform her if he was taken ill? Of course not. They don't even know that she exists, let alone that Andrei's living here –

A voice stirs beside her. It's Marina.

'Let's talk. It'll pass the time.'

'What?'

'You're awake, aren't you?'

'Yes, I'm awake. What time is it?'

'Half past eleven.'

'Only half past eleven.'

'You've been asleep.'

'Have I?'

'Yes. You were asleep when I got up.'

'Marina, you've lit the *burzhuika*!'

'I had to make tea for your father.'

'What did you use?'

'The encyclopaedia.'

'Oh.'

'I thought it was the one he'd miss least.'

'I suppose so.'

'And there are twelve volumes.'

They speak quietly, although they lie on the same mattress, because Kolya is between them. But he is deeply asleep, with the flaps of his fur cap muffling his ears. And then the cold space on Anna's other side, where Andrei should be.

'So many hours, before it gets light,' says Anna.

'Your father's been awake too. He only went back to sleep about half an hour ago. We've been talking for a long time.'

'It's strange, how he only talks when no one but you can hear him,' says Anna. Her heart beats fast as she waits for Marina's answer.

'You think he doesn't talk to me? You think I'm lying?'

'No, not that –'

'You think I invent it?'

'Maybe.'

'Why should I do that?'

'Because you want him to talk to you.'

'There are a lot of things you don't know, Anna.' Her voice is sharp in the darkness.

'I know,' says Anna. 'People have been telling me that all my life. I never had time to finish my education.'

'Shall we talk properly, then?' asks Marina, her voice changing. 'Shall we stop all this? I could tell you a story.'

It's still only half past eleven. Six and a half hours before the bakeries open. The night hangs like lead.

'All right,' says Anna.

'You know the people in my story. You'll have your own version. But let me tell you mine, and then you can tell me yours.'

Anna draws up her knees and pulls Kolya more deeply into the bony cradle of her body, under the layers of blankets. She tucks his hands into her armpits, where they'll be warm. He sleeps on.

'You realize that your father and I have known each other for a long time?'

'Of course.'

'I was thirty-two when I first met him. He was a couple of years older, with a wife and a four-year-old daughter. Your father was very interested in Tairov's work – you'll have heard of Tairov. He was in Moscow, directing at the Kamerny theatre, which he'd founded just before the war. Misha had been reading Tairov's book, *Notes of a Director*. It wasn't long after he'd staged *Phèdre*. I remember that the first time we met, we argued about that production. We'd both been to Moscow to see it. Your father was still hoping to write for the stage then.'

'But he never did.'

'No. So, we argued. He told me straight away that he was married, and about you. He used to tell me how clever you were, because you could already read when you were only four. But from what I could see he wasn't at home very much. Those were such different times, and although it's only twenty years ago it's passed away so completely you can't guess what it was like unless you remember it.'

'There's nothing so very different,' says Anna, 'about men who get married and have babies and then find that they don't want to be at home very much.'

'It was a new world,' says Marina. 'That's what we believed. Everything had changed so fast, and it was still changing. The theatre was right in the heart of it. It was 1922. For the first time ever we had a mass audience, we had soldiers and factory workers coming in with free tickets they'd been given. Theatre was going to be for everyone. They came to everything, they listened to everything, they talked about everything. They ate and drank as if they were in their own homes and they didn't dress up. They just poured in, in their boots and overcoats. They wanted theatre, because they'd never had it before. Everybody wanted it. Everybody wanted us. Ensembles sprang up, actors flung ideas at the audience, there were experiments going on everywhere. Some of them worked and some of them didn't. The whole of theatre turned into a giant stage where you were always in danger of being pushed back into the wings if artistic politics left you behind. The spotlight might suddenly shine on you, or it would go off and you'd be alone.

'And yet there was so much freedom. We didn't live in a fog, stumbling with one arm in front of our faces to ward off what was coming next. We knew the future was rushing towards us and we raced to embrace it. I sleep a lot now, but in those years I hardly went to bed. I'd go to sleep at two in the morning, and at seven I'd snap out of bed wide awake and run to rehearsals. And everyone else would be up too. Imagine actors getting up before ten. And yet they didn't look worn out and grey. Everyone looked beautiful, even those who were ugly.

'You've no idea, Anna, because you've grown up with what came after. The time of hope didn't last long. Everything solidified so quickly, after only a few years. They closed down one of Bulgakov's plays, and banned *The Crimson Island*. It wasn't allowed a single performance. By that time people were measuring what they said, and thinking about where to align themselves. There was such fear. It's one thing for a poet to speak out. He can always write poems. But an actor or a director has got to have a theatre. He has got to be part of something, or else he's nothing. People saw that they'd be out in the wilderness if they made the wrong choices.'

People, thinks Anna. Always *people*. I want to know about you, not about *people*.

'I thought you were going to talk about what happened between you and my father.'

'Yes. But this isn't background. It's all part of it.'

Those rounded, authoritative syllables. You have to believe her. But don't forget that Marina has been trained to make people believe what she says.

Kolya sighs, and shudders. A bad dream, nothing more. Anna pushes her hand under his coat and rubs his back, over the knobs of his spine, across his ribs, up to the wings of his shoulder-blades.

'There, sleep now. Sleep.'

'In the second year, I became pregnant,' says Marina. 'By that time I knew your mother. We'd been introduced, we liked one another. I used to come to the house. We were becoming real friends, kitchen friends.'

'And what?'

'I had an abortion, as everyone did. It was perfectly normal. I didn't tell your father until afterwards.'

There is silence for a while.

'What did he say?'

'He was angry.'

'So, he wanted another house, and another baby not to go home to. Was that it?'

'No. He said it was our baby, part of our life. He said I should have told him before I had the abortion.'

'But he wouldn't have done anything.'

'Of course not. He loved your mother. I knew that by then. But he was still angry with me.'

'It's true, he can stay angry for a long time.'

'He asked me if the foetus was male or female.'

'What did you say?'

'I said I didn't know.'

'Did you?'

'It was male. I was four months pregnant.'

'You left it late.'

'Through stupidity. Thinking I might tell him, and then pulling back from it, and then thinking again that I might tell him.'

'But you didn't.'

'No. It's finished. It's a long time ago. But that was the end of things between us. After that we were friends.'

'That wasn't what you wanted.'

'No. But I could tell that it was an effort for him to touch me. So I preferred not to be touched.'

'When my mother died, did you ever think —'

'No. I never thought of it. I knew it would not happen.'

She says it coldly and clearly, as if she's giving a statement to the authorities.

'So there you are,' says Marina. 'That's my story.'

They lie silent, in the dark. Her father breathes snoringly. Kolya twitches, then goes still. The room smells of the books Marina has burned.

'How many volumes did you burn, Marina?'

'Two. It's good paper, and the boards are almost as thick as wood.'

'We'll burn two more in the morning.'

Anna thinks of the bright hot flame that will spurt from those books. She'll hold her hands so close that her bones show through the flesh. The flames will lap at her palms. Who could have ever imagined such ecstasy, while the radiators still worked? Her whole life will be in her hands, and Kolya will sit between her knees, his face lit, his candle-pale skin flushed to rose.

'Of course, that wasn't the truth,' says Marina.

'What?'

'Do you want the real story?'

'Yes.'

'We recognized each other right from the first moment. We hadn't any choice, that's what I thought. He's dying now, and perhaps I'll die, too. Nobody will ever know what happened. There was no child, and now there's not even any story left. Everything will be rubbed out. That's what they do to enemies of the people, isn't it, Anna? They are erased from the records. So I'll tell you, even if you don't want to hear. Even if you think I'm your enemy.

'I was already well-known. I was used to things being as I wanted them to be. The roles I wanted, the tables I wanted in restaurants, summers in the Crimea. I was used to respect. Nothing had ever caught me and held me and made me do things I didn't want to do, and go to places I didn't want to go.

'But your father did all that. He captured me like a fish and then he tried to throw me back into the water, but it was too late. I'd spent too much time up in the air and I was damaged. I wasn't as beautiful any more, either to him or to myself. I couldn't repair myself. I couldn't even swim away. I sank to the bottom of the water and I hid there, in the mud. I believed that the mud was where I belonged.

'I wanted the child, but I knew that your father wouldn't be prepared to become its father. He would stay with Vera, and with you. My child would depend on me for everything. Once or twice I imagined telling him, in the heart of the night, after hours of sex, when you seem to be out of your body. I know, he's your father. I shouldn't be telling you this. I would imagine us talking soul to soul. Of course it never happened. I didn't have the courage.

'The doctor I went to was not a pleasant individual. He knew who I was. He kept telling me about how much he loved the theatre, and which roles I should take in the future. Plenty of excellent, fatherly advice, but his eyes weren't fatherly. We were in his consulting-rooms. He owned me, for a while. He was full of understanding for what he called my "predicament". What he wanted was for us to conspire together, and maybe for me to weep tears on his shoulder. But I wouldn't. I had to open my legs for him but I would not open my mouth. He actually said to me that he would be interested to come to my next performance, to find out if my experience had affected my art.

'Your father, of course, knew nothing about any of this. When I told him that I'd had the abortion, later on, he wrote a series of poems. They were very good poems.

'Vera read them. There was never any quarrel, nothing was said. She simply withdrew. She could be in the same room, and it would seem as if she wasn't there. You know how she always read all the drafts of your father's work? At that time she used to write her thoughts on small sheets of yellow paper – often very good, clear, technical comments – and then she'd clip the yellow sheets to his manuscripts. She never wrote on the manuscripts themselves. Your father showed me what she'd attached to the manuscript of the poems he wrote after we'd separated. It was just a short note. "In my opinion these poems, excellent as they are, strike a false note." That was all she ever said.

'I spent a long time down in the mud, thinking about it all. I thought a lot about your mother, too. I wanted her friendship even more now that I'd done this to her, but I couldn't get it. She didn't try to stop me seeing him, nothing like that. She didn't need to.

'I had to understand that I'd been mistaken from the beginning. We hadn't recognized each other. I'd recognized him, but he'd thought I was someone else. And I saw what a relief it was to him, when he believed I wasn't in love with him any more. He really loved me, then. He was so grateful to me for having got over him that he built me up into something remarkable.

'I remember the tone of the doctor's voice exactly. "It was a boy," he said. He wanted me to know that. Not, not so fatherly at all.

'And all those letters your father sent to me. The most wonderful letters, years and years of them. I've kept them all. Is Kolya still asleep?'

'Fast asleep.'

'That's it. Now it's time for you to tell me your story.'

'There isn't one to tell.'

'Of course there is.'

'No,' says Anna, 'because it's still happening. It hasn't turned into a story yet.'

Marina laughs. 'How like your mother you are.'

'I hope I am.'

She's solid, like Vera. She doesn't know what she wants yet, but when she does know there won't be any hesitation. Why did I tell her all that? Because she's going to survive. You can see it, it's written in her face. Though thousands shall perish around thee, it shall not come near thee. *God knows why that is.*

I didn't tell her everything. Perhaps it wasn't a true story at all. There are only two things I want to remember.

One night I got out of bed and went to the bathroom. He had fallen asleep. I filled the basin with warm water and soap and slowly washed myself, as if I were washing someone else. My thighs ached, my whole body was damp with sweat. It was summer, and still light, and I could see myself in the mirror, washing away the smell of sex, squeezing out my sponge, and soaping it again. My face was pale and my eyes were dark, and my reflection seemed to flicker, as if it wasn't quite real. The mirror reflected the window behind me, and a bat flew past, against the late-evening sky. It flew straight, then it jinked sideways as if it had sensed me. Suddenly I was terribly hungry.

And then it finishes. I don't remember what came next.

The second time, I was alone. I had gone back home after visiting the doctor who performed the abortion. I had no idea what to expect. Again it was summer. I sat by the window, waiting. I had no pain yet, but my body felt wrong. I was waiting and waiting, checking every grain of sensation, waiting for it to begin. I'd said to the doctor that my old nanny would be at home with me. But I hadn't told her anything. She would have looked after me, but she would have been sorrowful. I didn't want that. She would have prayed for me when she thought I wasn't looking.

Another pale, late sky. There was a heavy scent of jasmine, and it irritated me, although normally I like jasmine. It smelled artificial, as if someone were pumping the scent into the room. I got up and opened the window, but of course the scent grew stronger. I looked down and there it was, deep, dark green that was disappearing in the summer dusk, and white flowers like stars. Wave after wave of scent came up as the breeze turned. I leaned out, and that was when I felt the first pain, not strong at all but final, like something ripping inside me that could never be put back together.

She says she hasn't got a story. Andrei comes home and says to me, 'Hello, Marina. How have you been?' I exist for him, but only because I'm connected to her. They lie on the mattress together, with the child between them. Sometimes I hear them whisper. When he comes into the room his eyes pass over me as if I am furniture, until he finds her face. She is like Vera.

23

She's come at last. I don't say anything, but I hold out my hand. I say her name, those two syllables that mean truth. Ve-ra. Her name makes no sound, but she smiles as if she's heard it, and sits on the sofa beside me. It doesn't hurt. All the others hurt me when they come near me. But when Vera sits beside me, I feel nothing but lightness and warmth. Even though I know it's winter, she's wearing her sunflower cotton dress.

I don't open my eyes, but I know when I do the sun will be shining behind the curtains. I was wrong. It isn't winter, it's summer. It's so early in the morning that the garden will be soaked in dew. When we walk, we'll make black footprints. I know the exact shape of Vera's footprints on wet grass. They are firm, and not too small, and she's wearing the low-heeled shoes she always wears to work.

Something wonderful is about to happen. I'm trying to remember what it is, but I can't remember. Without opening my eyes, I can tell that Vera is smiling.

'You came at last,' I say to her.

'Yes.'

'But what took you so long?'

'Don't be silly. It wasn't any time at all.'

'You remember that first time we went dancing?'

'Of course.'

'I can't dance,' I said. She looked at me, and there she was, quite suddenly the most important thing I had ever seen. She was strong and supple, her waist deeply marked, her breasts round and full, her hips already moving to the music. She was laughing at me, because of what I'd said.

'Don't be silly. Everyone can dance,' she said.

'Not me. I'll only tread on your feet and pull you over.'

She took my right hand in her left. Her skin was warm and moist. She took my other hand and moved closer to me. Now I could smell her. A warm, powdery smell, then the smell of her hair which had had the sun on it. Vera loved sitting in the sun.

She wasn't laughing at me now. Her face was smooth and serious.

'Of course you can dance. You just have to let yourself move to the music,' *she said.*

What we did wasn't really dancing. She drew me close and we swayed to the music. The band finished that number, and started another, and Vera said, 'I love this one.' We never stepped out on the floor. 'Next time,' she said, 'we'll dance properly. I'll teach you.'

But I don't think we ever did. As I remember, we went to a café and I talked for a long time about Mayakovsky. I would have had to go to dancing lessons, and I didn't want to. There were more important things.

She's still there, still smiling, waiting. I can see her breasts and her hips, which I haven't yet touched. I believe that she's a virgin, and I'm right. Her life has been work, friends, dancing. But she is ready to move on. I can see her clear, serious face with the half-smile on it. One of her hands is lifted, ready to settle on my shoulder. If I made the slightest effort, she would dance away with me. But I stand still.

She's still here. She must have been sitting beside me for a long time, because I've been asleep. One of those others came up and did things to me. I can't see them clearly. They are like clouds I could put my hand through. But Vera is solid, and sharp. My eyes fill with tears, and I put out my hand to touch her. The weight of her thigh presses down my blanket.

'Did you go away?' *I say.*

She shakes her head and smiles. 'I've been here all the time.'

She uncrosses her legs and glances away from me, at something I can't turn my head to see.

'Don't go, Vera,' *I say.*

'Don't worry. When I go, you'll come with me.'

She smiles. She raises one hand, as if to settle it on my shoulder. It touches the open wound there, but I don't flinch. I want her to touch me. I want her to dance me away from here.

'Don't worry,' *she repeats.* 'This time, you'll come with me.'

I can't see Vera any more. They're all like clouds now. My feet have been cold for a long time, but now the cold has reached my knees.

'Vera.'

She doesn't answer, but she squeezes my hand.
'Cold,' I tell her.

Marina straightens up from Mikhail's side. How awful she looks, Anna thinks. If only Andrei could get something for her cough.

'What did he say?' she asks.

'He's cold.'

'But I can't light the *burzhuika* again. There's only enough to heat the room up a bit before we sleep.'

'I know.'

'He doesn't recognize me any more.'

'He doesn't recognize me, either.'

'But he spoke to you. He took your hand, I saw him.'

'He thought I was someone else. You know that your father's going, don't you?'

'Yes.'

'He isn't suffering, that's what matters,' says Marina, almost to herself. Anna looks at her father's face, carved, yellowish, like a mask of wood. His mouth gapes a little.

'He can't go on like this,' she says.

'No. He can't and he won't.'

On the mattress, Andrei is showing Kolya chess moves. He has made a chessboard from paper, with tiny paper pieces which Anna drew and cut out. They have had to burn the wooden chess set in the *burzhuika*. Andrei's legs are too swollen for him to get to the hospital today. Kolya watches the movement of the paper chess pieces. Andrei isn't playing real chess: his knights thunder freely over the field, snatching pawns, stymying kings and bishops.

'The horses are hungry,' says Kolya. 'Give them something to eat.'

'Of course. Here's their hay, and here are their oats. You hold out the oats, Kolya, with your hand flat. Like this, then they can't nip your fingers by mistake. Perfect.'

'They're gobbling it all up! They're trying to eat my fingers!' says Kolya. There is a gleam of pleasure in his wasted face.

'Hold out your hand and give them this apple, and then they'll be ready to fight again.'

Marina puts another blanket on top of Mikhail. She folds it under his chin.

'It's time to turn him again,' Andrei says from the mattress. They are turning him every two hours now, to relieve his bedsores.

'No,' says Marina, 'I don't think he wants us to touch him any more.'

'His skin's like paper. It's got to be looked after.'

'I think he's going, Andrei. Have a look.'

But before Andrei can heave himself off the mattress, Mikhail begins to snore, deep in his throat. A long, snoring breath, a pause, then the gravelly start of another snore.

'You're right,' says Andrei. 'There's no need to turn him.'

'Why's he making that funny noise?' asks Kolya.

'He's very ill.'

'I know *that*.'

'He's dying.'

'You didn't have to tell me. I knew without you even telling me,' says Kolya coldly. He bends over the chess pieces, excluding the rest of the room. 'Would you like another apple? You're still hungry, aren't you? Come on, boy, co-ome on. Don't be frightened.' He picks up the paper knight on horseback, holds him close to his lips and disappears with him under the blankets. As Mikhail continues to snore, they listen to Kolya whispering to his little horse.

24

It's on her way back from the bread queue that Anna meets Fedya, dragging his loaded sledge. For once he doesn't try to avoid her, but stops and stands planted in the snow before her. There they are, for the first time, face to face like real neighbours. Hunger has eaten out hollows in his face, and greyed his skin.

'I took our little one to the cemetery today,' he says. 'Zina wanted to come, but she wasn't equal to it.'

There is nothing to be said. It was just a few months ago that Zina came out on to the landing to show Anna the new baby, swaddled deep in his cream woollen shawl, fists crossed on his chest. It was another world. Sunlight glowed outside the dirty landing window that no one could climb high enough to clean. Anna leaned over the baby and smelled his warm, damp, powdery smell.

It should have happened again and again, for years. Zina would have come out on to the landing with the latest bulletins, when Fedya was safely out of the way. Vanka's first tooth, Vanka pulling himself up on the furniture, Vanka's first tantrum. *He rolled over today, all on his own. When I turned around, there he was, lying on his tummy.*

He knows Fedya already. He always gets excited when his daddy comes home, don't you, Vanka?

He's dribbling so much — look, this jacket's soaked through. Do you think he can be getting a tooth already?

But little Vanka, lifeless as wood, has already joined the queue at the cemetery. Not many people get buried these days, with the ground like iron. Bodies pile up in the frost, outside the cemetery gates. Some don't even get that far. They stay at home in their beds, because no one has the strength to drag them to the cemetery. The living rig a curtain round the dead, in their corner of the room.

'I'm so sorry,' says Anna. Fedya spreads his hands and looks down at them as if he's surprised they're empty. Then he clears his throat.

'There's an apartment building down by the Baltic station that's been shelled. Overlooking the canal. A mate of mine told me about it when I was on my way back from the cemetery. It was on fire, but they managed to put the worst of it out before the whole building went up. There's a reception floor made of wooden blocks. Most of it's still all right.'

Now that he says it, she can smell the stink of charred wood. He's lashed a blanket over his heaped sledge.

'Was there much left?' she asks.

'Could be as much as a sledge-load, if you get a move on. The building's safe, but watch out for yourself. There've been a couple of fights over there already. One guy had a knife.'

'Thanks.'

His big hands pull at the sledge ropes. 'Zina's very taken with that likeness you did of our Vanka. She keeps it by her all the time. I've got to get back to the works now, but I'll be leaving her with the wood. And she's got her ration card safe.' He clears his throat again. 'She wanted to keep the baby at home with her, so I had to tell her it wasn't the proper thing. She's not herself. But I don't know when I'll be able to get home again. The way we're fixed at the works, there's no time for that. You get a few hours' kip if you're lucky, then back on shift.'

They are still rolling tanks off the line at the Kirov works, she knows, even though the workers there are dying like everyone else. Fedya has become exactly the kind of heroic worker Zina's always believed him to be. He's taken his baby son to the cemetery, and now he'll go straight back to work.

'Don't worry. I'll keep an eye on her,' says Anna. She looks straight at him. 'You know Zina's always welcome to come in to us, if she wants.'

Fedya looks down at his hands, with the delicacy of a decent man. She always knew he was that. 'No. No, best she doesn't. She'll be all right on her own.'

'If you say so. My father's dying, so maybe you're right.'

He nods. 'Zina told me.'

But he can't do it, even now, thinks Anna, watching him. He can't bring himself to say he's sorry that my father's dying.

'Those Fascist bastards don't know what's coming to them, excuse my language. They don't know what they've got themselves into.'

'*We'll find them space in Russian earth,*' Anna says.

'You're right there.'

'It wasn't me who said it. It was Pushkin.'

'Well, he knew what he was talking about. There's space all right. We'll bury them.'

They stare at each other in sudden, savage unity.

'You don't go down as far as the station, it's on this side of the canal – the Obvodny. You can't miss it.'

'Thank you.'

'Zina told me what you did for our little one about the sugar.'

'It wasn't much.'

Fedya's fists clench on the rope. 'Nothing could've helped him. They made sure of that. They might as well have put their hands round his throat and squeezed. Our Vanka didn't stand a chance.'

Back in the apartment, Anna and Marina calculate. Her father's breaths are noisier now, more widely spaced. A thread of pulse jumps in his wrist. Before Andrei left for the hospital, he raised Mikhail up on a heap of pillows, to ease his breathing. Mikhail's skin is darkening, growing dusky around mouth and nose.

'It'll take me at least an hour to get there,' says Anna. 'Maybe more. I'll have to stop and rest. And then I've got to dig the blocks out . . .'

'Is it worth it? You'll wear yourself out, and there might not be any wood left by the time you get there.'

'We've got to get fuel. I'll take some of my ration with me.'

'Here, have this half-slice before you go.'

'I can't take your bread, Marina.'

Because once that starts, it's the end. If you even let yourself begin to imagine getting more than your own ration, it's like rousing up a wolf inside you. People collapse in the street, and straight away there's someone else on top of them, going through their pockets for bread or a ration card. If you go too close, they snarl you away.

You could lie all night long, dreaming of the crust you've put aside for Kolya when he wakes up. Anything, so that he won't cry and cry. Without knowing it, your hand could slip out and touch the surface of the bread. The bread feels as warm as life in the room's glacial midnight. Just a touch can't do any harm, you'll tell yourself. So you touch it. Your fingers work away at the rough surface. A few crumbs loosen and are carried to your mouth on a finger damp with saliva. In the morning the bread's gone, your hand is empty, and Kolya cries.

'Go on, take it, Anna. Think of all the calories you're burning, getting our bread and now our wood. You're keeping us alive. And what if you were to collapse out there, what would become of us all?'

She should keep on refusing, but she doesn't. This morning, on the way to the bakery, she found herself leaning against a wall, pressing her forehead into it. Already the cold of the stone was branching into her brain, making its home there and telling her she should rest, rest, until cold became warmth and sent her to sleep. The silence of the city gathered around her, fold after fold. The city put its hands over her lips. *Listen. Can't you hear that we're all sleeping? Why wear yourself out struggling, when you could rest, too? Come here. Lie down.*

But she crushed a handful of snow and rubbed it over the inside of her wrists until she couldn't hear the voice any more. She tricked herself by saying she would only walk ten steps, then she would rest again. She counted the steps as she used to count them with Kolya. And *one*, and *two*, and *three*, and *four* . . . When she got to ten she didn't stop, but counted another ten steps, and another, until she reached the bakery.

Marina's bread dissolves on her tongue. Marina watches in a way that seems familiar, although Anna can't place it. That fiercely focused gaze, those lips working a little, as if Marina is eating too, nourishing herself on what she's given away . . .

*

224

It's half past two, and already growing dark, by the time Anna sets out with Kolya's empty sledge bumping behind her. She has a couple of empty sacks too, and some twine to tie them on to the sledge once they're filled. It's only a child's sledge, but it'll carry a fair load.

The streets are almost empty. She passes the hump of a body frozen into a doorway, covered with drifted snow. It looks like a bag of rubbish, but Anna knows it's a body because she saw it before the snow hid it. It's an old woman. Maybe she stopped to rest on the way back from fetching her ration. Anna doesn't like going past the park any more. There are people sitting on benches, swathed in snow, planted like bulbs to wait for spring. They stay there day after day. No one comes to take them away.

It's cold, so cold. Anna adjusts the scarf she has wound around her face. She'll rest for a couple of minutes. No longer than that, because in her weakened state the cold could easily finish her off. The scorching frost goes down into her lungs like a knife. She coughs, gasps, shifts her weight from foot to foot, and bats her hands together. Her gloved hands make a muffled, ghostly sound. She thinks of the bulbs under their coverlet of snow, and shivers.

Nothing seems surprising any more, not even the bodies piled by the Karpovka canal, or outside the cemeteries. Andrei has told her about them. They are like two walls on either side of the road. It is not surprising that her father is dying while Andrei makes his way to the hospital to work, leaning on the cherry-wood stick which he needs more than Anna does now. On his swollen legs the skin is drawn and shiny. He labours on, as she does, ten steps and then ten steps more, passing the bodies of the dead. They lie exposed, charred by frost until the next snowfall covers them.

Being dead is normal. You have to patrol yourself all the time, to stop yourself slipping over the border between this world and the next. If you let go, and sit down in no man's land, the snipers of cold and hunger will soon finish you off.

She walks on through lifeless silence. There are no dogs, no pigeons, no cats, no plump, rosy-cheeked children screaming with excitement as their sledges hiss over the frozen snow. And then home to a bowl of hot milk, or a piece of gingerbread as big as your hand.

Anna's stomach gripes, and she swallows down the taste in her mouth. Her father has always chewed liquorice root to keep his teeth strong and white. She found two sticks of it in his camphor-wood box, when she was taking down the box to burn it. She made Kolya chew on the liquorice root too, although he cried and said his teeth hurt and there was blood in his mouth. When she felt his gums, he was right. There was blood on her fingers, and his front teeth were loose. Perhaps his second teeth were pushing them out? After all, at Kolya's age you expect wobbly teeth.

The liquorice root has become yellow and stringy, and it hardly has any taste left, but they keep on chewing it. It's good to have something in your mouth. There are three things which she can give to Kolya when he cries with hunger and there is no food. One is the liquorice root. The second is a strip cut from an old leather school-bag. Anna has already boiled the leather for stock, but the softened, chewy strips that remain seem to comfort Kolya, and perhaps there is still some goodness in them. The last thing she offers, when everything else has failed, is her own finger. He sucks it, clutching her hand with both his hands, and sometimes he goes to sleep.

'Yes, sleep,' says Anna aloud as the image of Kolya dissolves into the snow. 'Sleep all winter and wake up when spring's come.'

If only she could do that for him. Wrap him up like a squirrel and put him to sleep until all this is over. It's unbearable, the way he wakes up and tells her, 'Anna, my stomach hurts,' as if she doesn't already know. He looks at her, accusing her.

'Guess what, Kolya, it's time for your honey,' she says, and he follows her with his eyes as the honey jar comes out, and the special pewter spoon, chosen because it is the smallest they have. But the honey won't last for ever. What about when it's gone, and there's nothing left to distract him with, at the start of a day which will only bring him two slices of bread and a couple of hours' warmth?

'Can't I have two spoonfuls? Just today? I promise I won't ask for it tomorrow,' he bargains. Calculation flashes in his eyes. Hunger's making him older than he should be.

She shakes her head. 'We've got to make it last, Kolya.' The life dies out of his face and he watches as she puts the honey high up, out of reach and out of sight. He's a good boy. But one day he clawed at her legs, trying to drag her down so that he could climb and get at the honey.

Those snow devils are dancing again. It's only the wind spinning off the drifts. But the devils have faces, and they take on the shapes of people she knows. There's Evgenia, tossing a clod of earth over her shoulder. There's Katya, shaking back her hair. There's her father, sharp against the evening sun, holding a trout he's caught.

I'm not going crazy, it's just hunger. Let's see what I can remember. Facts. Measles can be identified by white spots on the inside of the mouth. What are those spots called? Elizaveta Antonovna always checks in the mouth if one of the children develops a rash with fever. Sometimes their mothers bring them in with fever, and rush off before we can call them back. But you can't blame the mothers too much: they have to work. They can't take endless days off. The children never disobey Elizaveta Antonovna when she tells them to open their mouths so she can look inside.

'Hmm. I thought so. Koplik's spots. Isolate this child immediately, or we'll have an epidemic in the nursery.'

And off she goes to fill in her report in triplicate, leaving the child standing there, flushed and dazed, mouth still open.

'It's all right, you can shut your mouth now,' I say, and that's when they start to cry.

Did I really work there all those years? Imagine what Elizaveta Antonovna would say if she saw Zina's dead baby.

'Definite signs of maternal neglect. I shall be making the fullest possible report to the Committee.'

Or Kolya chewing my old school-bag . . .

'A highly inappropriate diet for a child of this age-group. Kindly report to me for nutritional re-education, Anna Mikhailovna.'

One thing's for certain. Elizaveta Antonovna will survive. If she's not on special rations, she'll have wangled her way off to Moscow on a military flight. She'll be there sure enough, making the fullest possible report of a highly confidential nature.

(At the street corner, a man carrying a Bokhara rug glances across at the bundled figure pulling an empty child's sledge. Is it possible that he heard a laugh? People are going crazy in the streets these days.)

What did I say to Fedya? *'We'll find them space in Russian earth.'*

Space – yes – and vengeance. I didn't even know I was going to say it, but the words jumped out of my mouth. I know it's Pushkin, but I can't remember what poem. My father would know. Let's see if I can remember any more.

> You hate us anyway . . .
>
> And for what? Answer me.
> Because, in the blazing wreck of Moscow
> We blanked the insolent will
> Which made you tremble? Is that why you hate us?
> Because we made our earth swallow
> The juggernaut which crushed nation after nation
> And with our blood redeemed the freedom,
> Honour and peace of Europe?
> Is that why you hate us?

But there's a lot more. I'll remember it in a minute. *One* and *two* and *three* and . . . We must have had to learn the whole thing at school. Funny how things sink into you when you don't even know that you know them. It's a safe bet that it's Pushkin. Yes, he's right, that's all we want: freedom and peace. So it's all happened before, that's what he's saying. The same suffering, the same invasions and battles. We've had to face it once and now we're facing it again. Only the people are different. Everything's happened before and will go on happening.

Yes, it's coming back! I wish he could hear me reciting poetry like this.

> Will Russian earth not rise and bristle
> With steel stubble-glitter?

It's all exactly like now. You'd think Pushkin had visited the Kirov works. You'd think he was with us, watching all this. I must write it down when I get home, before I forget it again. *Steel stubble-glitter*, that was it. I wish I'd remembered that line before, when I was talking to Fedya. He'd have liked it.

25

It's dark by the time Anna reaches the burned building. The charred stench of it catches in her throat. She stands a hundred metres away, watching. There are shadows on the snow ahead, and a couple of bobbing lanterns. They seem to spill light and then wipe it up again without illuminating anything. She grips the rope of her sledge as she approaches the building. Part of the roof has caved in where the shell hit it, and the second and third floors of the building have collapsed along a third of their width.

Heaps of rubble lie on the pavement, but the main entrance has been cleared. As she watches, a shadow flits inside. If people are still going in, then there must be wood left. She moves forward over rough, blackened ridges of ice, where snow has been melted by the fire, and has frozen again. She pulls her scarf closer over mouth and nose, steps across the threshold, and lifts the sledge behind her.

There's someone in front of her, carrying a light that throws his shadow back over her. She does not think of speaking. Each of them moves like a ghost through the ruins, lost in its own dimension. The figure darts sideways, and his light disappears.

But it's still not quite dark. The space closes around her, packed with shadows. On her right a goblin-red light jumps from another doorway. She edges forward silently, and peers into the small room which must have been a vestibule. The floor is churned up, and in the middle a little fire burns, close to a woman who's hacking at a thick column of wood, more than two metres long. The woman's saw looks as if it comes from a child's carpentry set.

'Fuck off out of here. This is mine,' says the woman. She stares up at Anna from where she's squatting over the wood. Her shawl has fallen back on to her shoulders, exposing her face. She looks old, but probably she is young. The saw won't cut, not only because it's a child's toy rather than a tool, but also because the wood is hardwood. Mahogany, probably. A newel post or something like that, put into the house when it was young and magnificent. That woman will never be able to cut it up, and she won't be able to drag it home in one piece, because she's as weak as a cat. But she won't leave it, either. She stares up at Anna, not aggressive any more, and certainly not asking for help. There are only three things to deal with here: the wood, the cold, and her own weakness. None of them is negotiable.

Anna backs out of the room.

She's in the big, bare, stone-floored hallway that stinks of smoke. She feels her way to the stairs, in case the banisters are still there, but her hand touches nothing. Upstairs, something settles with a wheezing sound. There might be stuff worth having up there. It's too late to hope for furniture, but some of the wooden fittings might have been missed. But she stays still, pinned at the foot of the stone stairs, listening to the noise of the building as it settles on itself, dust teeming into crevices, cavity rubble slipping down the inside of walls that hang at crazy angles. If she climbed to the turn of the stairs, she'd be able to look up straight through the gash in the roof.

A door slams. There can't be people still living up there, surely, in the undamaged rooms? No, it's one of those tricks of sound that makes you hear life long after it's finished.

That's why she can't move. It's her father's breathing, back in the apartment, that keeps her pinned here. All her life he's been breathing. Why didn't she count those breaths when she had the chance? Why didn't she stop still and listen, on just one of those bad-tempered mornings when she was late for work and Kolya was whingeing that he didn't want his porridge because he always had porridge every single day? She'd never once stopped to bless the fact that her father still breathed. She certainly never stopped to bless the everyday porridge. Instead she hustled Kolya into leggings, tied his scarf crosswise over his chest and back, crammed him into jacket, fur cap, mittens – and don't forget the extra pair of socks in case the ones he's wearing get wet if the snow goes over the top of his boots – and then hurried him out of the door before he began to sweat. In a rush of spite, she'd even slammed the door as she went out, so that it would wake her father. Why should he sleep?

Anna listens to the noises of the burned building. There's her father's pulse. Weak but steady, it ticks on, like drop after drop of water falling into a basin. Anna shakes her head to get the sound out of her ears, but it goes on. She can't tell if it's real. Perhaps the whole of the city is thinning into a dream, becoming transparent as it starves. In a few more days, if she lives, she'll be able to walk through walls, skim the surface of the Neva, and glide from one side of Leningrad to another at the speed of her own thoughts.

The sound of her father's pulse continues, and she listens. Is she even alive herself? She rolls back the thick cuff of her coat and feels under it. Her arm is thin and cold, but soft. When people die, they go hard as wood. She strips off a glove and puts her hand against her mouth. Yes, she is breathing.

The pulse-sound shifts, steadies, and resolves itself into the tick of a clock, which has survived shelling and fire, and goes on telling the time to no one. The tick grows louder, elbowing her out.

She'll go. She'll get out of this tomb, never mind about the wood. It will all have been taken already.

But as she turns a man comes from the back of the hall, holding a candle, hauling a sack. He stops beside Anna. 'You don't want to hang about here,' he says. 'You want to get off home quick.' Then he too catches the sound of the clock. 'Keeps on going, doesn't it, even though there's no one to wind it up. Stupid, just like us.'

How long has she been standing here? She's wasted too much time already. Whatever made her think she could leave without getting any wood for the *burzhuika*? She must have been crazy. By the retreating light of the man's candle, Anna picks her way to the back of the hall and into the reception room. The light of several candle-stubs sends a dozen shadows swooping up the walls and folding across one another. Heaps of rubbish on the floor turn into women, who crouch there, grunting as they lever up the last few blocks of wood. How vast this room is. It falls away into blackness like a cave. Surely this can never have been an apartment? It's a ballroom, from more than fifty years ago. People would have crowded in here under chandeliers, the naked white shoulders of women gleaming against the men's stiff black. They danced on this floor, those former people.

In the candlelight the diggers look like women on a battlefield, stripping clothes and rings from the dead. The air is thick with effort as they scrabble in the dirt, trying to prise up the wood that remains. When Anna goes too close to a pram which contains five or six lumps of wood, its owner spits like a cat.

But here there's a space. Anna kneels, and harnesses the sledge securely around her waist. She sweeps her hands across the floor in front of her. Nothing but empty grooves where the wood was laid. She twists round and sweeps behind her. Again, nothing. She'll try closer to the wall.

As she crawls, her hands strike a block. Just one. She pulls, but it won't give way. It's firmly stuck, and that's why it's been left for easier pickings. Anna takes out the chisel from the bag around her waist, and begins to lever. There's a suggestion of give, like the first weakness in a sound tooth. She levers again, until the chisel slips and drives into the side of her other hand. Breathing quickly and shallowly to dull the pain, she pulls off her glove and brings her hand up to her mouth. The taste is warm and salt, but as she lips it carefully she can tell it's not a bad cut. Lucky she kept her gloves on. She sucks again, drawing in the taste of her own blood. It tastes good . . .

Now she pulls the glove off her other hand and holds it between her teeth so that she can gouge at the underside of the wood with her bare hand. The block comes out of its socket so suddenly that she falls backward, still clutching the chisel. Anna stuffs her prize into her sack. But she mustn't drag the sledge behind her any more. One of the other women could creep up and take the wood out of her sack without her seeing. Anna crawls forward again, but now the sledge is in front of her, shielded by her body, as she gropes across the ashy, stinking ground.

People are all around the walls, levering up half-charred blocks that remain where fire must have swept around the side of the room. Anna finds her own metre of space, and squeezes in, wedging herself against another woman who's trying to prise up blocks with a knife. She's lit a whole candle, and in its light Anna can see that she's using a solid silver knife with initials twined just above the blade. She doesn't look the monogram type – but then gold and silver travel like lice these days. A silver knife's no good for this anyway. Too soft. She needs a chisel to get those blocks up. Stealthily, Anna applies her own chisel, shielding it with her body so the woman won't spot it. Block by block, the burned wood comes up. It's badly charred, but at least a third of it will still be good for burning in the *burzhuika*. She prises out a couple more. They are looser here, and they come up as sweetly as new potatoes.

'Comrade.' The whisper is hoarse. 'You've got tools, haven't you? Give me a lend of them, just for a minute. I swear I'll give them back.'

Anna's hand tightens on the chisel. Once it's gone she won't get it back. The woman's big, and better fed than Anna. Maybe she's got a knife, a real one tucked away in her belt. Maybe she's seen that Anna's sack is already half-full. Anna does not answer. The whisper begins again, whingeing, singing, and the woman's body barges against hers.

'I swear to God you'll get it back. Let me just get up a few blocks.'

Anna stuffs the chisel under her coat, her skin prickling. A wash of dirty breath flows over her face as the woman's voice rises. 'Igor! Igor! Over here quick! She's taking my wood.' But the woman has been kneeling too long, and her legs have gone to sleep. As she lunges after Anna she loses her balance and falls, snuffing out her own candle.

Now the shadowed hall is safety. Anna flattens herself against the farthest wall, and listens. The woman's voice has died away. No sign of Igor, if he even exists. Anna has the chisel, the sledge, and her half-full sack of wood. That's enough. It was stupid to imagine

I could ever carry two sacks home, thinks Anna, as she ties the sack on to the sledge with her twine. This weight is going to be enough. She'll go a few hundred metres, then she'll have a quarter-slice of bread. That'll be enough to turn the air back into air, instead of thick, resistant glue that leans against you as you try to go forward.

She stiffens at the regular tramp of boots outside the building. Soldiers on patrol. The ones Evgenia talked about, who'll stop you and shoot you on the spot if you've got more food or ration cards than you ought to have. And here she is, in a building she's got no right to enter, with a load of looted wood. But the footsteps don't slacken, although a splodge of light hits the entrance to the apartment building. Imagine, they've got torches. She can even hear their voices, low, hurried and perhaps a little frightened. Yes, you're right, you should be frightened. We should all be frightened of one another these days. And we should be frightened of ourselves.

Now they've passed, and it's time to go out on to the street, into the blessed night air.

They're shelling again. She pauses to get the direction, but it's all right. Nowhere near home. It's coming from over towards Smolny again, by the military headquarters. It's going to be one of those iron nights the bombers love, with a frost so deep that everything can't help sparkling, even when there's only a quarter-moon. The sledge-runners squeak as Anna makes her way slowly down the pathway between drifts of uncleared snow. The streets are empty. It's too cold, and too dangerous. Everyone's indoors, although it can't be five o'clock yet. They are curled in their beds, conserving body-heat while another layer of frost grows on the window-panes. Every window she passes is blank with blackout. It's impossible to tell if the people in the houses are living, or dead. In all the city it seems that she's the only one moving, creeping forward with her load of wood.

But of course, she isn't. At the next crossroads a shadow comes away from the wall and crosses into her path. A man in a fur cap, with a candle-lantern slung over his arm. He opens his lantern, takes out a match, strikes it on the heel of his boot, lights the wick, closes the little glass door again, and holds the light up to Anna's face. He's wearing steel-tipped boots, not felt boots, thinks Anna, hypnotized. Why isn't he wearing felt boots? His feet will freeze.

'Hello, what've we got here?'

His face looks strange. After a second she realizes that it looks unfamiliar because he is fully fleshed. It's a long time since she's seen anyone who looked well-fed.

'What's that in the sack?'

'My brother,' says Anna. 'I'm taking him to the cemetery.'

His eyes are set deep in folds of flesh, and she can't see his expression.

'Poor kid. Littlun, was he?'

'He was five.'

'He looks like a littlun. And that's all you got in there, is it?'

'Of course it is.'

''Cos the reason I ask, is I wouldn't like to think you were telling me the tale. Nice-looking kid, was he?'

'Yes.'

'Let's see, then.'

'No! You can't do that to him. I told you, he's dead, leave him alone.'

For a moment it is Kolya lying on the sledge, like so many other children, stiff and blue. Perhaps her words have killed him.

'No, I won't let you touch him!'

'I won't do your brother any harm. Just having a little look, that's all.'

He's playing with her. He's got the energy to do that. He's not starving. He puts a hand on her arm and she pulls it back.

'Don't worry, darling. I'm not interested in you. A little crow like you's not worth a bite for a man like me. No, it's your brother who's got me all curious.'

He lifts the lantern higher and his eyes glisten at her. They're human eyes set in folds of human flesh, but her skin crawls. Something has been wiped from them, that should be there. He could do anything. It's only chance that'll hold him back. She stands quite still, retreating deep inside herself as his lantern light moves over her. After a long time, he puts his lantern down on the packed snow, and kneels by her sledge. Expertly, he unties Anna's knots, and opens the sack.

'There you are. I knew you were telling me the tale. Funny sort of dead brother this is.'

He upends the sack and tips the wood on to the snow. Thought flickers on and off in Anna like a faulty light. *He'll kill me. He won't kill me.*

'That all you got? Pathetic, I call it. Thought you might have something worth having tucked down the bottom of the sack, but no, you're a real little crow all right. All the same, wood's worth something. Pick it up and put it back in the sack.'

Her fingers blunder. He'll get angry. She's crouched in the snow and he looks down on her from his height. His right leg is by her cheek. The steel-tipped boot shifts, touches her, shifts away. He could smash her skull like an egg. The boot shifts. She shovels wood into the sack. I must live. Kolya in bed, twisting to look at the door, asking where I am. If I die he'll die.

'Not trying to shove a bit of that wood up your jumper, are you?'

'No, no –'

''Cos if you did, I'd have your clothes off you as well.'

He says it calmly, almost pleasantly. The wood's all back in the sack now. She crouches on all fours, looking up at him, not daring to stand until he gives the word. The man lashes the sack of wood back on to the sledge, picks up the rope, and slings it over his shoulder. Without saying anything more, he turns and heads off in the direction from which Anna has come. Anna listens to the squeak of the sledge, until it fades into silence. Stiffly, she scrambles back to her feet.

But he didn't get the chisel, she tells herself. He didn't get the last quarter-slice of bread. She crosses her arms on her chest and beats her hands against her arms to warm herself. She wants to run but she's too cold. At least, he doesn't know where she lives. She swallows down the taste in her mouth, then takes out the piece of bread and cradles it in her hand as she begins to walk down the bare, blank street, grating off crumbs with her teeth and softening them with her tongue.

26

It is much harder to walk without the sledge. Strange that it should be so, when the sledge was heavy to pull. But without its anchor, she might drift anywhere. She might even stop moving, and not know it. No regular squeak of runners behind her now. Only herself, empty-handed, stumbling home through ruts of frozen snow. To the next lamp-post. To the next. To that corner. To the second courtyard entrance.

She passes two more soldiers in their long coats and felt boots, who look at her but don't speak. Shelling's begun again. The air shudders, but nothing comes near. It's not far to go now. A kilometre, no more, and she'll be home.

Behind her, a cough. She turns, and there's the flicker of a candle-lantern. He's after her. He's followed her. She's got nothing, he knows that. Now he's taken her sledge and her load of wood, what more does he want? *I'll have your clothes off you as well.* Anna reaches under her coat and grasps the chisel.

'Anna?'

The voice wavers across the wasteland of ice that separates them. 'Anna, it's you, isn't it? It's me. Evgenia.'

She would never have known that voice, hoarse and cracked like an old woman's. But if Evgenia says so, it must be her. Anna shakes her head to get the numbness of cold out of it. The figure glides across the snow towards her, holding up its lantern.

'Thought it was you. I've been following you, didn't you see me? You've been weaving about all over the place.'

'Have I?'

'Yeah. Let's have a look at you.'

For the second time, a candle-lantern swings up to Anna's face. But now there's Evgenia's sharp yellow face behind it, and her human eyes.

'Here, take my arm.' She links arms with Anna, as if they're two girls off to a dance together. But it's nice, the feeling of Evgenia's arm across her back, supporting her. 'Come on. It's not far.'

'But you're heading the wrong way, Evgenia. I'm going home.'

'You'll never make it like that. We've got to get you warmed up or someone'll find you flopped in a snowdrift tomorrow.'

'I'm not cold, Evgenia, I'm warm.'

'Yeah, you feel warm, but you're freezing. That's what people feel like just before they snuff it. Come on.'

They go on past heaped, dirty-white snowdrifts that gleam in the light of Evgenia's lantern. There's a man propped against the drift, head sunk on to his chest. A rind of yesterday's fresh snow covers his feet. His boots have gone. They turn off the avenue, into a narrow street and then a narrower one. Anna knows these streets. Off the broad public avenue, where the trams run and people walk to shops and offices with quick, firm purpose, into a world of children screeching from apartment window to apartment window, women on doorsteps who stop talking and stare as you pass, and a drunk snarling at nothing.

Now, there isn't a flicker of movement. The streets are canyons of uncleared snow. The windows are masked with blackout. An entire house has been torn out by a shell. All around there's heavy, dead silence, the silence of a mother whom even her own children's crying can't wake.

'Here we are. Up these steps. We're on the third floor.'

The two women pass through a doorway which is fantastically looped and wreathed in ice from a burst pipe above. A stalactite stabs the side of Anna's head. The stairway to the third floor is raw and damp.

'This is us.' Evgenia unlocks the door, and they go in.

The room is warm. Smells of smoke, warm flesh, frowsty bed-clothes, lamp-oil, fat and old boots wash around Anna. She'd almost forgotten it. This is what life smells like.

'Sit down on here.'

It's a bed, covered with heaps of coats. Evgenia kneels down, pulls off Anna's boots and begins to rub her feet.

'How long've you been wandering about like that for? Your feet are like blocks of ice. Let's have a look. No, you're not too bad, you're not frostbitten, but don't go near the stove yet.'

Her feet are hurting now. They didn't hurt all that time when she was walking. Evgenia's pulled off her gloves as well, and now she's rubbing Anna's hands between her own.

'You shouldn't be out after dark. I told you before, it's dangerous. You don't know who's out there.'

'I do know.'

Evgenia looks up. 'What happened?'

'A man took my sledge and the wood I'd found.'

'Yeah, I thought something must've happened. You didn't look like yourself. Did he beat you up?'

'No.'

'You were lucky then. We may have eaten all the real rats, but we've still got the human ones around. He could easily have knocked you over the head. That's all it takes. One shove and you're in the snow and you don't get up.'

'When I saw you, I thought it was him again.'

'I thought you didn't look too pleased to see me.'

Evgenia's voice is so different. Where it used to be full and deep, it's hoarse, as if she's been ill. She looks different too. Thinner, of course, though nowhere near as thin as lots of people. She's not starving, and she's not short of wood either. Just think of leaving a stove lit when you're not even at home. She must have plenty of wood. Yes, there's a pile at the foot of the bed. Good stuff, too. It looks like sawn-up planking from one of the old wooden houses they're tearing down.

'You're still working?'

'Yeah, still working. Though now that the factory's down to twenty per cent production, I do most of my work here.' She points to a corner of the room which is curtained off by a sheet.

'You bring them back here?'

'Well, their balls would drop off if we did it in the street. Besides, they like their home comforts, samovar lit, stove burning and all that. They're a bit more free with their money then.'

Evgenia's teeth show. 'Funny, isn't it, how the real dirty bastards are always the ones who are soft about home and their mothers? Not that they give a flying fuck about anybody else's. I look at some of them and I'm thinking: *Your soul's been squeezed out. There's nothing left in it any more.* But I don't ask them anything. I don't want to know. I tell them Mum's here when I bring them back, so that keeps them in order a bit.'

Anna looks carefully around the room. 'Your mum's here –?'

'There.' Evgenia points to the bed where Anna's sitting. 'Under those coats, up against the wall. She always creeps up close to that wall in her sleep. She sleeps most of the time now.'

'Is she ill?'

'No. She just wants to sleep.' Evgenia is still holding both Anna's hands. 'Things've been hard for her, you see.'

A flash of understanding passes between them. Anna moistens her lips. 'Your little boy?'

'Yes. He had enough to eat, it wasn't that. It was his cough. It went down on his chest. I paid the doctor to come here, but he didn't have anything to give him. Mum sat up holding him for three nights.'

I had a kid, but my mum looks after him, and now he thinks my mum's his mum, if you see what I mean. So I don't interfere.

'What was his name?'

'Gorya. He had a proper burial, I made sure of that. I didn't dump him at the cemetery gates. Mum couldn't come because of her legs, so it was just him and me. I paid a bottle of vodka for them to dig the grave, and I stood over them and made sure they did it right. He was all wrapped up warm. I took him there on the sledge, but it was a long time to wait while they dug because the frost'd gone so deep into the ground. But I wasn't going to go until I'd seen him safely buried. I picked him up and held him. It was just him and me then.'

'When all this is over, you'll set a gravestone for him.'

'Yeah. You know, Anna, the worst bit is, I keep thinking that when all this is over it'll go back to how it was. The dead aren't really dead for ever, only for the duration, if you get what I mean. Like when a kid's playing hide-and-seek and they hide for ages, dead still, until you shout, "It's all right, you can come out now." And they do come out. I think like that even though I saw him buried. And then I start going crazy and thinking maybe it wasn't him. Maybe I only thought it was me standing there holding him. But I don't feel it properly. I think, "Gorya's dead," and that seems normal but not true at the same time, if you see what I mean. And then I think, "What if I start feeling it?" You know, when things are different. When all this is over.'

Anna turns Evgenia's hands over and strokes the palms. 'We can't think about it.'

'You've warmed up a bit, anyway.'

'Yes. I must go soon. They'll be frightened about me at home.'

'It's nice, though, just sitting here talking. I never have time. You sit here for a bit, while I make the tea.'

The room swims in warmth. I'll rest, just for a minute, while she makes the tea. Imagine, a stove with a pile of wood in the corner. And they're eating, you can tell that.

But snow has got into the room somehow. It dances in front of her, and out of it comes a figure, man or woman, walking towards her. The sledge squeaks . . .

'Here. Don't drop it.'

Evgenia places the glass of hot tea in Anna's hand. Its fragrance wreathes around her face. She sips. It's real tea, hot and strong, and there's sugar in it.

'One of my clients gave me half a cup of sugar. Well, if someone gets so drunk he can't see, then he's going to lose stuff, isn't he? I've still got Mum to look after.'

There's a note in her voice Anna's never heard before. Harsh, defiant, but shamed.

'It's these times,' says Anna. 'There I was earlier on, crawling round on the floor of a burned-out apartment building, digging up half-burnt blocks of wood. This woman wanted to borrow my chisel, and I didn't let her. But it's not just that. I'd have stuck the chisel into her if she'd tried to grab it. You find yourself doing things you'd never have thought you could do.'

'That's it. You know you're changing, but you still think you can find the way back to what you used to be. Then one day you know you can't. You've gone through a drunk's pockets and stolen his stuff, and then tipped him out of the door into the snow. And not cared if he froze to death. Well. So how are things with you?'

'My father hasn't got long now. With the rest of us it's only hunger, the same as everyone.'

'I can let you have some wood.'

'But you need it yourself.'

'I can get more. As long as I've got my clients, we're better off than you are. And everyone knows me. Besides, they don't want to come back here and get frostbite in their wedding-tackle, so I usually get to hear of it if there's a wooden house being torn down.'

'Wedding-tackle! Is that what they call it? They don't sound the marrying kind.'

'It's the same as the way they all have a thing about their mums: they like talking nice when they get a chance. Shut up about it now, Anna, Mum's awake.'

The coats stir as if an animal is digging itself out of hibernation. Two small, sharp eyes regard Anna.

'Who's this then, Genia?'

'This is Anna, a friend of mine.'

Evgenia's mother pushes off the coverings and painfully edges her scrawny body off the bed.

'I had such a sleep . . .'

'I know you did, Mum. You've been asleep for hours.'

'I kept hoping I'd dream, but I didn't dream. Is it morning yet?'

'It's evening, Mum. It's not late.'

The old woman hobbles over to the far, shadowy side of the room. She lights a second candle, and Anna sees the embroidered cloth, the little lamp, the icon, the small photograph of a child.

'When are you going to get oil for my lamp, Genia? My beautiful corner's not right without it.'

'When I can, Mum. You know there's no oil in the market now, and we've got to keep what's left for the big lamp. You've got your candle.'

The old woman heaves herself to her knees in front of the icon, and crosses herself repeatedly.

'She's a believer, you can't change that,' says Evgenia quietly. 'That last campaign against backwardness we had, they called us in one by one at the factory and asked if our children were baptized, and if there were any icons in the house. So what could I do? I had to lie. I didn't baptize Gorya, but Mum crept off somewhere and got him done, just like I knew she would.'

Slowly, tremblingly, the old woman leans forward until her lips touch the painted feet of the infant Christ in his mother's arm.

'I must go now.'

'I'll walk with you as far as the Cathedral. Then you'll be all right.' Evgenia bundles wood into a hemp bag.

'Not as much as that, Evgenia.'

'Kids can't keep themselves warm like we can. Take the rest of this sugar for your Kolya.'

Anna watches as Evgenia pours the remaining sugar carefully into a cone of newspaper, and twists the top. 'Evgenia, what about your mother? She'll want that.'

'Look at her.'

The old woman is still keeled forward, whispering.

'You know what she's saying?'

'Evgenia, don't, she'll hear you.'

'She won't. She's deaf. She's giving them her instructions about Gorya. Mind he keeps his jacket buttoned up, and he doesn't like parsnips, so please, merciful Virgin, give him carrots instead. Then at bedtime he has to have his cod-liver oil and he sometimes tries to spit it out, so, my dear one, make sure you watch him till he swallows it.

'It's as much as I can stand to listen to her sometimes. They're a lot more real to her than I am. It's them she wants to be with. I put good food in front of her and she just stares at it as if she doesn't know what it is. Then she goes back to bed, and sleeps, like you saw. Because she doesn't want to live any more. She wants to be with them. But I don't, and I don't know if that's right or wrong. I do want to live. I don't care how bad it is, I still want to live.'

'I know.'

'I knew as soon as I met you that you were like that too. You can tell straight away. Some people don't have it in them, and they just fade away. I could have looked at you and Katya, out there, and known straightaway who that wall was going to fall on. It's not even something we want, it's the way we are. We just have to keep on. Often I think it would be easier to be like Mum now. Only I can't be. So everything I do now, I'm going to have to live with for the rest of my life.'

'I don't see how you can be sure,' says Anna, but even as she says it she knows that Evgenia is right. One look at Evgenia's tough, strong-boned face, and death would back off to find an easier target. God knows there are plenty.

'Mum says these are the latter days,' says Evgenia.

'What does she mean?'

'She's got a little book of prophecies. It says that in the latter days two giant serpents shall do battle until they devour the world with fire and thunder.'

'I can't think who those two serpents could be.'

'Me neither, I keep telling her it's a load of cobblers.' But Evgenia's sharp, ironic eyes are gleaming. 'Still, it wouldn't be a bad bargain if we got rid of two serpents for the price of one, would it?'

'But they'd have already devoured the world.'

'Yeah, there is that. But still . . . *In the latter days, in the time of blood,*" Evgenia quotes. 'That's what her book says.'

They go to the door.

'She'll be there for hours,' whispers Evgenia, glancing back at her mother.

'It's hard for you.'

'I wish she'd just talk to me.'

'A doctor I know says it's hunger that's making everyone so strange. It's nothing personal.'

'She's not hungry. I make sure of that. But what's the point of me doing all this, if she won't eat?'

'Evgenia –'

'It's all right. I'm just being stupid.'

They are in each other's arms. They are rocking each other.

'It's all right, it'll all be over soon, it'll get better, have a good cry . . .'

For a long time they cling. Five minutes, maybe ten. The minutes belong only to them. Then Evgenia draws away, wiping her cheeks.

'We'd better get going. I'll see you on your way.'

'I'll be fine.'

'I know. As long as you don't –'

'– waste –'

'– bloody –'

'Was it bloody she said, or fucking?'

'Bloody.'

'*Sausage,*' they say, both together, their faces only centimetres apart.

In the latter days, in the time of blood . . . But here, there's no blood. Snow lies congealed on the roofs, and blood congeals in the bodies that loll in frozen parks. Not a drop spills, all through the long night. This is Peter's city, built on the marshes of the Baltic. Labourers brought soil to build it on, carrying soil in the hems of their cloaks. They laid down their bones and the city walked over them. They sank down. When there were enough of them, Peter had his foundations.

Late in the morning a lilac-coloured dawn will come, with burning frost that glitters on branches, on spills of frozen water, on snow, cupolas and boarded-up statues. Nothing has ever been more beautiful than these broad avenues, the snow-coloured Neva, the parks and embankments. Only the people mar its perfection as they crawl out of their homes into the radiance of snow. Perhaps today is the day when they'll fail to reach the bread queue. So they move on, flies caught between sheets of glass.

27

The December death-toll is mounting. The figures can't be accurate, because not all the dead find their way to cemeteries or to common graves dynamited out of frozen earth. It's impossible to count those who lie frozen in their homes, or covered in snow, on their way to a destination nobody remembers. Pavlov sees them, as everyone else sees them. A foot sticking out of a snowdrift here, a bundle face-down on the Neva ice. Those dead don't go away. They aren't buried, and they won't decay. There will be a major public health crisis once spring comes, thinks Pavlov automatically, then he turns his mind away. That is not his problem.

Pavlov's problem is the next day, and the one after. His job is to inch Leningrad towards life. His job is life, although he understands that there must be death, and sometimes there is so much of it that it seems to come off on his hands, like newsprint.

On available statistics the deaths for December look as if they'll be four or five times November's figures.

'We're coming up to forty thousand.'

'Are you sure? Have those figures been checked and confirmed?' raps out Pavlov. 'I need an accurate picture.'

He's got to know how many ration cards will not be re-registered at the beginning of next month. Now that everyone has to appear in person to re-register his or her card each month, the dead can't distort the system with their 'ghost' rations. It makes fraud more difficult, although still not difficult enough.

Fraud, black market and theft are distorting his statistics. Pavlov rubs his eyes. The penalty for any misappropriation of food must be summary. That is no problem. That is already happening. Black-marketeers, thieves and ration-card forgers can expect no mercy. Those who manipulate the system from within are the worst, and must be punished most harshly and publicly, so that examples are made. The problem is that when so many are dying, the death penalty loses its edge.

So much flour, so much sugar, so much fat. High-protein airlifts are coming in, but quantities are pitiful. Fifty or sixty tons of high-calorie food a day, against a target of two hundred tons. Sometimes the planes are grounded, and nothing arrives. But whatever the military airlift brings, it won't fill those millions of mouths.

The ice road over Lake Ladoga is what's going to save the city, if anything will. But progress on that front is still slow. So many trucks have gone through the ice, or broken down, and those that are left take nearly three times the projected journey time. Blizzards often make it close to impossible for trucks to navigate from one station on the ice to the next, and when the sky's clear, the German bombers come. It's a heroic struggle, of course it is. Everything's heroic. You can take that for granted, but it's not the point. Pavlov's pen rests on his paper. He looks up, calculating. His eyes are reddened with smoke and lack of sleep, but he's a strong man, and he knows how far he can drive himself.

The Kirov works have just had to stop production, although the workers are still there, heroically defending the factory, sleeping in shifts, staying at their posts even when they can't stand up. But producing nothing.

We don't need any more heroes, we need tanks. We need anti-aircraft batteries, and engineers with spare parts. Even when supplies have got safely over the ice, there's the nightmare of the single-track line from Lake Ladoga to Leningrad. Railway staff are starving like everyone else. They can't keep the line clear, and it needs constant repair after regular bombing raids. There's not enough fuel for the engines, there's a shortage of skilled manpower, and they can't even get together enough up-to-strength gangs to clear the lines and points.

'Here are the latest figures.'

More figures on thin paper in front of him. Hungrily, his mind seizes on the statistics. That's Pavlov's gift: figures don't overwhelm him, they sharpen him. At once the new figures slot into their place in the latest of the plans he's had to make on the wing fifty times this winter. He knows they call him the Food Tsar behind his back, but he takes it as a compliment. Besides, he doesn't underestimate his enemy. Pavlov knows his Nekrasov. *The greatest Tsar of all is hunger* – Nekrasov got it right about that. But it's no good cowering before hunger. No, you've got to keep your head and attack, before it's too late. Get that Irinovsky line going, no matter what it takes. Get the ice road up to full production, the way it should be. Never mind if those bastards bomb the railway night and day. Get the gangs on to the line and repair it every time. If those in charge can't organize, shoot them.

Of course there'll be losses. So do it now, before the deaths rise any more. Corpses can't clear railway lines, or man the stations on the ice. He knows that military command is with him on this. He's talked to Zhdanov.

Those on the lowest ration-level can't live for long, unless they have private stores of hoarded food. It's unlikely that they'll have such stores, after almost three months of mounting hunger, any more than they'll have fat left on their bodies. The fat is all burned off. The cupboards are stripped. These people now receive two slices of adulterated bread each day. Because their body-fat has gone, their muscle is being consumed by the engine of their bodies. They drop dead from hypothermia, heart failure, exhaustion, and all those diseases that have a thousand names but come to the same thing: starvation.

'Deaths reported from dystrophy and other starvation-related diseases . . .' drones a voice behind him.

'Kindly don't waste my time giving me that information again,' snaps Pavlov. 'I am familiar with the pathology. I want precise figures for the amount of flour in storage at the West Ladoga warehouses. It is essential that all possible efforts are made to increase the volume of supplies brought in over the ice road.'

Like body-fat, the number of those into whose mouths he must put food is melting.

'Thirty thousand deaths, you say? Forty? Forty-five?'

The numbers are written in columns. In other columns, the tonnage of flour, fat, sugar, meat is noted just as meticulously. When he cut the ration at the end of November, a raw stenographer blurted out, 'But people will die!' and then went white, realizing what she had said. There was no one else in the room. If there had been, he would have had to take action.

'Do you think I have no human feeling?' asked Pavlov quickly.

'No – of course not – I didn't intend –'

'I take responsibility, do you understand that?'

'Yes –'

She doesn't understand, and she can't understand. To be the one who writes the order is not pleasant, even when you know it's the only thing to be done. He's writing history, but at the same time history is writing him. He hasn't got the choice that girl thinks he has. And back in Moscow, the Boss is watching him.

But things will change. They have got to. Pavlov can sense a change which can't yet be seen or heard or felt. It's like a certain rawness in the air after months of dry frost. Hundreds of kilometres to the south there's a warm wind stirring, although the frozen river doesn't know this yet. These are not things you can know or understand, but you sense them, and your blood stirs with them. No, it's true, these really are the greatest pleasures of all, those pleasures you don't really understand.

Pavlov has leaned forward. His hands grip the desk. He is not in grey, winter-haunted Leningrad now, but in a village eighty miles south-west of Moscow, standing on a shallow cliff above a river where the ice is breaking. Thick sheets of ice bump and grind against one another. Some are forced underwater by the pressure of the current racing over them. The air's full of the noise of water, rushing and urgent, and all at once he realizes how long and silent the winter has been. A bird flies low over the surface of the river, skims it, and then rises over the wooded opposite bank. There's a smell of mud, and raw, churning water, and surely the light over those folded hills is clearer now? It picks out their curves like a promise.

So many tons at West Ladoga, so many tons stored in Leningrad, so many on their way to Leningrad across the ice road. It's the third week in December, the coldest and darkest week of all, when the pulse of life sinks lowest. It's not dramatic to die of hunger. No one has the strength to run into the streets, bleeding and cursing. This is an invisible disaster, like the death of a hive in winter. But when it's spring and the hive's opened, it will all become clear. Like cells, the apartment houses of Leningrad will be packed with bodies, shrivelled and blackened with frost.

Pavlov pulls another piece of paper towards him. On it he sketches a graph plotting the rise in the death rate against the cuts he has made in rations. He arrives at mid-December, pauses, then continues, extrapolating into the January that has not yet arrived. Assume no rise in the ration. Assume that the death rate follows the December pattern. No further cuts, but no rise. Dependants remain on 125 grammes of bread per day. On through January, into February. The angle of his graph points at the sky, carrying the lives of more than half the population of Leningrad with it. It goes on up. They die faster.

He looks again at his up-to-date lists of reserve food supplies. His reserves are pitiful. All they guarantee is a few more days' bare survival. If he increases the ration by as much as twenty grammes, the risk is appalling. But leave it like this, and the citizens of Leningrad will die anyway. There's only one thing that gives him any room for manoeuvre, and that's the potential of the ice road. Not what it's done for Leningrad so far, certainly: but what it might do. He lifts the telephone, pulling graph and statistics in front of him, and makes a call to Zhdanov and the Leningrad Military Command.

Hours later, Pavlov picks up his graph of the projected Leningrad death rate and scrutinizes it again. Then he strikes a match, holds a corner of the paper to it, and lets it burn. He doesn't need it, because the figures are printed on his mind. And besides, it's a document that doesn't need to be seen by anyone, especially by that stenographer with the white face who said, 'But people will die!' Blackness scrolls up the side of the paper. Only when the flame is about to touch his fingers does he blow it out, and crush the burnt paper to ash.

On the twenty-fifth of December, the daily bread-ration will be increased by a hundred grammes for workers, and seventy-five grammes for dependants.

*

But the stenographer was perfectly right. In another part of Leningrad, on Vasilievsky Island, three days later, a child opens her notebook. It's a small notebook, made to fit in a pocket, like an address book. The letters of the alphabet run down the right-hand side. In the clear handwriting of a well-taught eleven-year-old she writes her first entry.

Zhena. She goes back and underlines the word, *Zhena*. *She died on 28th Dec. at 12.30 in the morning, 1941.*

In future entries, she will not underline the names. She will record the deaths of her family one by one, until they are all there. At the end she'll write: *The Savichevi are dead. They are all dead. Only Tanya is still here.*

Pavlov, too, is perfectly correct. He's writing history, while history writes him. He rubs his eyes. His colleague watches from across the room. Pavlov frightens him, but it's not fear he feels at this moment, but something else, closer to pity.

28

It is ten past midnight. Darkness, stillness, cold. A savage cold that is strong enough to halt the beat of blood, strong enough to turn the dead into logs of frost.

All four of them huddle together, sharing their body heat. They're fully dressed down to hats with ear-flaps, gloves and scarfs. At the foot of the mattresses four pairs of boots stand ready. The ventilation window has been mended with layers of cardboard where a shell-burst shattered it two weeks ago. The other windows are crusted with frost, inside and outside. Outside, an ice-laden wind sifts the snow into whirling demons at empty street-corners.

But it's dark, dark. Nothing of this can be seen. There's only the savagery of cold, like an animal prowling the room, lashing every inch of exposed skin. Outside, the midnight temperature is eighteen degrees below zero. It has been dark since three o'clock, and it will be dark late into the morning. Long, long hours when there's nothing to do but cling together and keep alive.

If she touched the *burzhuika* now, its freezing metal would stick to her palm. Tomorrow they'll burn more books. Thank God there are books to burn.

He doesn't see the burning of his books. Four people lie together in one room, but in the next he's alone. He lies on his back, his nose jutting into the cold. His hands are folded on his breast, and they hold a book. His skin is glazed solid. The cold can rage around him as much as it likes, but it can't do him any harm. He's part of it now. It has cauterized his wounds. There's no smell of sickness any more, and although death has come into the room it too remains frozen, dormant, like a winter visitor who will only come to life with the spring.

'Are you asleep?'

'No, are you?'

'No.'

'How's the little one?'

'Sleeping.'

'You're sure?'

'Yes, sure. But his feet are cold.'

'Give me your hand.'

In their cave of rugs and blankets, two hands meet. There is no warmth in the touch. Two hands, stiff, chill, claw-like, fold into one another. They are not male or female any more. But they are alive. One hand stretched out to another, touching. From the child there is a sudden, spasmodic explosion of coughing. His body shakes, his chest rattles, but he doesn't wake. Andrei and Anna press closer, one on each side of Kolya's body, warming it as much as they can.

'Marina's sleeping?'

'Yes,' says Anna. 'She's sleeping. It's only sleep.'

Kolya shakes and coughs. Anna undoes her coat and pulls him inside. Slowly, with stiff fingers, she buttons her coat back over them both. He burrows into her, choking against the skin of her neck. She rubs his back and tucks his feet between her hollow thighs.

The four of them, musty in clothes that they don't take off at night. Four pairs of boots stand by the mattresses, and when they crawl from their cave of blankets into the freezing room, all they have to do is step into them. But everything takes so long. It hurts to breathe. You get palpitations.

Marina is curled into a ball at Anna's back, turned away from the others, her fist pressed into the hollow under her cheekbone. Imagine being asleep, and dreaming. Dreams of food. Dreams of fragrant, smoking-hot soup made with dried mushrooms. Tiny dumplings float on top of it, golden and puffy . . .

Kolya's honey. The glass jar is almost empty. Only one spoonful left.

Things will get better. They've got to. The blockade will be lifted. Our forces will take back Mga and the Moscow railway will re-open. The circle of siege will break.

Only Kolya's honey stretches between this time, now, and then, when things will be better. A thin, dark, sweet thread, smelling of heather and smoke. One spoonful. They'll all watch, while Anna lifts the spoon to Kolya's mouth.

'There, slowly, don't gobble it.'

In go the precious calories and vitamins. Is it their imagination, or is there a little more colour in Kolya's wasted cheeks as he swallows? Anna reaches out, catches on her finger a drop which has fallen from the spoon on to the side of the glass jar, and puts her finger into the child's mouth to suck. He sucks and keeps on sucking long after the sweetness has gone. On these threads they hang.

The honey jar is here, wedged against the mattress. If thieves broke in, they wouldn't find it. Anna fingers it. The pain in her stomach sharpens. She snatches her hand back into the cave of blankets.

The cold, dead rooms of the apartment lean over her. Each frozen cell hangs suspended in the comb of the apartment building. Below, there are the icy, ringing staircases, the courtyard shrouded in snow, the unswept pavements, the shell-damaged buildings, the bomb-sites, the inner-city defences she helped to construct back in September, in another life. Beyond them, the iron ring of the invading army, pressing on Leningrad's neck. There is Leningrad, paralysed like her own flesh and blood.

Kolya is sucking in his sleep. His lips move against her neck, rooting for food like the baby he was five years ago. Andrei is silent. He's asleep again, like Marina. His hand has fallen away from hers.

These are the most difficult hours, the hours after midnight, when day is still unimaginably far off. Anna drowses, jerks suddenly out of sleep, then drowses again. Her stomach hurts. She draws up her knees, cradling Kolya. Her toes are itching, but she can't reach them.

It sounds as if death is walking about in the next room. Its footsteps are clear, and close.

Tomorrow, the fight for food, for warmth, for one more day's survival. Tomorrow, once again, they won't take her father's body to the cemetery. If Kolya's little sledge hadn't been stolen, they might have managed it. Her father will have to stay here, and it's been six days now. Or is it seven? Time's slipping, like the mat of blankets. She begins to count back. It was on the Thursday – no, the day before –

Tomorrow the honey will be gone. Don't think of it now. Kolya's heart ticks against her breastbone. Do children's hearts normally beat as fast as this? He whimpers, but doesn't cough. That's right, sleep, sleep. They can't blockade your sleep.

The night passes.

Then it's night again.

Nine days now since her father's death – or is it ten? It's two o'clock in the afternoon. The sun comes out, and its light pushes through crisscrossed paper into the room where Anna's father lies. The room grows radiant. Shadows of frost leaf and frost petal settle on the mound of Mikhail's body. His beard sparkles, but he sleeps on in frigid silence, as he has slept for ten days now. Or is it nine? Now the sunlight vanishes as the sky grows yellow with coming snow.

The bakeries opened late again. Today it was because a shortage of water delayed the baking of bread. When Anna got back with the rations, Andrei was already home from the hospital, after a night shift. He ought to sleep there all the time, like the other doctors, but he still insists on coming home whenever he can. He got a lift on a truck this time, he tells her. It's crazy to use up his energy like that, but she's given up arguing about it. She only argued from duty: she wants him here.

Andrei is asleep, with Kolya in his arms, when Anna comes in. She stoops to check Kolya's breathing. His face is peaceful, locked in sleep. His cough's getting better now. This is his best and deepest sleep, the midday sleep after the midday meal of bread soup. He'll have had a couple of spoonfuls of buckwheat porridge today, as well. They've got into a system of eating half their rations as late in the evening as they can, and the other half at noon. That way, it doesn't matter how late Anna gets backs with the bread. They've at least got something to eat at noon. And if, one day, the bakery doesn't open at all, or something happened to Anna, they could keep going until the following day. They would never have to say to Kolya: *There's nothing to eat today.*

Seventeen hours to endure, between seven in the evening and noon the next day. This morning Anna rinsed the empty honey jar with hot water for Kolya. The rest of them had hot water flavoured with nettle tea that Anna dries after use, and then re-uses. She puts a pinch of salt in the tea. Salt stops you feeling dizzy.

If only her father hadn't died so close to the end of the month. They were only able to claim his ration for a few days after he died, then it was re-registration time. Everyone must re-register in person. If someone dies at the beginning of the month, just after registration, you do well. As much as thirty days of extra rations. As it was, Anna dried a half-slice of the extra bread from her father's ration over the *burzhuika* each day, and put it away. The seven half-slices are hidden in a vase with a heavy plate over it. She checks them every morning to make sure mice haven't got at them, although there don't seem to be mice around any more. Cats, crows, dogs and pigeons have all been eaten. People are eating rats, and rats are eating people, in apartments where the dead lie on the floor in puddles of ice.

Perhaps someone in their apartment building has trapped and eaten the mice. Or more likely, the mice know that there's no living for them here, not even a crumb. They've broken the blockade and gone to the German lines.

She lifts the plate. There is the dried bread, untouched. If the ration's cut again, or Kolya gets another illness, at least she's got something in reserve. Or if he cries too much. Now that he's getting over his illness, he cries more.

'Anna,' he said one day, 'when are you going to make my soup?'

'What soup, Kolyenka?'

'You always make me soup when I've been ill, to build me up again.' He looked at her reproachfully, like an old man. He remembered the chicken soup she used to make after anyone had been ill, flavoured with parsley and a handful of dried chanterelles. It was golden, flecked with green, with the faintest pearling of chicken-fat on its surface. If she had the flour she would make wheat dumplings as well, feather-light and floating. Kolya used to love it when he was allowed to lower the dumplings one by one on their slotted spoon, and watch them sink to the bottom of the pan before they swelled and rose to the surface. The dumplings absorbed any excess fat so that the soup's texture was perfect.

Kolya was still talking. '*You know*, Anna, your chicken soup. I like that soup.'

Anna swallowed the gush of saliva in her mouth.

'I'll make you some soup.'

She made him bread-soup, crumbling a half-slice in water and heating it over the stove with a pinch of salt. He drank it greedily, like a convict, clutching the cup to him.

Yes, Kolya's getting better, but he's so weak they don't let him out of the one room they can keep above freezing. The pipes in the bathroom are frozen anyway, so he doesn't need to go in there. The toilet's frozen too. They use an old chamber-pot which Anna empties into a snowdrift in the yard. Sometimes she hasn't got the strength to carry it downstairs, and then she puts the pot out on the landing, its sullen stew of urine and faeces covered by a tin plate. It's so cold that soon the chamber-pot freezes, too, and the next time she goes down to the yard she has to hack out the frozen sludge before she can throw it away. Everything takes so long. Every day she is slower. Her hands are stiff, joints swollen, fingers raw. She cut the web of skin between thumb and finger on her left hand, when she was chopping wood, and it won't heal. She's never been clumsy like that before.

Evgenia's wood is all gone, but Andrei got another sackful when the wooden fence around the hospital was torn down, and there are still books to burn. Her father's Shakespeare is on the shelf above his bed.

Anna draws the quilt up around the back of Andrei's head. But where's Marina? The *burzhuika* is almost out. Anna opens the stove, where the fire is down to red ash. Kneeling, she teases it with scraps of paper and splinters of wood until flames lick up out of the ash. She makes a little wigwam of kindling, and then adds two larger chunks of fencing. Even in here, with the stove going, the windows are blank with frost. Yesterday the temperature outside fell to twenty degrees below zero. The radio says that newspaper pads should be used to wrap children's chests. Newspaper, because of its insulating properties, provides excellent protection. If you have no newspaper, you can take a book apart and stitch layers of pages into a child's vest. You might think it was better to burn the book as fuel, but in the fight against cold you need long-term weapons as well as short-term ones. A paediatrician gave details of how she had stitched together layers of Tolstoy into a vest for her six-year-old son.

The door to the kitchen is closed.

'Marina?' But no one answers. Perhaps she's gone down for water. But what if she can't carry it back up, the way she couldn't last time? What if Anna's got to haul the water upstairs and support Marina as well? It's bad enough to make the ascent alone with a bucket of water. She has to grope her way upwards because the lights don't work, stopping every few steps, terrified of slipping on a patch of ice left where someone else spilled their water. Tears of anger and weakness spring to Anna's eyes.

'Marina?'

'I'm here,' answers Marina, from behind the closed door of Anna's father's room. Anna hasn't been in there since he was laid to rest. She pushes the door, and it opens easily, sending out a coil of freezing air. Quickly, she steps inside and shuts the door behind her so Kolya won't be chilled.

There's a light fur of frost on her father's face. He lies on his back, with a book between his hands. It's a battered volume of Pushkin, folded there by Marina before Mikhail's body stiffened. Marina, wrapped in coat and shawl, sits beside the bed. The shawl is wound around her face, so that only her eyes show as she turns to the door. But her hands are bare and they are wrapped around Mikhail's.

'But Marina, your hands – you'll get frostbite. You mustn't stay in here.'

She lifts Marina's hands. They are stiff, marbled blue and red.

Anna rubs them between her own, as Evgenia did. Marina's hands feel dead between hers.

'It's all right,' says Marina. 'I've only just taken off my gloves. I wanted to touch him.'

Anna continues to rub for a while, then fumbles Marina's fingers back into their gloves. Marina doesn't help her. She seems not to understand why Anna is moving her hands about.

'We can't stay in here. You could freeze to death.'

'It's all right. You go in the other room. It's just that I wanted to be with him for a while,' Marina explains, as if everything is perfectly normal.

It's normal for a dead man to stay in the next room until he's covered with a pall of frost. It's the same in rooms all over Leningrad. Anna knows that, because she's talked to other women in the queues.

'I'm alone now, but he's still with me. I've made a corner for him.'

In some rooms, whole families lie and wait for spring.

They can't bury her father yet. The ground's too hard. Crowds of bodies are piled at the cemetery gates, waiting. And even if there were graves, their combined strength wouldn't get her father down all those stairs. And there's no sledge, she finds herself explaining to him. And so we've got to keep you here, we can't help it –

He has drawn her close to him, too. She's right by the bedside now. There's the Shakespeare on the shelf above her father's head. Seven volumes, with their red leather covers and thick, creamy sheets of paper. Marina sees her glance, and says, 'But it was his Pushkin he wanted.'

'Did he tell you that?'

Marina pulls her shawl down so her mouth is uncovered. 'No. But I knew.' Her pallid, drawn face lightens. 'Do you remember what happens after the duel?

> Onegin rushes to the youth,
> Peers at him, calls his name – useless:
> He's gone.

And how Zaretsky puts Lensky into the sleigh, cold and dead? Remember that? And so it's all happening again, exactly as Pushkin said. It happened to Pushkin, and it's happening to your father. The snow, and the sledges, and the dead man. Did you ever hear your father read that passage?'

'I don't remember it. But he was always reading Pushkin.'

'Of course. I remember him reading it aloud one evening. No, he

261

wasn't reading, he was reciting it. He had the book in front of him, but he knew it by heart. His eyes were closed. He didn't need the book, but I think he liked the feel of it in his hands.'

'Yes, I remember. He used to say his memory was going, and that's why he always had the book.'

Her father in his chair, perfectly upright, face raised up a little, eyes shut, mouth faintly smiling. He would begin to recite, and she would listen for a while and then become bored – or perhaps not bored, exactly, but restless. She'd want to be elsewhere. And then Kolya would clatter in wanting something to eat, and she'd have an excuse to get away. All those pieces of paper he was always writing on. What was going to become of them? She'd tried to read his stories, but she had never enjoyed them. Everything in them had to be explained to her.

Don't think of that now.

'He didn't recite like an actor, so that you became aware of him and his personality,' said Marina. 'He had too much respect for the life of the poem.'

'Marina, you must come out of here.'

'Could you draw him for me now, Anna?'

'What? As he is?'

'Yes.'

'I can't.'

'He'll be forgotten. All of it will be forgotten and they'll say it never happened.'

'You've got to stay alive yourself, if you don't want things to be forgotten.'

'Get your paper, Anna. Please. Just a quick sketch. We've got to have a record.'

'My paper's finished.'

'You could draw in one of his books. The Shakespeare. That's got wide margins. And the end-papers are good.'

Stiffly, Marina stretches up and lifts down the book. 'Look, I've even got a pencil. Draw him. Please. Otherwise it will all disappear.'

'You promise you'll come out of here and sit by the stove when I've done it?'

'I promise.'

Anna draws badly, with gloved hands. She's not going to risk frostbite for this. And she's angry with Marina, for making her look at what she doesn't want to see. The trouble with drawing is that you have to look, if it's going to be any good.

Her father, who is now iron flesh on an iron bed. His head is uncovered, and there's ice in his hair. She draws the wasted lines of cheek and jaw, the jut of his nose, and the bony hollows of his temples. She draws carefully, as if she loves what's lying there. But she doesn't. He's gone, and Marina suffered for nothing when she touched him with her bare hands like that. He's somewhere else, not thinking about them at all.

But Marina — no, Marina doesn't understand that. She believes that they are together, her and Misha, as she always calls him now. She's not afraid of him. She leans forward to watch the lines as they sprout from Anna's pencil.

'That's him,' she murmurs. 'You're right, do it like that.'

The sketch is done. Anna hands the book to Marina, averting her face from her father.

'You promised you'd come away now.'

'Yes, I will. You don't understand how important this is, Anna. I can see that you don't like it. But that's because you don't understand, not because I'm wrong. Your father was a great man.'

And suddenly everything changes. Anna turns and looks at her father, but this time without anger. He's gone, he's where he wants to be. And he's a lump of frozen meat, but also he's magnificent, with the book between his hands and his nose jutting at the ceiling. He is what he is. He hasn't changed.

'Maybe he was born to bring a blessing
Or even great things to this world.
His silenced lyre might have sent music echoing
Through times to come like thunder. For this poet
Maybe, on the ladder of the ages
A high rung waited. Maybe his martyr's spirit
Carried away with it a holy secret . . .'

263

goes on Marina. 'Surely you remember, Anna, how your father used to recite that passage?'

'Yes, yes, I think so,' answers Anna, and this time she really thinks she does remember. And now it doesn't matter that Marina's wrong, that her father's stories are dull and hard to understand, and that even if they keep all those pieces of paper nobody will want to read them. He wasn't a great man, but that's of no importance at all.

She does remember. At the dacha, under the honeysuckle, her father with his book, a heavy cloud of the Sokolovs' bees booming in the blossom, and then the words spilling quietly out from the shade where he sat to the verandah where Anna stirred her cloudberry jam over the stove. Her father, upright, preoccupied and slightly absurd, turns and gives her his rare, sweet smile. *'How's that jam getting on? It smells wonderful. Cloudberries always make the best jam of all.'*

Was that what he said? Something, anyway, that made her wave the wooden spoon at him in greeting so that little drops of cloudberry jam spattered her blue cotton dress.

'Yes, I remember,' she says. Marina nods, satisfied.

29

Marina is so cold she's barely able to reach the stove. She hobbles across the room, leaning on Anna. Shudders run through her and into Anna.

'Here. Sit down.' Anna speaks gently, although she wants to shake Marina off and push her into the chair. But Marina continues to stand stiffly. The cold has got into her, as Anna knew it would. She's been holding hands with the dead, and you mustn't do that. You must let go straight away, as soon as they touch you.

Anna presses her down into the chair.

'Stay there, warm yourself,' she says. But she can't leave Marina. They are trapped together, in their dark wood. There, the trees grow so thickly that rain and sun don't spill through. There's a bed of brown needles, and sometimes the skeleton of a bird that has hidden itself away to die. Anna stares around for rescue, and there is the heap of Kolya and Andrei, sleeping. She can only see the back of their heads, in their fur caps. Kolya always wears his fur cap now without any arguments, because Andrei wears one.

'At home, hunters always sleep in their clothes like this. They make a shelter out of pine bark, and they plaster it with snow, and then they're quite warm. Snow is an insulator, you see, Kolya.'

'Is it? Can we make one of those shelters?'

'Yes, why not? When it's safe to go out in the forest again.'

'You and me and Anna.'

The birds will come back. There'll be orioles in the woods again, and corncrakes where the meadow flows into the stream, down by the Sokolov farmhouse. There'll be the upheaval of spring again. Tumult of birds drilling out song in the wet branches. There'll be ice breaking on the Neva, sparks of green on black earth, morning light as sharp as lemons, and a rush of brown froth where snow-water melts. It will all come back again. I believe in it, says Anna to herself, folding her hands around Marina's knuckles.

'What a beautiful colour,' says Marina. She's looking intently at the scrap of Turkish rug under her feet. It's almost threadbare, but it's been an article of faith all Anna's life that 'It's valuable, you know. Hand-made. You can't get rugs like it now.' The colour is dark, subtle crimson, shading into deep brown. 'Really beautiful.'

'It's worn out,' says Anna.

'But I'm glad you use it. You should use beautiful things, not put them away.'

Andrei and Kolya have woken. Andrei takes off his blanket, warm from his body, and wraps it around Marina so that she's tented from head to foot, with an open flap to gather the heat of the stove. Anna puts water on to heat.

'Tea, Marina. That'll make you feel better.'

'Look in my boots,' mumbles Marina from inside her blanket cave.

'In your boots?' All this has finally sent her crazy. 'Your boots are on your feet, Marina. Your feet are in them.'

'Not these. My other ones.'

'She means her felt boots,' says Kolya, in the languid, unchild-like voice that makes Anna's hair crisp with fear. 'They're in the kitchen.'

They aren't really Marina's felt boots. They were Vera's. They were always too small for Anna, but they've been kept for years, carefully packed with newspaper and camphor balls. Who would ever get rid of a pair of felt boots? When the first snow came, her father had remembered them for Marina. To Anna's annoyance, they fitted Marina perfectly.

'Yes,' says Marina, 'in the kitchen. Look inside them, Anna.'

The boots are behind the kitchen door. Anna lifts them. They're heavier than they should be. She puts her hand into the right boot, and her touch meets cold glass. She draws out a small pot of jam, labelled in Marina's bold, spear-like handwriting: *Raspberry jam, 1940.* She reaches into the left boot, and there, too, is a jar. This time, the jam is cloudberry. They are small jars, holding about four hundred grammes each. How has Marina done it? How has she had the strength to hold these back?

'Marina!'

'Bring it here. We'll have tea with jam. But this is the last of it, Anna, it's all I've got. I hid them away. But now's the time to eat it, because it won't get any worse than this.'

'What is it, Anna?' calls Kolya, looking at his sister in the doorway, her face blazing, tears sliding down her cheeks as she holds up the two jars of jam, one in each fist, like a boxer in triumph after the last, bloody, flesh-pulping round.

'Jam.'

'Jam!'

They swoop on Marina, clutching her, hugging one another, on their knees and tangled in blanket. Kolya butts his head into Marina's lap. 'Jam, jam, jam!' He shoves against her. He claws at her clothes. 'Jam, Marina! Jam!'

'Look, raspberry jam!' Anna holds it up to the light and the seeds hang like points of straw in ruby flesh.

'And cloudberry . . .' says Andrei. 'Cloudberry – it's my favourite.'

For weeks they haven't dared let such words out of their mouths. They don't dare talk about the food of the past, though they're obsessed by it. Each one of them is locked in silent, separate craving. Little savoury pasties packed with jelly and rich meat. Blini with red caviar and white sour cream. 'That ice-cream I had last summer – and I didn't even finish it.' And the ice-cream marches across your mind to torment you. Chocolate Eskimo, glistening, rich with cream and sugar, scented with vanilla, sliding across the tongue, dripping to the ground, half of it wasted, not even thought about – how could you have done that?

Raspberry, cloudberry. They sit between her hands, dark, glistening, packed with sugar, sealed with transparent circles of waxed paper.

'Look at it. See how clear it is.'

'Packed with vitamins,' says Andrei, examining the jars. His fingers shake and the glass chinks lightly. 'Anti-scorbutic – and so much nicer to take than boiled pine-needles.'

Many of his patients have scurvy now. In hospital they are given essence prepared from pine-needles. Andrei has obtained the formula, and made an evil-tasting liquid which everyone has to take daily.

'Careful, be careful with those jars. Wait, I'll get saucers and spoons.'

Anna comes back with four spoons, and twists the cap on the cloudberry jam. 'We'll give Kolya his first. Here, open your mouth.' He tips his head back, opens his mouth wide, and shuts his eyes. His foul, starved breath makes Anna's eyes sting as she carefully places the spoonful of jam in his mouth. 'Don't swallow it all at once. Taste it.'

The child's body shudders all over. He holds the jam in his mouth heroically, his eyes watering, then he gulps it down. He opens his eyes. 'More.'

'In a minute.'

'More.'

She spoons in more.

'Now wait. It's not good to have too much at once.'

The adults hold back until the water has boiled and Anna has made tea.

'You're a real Stakhanovite, Anna, making all this tea out of nothing.'

'Yes, I should send a sample to our great leader. *Life has become better, life has become more cheerful.* And here's the proof of it. Here, Kolya, your tea. And which jam do you want this time, raspberry or cloudberry?'

Kolya frowns, savouring choice. 'Raspberry. But, Anna, I don't really remember what raspberries taste like. They don't look like I thought.'

'Here you are. Open your mouth for a spoonful and then I'll put some on your saucer.'

'Not too much,' says Andrei. 'He's not used to it. Take it slowly.'

'There now, good boy, you've had two spoonfuls. Slow down a bit. Smell it first. Isn't it wonderful?'

Kolya lifts the saucer to his nose and snuffs the fragrance of raspberries trapped in sugar. 'I'm going to eat all round the edges, then I'll eat the middle, then I'll lick the saucer until you can't see anything.'

Andrei poises his spoon over Anna's saucer. 'Which will you have?'

'Cloudberry.'

'Me too.'

You could get drunk on such sweetness. The jam syrup slides over tongue, palate, throat. You feel suddenly warm, as the sugar hits you, and the touch of acidity that the best cloudberry jam always keeps. And then a sip of scalding tea. You feel your cheeks flushing. Surely, for a moment, you look like yourself again, as you scrape up the last quarter-spoonful. You are young again, with smooth, full flesh. You wipe the saucer clean with your finger, and suck it.

'Cloudberries remind me of home,' says Andrei. 'And black-berries, too. When blackberries are ripe in hot sun, they already smell like jam.'

'But you don't have hot sun in Siberia.'

'Of course we have. No one has a summer like ours. The sun comes down to the earth, to where we are – it's not like your high-up Petersburg sun. And it really burns. We roll around in it, just as we roll in the snow in winter-time. You don't know anything about it, Anna, until you've been there, but I'll show you. Just wait.

'We'll take bread and goat's cheese, and a berry-pail. Even in winter you can find berries under the snow, if you know where to look. The snow lies deep on them. There's an ice-crust, and when you break through it, there's fine soft snow, like powder. You have to dig down, but lightly, with your fingers, so that you don't crush the berries. When the snow's cleared away, the bushes spring up, and the berries are there, coated in ice. The ice preserves them. You can walk all day out there, and feel better than you did when you set out.'

'Yes, goat's cheese . . . Do you think we could have another spoonful, Marina, or should we save it?'

Marina seems not to hear the question. She's turning her saucer round in her hand, but not eating it.

'Marina, aren't you going to eat yours? You must eat.'

'Not now. I'll drink my tea. But you eat. Take another spoonful. Kolya, have a little bit of mine, and see if you remember what cloudberries taste like. You know what this reminds me of?'

'What?'

'Easter.'

'Easter! Why?'

'You're too young, all of you, to remember. We'd fast for six weeks, even in the theatre we'd fast, when I was twenty or twenty-one. And then suddenly you'd know that things were changing. It was exactly the feeling that you get when the wind changes direction, and begins to blow from the south-west. And then Holy Week came. Holy Thursday was the day I loved most, when we'd boil onion skins and dip our eggs in the water to colour them. There was such an atmosphere. It grew day by day, mounting up until you knew things couldn't possibly go on like this. Down by the river you could already hear water running strongly, under the ice. And the surface of the ice had that grainy look it doesn't have at any other time, except just before it melts.

'We'd go to confession, all of us, even those who weren't really believers. Even if you didn't really believe, you'd feel sure that something had happened. It was like winter lifting from your soul. You would notice everything: little children running about with red cheeks, fresh as bread, and the way ice stayed thick and dirty in the lee of walls, where the sun didn't come.

'I had a pair of black suede boots with little heels, and I remember picking my way to the theatre and watching the little square tips of the boots and thinking how perfect they were, and how much I liked the noise of my heels tapping on the pavement. Suddenly we were all eager to help one another, even those of us who were rivals for parts. Of course it didn't last. And when Sunday came everyone would greet you, and you'd greet everyone: *Christ is risen!* And they'd answer: *He is risen indeed!* In our house, when I was growing up, they always served cloudberry jam with the pashka on Easter Day.'

'Marina, eat it, please.'

'I'll eat it later. I'm so tired, I've got to sleep now.'

'Just a little. Here, smell it.'

Anna holds the spoon to Marina's mouth. Marina's mouth wrinkles, opens a little, then closes. With all her heart Anna wants Marina to swallow, and to eat her share. But with something else, which doesn't feel like her heart at all, she reasons, 'If Marina doesn't eat, there will be more for Kolya. And it's not as if I haven't tried to make her.'

'Don't, Anna. I want to lie down. I'm really not hungry.' They help her into bed, and cover her with the stove-warmed blanket. Her eyes close at once, and she sinks away from them into sleep.

'Now, Kolya, let's get you settled on the sofa . . .'

Kolya curls up in his nest, with the chessboard and paper pieces. '*And then the bad horse comes up and tries to swallow all the people, but they don't let him, they run away and their friends help them . . .*'

'It's a bad sign,' says Andrei quietly.

'What? But he's looking so much better. More energy –'

'Not Kolya. Marina. Not that she didn't eat, but that she's not hungry. It's a recognized stage in the physiology of starvation.'

And in spite of himself, and for all his warm sympathy towards Marina, Andrei can't help a faint gleam of satisfaction crossing his face at his accurate, professional diagnosis. He'd understood her condition, right down to the torrent of memory she'd let loose. That was all part of it, too. He knows what is happening and he has the right words to describe it. That was what his professor said, two days ago: 'You've already experienced what very few doctors ever experience. If you live, you'll become a good doctor.' And he had glowed with it. Yes, in the frozen corridor, where corpses lay like wood, he had been elated.

But it's *Marina* he's talking about. She's always scared him a bit, but she's part of this 'home' where in weeks they've grown into one another more closely than a family of forty years. It's the place where Anna bends over Kolya with her lips moving as he eats, where Marina and Anna pass a sliver of scented soap between them. It's a place of books, drawings, ancient rugs that are loved all the more because they are worn out, and of meticulous sharing-out of soup and cereal into equal portions which are then sabotaged by both women's determination to give Kolya that featherweight on the scales which may add up to his life.

It's where Anna sets out for her hours of queuing in savage cold, where she jots down for him items of news she's heard on Radio Leningrad, because otherwise she'll have forgotten them by the time he gets home. She worries about not being able to remember things, but he tells her that it's only a temporary symptom. Her diet is lacking in important minerals and vitamins, he tells her solemnly, and they both laugh, but he knows that she's relieved. And then she presents him with an insulating lining for his boots, which she's made out of the felt underside of her father's desk blotter.

He should not have spoken of Marina like that, as if he were on a ward-round and she were any anonymous patient. Quickly, to blot out his words, he says, 'We mustn't let her sleep too long. We must rouse her in not more than an hour's time, and feed her. And we must keep checking her temperature.'

'She's exhausted, that's all,' says Anna. 'I don't know how long she was sitting in that room.'

'No.' He frowns, lost in his own thoughts. 'We shouldn't have let her go on talking like that. She's too weak.'

'She wanted to.'

'Yes, people get like that. The past is clearer to them than the present. They have to speak about it. And then they stop talking, and you know they aren't remembering any more. They've gone back there.'

'. . . and the horse stamps his feet so hard that all the people are frightened and they hide in their houses, right back here where the horse can't get at them . . .'

'Anna. Would you do that?'

'Do what?' she asks, to gain time, because she thinks she's already understood the question.

'If I were dead, and there was nothing you could do for me any more, would you still go and sit with me?'

'We're not like them, Andrei.'

'I know we're not.'

'We've had different lives. And they were born in such different times. They try to belong to the present, but they can't.'

'They loved one another.'

'She loved him. I'm not so sure about my father. Perhaps he loved the fact that she loved him.'

'But she kept on.'

'Yes. And she won't stop. She'll go on until she dies, too.'

'Why do you say that?'

'It's true.'

'You sound so cold, Anna.'

'I'm not cold. It's only that I don't believe in sacrificing yourself, when the sacrifice doesn't benefit anyone.'

'It's what she wants.'

'I can see that.'

'So you wouldn't sit beside me?'

'Andrei, you're asking me something that doesn't make any sense. I'm not Marina. I've got Kolya to think of.'

'I know you have. It's not that I don't understand that, it's just –'

'I know. You wish that I hadn't got him. You want us to start together from nothing, together, with nothing to think about but each other. I don't blame you. Elisaveta Antonovna, at the nursery, always used to get angry about the way I was with Kolya. *"Really, Anna Mikhailovna, anyone would think that child was your own son. Don't you realize what a bad impression you're making?"* She didn't think any upstanding Soviet citizen would look twice at me. My class origins for a start, and then a child in tow . . . Well, maybe she was right.'

'How can you say that? You know that isn't what I mean. I'm talking about you, not about other people.'

'Yes.'

Kolya's voice has faded to a murmur. He's tired, too, after the burst of energy that the jam has given him. He lies back on the sofa cushions, his face wiped clean of mood, his eyes unfocused, staring at the paper strips that crisscross the window. His lips move.

'Kolya, what are you talking about?'

'I'm talking to my little horse. I'm telling him to be brave, because the big horse has hurt his head. He kicked him.'

'That wasn't nice.'

'No. You shouldn't kick people. Anna, is Marina dead?'

'No, of course not. What made you think that?'

'Only she looks dead.'

'She's sleeping. She's very tired.'

'Like Daddy.'

'He's dead, Kolya.'

'I know. But he was tired as well.'

'You remember, you said goodbye to him.'

'Of course I remember. I'm not a baby. Anna, do a lot of people always die?'

'No, not like this. I told you. It's because of the war. Usually, people don't die until they get old.'

'Oh, I forgot you told me that.'

'I'll play a game of chess with you, Kolya,' says Andrei, 'and then I've got to go.'

'To the hospital?'

'Yes, to the hospital.'

'Andrei?'

'What?'

'Are we – you know – like Daddy and Marina?'

'You mean, are we going to die?'

Kolya presses his lips together, and nods.

'No,' says Andrei. 'We're not going to die. Not you and me and Anna. We're going to live.'

Kolya's lips purse in an exaggeratedly nonchalant, soundless whistle. 'It's only that I wasn't sure, so I wanted to know,' he explains.

Andrei sets out the paper chess pieces, going over their positions with Kolya. 'Now you show me, Kolya, where your king goes, and where your queen goes.'

They play for ten minutes or so, in the guttering candlelight. Anna watches without speaking. Soon, she will have to move, but not just yet. She has found a leather manicure case which belonged to her father. He must have forgotten about it, because it was in the pocket of his dressing-gown. It is pigskin, she thinks. She has emptied out scissors, clippers and emery board, and removed the metal fastenings. Now she must fetch water, and put the manicure case on the stove to make broth from it. It will take a long time before the pigskin softens, but it will be worthwhile. There'll be nourishment in it. They'll drink the broth, and Kolya can chew the pigskin.

Andrei glances up. The angle of candlelight flushes his hollow, old man's face with youth. He smiles at her. Although his eyes are only shadows in this light, she knows their exact colour. They are blue-black, like the waters of Lake Baikal. Andrei says that Lake Baikal is ten kilometres deep. No one knows what is down there, though they say that Baikal sturgeon can live for three hundred years. The waters of the lake are pure and life-giving. Even the stones from its shores bring luck.

How much you could hide, in water ten kilometres deep. But Andrei's eyes don't conceal anything from her in their depths. However deep she goes, there is still love, so complete and undistorted that it frightens her. She is used to living with tangled people, and their tangled stories. But Andrei isn't like that. *I love you, I want to be with you, come with me.* She hasn't grown up with such words. Maybe that was why she turned him away when he asked his question. Maybe he frightens her, just a little, because he's at ease in such deep waters. He is going to make her join him there. And he asks her questions no one has ever asked before. *'So you wouldn't sit beside me?'*

'You look so nice,' she says now, 'you and Kolya.'

Andrei smiles without answering.

'Yes, I would,' she goes on, so quietly that he can't possibly hear her. But he does.

'What would you do?'

'Sit with you.'

*

275

Outside, the wind whines. It brings snow with it, which will swallow up Andrei as soon as he steps out of the apartment building's shelter. It will buffet him, blind him, cover his cap and his eyelashes. It will sting his eyes with particles of ice. He will stumble on, hugging walls, and feeling for the edge of the pavement with his cherry-wood stick. It's a blizzard in which anyone could be forgiven for dying.

'Anna, when's Andrei coming back?'

'Not until tomorrow. I've already told you, so don't keep on asking. He's doing the night shift.'

'He's been gone ages.'

She blows out the candle, and lifts a corner of the blackout. But there's nothing to see.

'Is it still snowing, Anna?'

'Yes, it's still snowing. Go to sleep.'

In the German lines sentries stamp their feet. Christmas is over, and here's a new year of filthy Russian weather. We should have been halfway to China by now. Soon will be. A few more weeks ought to do it.

In Leningrad, a tank rolls down towards the Moscow Gates, on its way to the front line. Its thirty tons of steel rock and grind over the tramway. From city to battle is no distance at all.

By the Baltic shores, the sea is frozen, too, and snow lies so thickly on it that it's impossible to tell where the sea ends and the land begins.

Snow falls between the birches, and on to the frozen Neva. It covers the rubble of shelled apartments, and the burned-out farmyard where Mikhail bought his eggs. It drifts into abandoned, looted villages, hiding shallow graves. Two armies stare through the blizzard, straining for enemy movement. All planes are grounded, and there will be no bombing tonight. Over the ice road, the road of life, lorries move slowly forward from control post to control post. The ice is thickening every day, as winter grips more deeply. The ice road is beginning to do its job.

*

Vasya Sokolov never expected to end up driving lorries over the ice road, but that's where they've posted him, and that's what he's doing. He knows he's lucky. He's kept hold of the Sokolov luck. He hasn't ended up on the front line. This is his second crossing of the day, loaded up with flour and ammunition. He's going to be several barrels above plan if he manages a third crossing. *Comrades! Every extra bag of flour you carry will save a hundred Leningrad children from starvation!* Yeah, but you can't think like that. Not all the time. Not when there are delays, and the bags of flour sit on the back, getting nowhere.

This lorry's a bastard anyway. Something's been wrong with the steering all week. Vasya smashes his hand down on the steering-wheel. Don't play tricks with me, you fucker. People are getting shot for less. The lorry groans and heaves itself on over the rutted ice, slipping and sliding. Still dragging to the left. How far back was that repair station? A couple of hundred metres? Could head back there. No. Go on, you bastard. Don't fuck with me.

The lorry mounts a ridge of ice. Its wheels spin, then catch. The engine labours. At that moment the lorry's juddering loosens a connection. The electrical spark can't quite jump across. The engine stops.

Vasya knows immediately what the problem is. It's happened before. All he has to do is get the hood open and restore the connection. Vasya's got a real feel for engines and he's done a maintenance course. It won't take him five minutes to get this bastard going again, at least for long enough to push on to the next control post.

It's very quiet. Snow sifts across the windscreen while Vasya fastens his ear-flaps and reaches down for the screwdriver. He opens the door and the wind hits him. A wind straight from the north, stinging with snow. Thirty below, fifty with this wind. It's like being skinned. A shocked sound comes out of Vasya's throat. He shuts his mouth, and feels his way round to the front of the lorry, keeping one hand on the metal. In this whiteout he could be five metres from the lorry and lost for good.

The hood creaks open. He props it and clambers up to peer

inside, but snow's falling so thickly he can't see the wiring. He wipes his face and starts again. It's not the same connection. He tugs gently, but these wires are secure. Right. Try again. Snow spits and melts on the warm metal. There it is. The wire's snapped and he can't see the end of it. It's frayed now, and too short. It won't reconnect. Still, that doesn't matter, all he needs is another piece of wire, and he's got some back in the cab. No problem, now he knows where the problem is. He feels his way back to the cab, gasping with the punch of the wind, climbs up, and looks for his wire. Nothing. Some bastard's nicked it.

No. It was him. He used the wire yesterday and forgot to replace it. Vasya's face darkens but he doesn't do anything, doesn't punch the steering-wheel this time.

Got to think of something quick. Any piece of metal'll do. Wire securing the crates in the back, maybe.

A hair-grip would do. What if he'd had a girl in the cab and her hair-grip fell out when they were doing it and he found it now, closed his hand on it, just the right length. He could get the job done in no time.

Round the back, untie the straps over his load, get a look at those crates. Suddenly he thinks he hears an engine. Coming closer, someone behind him, one of the boys, maybe Ugly Yuri or Mitya.

'Here, mate!' Vasya shouts. 'I'm over here!'

And he's let go of the straps, he's waving his arms, he's stepped away from the lorry towards the engine noise. He'd never have done it if it hadn't been for the wind knifing up his brain.

He's on his own. He's left his load. People get shot for less. He reaches out, sweeping about him with his arms. Snow that way. Is that the way the engine noise came? He can't hear it now. The wind's so loud, beating into his skull. Snow this way. He takes another step, reaching out for metal. Snow falls into his arms.

His sacks of flour with the stamps on them: FOOD FOR LENINGRAD. He won't be above plan if he doesn't get a move on. Get back to the lorry, find a piece of wire, make the connection, start the engine.

But he can't find it. His lorry won't tell him where it is. It stays quiet, playing hidey in the snow.

'Where are you, you fucker?' shouts Vasya Sokolov.

The wind drives. The snow pours on to him. He puts up his hands to shield his eyes but the snow stings its way into them. Now he doesn't know where he is.

A hair-grip, that's all he wants. Like little girls wear to keep their hair back. They're always losing them and then their hair flops over their faces.

'Vasya, Vasya, can you see my hair-grip? It's fallen in the water. I've got to find it!'

Who said that?

Andrei stops in the shelter of an apartment doorway. He knows where he is. Straight on, third turning on the right, and down to the hospital. He can find his way, even in this whiteout. Perhaps he could let himself rest for a few minutes. If he kicks the snow off these steps, and sits down, just for a little while, it will be quite easy to lever himself up again. He's got the stick to help him.

He's used to worse blizzards than this, and he knows what to do. He doesn't come from Irkutsk for nothing. It's peaceful here, in this little doorway which is fantastically hung with icicles. Here, there's time to think. Imagine little Kolya, asking if we were going to die, just as if he were asking about a trip to the zoo. And I said no.

But in the hospital there'll be more patients than ever. Children with shiny skin stretched over swollen bellies, old men dead in corridors, fever, dysentery, dystrophy, frostbite, failing eyesight, suppurating gums, tuberculosis, pneumonia. Most of them will die, but before they do they need a doctor there to look carefully into their eyes and mouths and ears, to sound their chests, to take their pulse and offer water, and such drugs as we have. They must have what there is. There must be someone who is still on his feet, to take the baby out of the arms of its dying mother and tell her, 'It's all right, we'll take care of him.' We are men, not beasts.

Andrei heaves himself up. As he emerges from the shelter of the doorway, a blast of wind hurls snow into his face. He blinks, hunches his head between his shoulders to protect it, grips the cherry-wood stick, and walks into the wind.

30

It is May. The sky is a high, clear blue, and although there are a few white clouds floating at the horizon, towards the Gulf of Finland, they never cross the sun or dim the radiance of summer light.

In streets, in parks, on bridges and along the water, people are strolling. They blink in the bright sunlight. They are thin, marked by sickness and weakness. Some lean on sticks, although they are young. They keep away from the side of the street which is signed as the most dangerous in case of shelling, even when this means that they must walk in shadow. Leningrad is still under siege.

But there is food. These are people who have eaten this morning, and will eat again tonight. They're hungry, they're underfed, but they're not starving any more. Trams are running, electricity is flowing. In January the ice road began to fulfil its promise. All through the rest of the winter, and until the ice thawed, it brought in food and fuel. Most of those who are still living will now live.

There's a new military commander in charge, an artillery specialist. Govorov, he's called. 'Let's hope he gets our guns talking a bit louder,' people say, when they learn their new commander's name. He's a real strategist. When it comes to shelling the German positions he's a tiger. Doesn't wait for their guns to open up, but belts into their artillery first. Well, that's clear enough; anyone can see the sense of that, provided you've got the guns to do it. And Govorov seems to have the knack of getting the guns.

But on the ground he's more of a puzzle. His line seems to be that sometimes you have to fall back, in order to attack. But you wouldn't think there was anywhere to fall back to, what with the Germans so close, shelling us from the Pulkovo Heights, making camp in the Peterhof Palace. Soldiers on the front line say they can hear the Germans yelling sometimes, in what they think is Russian.

'All Russkies kaput! Stalin kaput, Leningrad kaput!' Funny to hear them bawling away about you-know-who like that.

Govorov's already pulled the 86th back from Nevskaia Dubrovka, our foothold on the other side of the Neva, from which maybe, one day, we could have pushed outward, deep into German flesh. Nevskaia Dubrovka had already used up so many lives. Surely we should never have abandoned it. Surely you've got no choice but to keep on paying for a piece of land, once it's already cost you so much in blood. You'd have thought Govorov would have held on to it, whatever happened. Doesn't he know how many men have coughed up their guts into that soil, and laid down their bones for the next man to walk on, as if they were building Petersburg all over again? But what does Govorov care about that? He's been airlifted in, another high-up with his orders straight from God.

'Govorov's all right. Govorov knows what he's up to. You'll see, he's got a plan,' say the infantry of the 86th, who might have had enough of being the symbol of Leningrad's heroic resistance.

The shelling is not so bad today. The sheer, sharp quality of light bathes everyone and reveals everything. These are the survivors, emerging from their winter of starvation. Lips are pale and cracked, faces drawn into triangles, hair dry and dusty. The siege has gutted them.

It's not half over yet, or even a quarter over. The radio keeps telling them to brace themselves, go forward and continue their heroic resistance. The Germans are still advancing deep into Russia. Intelligence suggests that a new German offensive on Leningrad is planned, and meanwhile the blockade continues to grip. But there are supplies in hand now. Even now that the ice has gone, there'll be shipping to transport food and ammunition into the city.

Pavlov is no longer walking a bare wire. He has got figures to add to his columns now. Already it's vanished, the terror of nothingness that gripped Leningrad that winter. *That winter.* To speak of it, or not to speak, that's the question. It's too close, too vast, like an immense fall you have only just not fallen. Behind, there are the sheer, icy sides of the pit that might have swallowed you.

The dead are gone from streets and houses. Heaps of snow and filth have been cleared. The Neva sparkles blue, where women crawled across wastelands of ice, with buckets of water that smelled of corpses.

There's another factor that doubles the survival chances of those who have survived so far. There are fewer mouths to feed now. No one speaks of it, but the truth is that Leningrad's population is down to half of what it was. 'Of course, they've evacuated thousands over the ice road – hundreds of thousands,' people say to one another, and this is true. They know, and do not say, how many more death has taken.

From every row of wooden houses, from every apartment building, shop, museum, library, factory, hospital, orphanage, school, the corpses of winter have now been removed, leaving empty, sunlit apartments, unswept doorsteps, classes without their teachers, teachers with classes of ten children instead of thirty, empty seats at library desks, shops that don't open, poems that will not be written, operations that will fail to be performed, and little boats that will not, this season, be uncovered, repainted, and launched from shallow, sandy shores on to the waters of the Baltic.

The sun shines. Everything's possible now that the sun is here, warming flesh and drawing dandelions and nettles out of wasteground. As long as you can still walk, no matter how slowly, and pause from time to time to hold up your face to the sun and let a haze of glowing red soak through your eyelids, everything is still possible. Radio Leningrad advises mothers to expose their children's skin to the sun, because it's a valuable source of vitamins. It seems impossible, but children are still being born.

An old couple shuffles into the sunlight. Now that they are close, you can see that they are in fact young. He wears a cap which sits oddly on his huge, exposed skull. She wears a headscarf with a pattern of roses. They walk in step, supporting each other.

'Look,' says Anna. 'Isn't that Zina and Fedya?'

'I don't think I know him.'

'He's changed . . .'

Yes, he must have been ill. He's wearing slippers on swollen feet, and Zina's the one doing the supporting, not him.

'Zina?' she calls uncertainly.

'Is that you, Anna?'

'Yes, it's me.'

'Forgive me. It's only that everyone looks so different.'

'How are you?'

'We're alive. I thought I should lose Fedya as well, but look, here he is.'

And here he is. His powerful body has disappeared. Skin stretches like paper over his nose and jaw, but his legs and feet are swollen. His thick, fair hair has fallen out.

'Yes, he's been very ill. He's been in hospital. Anybody else would have died, but not him. You weren't going to let it happen, were you, Fedya?'

She covers his hand with her own. Her smile is proud, tender, maternal. He's not only lived, but he's brought her back to life. Without his illness, she would have followed Vanka.

'I like your scarf,' says Anna.

'I know, it's pretty, isn't it? I love roses. When all this is over, Fedya's going to buy me some real roses, aren't you, Fedya?'

He nods, but doesn't speak. The effort of standing is enough for him.

'And with you,' asks Zina delicately, 'how are things?'

This is how you put it these days. You never ask directly.

'My father died, and Marina Petrovna died.'

Zina puts her hand on Anna's arm. 'But your little one?'

'He's over there.' Anna points down the sunlit street, where two little boys are playing by a wall. They are crouched down with their heads close together, and they have wiped from their minds everything in the world but their game.

'It's nice for him to have someone to play with,' says Anna.

'So he lived,' says Zina.

'Yes.'

They stand in a silent group. Winter is over, and the dead are still dead, because it was never true that they had only died for the duration. The mounds of bodies are being buried as fast as the authorities can handle them. More than a hundred thousand were buried last month. The streets are quiet and people walk in little groups, not crowds. They say a million have died. But the figures are only approximate.

The bird-like cheepings of Kolya and the other child suddenly darken.

'It's my turn to attack!'

'No it isn't.'

'It is. You're a liar.'

'Give me back my truck then, I'm not going to play with you any more.'

A mother appears in the entrance to the apartment house, shading her eyes. 'Now that's enough – can't you ever play for five minutes without arguing, Grisha? You've been moaning about having no one to play with for long enough.' She looks up the street, catches Anna's eye, shrugs and calls across, 'Kids! They never give you five minutes' peace, do they?'

'Kolya, if you don't want to play, then don't play. But if you're playing, play nicely.'

The children stare up at her with their sharpened faces. They know what grown-ups can do, and what they can't do.

Out they pour, the streams of banality that have made up Anna's life for years. 'Socialization', Elizaveta Antonovna calls it, though she does very little of it herself. But although the nursery has re-opened, Elizaveta Antonovna's not back from Moscow yet. She's too important where she is. There will be a new director, but so far one hasn't been appointed. It's hard to find anyone.

'Are you going to evacuate your Kolya, now that there's the chance?' asks Zina.

'No. He stays with us. Andrei's got us a little plot of land behind the hospital, and we've planted potatoes and cabbages.'

'We must be getting on,' says Zina.

There was something she wanted to say to Fedya, Anna remembers. Something she'd forgotten. But she can't remember it now. She hopes Andrei's right when he says it's lack of vitamins that makes her forget so much. Her brain only seems able to hold one idea at a time.

'Fyodor Dimitrievich . . .'

His eyes turn to her, dull with sickness. Of course, that was it. When they last faced one another, in the snow, when he was bringing home the wood on his sledge. After Vanka died. She almost steps back as it rises up and possesses her. The snowy street, the houses packed with dead, the man who put the steel tip of his boot by her head. It isn't the past. It isn't history and it never will be. But what is it then?

Don't think of all that now. Here's Fedya, not handsome any more, looking at her without curiosity. She'd told him a line from that Pushkin poem. *'We'll find them space in Russian earth,'* she'd said. And there'd been a flash of understanding between them, as if at last they knew they were the same kind, fighting the same thing. He'd answered, 'You're right there. We'll bury them.' But it was only later that she'd remembered the rest of the lines.

'Listen,' she says, 'I remember it all now. The whole poem.'

> 'Because we made our earth swallow
> The juggernaut which crushed nation after nation
> And with our blood redeemed the freedom,
> Honour and peace of Europe . . .'

Fedya still doesn't speak. Perhaps a shade of lightness crosses his face.

On the landing, Fedya with his towel slapping his bare shoulder, in singlet and trousers, pushing into the bathroom first. A real Leningrad boy, a boy of the courtyard. Grey eyes, muscled shoulders, and thick fair hair.

'Come away now,' says Zina to her husband. 'You'll wear yourself out, standing here. There's nothing more tiring than standing. You know what, Anna, my Fedya was defending the Works right up to the day they took him off to the hospital. They had to stop him, he wouldn't stop himself. He ought to get a medal.'

'Yes, he ought,' says Anna. The May sunlight is piercing her eyes and making them sting. Zina's right: standing here like this, talking to old friends, is the most exhausting thing of all.

Anna and Andrei watch as the couple shuffles away.

'Kidney disease,' says Andrei.

'You can't know that.'

'No,' he agrees, 'you're right. I can't be sure.'

They call Kolya to them, and walk on.

'Look, dandelions!' says Anna, and kneels to grub up a handful of leaves. 'Keep a lookout for more, Kolya. You're closer to the ground than I am.'

He runs off to scavenge between stones, while she examines the new green leaves. This colour won't last. As the sun grows stronger, so these leaves will darken and toughen. The indented pattern is cut into the leaves like toothmarks, just the same as every other year. She lifts a leaf to her lips and nibbles it.

'Full of vitamin C,' says Andrei. 'And I think there may be useful traces of folic acid as well.'

'If we find any more, I'll prepare a salad. We've got enough oil to coat the leaves.'

'Yes, a salad's better than soup. It preserves the nutrients.'

'Andrei, will you please stop talking like that?'

He smiles at her. She's wearing that green dress again, her favourite dress. She put it on so carefully, patting the folds into place before drawing the belt tight around her waist, and then loosening it again. It looked better loose. He could see her thinking that. She was still very thin. When she stood naked he saw her ribs rise and fall with the quick pants of her breath. She got out of breath so easily. And her breasts were shallow. She felt him looking, and quickly huddled on her dress. But the image of her hung on his mind like a photograph: her skin winter-pale, her pelvic bone showing, her knees startlingly bony and protuberant.

When she had the dress on she turned and looked at him, and smiled uncertainly. 'It's the first time I've worn it this year. Does it look all right?'

Her thin, pale arms hung down from the too-large sleeves of the dress. She made a gesture with her arms, as if offering up what she was to him. 'I know I look terrible.'

'No. You don't look terrible.'

'It's no good saying that, Andrei. I've got a mirror.'

'I look just the same.'

'Do you think we're ever going to be ourselves again? Look at my hair. Every time I comb it, more falls out.'

'It'll grow. All you need is protein – and minerals –'

'I know that.'

He touched her upper arms, where a fine down of hair caught the light falling through the window. Another sign of malnutrition. And his own hands looked enormous, with lumps of bony knuckle sticking out, and great raw wristbones. Who would want to be touched with such hands? But Anna closed her eyes, and sighed, and leaned towards him. And although his hands shamed him he felt them tightening on her. All winter they had slept cupped into one another and felt nothing. He pulled her closer. She put her lips on his, dry and searching. They kissed. After a while he said, 'You taste different.'

'I know. My breath doesn't stink any more.'

It was true. The graveyard smell of starvation had left them. Her lips were dry, but not cracked. It must have been the nettle soup she'd been making, and the increase in the rations. The inside of her mouth was moist. They tasted each other again, exploring, her thin body pressing against his through the folds of her green dress and the folds of the shirt that hung on him. Their bones were sharp, but they pressed closer. She moved a little, fitting him to herself.

'Yes, you taste right,' she said. 'You taste of yourself again.'

Anna has collected a fat bunch of dandelion leaves. Ahead of them, Kolya runs to a heap of rubble where a wall has collapsed under shelling. Nettles are sprouting, and dandelions, and tufts of new grass. Kolya darts here and there, picking leaves.

'There are loads here, Anna! Millions!' He waves a bunch of leaves at her, then kneels to grub up more. Anna looks down at the dandelion leaves in her hand. Sun glistens on them. They are so fresh that they look as if they are still unfolding. Anna eats another leaf. The taste is sharp and peppery: the taste of life, and not of death.

Marina and Mikhail lay side by side for a while. Now, although they lie in the same grave, they share it with thousands of other Leningraders. Perhaps, by accident, they were flung together, and they touch, as Marina would have wished. More likely, they are quite separate.

Already, new grass is furring the mound of the mass grave where they lie, just as frost furred their bodies in the room where Anna and Andrei laid them side by side, touching, on Mikhail's bed. Anna could not bring herself to lay Marina on the floor. She looked at them, side by side, their noses pointing at the ceiling, and then she shut the door. She didn't believe that they were together.

Their grave will be much visited. Fifteen years later, work will begin on a memorial to the victims of the Leningrad Blockade. Generations of Leningraders will come here, to Piskarevsky Cemetery. They'll stand for a while, stare at the eternal flame, read the poem engraved on the memorial stone, and lay flowers. In the earth, slowly, imperceptibly, separately, the flesh of Marina and Mikhail will part from its bones, and dissolve into the flesh of all those other Leningraders who died of hunger in silent, frigid rooms. The mummified babies who barely had time to emerge into the light before they were snuffed out; the students who walked arm in arm through the Summer Gardens, eating Eskimo ice-cream; the professors; the refugee peasants who fled to Leningrad pushing their possessions in handcarts, hoping to save their lives; the orchestra members who kept on practising in fingerless gloves as the temperature in their rehearsal rooms sunk beyond zero; writers, lathe-turners, museum curators, engineers, street-cleaners, schoolchildren. There are so many of them, such an unearthly number that the mind also dissolves at the thought of it. The memorial stone will swear that they will never be forgotten, and this may be true.

Is that enough for them, those ones under the grass? They're Leningraders, after all. They know the score. Leningraders will always be aware that stones can be lifted, statues can be felled, names changed, engraved words erased overnight. Invaders can come again. There's no use relying too much on a memory that's only set in stone.

In another part of the city, a red-haired woman with strong, bared, freckled arms is digging. Rows of young cabbages are being planted out where the park's turf has been removed. Every square metre of open land in the city must be prepared for food production, against a second winter of siege. The beets are already in, and the potatoes. The woman bends forward, thrusts her spade deep into the earth, loosens it with a practised jerk of her foot, and brings up the heavy spadeful. It's city earth, used to growing grass and flowers, but it has the same smell as earth in spring everywhere. It is sour, fermenting, full of promise. It crumbles easily after the deep frosts of the winter. Evgenia moves sideways, and drives her spade in again.

A couple of men in uniform stop to watch her. The sun is behind her, and it turns her red hair into a blazing halo. She's taken off her headscarf, and rolled her sleeves up above her elbows. Evgenia has always liked the feeling of sun on her bare skin.

The men watch Evgenia. Her clumsy jacket and trousers hide her body, but they can tell she's just the kind of woman they fancy. They can picture the strong socket of her waist, bent at work, her hips, her breasts. They admire the strength of her white arms. Not too skinny, either: she's managed to keep a bit of flesh on her.

'She looks as if she could carry on like that for ever,' says one of them.

'Yes, she's a real worker, that one.'

Evgenia's spade slices cleanly into the earth. Up comes another spadeful, with the moisture of spring still on it, making it glisten like chocolate. Now the sun and rain will sweeten it. The young cabbages will spread their roots and drive deep, fattening themselves on the endless sunshine of white nights. These cabbages will have to work hard. They must pump themselves full of life in the brief, dazzling Northern summer, before the frost comes round again and turns their stalks to blackened slime.

A patch of sweat spreads between Evgenia's shoulder-blades, and she wipes her face, streaking it with fresh earth. She glances behind her, but the men have moved on. She had the feeling that someone was watching her, and she doesn't like that. Four more rows, and then she'll rest. Or perhaps she'll carry on a little longer. After all, you don't get many days like this.

Three people stroll along the embankment, close to Lieutenant Schmidt's bridge. The late sun strikes towards them, bouncing off the water so that they squint and shield their eyes. The man and woman walk close, touching at shoulder, hip and thigh. They are enlaced, lazy, only just keeping an eye on the little one scooting along the kerb ahead of them. Is the child a girl or a boy? The three of them are far off, and it's hard to tell. Suddenly they move into a bar of light reflecting up from the water. Broken, shivering pieces of light run up and down their bodies. They look as if they are dancing.

They are mother, father and child out for a walk on this beautiful May afternoon, as Leningrad settles like a swan on the calmest of waters.

But, of course, they are not.

'Нет, весь я не умру . . .'
'No, I shall not wholly die . . .'
Alexander Pushkin

Select Bibliography

I am indebted to the authors of the following books:

The Road to Stalingrad by John Erickson, Cassell & Co., 1975
Russia's War by Richard Overy, Penguin, 1998
The Siege of Leningrad by Harrison E. Salisbury, Secker & Warburg, 1969
The Russian Century by Bryan Moynahan, Chatto and Windus, 1994
Leningrad v. Period Velikoy Otchestvennoy Voinny 1941–1945, Leningrad Historical Museum
Notes of a Blockade Survivor by Lydia Ginzburg
Everyday Stalinism by Sheila Fitzpatrick, OUP, 1999
Stalinism, New Directions, ed. Sheila Fitzpatrick, Routledge, 2000
Life and Terror in Stalin's Russia 1934–1941 by Robert W. Thurston, Yale University Press, 1998
Stalingrad by Antony Beevor, Viking, 1999
Reinterpreting Russia by Hosking & Service, Arnold, 1999
Echoes of a Native Land by Serge Schemann, Abacus, 1998
Soviet Women by Francine du Plessix Grey, Doubleday, 1990
A Week Like Any Other by Natalya Baranskaya
The Making of Modern Russia by Lionel Kochan and John Keep, Penguin, 1990
Into the Whirlwind and *Within the Whirlwind* by Evgenia Ginzburg, Collins Harvill, 1989
Hope Against Hope and *Hope Abandoned* by Nadezhda Mandelstam, Harvill Press, 1999
A People's Tragedy by Orlando Figes, Pimlico, 1997
The Rise and Fall of the Third Reich by William L. Shirer, Secker & Warburg, 1960

*

The poems, in various editions and translations, of Alexander Pushkin, Anna Akhmatova, Marina Tsvetayeva, Nikolai Gumilev, Vladimir Mayakovsky, Osip Mandelstam, Boris Pasternak and Alexander Blok.

The Cambridge Companion to Modern Russian Culture, ed. Nicholas Rzhensky, CUP, 1998

Art Under Stalin by Matthew Cullerne Bown, Phaidon Press, 1991

Modern Poetry in Translation No. 15, ed. Luca Guerneri, 1999

Pushkin's Button by Serena Vitale, Fourth Estate, 1999

Introduction by Lydia Pasternak Slater to *The Poems of Boris Pasternak*, Unwin Paperbacks, 1984

Pushkin, Selected Verse by John Fennell, Bristol Classical Press, 1991

Mandelstam Variations by David Morley, Littlewood, 1991

The translations from Pushkin (passages taken from *The Bronze Horseman, Eugene Onegin, To the Slanderers of Russia* and *Exegi Monumentum*) are my own.

Some characters in this novel, for historical reasons, take an unfriendly view of their Finnish neighbours. I do not share this view. It was through living in Finland that I first came to love the brief, astonishingly beautiful Baltic summers, and sombre Baltic winters. This book owes a debt to the Finnish landscape and people, along with its heavier debt to the landscape, the history and the people of their great neighbour, Russia.

refresh yourself at penguin.co.uk

Visit penguin.co.uk for exclusive information and interviews with
bestselling authors, fantastic give-aways and the
inside track on all our books, from the Penguin Classics
to the latest bestsellers.

BE FIRST ⊘

first chapters, first editions, first novels

EXCLUSIVES ⊘

author chats, video interviews, biographies, special
features

EVERYONE'S A WINNER ⊘

give-aways, competitions, quizzes, ecards

READERS GROUPS ⊘

exciting features to support existing groups and
create new ones

NEWS ⊘

author events, bestsellers, awards, what's new

EBOOKS ⊘

books that click – download an ePenguin today

BROWSE AND BUY ⊘

thousands of books to investigate – search, try
and buy the perfect gift online – or treat yourself!

ABOUT US ⊘

job vacancies, advice for writers and company
history

Get Closer To Penguin . . . www.penguin.co.uk